Long Story

By the same author

Reality Check

Long Story

VICKI NOTARO

SANDYCOVE

an imprint of

PENGUIN BOOKS

SANDYCOVE

UK | USA | Canada | Ireland | Australia
India | New Zealand | South Africa

Sandycove is part of the Penguin Random House group of companies
whose addresses can be found at global.penguinrandomhouse.com

Penguin Random House UK,
One Embassy Gardens, 8 Viaduct Gardens, London SW11 7BW

penguin.co.uk

Penguin Random House UK

First published 2025
001

Set in 13.5/16pt Garamond MT Std
Typeset by Jouve (UK), Milton Keynes
Printed and bound in Great Britain by Clays Ltd, Elcograf S.p.A.

The authorized representative in the EEA is Penguin Random House Ireland,
Morrison Chambers, 32 Nassau Street, Dublin D02 YH68

A CIP catalogue record for this book is available from the British Library

ISBN: 978–1–844–88688–3

Penguin Random House is committed to a sustainable future
for our business, our readers and our planet. This book is made from
Forest Stewardship Council® certified paper.

FSC www.fsc.org MIX Paper | Supporting responsible forestry FSC® C018179

For Denise and Eugene, who have always believed in me

'Friendship is constant in all other things
Save in the office and affairs of love.'

Much Ado About Nothing, William Shakespeare

1. Tara

@TMZ: Action man Rory Vaughan was pictured enjoying a cosy dinner last night ON VALENTINE'S DAY at Giorgio Baldi in Los Angeles with his latest co-star, pop sensation Allegra . . . The pair are starring together in the forthcoming erotic heist movie EMBROILED, based on the smash-hit novel of the same name. Their characters spend most of the book in steamy clinches, and studio execs are surely hoping that Allegra's big-screen debut means the movie version will be just as raunchy as her music videos. Vaughan, who turned 48 this week, is married to superstar actress Tara O'Toole (35), but looked thrilled to be in the company of the sexy 26-year-old starlet! Click on the link in bio for everything we know about the film so far . . .

I rolled my eyes, but my stomach contracted a bit. Throwing down my phone, I lay back on the couch in my trailer, swallowing the nausea that had suddenly rolled up from the pit of my stomach. Rory hadn't called me since the previous morning, which wasn't like him. He also hadn't sent his usual huge display of magenta roses to celebrate 14 February, but I knew, like me, he was working long days on a film set. He wasn't too busy to go for dinner with Allegra, though, my brain whispered. I shushed it. Being seen out and about together was all part of building the lore around the movie; everyone knows that. He could have called, though.

It's a total nightmare being in the public eye sometimes – I mean, the mere act of looking at your phone can be highly dangerous. I can't count the number of times I've casually glanced at a notification only to be presented with pictures of myself on gossip sites I didn't even know had been taken. There was the time my skirt was tucked into the huge, pink granny pants I was wearing because I was on my period – that didn't do much for my sexy image. Or the time a creep with a long lens took shots of me scoffing a doughnut down the Cape with visible cellulite on my thighs, with an accompanying headline shrieking about how I'd let myself go that summer. That granular level of scrutiny is one thing nobody tells you about being famous, and it's difficult to understand until it's your own arse circled in a magazine for all to see and smirk at.

For normal people with regular lives and jobs, getting an email or a text that truly stops you in your tracks and derails your best-laid plans is maybe a once-in-a-blue-moon occurrence. For me, well, there's a new story to either deal with or avoid almost every single day.

Of course, I've learned to assess and compartmentalize them. My therapist, Samuel, taught me to ask myself, will this disrupt my hour, day, week, month, or the rest of my life? – and act accordingly. It's why lots of other actors don't dare look at the internet, and let their publicists deal with everything. Sandra Bullock uses a Nokia, for god's sake. I can't help it, though. Maybe I'm a glutton for punishment, maybe I'm just a nosy bitch, but more often than not you'll find me glued to my iPhone.

'I'll never learn,' I sighed, berating myself. My trailer was a quiet, safe space at Pinewood Studios in London, and I was gratefully alone for the first time in hours. It was my last day on set for a lovely little romantic comedy called *Mind the Gap*. To be honest, it was the kind of movie I could do with my eyes closed, but I give every project my full commitment. This sort of light, escapist film was my bread and butter; it's what the people want from Tara O'Toole.

I'd been looking forward to wrapping, and I had a fun girly weekend planned with Alex, my closest and oldest friend. There were two scenes left to film and I knew I had my lines down, but seeing the post about Rory on Instagram had thrown me.

I was prepared for there to be rumours about my husband and Allegra (no surname necessary) – if there weren't, they weren't selling the movie convincingly. She was the pop star *du jour*, one of the biggest female recording artists in the world and incredibly sexy in her sultry, serpent-like way. I always think of a boa constrictor when I watch her perform; coiled, ready to pounce and squeeze the life out of her prey.

But if not Allegra, it would be somebody else equally hot. I'm a professional, and I understand the job. And, of course, I trust my husband.

It was hard, though, being far apart for so long. I'd missed his birthday due to filming, but he'd left a love-heart emoji on my gushing celebratory post. When had I last seen Rory? I bit my lip as I counted back . . . it had been about five weeks since I'd been with him in person, but we talked all the time. Granted, it was snatched conversations here and there, but when we both wrapped our respective projects, I was looking forward to some downtime together. Maybe we could go to the house on Cape Cod for the whole summer this year; I'd personally prefer Barbados, but being in his home state would relax my husband, a New Englander through and through.

I couldn't stay away from Instagram, though. I scrabbled for my phone and quickly scanned the comments below the post. '#RORA for ever!' one user wrote, using our cute couples moniker coined by the fans. 'Tara O'Toole is FAR sexier than AllegrASS,' said another, clearly not enamoured with my husband's co-star's infamous behind. I felt a bit smug then, even though I knew it wasn't empirically true. My brand has always been wholesome with an edge – the girl next door who you secretly suspect to be a tiger between the sheets. I'm not a femme fatale, nor would I want to be. It sounds exhausting.

Slightly placated by the comments, I rallied a bit. It was just a stupid publicity stunt for the film. I had nothing to worry about. Mollified, I spent a few minutes throwing out a few likes from my burner account. I can't post freely from my official

Insta, but as @RoryLover1987 I can do whatever I want. I love going on a liking spree – here, you get a heart! And you! Like a benevolent, anonymous Oprah.

There was a knock at the trailer, and Sara, the perky second assistant director, poked her head around the door. 'You're needed back on set, Ms O'Toole!' she beamed. 'Five minutes, if you can.' I smiled back and nodded my assent.

I sent the Instagram post to Rory, accompanied with a few shocked face emojis and then a wink. 'Something to tell me???' I wrote. It didn't deliver immediately. Shrugging, I shook out my hair in the mirror, blew my reflection a kiss and headed back to the set.

Sets are my happy place when the movie is going well. Everyone there has a job to do, and every one of those jobs hinges on the actors in front of the camera.

'Here she is, queen of happily ever after!' my co-star called when he saw me, and I laughed. Chris Adams devised that nickname for me on our first day shooting, after he spent weeks watching my movies in preparation for the role. He thought it was amusing that even in my genre films, my characters never came off too badly in the end. 'Do you have a clause in your contract that you don't get maimed, murdered or maligned, Tara?' he'd asked that first morning. 'Or is it just that nobody wants to harm one of those famous hairs on your head?'

'Yeah, that's it,' I'd laughed back. 'Covet Cosmetics won't allow my hair to come to any harm whatsoever – didn't you hear it's insured for $5 million?'

That's actually true, you know. My hair is one of my greatest assets. My mother was Latina and my father is Irish, and I'm a mix of them both. As a child I bemoaned my looks – my formerly frizzy auburn mane was the bane of my life until I used it to my advantage. Now my hair and freckles are what score me big money in beauty campaigns, a handy side hustle to my acting career.

I strolled on to the sound stage, ready to get back to work. The make-up girl fussed with powder and lip gloss and fluffed out my hair while I talked to the assistant director of photography about blocking for the next scene. The movie was set at a newspaper headquarters in the 90s so I was in my element, rocking my natural curls, with brown lip liner and a lot of trouser suits.

Chris was playing my older boss who was trying desperately not to fall for me and failing. He was doing great, considering this was his first romcom – he's usually more of an action man, but getting on a bit now for the high-intensity stuff. Our pairing was providing just the right amount of sexual tension; that much was apparent in the dailies. Too much chemistry, and the audience would suspect you of pulling a Brangelina. Too little . . . well, I don't know. That's never happened to me.

The director was giving Chris a pep talk, explaining how he was going to edit the sequence with flashes of me strutting through the office in slow motion, and how no man alive could possibly resist my radiant allure. 'Just give in to desire, Chris,' he was saying. 'Every man and woman in the movie theatre will totally understand where you're coming from.'

These things might go to someone else's head, but not mine. I learned a long time ago that who I am on the outside has very little to do with my true self. I put what I'd seen online out of my head. Focus. It was time to work.

I was gearing up for my big parade through the office when a hush descended on the sound stage. The bright lights were blinding me, so I couldn't see what everyone was suddenly looking at off camera. Then I made out a tall figure hugging Chris. Was that . . .

'Ohmigod! Rory!' I shrieked, and ran full speed at my husband, work forgotten. He'd flown from LA all the way to London to surprise me! Forget pink roses, forget phone calls, this was what it meant to be a great husband!

Rory gave me a quick hug, but I could tell he didn't want to interrupt the shoot. He's incredibly professional, and known for it in the business. He leaned down to murmur in my ear. 'Finish what you're doing,' he said softly. 'We can catch up after.'

Knowing my husband was sitting watching the monitor behind the camera added more than a bit of sparkle to my final two scenes. I felt like I could burst with happiness, realizing only when he appeared how much I'd really been missing him.

Once the takes were in the can, I endured the cake, champagne and multiple rounds of applause that come with a star's last day on set, dying to be done and alone with Rory but never, ever rude to the crew. I listened to their speeches, accepted their gifts and was as gracious as my mother always taught me to be.

'Finally!' I exclaimed as I threw open the door to my trailer. 'Just the two of us!'

Rory followed me inside, oddly quiet.

'I can't believe you got the weekend off and came all this way,' I was prattling as I shimmied out of my costume and pulled a T-shirt over my head. I still couldn't quite believe that Rory was there, and I was fizzing with excitement.

I realized then that he didn't have any kind of bag on him and that he was shuffling nervously near the door. 'Hey, sit down, relax, I won't be long,' I said, gesturing at the heavily cushioned sofa by the window. 'Did you leave your stuff in the car? You remember, I had planned to spend Sunday and Monday with Alex, but I'm sure she'll understand me changing our plans because you're here. Or maybe I can even move a few things around and go with you to LA!' I chattered on nervously because I was sensing a strange vibe from my husband. Something wasn't right.

Rory sat heavily on the sofa. 'Tara, come here.'

I did what I was told and sat down next to him. Even after twelve years together, I find how gorgeous Rory is shocking, especially when I haven't seen him for a while. My husband is a fine specimen of a man, tall and thick and strong, and his energy takes up a lot of space in a room. He looked exhausted up close, though, and seemed jittery. When I went to plant a kiss on his lips, he shunted his body so I missed his mouth.

Okay, so that was it. He was still mad at me. Had he come all this way to keep fighting?

'Tara, we have to talk.'

'I know, but at least let me give you a kiss fir—'

'Actually, I need to talk. And I need you to listen.'

I forced a breezy laugh. He was definitely still pissed at me, so I decided to play it cool. 'Okay, if you want to play it like that. I'll listen attentively, like a good girl.' I sat up straight and prim and batted my lashes at him – coquettishly, I hoped.

'Knock it off, Tara,' he barked. 'I'm not joking.'

My stomach lurched. He never spoke to me like that. 'Rory, what's going on?'

'Uh . . . I came to see you in person because I've made a decision. This will be difficult for you to hear, but I'm going to do what has to be done and be the one to end things. It's over, Tara.'

My vision blurred and I heard myself laugh from what felt like very far away. I could feel the high of the surprise ebbing away, a cold, nasty feeling in my chest replacing the euphoria. 'What? What's over?'

'Our marriage. I'm done with pretending, with playing games.' He looked at me coldly, and I felt a shiver deep inside. I'd never seen his eyes look like that when trained on me. It was like I was watching Rory perform, not having a real-life conversation with him. He looked like my husband, sounded like him even, but in all the time I'd known him, he'd never been this icy. Was this a pod person? An alien wearing Rory's skin?

'I don't understand,' I managed. 'Has something happened? Something I'm not aware of?'

Rory blushed then, a deep red that crept from his neck all the way up his face. It's always been his tell, when he's trying to keep a secret or when he's embarrassed. It's one of the most adorable things about him, this big, strapping guy who blushes like a six-year-old. Suddenly, I remembered the Instagram post and a sickening clarity began to descend on me. Rory was so moral, so upstanding. Surely he couldn't be . . .

'Oh my god,' I blurted as I leapt up. 'It's true, isn't it? You're sleeping with Allegra!'

He wrung his hands, and I knew in that instant I was correct.

'I'm not sleeping with her, it's . . . I'm in love. I've fallen in love with Allegra.'

The statement hung in the air, which immediately felt thin, and I gasped for breath. Rory grabbed my wrist and guided me back to the sofa next to where he was sitting, and I went as if on autopilot. I was blinking hard, as if trying to wake myself up from a nightmare.

'Look, Tara, I didn't want it to come to this. And I didn't want you to hear it from anyone else. It was important for me to come and tell you face to face.'

'What, that you don't love me any more?'

He drew his lips in a thin line. 'My feelings for Allegra are very powerful. I couldn't keep that from you.'

My brain was scrambling to make sense of what Rory was saying. Okay, so he'd slipped and shagged his co-star. It happened, especially when it was a sexy film. Rory was such an ethical guy he wouldn't be able to live with a lie. So he'd been honest, he'd told me. I could deal with it. It didn't have to be the end of us. I was formulating the right thing to say in my head, but what escaped my lips was more like a desperate plea.

'Don't be so hasty, Rory. It's just a crush, it will pass. These things happen when you get a bit older . . .'

'It's not a crush, Tara. I'm a forty-eight-year-old man, not a schoolboy.'

'Then why are you acting like a hormonal teenager?' I roared, shocking us both. Go easy, Tara, I told myself. Don't push him away. 'Look, it could be a midlife thing. I get it. You're not in love with somebody else. You can't be.'

But when I looked in Rory's eyes then, all I saw was pity. And that's when I clocked him, right in the chops.

PAGE SIX

15 February 2025

IT'S OVER! Rory Vaughan and Tara O'Toole SPLIT amid rumours of an on-set affair with Allegra!

News is reaching us this evening that everyone's favourite red-head, Tara O'Toole, has fled the London set of her latest film having been given the old heave-ho by her husband of eleven years, fellow actor Rory Vaughan.

The couple's marriage, long thought to be one of the most solid in Hollywood, has been called into question in recent days after Vaughan spent Valentine's Day in Los Angeles with his current co-star, Allegra. However, sources on set say that O'Toole was utterly blindsided by her husband showing up in London to deliver the bad news in person.

'Tara was so happy to see him, completely surprised and thrilled because she had just wrapped filming on the movie, but then a few minutes later we all heard screaming and shouting coming from her trailer. Rory eventually came out with a bloody lip, got straight into a waiting car and left.'

It's not known how Vaughan was injured or where he went, but we're told that not long after, Tara left the set and headed for a private airstrip nearby, where she was seen by paparazzi boarding a small jet. Insiders say she was heading to Dublin, where she grew up, but we're also receiving conflicting reports that she went straight home to New York.

More as we get it!

2. Alex

My phone was vibrating non-stop in the cup holder, distracting me from the road. Its flashing screen alerted me to incoming calls with country codes from the UK, US and even Australia, but I was ignoring it in an effort to concentrate on steering.

It was almost eight o'clock on a Saturday evening, but the news cycle is never-ending. I knew that every showbiz hack and tabloid editor I'd ever worked with would be trying to reach me to get the scoop on Tara and Rory, and I wasn't about to entertain them – especially when at that moment Tara was lying prone across the tiny back seat. I'd collected my best friend from Weston Airport, bundled her into my Mercedes coupé and sped off towards my apartment in Dublin's Docklands.

Now that Tara was safely with me, I could finally turn the damn phone off. The constant buzz was setting my teeth on edge. I work in the media as a writer and podcaster, but I'm a classic geriatric millennial in that I never have the ringer on loud – if my device dared to make a noise, I would likely fling it out the window.

'Are you sure you're okay down there?' I called, and heard a grunt of assent. 'You know, you don't have to lie half on the floor, Tara. I know you've been away a while, but we don't really have paparazzi in Dublin. Apart from that one weird guy who drives a moped.' She didn't reply, but I knew she was being hyper-cautious. In this day and age, anyone with a phone could be a photographer.

I chewed the inside of my cheek as I tried to focus on driving. The car had been an impulse buy when I signed my first sizeable advertising deal for my podcast, *Alex Knows*. I'm not a flashy person – I prefer to ride my bike because of crushing eco-guilt – but I've always wanted a sexy little Merc. I drive it so infrequently, though, it took all of my attention to control the bloody thing.

Tara wasn't manic, but that was frightening in itself. I'd expected her to be distraught, but she had been practically catatonic since she'd deplaned. I instantly knew that everything I'd read on social media was true when she was non-verbal. Perhaps she felt guilty about resorting to violence, but if Rory really had left her for Allegra, I didn't blame her one bit for thumping him.

Still, when I saw Tara in person I went from concerned to properly worried. Her reaction to any sort of trauma has always been to go completely mute, but it's a deathly calm before a motherfucker of a storm. Those storms are few and far between thanks to a lot of expensive psychotherapy and work on herself, but I hadn't seen her quite like this for a very long time – not since her mother died when we were eighteen.

I was stunned, too. Rory Vaughan was a stand-up guy, the kind of fella that seems too good to be true but is as sweet and sound as he comes across. Good on paper, and good in reality. I'd never held much faith in men or marriage in general, but Rory was the type of man who made me think that a loyal, communicative husband was possible to find. Had he fooled us all?

I just wanted to get Tara back to my place. It had only been a few hours since Rory had shown up in London, dropped a metaphorical atomic bomb on Tara and their marriage and scarpered as soon as he'd confessed his sins. I knew very little about what had actually gone on, besides what Tara's assistant, Felicia, had told me and what was in the public domain. Felicia had asked where she should direct the plane, and on instinct I said to me in Dublin. I was always Tara's go-to in an emergency, and this was DEFCON 1. I told Felicia to send Tara alone, too. I knew she wouldn't want an entourage. Her team of agents and her publicist, Giulia, would be in full-blown crisis-management mode; they could take care of the press.

It wasn't exactly convenient for me, however, although I guess crises never are. I was prepping for a huge interview, I had loads of washing to do and I hadn't been having the best day ever even before Felicia's call. Work was stressful; my listenership was down, and when your podcast has your name and face on it it's hard not to take that personally.

Plus, Tara's imminent arrival meant I'd had to cancel a date that evening with a cute videographer I'd met at an event. It had been a while since I'd seen a man naked, and it was beginning to show in my behaviour. As a single woman, I knew I had to stay in sexual shape with an actual human male from time to time in order to prevent full-blown cat-lady tendencies from emerging. They were always there, lurking just beneath the surface. It's why I don't own a vibrator – if I did, I might never talk to a man again.

My problems were small potatoes compared to Tara's, though; her marriage was crumbling out of the blue, whereas I'd never even stayed in a relationship long enough to swap keys.

I wanted to kill Rory with my bare hands. What the hell was he thinking? Tara wasn't naïve, she knew people got close on set, and particularly making a sexy, high-stakes thriller. We'd had discussions before about co-star crushes, how she could possibly reluctantly turn a blind eye to a short-term fling for the sake of preserving her marriage. 'Only because I understand it, Alex,' she'd enthused. 'I know you're a romantic, but I've been in love scenes where I'm not acting. It doesn't mean I love Rory an iota less, it's just purely physical.'

Tara thinks I'm a romantic because she presumes I'm holding out for The One. I don't have the heart to tell her that I don't believe in lasting love these days, and that I'm constantly being proven right.

But I was still horrified at this particular turn of events, and that unicorn husband Rory Vaughan was turning out to be just like the rest of them. For him to desert his wife for a woman he'd known for a month? A much younger woman with a terrible reputation and a string of broken engagements in her wake?

Allegra was a notorious man-eater. She even wrote the annoyingly catchy 'Love Bite', a blind-item song last summer about all the hot, famous guys she wanted to sink her teeth into. Tara had FaceTimed me from New York when it dropped to see if I thought the lyric 'oh, that Rory makes me so horny' was about her husband. I remembered her being pretty thrilled about it, squealing that her man still had it. Well, it seemed now that the Rory in question *had* been Tara's, and the siren Allegra had bewitched him with her song. I wasn't letting him off that easily, though. He was obviously open to bewitching.

I pulled into my space in the underground car park beneath my block on Charlotte Quay. There wasn't a sinner around, so I manhandled Tara out of the back seat and into the lift; she only had her Birkin with her, evidence of how quickly she'd fled the set.

Tara bought me an Hermès bag of my own once, for my thirtieth birthday. It's green calfskin and the most beautiful thing I own, so of course I never take it out of its dust bag for fear of destroying it. It lives a sad, lonely life in my wardrobe, never fulfilling its purpose. That depresses me, but not enough for me to actually use it.

When we reached my apartment and closed the door behind us I breathed a sigh of relief. My home is my sanctuary – everything has its place, it's quiet and orderly and I'd never leave it if I didn't have to. See? Cat-lady tendencies. Only I don't own a cat, because I have allergies and couldn't hack the fluff.

'Okay, you're safely here now and nobody saw you. You can exhale, Tara.'

As she let out a breath, she burst into heaving sobs. I gathered my friend in my arms; she felt frail, which isn't like Tara – she's never been a Hollywood sylph, she's too fond of carbohydrates. She recounted what had happened with Rory in between sobs, and when she got to the part about punching him, I hid a smile. Tara has always been feisty.

'But he didn't even get angry with me, Al. Even when he saw the blood, he just looked sad. He said he'd leave me to calm down and digest the news, and we'd talk later. He said he had to get back to LA. I asked him, did you really come all this way to end our marriage? And he said yes, that it was eating him up inside. He thought I deserved the truth. Then he was gone.'

I let Tara cry until she exhausted herself and eventually fell asleep on the couch. I stroked her dark red hair, noticing there were still tears leaking from her closed eyes as she snored and leaving streaks along her cheeks. With her face still and brow smooth she looked like a teenager, those famous freckles and excellent dermatology really proving their worth. Tara and I were born the same year, but her mother shaved a couple of years off her professional resumé when Tara was seventeen, swearing blind that she'd thank her later in life when it gave her career longevity. Thus we're both currently thirty-seven, but everyone thinks Tara is thirty-five as I'm about to turn thirty-eight. Just another example of the slight injustices that come with being the best friend of an acting superstar.

There was no point disturbing Tara to attempt to transfer her to the spare room – it wasn't even made up for a guest, because I hadn't been expecting anyone. I'd leave her be, where she at least looked somewhat peaceful. Poor Tara. My heart ached for her.

I called my mother from my bedroom. An Irish mammy and also a midwife, Deirdre Curtis always knows how to behave in an emergency.

'Sweetheart, I've been trying to reach you. Is it true about Tara and Rory?' Mam is unusually well versed in the internet for someone in their mid-sixties, so she'd already heard the news.

'Sadly it is, Mam. I got her here, so she's safe.'

'Oh, thank god. Eamonn,' she shouted, not moving her mouth from the receiver, 'Tara is in Alexandra's house! No, you can't tell anyone, you absolute eejit! I don't care if Maura from the golf club is wondering!'

My father has never really understood the concept of discretion when it comes to my famous friend. He likes to brag about her down the pub and has to be specifically warned not to divulge sensitive information. It's sweet, really. As Tara and I are both only children, she's something of a second daughter to my parents and I've always been happy to share them with her. It takes the heat off me.

'Is it true she gave him a box, love?' my mother asked, trying to keep the glee out of her voice and failing.

'It appears so, and from what she's told me, he deserved it.'

'So is it actually over, then? For good?'

'I don't know, Mam! It just happened.'

'Don't get huffy with me, young lady!' Her tone turned conciliatory then; she knew she had to keep me onside to get the gossip. 'Okay, I have experience with this sort of thing on a more local scale. When Bernadette Duffy's Dermot ran off with the divorced floozy down the road, the only thing that got her through the day was Valium.'

'She's already pretty sedate . . .'

'For now! Trust me, ring the D-Doc. Take her phone off her, and make sure you ring all her "people",' – I could practically hear my mother doing air quotes – 'and get their advice. Big stars have crisis-management teams, like on that show *Scandal*.'

This was surprisingly good advice, not that I needed it. Fifteen years of writing about celebrity culture meant I had a decent understanding of how to behave when the shit hit the fan, but I was impressed my mother did too.

'The other thing, love, is that you might not be able to keep her in Dublin. This city is like a village – the second anyone gets wind she's there, you'll both be persecuted. Bernadette Duffy isn't a bit famous, but she still couldn't go round the shops without getting hounded by "well-wishers".' There were the air quotes again.

My mother had a point. I had been so focused on getting Tara to my side, I hadn't really thought of a next move. If I was already getting calls from every Tom, Dick and Harry in the world's media, it meant people in the know were pretty sure she was with me.

I didn't want my apartment surrounded, because I wouldn't be able to protect Tara then. I didn't have a doorman, or a complex security system. My place was ill-equipped to act as a proper A-list hideout. Maybe I should have sent her straight back to New York, but in the moment I'd only been thinking of having her close by.

My mother was still talking. 'If you want my advice, you'll get her back to the States pronto. The Americans know how to handle this sort of thing. Sure, we don't have an Olivia Pope-type character knocking around Baggot Street you can call, do we?'

I suppressed a laugh. 'Thanks, Mam, but I'm not going to do anything just yet. It's all still too fresh, and the eyes of the world will be on her the second she makes a move. We're going to lay low together. This is the best place for her right now.'

'Okay, hon. I'll call over on Monday and sit with her. Jen is up to high doh with all of those children on weekdays, so don't bother her, and I know you have your huge day in London.'

'I was going to cancel—'

'Don't you dare!' she shrieked. 'You can't let them down with mere hours' notice – I raised you better than that. And it's not every day you get to meet a duchess!'

'Ah, she's a duchess in name only. Like Meghan Markle, but not as glam.'

'Still, she's royalty all the same. From what you've been telling me, the podcast needs this interview. And I'm dying to hear it! You'll get your arse on that plane, madam. Come back Monday evening sure; you'll only be gone a few hours that way. I'll come over as soon as my lunchtime Zumba class finishes.'

I mulled it over in my head, and decided my mam was right.

I'd change my flights so I was in and out in one day. So much for the fancy London girls' night out Tara and I had planned; I'd have to cancel our suite at the Dorchester and the tickets for the new *Devil Wears Prada* musical.

'Okay, okay. Are you sure you don't mind sitting with Tara while I'm gone?'

'Mind?! I'm dying to see her! And I'll make her feel better the way only a mammy can. I'm a professional!' she declared.

I thanked my mother and rang off, promising to keep her updated. It was niggling at me that perhaps I'd been selfish in bringing Tara here. In the coming days, getting her home to New York *would* most likely be the best thing for her – that's where Tara's stepdaughter, Storm, is, our close friend Darius, and her favourite therapist, Samuel. But I didn't want to be too rash. I decided that when the time was right to make the move across the Atlantic, I'd know.

But just in case, I did what I always do when I'm not sure about something. I rang our friend Jen.

'Oh, thank god,' she said as she answered the phone without even saying hello. 'I haven't wanted to bother you, but I've been dying for you to ring. Is it all true?'

Jen, Tara and I have the sort of communicative shorthand only very old friends have. I didn't need to ask her what she was talking about, and she was likely just as worried about Tara as I was.

'Ugh, Jen, it's bad.' I sighed, flopping on the bed.

'Is she talking?'

'A little, but not much.'

'Christ. The bastard! I can't believe it! Brian has never trusted him, calls him Flash Rory, but I always thought he was just jealous.'

'Ah, he is,' I agreed. Jen has been married to Brian Callaghan for fifteen years and with him even longer. 'I was a child bride!' she's been known to cry. 'It was a shotgun wedding!' Considering the fact that she was twenty-six and not pregnant, neither is true, but Jen doesn't let that stop her. Yet while Brian is a wonderful, steady man and an amazing father, he doesn't have Rory's charisma or washboard abs. 'And we can't blame him for being jealous. But it seems Rory's been flashing Allegra all right.'

I filled her in on what I knew, whispering in case Tara woke up and overheard me. She wouldn't mind Jen knowing; the three of us have been thick as thieves for eons. Still, I wouldn't like her to think I was gossiping about her.

'Your mam is right,' Jen said once she was up to speed. 'You have to bring her back to New York. I know you like your home comforts, but she needs you, Alex. I'd go with her myself – Jesus, I'd LOVE to go and stay with Uncle Dar for a while. But I'm trapped here with these poxy children while my husband buries every poor creature that kicks the bucket in North Dublin.'

Jen didn't really mean that. She absolutely adores Rex, Emily and Savannah (ages three, eight and thirteen respectively), but she likes to play the put-upon mother from time to time, especially in relation to the perceived glamour of my and Tara's careers.

Jen has always been our cool friend. At forty-one, she's a ceramicist and yoga teacher, has her own studio near her home in Stoneybatter and is the proud owner of an achingly hip shag haircut. Sometimes she tries to be a bit woo-woo, but she once left her crystals out to charge in the light of a full moon and had them stolen by a squirrel, which she said served her right. Brian is an undertaker, the fourth generation to helm a booming family business, and is always busy because as Jen says, 'People never stop fucking dying.'

Jen also attended her uncle Darius's stage school, That's D'Amore. That's where we all met, but she was older, cooler and wasn't a wannabe actor like me and Tara – Jen fancied herself a late-blooming contemporary Irish dancer until she tore her ACL attempting a flying leap. I remember her sinking into a deep adolescent depression at the time, watching her video of *Riverdance* over and over and weeping about never being the next Jean Butler. Tara and I had been deployed to cheer her up, and that's when we'd all really bonded. Jen's family home near Mount Jerome was walking distance from the school off Dame Street, and I'd take the bus from Phibsborough to Harold's Cross to hang out with my new Southside posse.

'So you think I should go back to New York with her? Would it be irresponsible to shove her on a plane by herself?'

'I think it would be unwise. Tara is famously co-dependent. I don't think she should be left alone for long. God knows what she'd get up to. And you can't expect little Storm to be the one to mind her!'

'Storm is twenty-three, Jen.'

'A twenty-three-year-old nepo baby means she's essentially fifteen in normal-people years. Now, I have to go and make sure my own teenage child isn't sneaking out a nagin to the disco. Talk to you later.'

After checking on Tara, who was still snoring, I allowed myself a brief reprieve to slump at my desk and figure out what to do. I think better in my desk chair; I had it ergonomically designed just for me, which is how I knew I was truly getting old.

Should I really up sticks and go with Tara back to New York? I'm not someone who's very spontaneous, but I would do anything for my best friend. I love Tara more than any other living person, besides Deirdre and Eamonn of course. This is something ex-boyfriends have resented, which is one reason I never kept any of them around for long. One even went so far as to claim that we were secret lesbians and Rory was a beard. We had a good laugh at that one – Tara may be one of the most beautiful people alive, but I have never had any desire to visit her nether regions.

I am the Hillary Whitney to her CC Bloom, something we decided and pinkie-swore on when we first watched *Beaches* aged twelve. Tara also made me promise that I would never die of viral cardiomyopathy, leaving her to raise my spoilt daughter alone. I agreed.

And like the fictional duo we emulated, we'd only ever had one semi-serious wobble, and it was over a guy. My throat tightened as I remembered the one time I thought our friendship might be over, and why. Thank god we'd nipped it in the bud.

The desk in my small home office overlooks the Grand Canal, a vista that never fails to inspire me. Work takes me all over, from the UK to Dubai, but Dublin has always been and will always be home. I like to sit in my special chair and watch the twinkling lights of the busy docks. It makes me feel grounded.

As I glanced around, my eyes landed on something I didn't want to see. The advance proof of Sean Sweeney's autobiography had landed a few days ago and given me an awful fright. I'd hidden it under papers on my desk, ignoring it until I felt emotionally equipped to deal with it. But in the kerfuffle, it had revealed itself to me once again.

His face always had the same effect on me – every time I happened upon a picture of him I'd experience a rush of adrenaline, a wave of nausea and a vague throb of desire all at once. Awkwardly for me, barely a day went by without a photo of Sean Sweeney entering my orbit so I was spending more time than I'd like feeling sick and horny.

I'd have to read the book soon; avoiding it was not an option in my line of work. Celebrity commentators have to be abreast of everything in the zeitgeist, even books by boys that stamped all over your heart seventeen years ago. Well, only when said boy turned into a major rock star and fashion darling, I guess. I shook myself off and took off my glasses, pinching the bridge of my nose. Sean Sweeney was a problem for another day. Right now, it was time to prep for my interview with the disgraced duchess, and then figure out what to do about Tara.

VIPMAGAZINE.IE

Monday, 17 February 2025

COMING SOON

PREVIEW: Interview with a Rock Star, *by Sean Sweeney with Fionn Farrell*

We've only been allowed to read an extract so far because this book is promising to be extra juicy, but we already know that musician Sean Sweeney's memoir will be the hottest celeb read this spring.

The Irish boy-bander-turned-multi-platinum recording artist and style icon has stories to beat the band (pun intended), which he gleefully shares with music journalist Fionn Farrell in this glitzy, gossipy tell-all.

Millennials will remember him as the quiet one in The Chancers, the all-male quartet designed to pick up where Westlife, NSYNC and 4PLAY left off in the mid-noughties, only with instruments.

Then Sweeney left the band suddenly, moved Stateside and reinvented himself as a serious musician and the frontman of rock outfit Higher Power. With a distinctly New York sound and clever collaborations with hip-hop and EDM artists and producers, the band is a stalwart of the rock music scene.

Famously private, Sweeney has managed thus far to keep details of his early life under wraps. Hailing from working-class Crumlin, his musical talents were honed at the city's famous That's D'Amore stage school alongside other well-known Irish faces, like his Higher Power bandmate Ciaran Doyle, morning TV host Tommy McGrath, journalist and podcaster Alex Curtis and Oscar-winning actress Tara O'Toole.

We're told it's a delicious, jaw-dropping read, and that Sean will reveal all about his love life, substance-abuse issues and family strife. It promises to be a rollicking romp for anyone interested in pop culture and the making of a global rock icon.

3. Tara

I woke up not knowing exactly where I was. For a few brief seconds after I surfaced from slumber, I felt great. Rested, calm, happy even. I had a feeling of safety, which made sense as I realized I was in Alex's guest bedroom in Dublin. As I fully regained consciousness, the shock and horror of the previous couple of days came rushing back at breakneck speed. Rory had left me. He was in love with that little tramp Allegra. Nothing was as it should be and likely never would be again. Suddenly, I was struggling to breathe.

I scrabbled desperately at the bedside table, my hands frantically searching for the pills that had been numbing my sensibilities. Blessed Alex had called in a favour from a music promoter she knows and got me a sneaky stash of diazepam without a prescription. I've never really been one for drugs, but the dreamlike, sleepy sensation they provided was a panacea for the open wound of betrayal. I greedily swallowed two pills with water and lay back waiting for the calm to descend.

I wasn't sure exactly what day it was, and was afraid to look at my phone to find out. There would no doubt be hundreds of notifications; I knew my publicist, Giulia, and Alex had been fending off reporters since some bastard on the set leaked what had happened between Rory and me. I wasn't even being afforded a centimetre of space to deal with what had happened before the vultures started circling. I loved my job, but sometimes I really hated being a celebrity.

Sometimes I wondered if I'd have become an actress if I knew what being famous was really like. But all things considered, I know I'd still want to be a star. Since I was a tiny kid, acting was all I ever wanted to do. If my parents thought sending me to stage school as a child would contain my dramatic energy, they were mistaken – all it did was exacerbate it. That's where Alex and I met, and soon became joined at the hip.

Thank god for Alex Curtis, I thought as I tried to regulate my breath. That was a familiar mantra, one I'd repeated to myself over and over for literal decades. I'm not particularly religious (although I dabbled with Kabbalah in 2010; the red bracelet was cute), but I have always thought that a guardian angel must have been shining down on me the day I met her, because she has been rescuing me ever since. She'd say otherwise, though. Alex doesn't like to take credit for anything, let alone bolstering my mental health.

I lay there waiting to be lulled back to sleep. The apartment was so quiet I knew Alex wasn't home. She was likely getting her affairs in order before she had to drag her poor, cuckolded best friend across the ocean. Then I remembered; it was Monday, and she'd headed to London at the crack of dawn for her sit-down with the former Duchess of Bicester, now the proud author of a big-budget bonkbuster. Alex wouldn't be back until the evening.

A wave of loneliness washed over me, followed by a fresh burst of pain in my chest that spread outwards, as if through my arteries. I popped another pill, but when sleep still wouldn't return, I decided to get up.

Alex bought her place when she moved home from London a few years back, and it's her pride and joy. When the weather is nice there's an amazing view of the so-called Silicon Docks, but on a grey late-February morning the sky looked like I felt – foggy and depressed.

I was wearing an old Trinity College T-shirt belonging to Alex and nothing else, so I rooted in the clinically neat wardrobe in her room for panties and leggings. Honestly, I wouldn't have been surprised if she had all her knickers hung on tiny hangers and colour-coded from light to dark. I was almost right – she had a panty uniform of all black bikini-style briefs with a hint of lace trim. Feminine, but practical. Classic Alex.

I spied something anomalous from the corner of my eye. It was a ridiculous feather-trimmed pink satin robe that was utterly out of place, and I immediately identified it as an unwanted gift from Deirdre. Alex is too sentimental to give away presents from her mam, but the little paisley number was far more my taste than hers. I felt a little better even just putting it on.

Trying to distract myself while the drugs worked their magic, I took the opportunity to have a nose through Alex's stuff. I checked out her perfectly organized skincare collection and dug around her make-up bag until I got bored – how many subtly different red lipsticks can one blonde own?

I came across a framed photo on the bedside table. It showed two smiling little girls wearing fairy costumes, one slight, fair and pristine, and one tanned and a bit feral-looking. I picked it up and examined it; I hadn't seen the photo in years and it was so old-fashioned it even had a little digital date stamp in the bottom-right-hand corner: 31.03.1999. We were eleven, going on twelve, and I could remember it being taken so clearly.

'Girls, say cheese!' Deirdre had been behind the camera, and I was already posing and throwing up a peace sign like I'd seen the Spice Girls do on *Top of the Pops*. Looking at the photo, I could practically feel Alex's little arm tight around my waist.

'What a pair of little posers,' Darius had said from behind us. 'Gloria, you've really got a live one there.'

'Don't I know it, baby,' my mother laughed, her broad New York accent loud and out of place in the room. 'Mark my words, that girl will have an Oscar before she's thirty.'

It hadn't been the first time my mom had ever said such a thing, but it always made me feel so proud when she did. Gloria had believed in me wholeheartedly, always. Ugh. It was always hard remembering my mother. It never stopped hurting.

I always felt different to the other girls. I liked how my freckles seemed to join up in the summertime, and how I could speak Spanish like my mother, but I didn't like the way my hair wouldn't sit right, or the way some of the other moms tutted when I was loud. I was always being told to calm down, speak softly.

I was jolted from my reverie by a buzzing noise coming from the spare room. I followed it and noticed my phone flashing from where it was plugged beside the bed. My heart leapt when I saw Storm's contact photo on the incoming call.

'Tara, oh my god!' she shrieked when I answered. 'I've been so worried about you! I must have called like thirty-seven times since Saturday!' For once, this wasn't Gen Z hyperbole; I had been ignoring everyone, even my darling stepdaughter.

'Sweetie, I'm so sorry. I've been hiding from my phone. Are you okay?'

'I'm fine, it's you I'm worried about. Alex has been keeping me posted, but I needed to hear your voice. Are you really coming home?'

'Apparently so, in a day or two.' I exhaled. I could feel the benzos starting to relax my muscles a little, and I rotated my neck in an attempt to loosen it. 'Alex is handling it all, but I'm told we're going to New York as soon as arrangements are made. I just don't want to be seen by anyone on the way, so it's a little complicated.'

'Oh, I'm so relieved. I'll feel so much better once you're back here and I can keep an eye on you. I'll, uh . . . I'll get your room ready. Put all my dad's stuff elsewhere.'

My heart nearly broke at how sad she sounded. I've been in Storm's life since she was eleven years old. Rory's first wife, Lana, had died when the kids were nine and fifteen; he was raising Storm and Xavier alone when we met. Yes, they are named after X-Men characters. My husband is that much of a nerd.

Could I still call him my husband if he'd left me for somebody else? I felt a stabbing pain in my chest as I listened to my stepdaughter tell me how she was getting the apartment spruced up for my return. I knew without her having to tell me that Storm was also utterly furious with her father, and feeling as betrayed as I was. After all, Allegra was only a couple or so years older than her. I felt the rage stir deep in my soul, muted only slightly by the narcotics.

'Thank you, my love. I appreciate everything.' I could hear my words slurring, just a little. 'I've taken something to go to sleep, so I'll say goodbye. See you soon. Kisses.'

Yet still, sleep wouldn't come. I lay there in a daze, but still totally conscious and feeling my very bad feelings. It was almost noon, according to my phone, and the day stretched out torturously. I wandered around the apartment, just for something to do.

Alex's place is nice, but not exactly cosy. She's a neat freak and likes things super organized and minimalist, whereas I prefer old homes, somewhere with a bit of history. My pre-war three-bedroom on the Upper West Side is all hardwood floors and high ceilings, while the LA house in Beverly Hills used to belong to Elizabeth Taylor. Rory bought it for me when we got married, knowing Liz has always been my hero.

Yet another stab of pain pierced my chest as I realized I may not be able to keep my homes if Rory divorced me. Maybe I should lawyer up? Nab Laura Wasser before Rory did. The panic was rising, so I scrabbled in the dressing-gown pocket for another pill; either Alex had got me a bad batch, or they just didn't seem to be working like before. Maybe I was beyond pharmaceutical help.

Out of the corner of my eye, I spied Alex's bar cart. A drink would encourage the diazepam to knock me out, surely? I poured myself a strong vodka martini, stirred not shaken. A lot of people don't know that shaking a cocktail waters it down, as it melts the ice. That's why James Bond likes them shaken – a kick of booze, but weak enough to have his wits about him in a high-stakes situation. I wanted my wits to go away, so I sloshed in some extra vodka just to be safe.

I couldn't sit still, so I reeled around the apartment, touching all my best friend's possessions. There were so many books, and framed movie posters on the walls. Alex is big into entertainment and pop culture, so I always get her to read a script before I sign on to a project. She has a knack of knowing what'll be a hit.

I always thought Alex would end up acting too. She was actually the more impressive thespian of the two of us, even as a little girl, but she'd had bouts of paralysing stage fright since we were teenagers. As we got older, she became adamant that she didn't have the personality to be a celebrity; now I am one, I'm inclined to agree. Being both famous and successful is about far more than talent, sadly – you have to have a big set of balls to succeed in the movie industry, and Alex is a bit too gentle for showbusiness.

She'd been successful in the media, though, there was no denying that. Living in London in her twenties was the making of her. I fingered the awards on her shelf: Best Podcast Series for *Alex Knows* from 2021, Irish Non-Fiction Book of the Year for her official biography of Colin Farrell in 2023. She left my brief dalliance with him out of the book, thankfully; I didn't even have to ask her to. I don't know if Colin even remembers, to be honest. It was back in the day, when he was out of his bin most of the time.

Slurping my drink and trying not to spill it – why are martini glasses so damned awkward? – I sat down at the desk. Sometimes when I'm feeling overwhelmed by fame and its trappings, I like to imagine myself living Alex's life. Celebrity adjacent, but not involved exactly. Her face isn't plastered on crappy tabloid magazines, but nor has she ever graced the cover of *Vogue*. She has written for them, though.

I wondered – would that kind of life be enough for me? One behind the scenes? My private life wouldn't be fodder for the masses, but then, I wouldn't get to do what I loved either. Acting, unfortunately, comes with notoriety, if you're doing it right.

'Shit!' I exclaimed aloud as I sloshed vodka all over the desk. I moved a sheaf of papers to stop them getting destroyed and uncovered something that caught my eye. Was that . . . Oh! Sean Sweeney's autobiography. Wasn't he a bit young to have a memoir? He hadn't even hit forty. I guess celebrity years are like dog years when you think about it.

Idly, I flipped to the index at the back, checking to see if my name was mentioned. Having known Sean for ever, I'd be surprised if I wasn't. My vision focused and I saw that I was mentioned quite a lot. Not on just one or two pages, but . . . sixteen times? Hang on, was that a whole chapter dedicated to me?

I don't know how long I sat there reading, but as I pored over the pages I grew cold with terror. Every mention of me I saw made my heart rise further up into my throat, until I felt like it was choking me.

Sean was never meant to tell anybody this stuff. These were secrets, deep secrets, printed in black and white for all to see. What had he been thinking? And how would Alex react when she read this?

I felt like I was going out of my mind, and simultaneously dulled by the sedatives and alcohol; crawling out of my skin at the thought of Sean revealing things we'd promised to keep between us for ever. I took another pill, and then a few of Alex's over-the-counter painkillers to attempt to dull the gnawing headache that was crushing my skull.

But nothing helped. I was pacing the length of the apartment reading, and the words were starting to get very fuzzy, when I tripped. The book flew out of my hand and across the room as I fell, landing with a thud on the coffee table.

I must have stumbled over to the couch, because I came to half hanging off it god knows how long later. I heard a faraway scream and blearily opened my eyes to see Deirdre Curtis staring at me in horror. Was she an apparition? Why was she wearing a neon headband? I tasted vomit on my tongue, and then everything went black.

4. Alex

I sprinted through Heathrow's Terminal 2 to make my 7 p.m. flight, cursing Tara under my breath with every step. She was fine, I'd been assured of that by my mother, and by the doctor to whom I'd paid a premium for a house call. They, along with Tara's private New York physician, concurred that she had accidentally taken a few too many pills and passed out, thankfully not before vomiting some of them up.

My mam was terrified that Tara had attempted to top herself when she happened across Tara's unconscious form, but I knew implicitly that she hadn't tried to end it all. She'd just had a very bad shock and was trying to dull the pain. She's always been the type that plays fast and loose with the rules; Tara viewed dosage information on medication as a mere guideline. She swore she was just trying to sleep, and I believed her. So, being safe in the knowledge that Tara was all right, I could afford to be angry with her for ruining my day. It had been dangerous, what she'd done. Perhaps Tara needed more help than we'd realized.

I was already in the process of getting my friend back to New York, having decided that Jen and Mam were right. Taras's team had managed to quieten the story about her punching Rory and were very much painting her as the injured party – which she was, of course. It was now a case of being as discreet as possible when crossing the Atlantic so Tara wouldn't be hounded. Felicia was helping with the logistics, and I'd stay with my friend until she was back on her feet, whenever that might be. In truth, I didn't trust her Manhattan friends to look after her properly. Not the way I would, anyway.

My flight to Dublin was boarding, and I made it with minutes to spare. I'd been so anxious I was going to miss it because of how chaotic my day had been. Normally I have a very exacting airport schedule in order to cope with the mild trauma that is flying. I finally let myself exhale the breath I'd been holding in all day once I fastened my seatbelt.

My mother's hysterical call had come mere moments before I was due to sit down with Sexy Sadie, the disgraced divorced duchess who had turned her own notorious sex scandal into a semi-fictional account just about to be published. She was doing the chat-show rounds to promote it and coming straight to me from a live interview on *Loose Women*. I had secured the only one-to-one podcast slot with her and knew it would be huge for ratings.

Podcasts are more intimate than television interviews because celebrities are more relaxed when it's just me and a microphone. No cameras, no glam squads, just me and my questions. Harry Styles once told me that the combination of my sweet, blonde appearance and blunt interview style is disarming; he called it a 'lethal combination', while giving me the glad eye. It's a story I get a kick out of telling at dinner parties.

Thankfully, the duchess had been late and I had time to establish that Tara was both alive and not actually trying to overdose before I had to start the interview. I'd arranged for my very discreet GP to remain on call, calmed poor Deirdre down and managed to wipe any trace of hysteria off my face just as Sadie arrived.

The duchess was great – indiscreet, hilarious and warm, and I knew the chat would attract a new strain of listeners. Thank goodness for small mercies.

The plane began trundling down the runway, something that always sets my teeth on edge no matter how many hundreds of times I fly. I don't like being so out of control, hurtling through the air in a tin can with wings, and I think that's a very rational fear.

I caught sight of my reflection in my iPad screen as we

levelled off and winced. I needed a top-up of Botox; I was looking haggard. I'm generally a very low-maintenance person and not very vain; I have the same Sézane shirt in fourteen different colours and prints, and I wear them with mom jeans, one of my many pairs of statement glasses and a swipe of lippie. Thankfully, that is enough to be considered a 'look'.

It's a good job most of my work takes place off camera; I'm not expected to look flawless 24/7, not like Tara is. The podcast being popular internationally means I do have to stay on top of my image, though – you can't look like hell and expect people to listen to your show and like your memes, that's the sad truth.

I'd ask Tara where was best for Botox when we got to New York. I don't know how she does it, being constantly switched on and looked at, but she does it with aplomb. Usually.

And I didn't mind going to New York, really. I was lucky, in that I could do my work from anywhere. I don't usually love my routine being impacted, but going to one of my favourite cities on earth to help my closest friend wasn't exactly a hardship. I could manage.

The plane bounced around a bit in turbulence, and I yelped loudly enough that the man next to me gave me a filthy look. Sorry for worrying about my own mortality, sir! I thought, closing my eyes. I couldn't help being frightened; it was baked into my bones at this point, no matter how many times I tried hypnosis for anxiety or breathing techniques. I've always been a scaredy cat, since I was a little girl. My mother says I came out of the womb nervous, my first cries meek until I was safe and swaddled in her arms.

Tara was actually my first ever proper friend. I'd spent my childhood being mercilessly bullied at school, perhaps because I was slight and sweet-natured. They called me Specky Four Eyes (original) and Casper (the friendly ghost) and, as we got older, it got more physical. I spent a lot of time feeling utterly alone.

Then Mam sent me to That's D'Amore when regular school had become a living nightmare, and it was the making of me. There, I met people like me who loved movies and music, and being friends with someone fabulous like Tara allowed me to develop a sort of confidence that bolstered me when I was rattled. So while she always says that I'm her guardian angel, the truth is, Tara saved me way back when and I've just been repaying her ever since. Ours is a friendship that pre-dates celebrity, that is predicated on a sisterly bond formed young and strengthened by everything we've been through together.

The plane lurched again. I know logically that turbulence is only air pockets, but my body still reacted to every jolt. I was trying to fully dissociate when the girl in the row behind me started blaring music from her phone – and not just any song, but the latest one by Higher Power. I sighed. Typical.

It was hard to think about That's D'Amore without thinking about Sean Sweeney, because that's where I also first laid eyes on him. Tara and I had been there a year when he'd joined, and he was just so . . . cool. He'd been held back in school, so although he was a year older than us, he was in the same class. He had a slightly rougher accent than my own and hailed from the exact opposite side of the city to me, a magical place I had never heard of called Crumlin.

Sean told us he had four older brothers and his 'ma' had sent him to stage school so he could channel his creative impulses. 'She's afraid I'll either start hanging around a group of gurriers like Anto, or get the head bet off me playing GAA like Paul.' I didn't have a notion about gangs or rough sports, but every word Sean spoke sounded like magic to my ears. I was spellbound.

Sean was also very talented. He could sing, dance and play the guitar, and everyone fancied him. Tara was the only one who wasn't really interested. 'Too full of himself,' she'd sniffed when I'd confessed my undying love for him. 'And he has weird hair.'

My adoration went unrequited. It wasn't like I even had much opportunity to get to know him on a deeper level; Sean didn't socialize much. I knew he worked with his uncle, selling fuel off the back of a truck in the small bit of spare time he had, and that money was tight. Still, he never missed a class or a production and I idolized him from afar throughout my adolescence.

Then, in our final year, Tara admitted that she finally saw what the fuss was about. 'He's grown into himself now he's eighteen,' she said. 'And he dresses better. I get it, Alex!'

At first I was thrilled that my best friend agreed with me. Then, when it seemed her interest was reciprocated, I became horrified. I'd catch Sean gazing at Tara as she danced in class and my chest would fill with a burning sensation, white hot and bitter in my throat. How could I ever compete with the dazzling Tara O'Toole?

Tara must have been able to sense my envy, and made a suggestion before our last Easter production. 'Let's make a pinkie promise,' she said at rehearsals when she caught me drawing love hearts around his character's name in the script. 'How about we both swear to never, ever go near Sean Sweeney romantically? That we'll never let him come between us, dreamy and all as he may be?'

She saw my puzzled frown. 'He's just a fish in the sea, Alex! You and me, we're only just getting started. There'll be so many more boys in our future we won't be able to cope.' Tara threw her arms out dramatically, and I couldn't help but giggle.

'Deal,' I agreed. As if he'd ever look twice at me anyway. This way, Tara would stay away from Sean and my heart could remain unbroken. She hooked her little finger with mine, we both kissed the other's finger, and a pact was made.

To my amazement, it didn't take very long for me to break it.

I finally arrived home around 9 p.m., tired and hungry. My mother greeted me at the door.

'Why on earth are you dressed like that?' I gaped, taking in her leg warmers and fluorescent leggings.

'I was at Zumba!' she yelped. 'Today's class was Barbie themed. I was mortified when the doctor arrived. I was planning on showering and changing when I got here, but I've been afraid to leave Tara for a second.' Poor Deirdre looked exhausted. I pulled her in for a big hug in the hallway.

'Thank you for being here today, Mam. I never should have gone to London. Tara was in no fit state to be left alone.'

'Nonsense, pet. It's not your fault. I'm just glad I got here when I did, but the poor child was a sorry sight. She vomited all over your lovely rug . . .' A puke stain wasn't quite as upsetting as my friend's precarious emotional state, but it was close. Still, I wasn't going to let on.

'Feck the rug. How is she? And how are you?'

'Sure I'm fine, I had a brandy when that nice doctor was here, once I knew she was going to be okay. Sorted me right out. Tara is another story,' she whispered, nodding towards the living room. 'I'd swear there's something else going on, something she's not saying. She's very agitated.'

'I think I'd be agitated too if my husband left me for a girl younger than his son,' I muttered.

'She was moaning about reading something when she was still out of it, but she's been sort of mute since she sobered up. Now, love, are you sure about going to New York? How long will you be gone?'

'Yeah, it's fine, I promise,' I placated her. 'I have no idea, but I'm always on FaceTime, okay? I'll keep in constant touch.'

'I know you will, pet, I just worry . . .' She sighed. 'When something happens with Tara, good or bad, you always jump in with both feet. I worry about you forgetting about your own life sometimes.'

I knew my mother was concerned about me always playing second fiddle to my friend because she often told me. Deirdre thought I was getting long in the tooth and should be focused on finding my own husband and family, like Jen and Tara had.

'This is what friends are for, Mammy.'

'I blame those shows you grew up watching. Bloody Rachel and Monica, and those *Sex and the City* wans. Friends are wonderful, Alex, but they're no substitute for a husband and children. And I say that loving Tara like a daughter of my own.'

'You'd walk through fire for Darius!'

'That's different!'

'It isn't a bit different, other than the fact that he's not a world-famous star going through a crisis. If Francisco left him for some young buck, you'd be on the next flight.'

She looked suitably chastened, and I heard her huffing under her breath.

'Now, you better be getting off,' I said. 'Dad will be starving.'

'Eamonn will be fine; I taught him how to use Deliveroo a few weeks back. He'll have ordered half of Nando's to the house, and it will reek of peri peri. Goodnight, sweetheart. Talk to you tomorrow.'

I waved her off, and finally entered the living room, where I found Tara curled up on the L-shaped couch, a blanket on her knees. She was pale and wild-eyed.

'Alex, I'm so sorry. I'm not able for these feelings,' she whispered when I sat down beside her and took her limp hand in mine. She was wearing the ridiculous feathered robe my mother had given me for Christmas, and there was a vague smell of vomit off her, but I said nothing. 'I keep calling Rory, and he won't even answer. How could he be so cruel?' she pleaded, her amber eyes brimming over with fresh tears.

I hugged her tight, whispering soothing affirmations. Rory had been ignoring my calls too; I suspected he had handed his phone off to an assistant so he could continue his sordid affair in peace.

'It's going to be okay, Tara, I swear. Tomorrow, we're going back to New York. You'll see Storm, and Darius will be there.

You'll be back with your dogs, your own things. You don't need any more pills to numb you out. I'm sorry, honey, this is one time when you're going to just have to feel it.'

When she finally looked at me, she seemed a little more frantic than I'd anticipated. Her eyes were wild, her teeth chattering. 'Alex, I need you to promise me something.'

'Anything.'

'Promise me you won't abandon me now, no matter what.'

'I won't.'

'No matter what, Alex!' She gripped my hand so tightly it started to hurt.

'Tara, I won't leave you, I promise. I'm with you through all of this, okay?'

She sank back against the cushions, the trembling easing slightly. She nodded, but her eyes were elsewhere.

'I'm going to pack, okay?' I said. 'I need to get my stuff together to be able to work from New York.'

Tara nodded again, but I could feel her watching me as I filled my bag (a re-gifted Louis Vuitton Neverfull from Storm, who had declared it 'SO not my style'). I collected all the things I'd need to do my job – portable mics, headphones, notebook, iPad, laptop, various chargers, my favourite pens and my trusty diary that Tara slags me about. I may live and work in the digital age, but I'm still a paper girl.

I paused, knowing I was forgetting something. Then my eyes fell on Sean Sweeney's autobiography. It was on the coffee table. I didn't remember leaving it there. Weird. I knew I couldn't avoid it any more, though. It was being published that same week. Tara's cushy private plane was the perfect place to get over myself, and dive in uninterrupted for seven hours.

I slid the book into my bag and met Tara's gaze. She looked even more horrified than she had moments before. 'What is it?' I asked, concerned.

'Uh . . . nothing. It's nothing at all.' She plastered on a smile, which didn't quite reach her eyes. 'Let's look at your clothes, shall we? You'll hate every single thing in my wardrobe, so we better bring lots of stuff for you to wear.'

She rose from the couch still wrapped in the blanket and shuffled into my bedroom, surprising me. Tara never showed any interest in my clothes – she thought I had the most desperately boring style on planet earth. But then I figured, any action was preferable to catatonia.

Tara's moods were bound to yo-yo, and perhaps rooting through someone else's wardrobe could rouse even the most depressed, betrayed fashionista from her misery. Her being engaged in slagging my clothes was preferable to another near-fatal accidental overdose. So I followed her in, daring to feel a tiny bit hopeful.

Extract from Interview with a Rock Star *by Sean Sweeney*

Chapter Nine

Me and Miss O'Toole

That's D'Amore continued to be an escape from home as I got older. When I first enrolled, Ma was under a lot of pressure with all the kids by herself and money was tight. Darius had taken pity on her when she begged him to give me a chance. I was displaying musical talent with the guitar my dad left behind when he moved out, so the big old softie created a scholarship so I could attend the school, and never let on to Ma that this was previously unheard of. She never would have let me go if she knew it was charity, and instead she got to be proud as punch of me being good enough for a free ride. I'll always be grateful to Darius for that. And Ma, I'm sorry for telling whoppers!

Throughout my teens, That's D'Amore was a break from the drudgery of regular school. I guess I was a late bloomer in most ways, purely because I never had time to think about life outside of helping Ma, working for my uncle delivering coal, or suffering through my education so I could get to stage school every Tuesday, Thursday and Saturday.

There were cute girls everywhere and, believe me, it wasn't that I didn't notice them. I simply could never fathom getting involved with anyone, or bringing them home to the chaos of my house. I saw friends enjoying first love and new experiences, but I felt like it wasn't for me; that I was an outsider.

Tara O'Toole was always the hottest girl in stage school. Even as a teenager she had that star quality, that smile that lit up her whole face, this mane of wild curls and – let's be honest – a fantastic body. She was gorgeous and popular, and I didn't think she'd be interested in a lad like me when she could have anyone.

In fairness, she didn't pay me a blind bit of attention until we were in our final year. I had become a bit more sociable then, realizing that all the craic of That's D'Amore would soon be behind me and I'd have to get serious about pursuing a career in music or come to terms with working for Uncle Ray for ever.

I was horny as hell by then too. It was like as soon as I allowed myself to even consider women, my hormones went wild. I fancied every girl I met – I didn't have a type; maybe I still don't – but I didn't have the confidence required to make up for my lack of experience, so I held back. This was the era of internet porn, the first time you could access stuff for free online, so that's where I directed my, er, energies.

It was at a New Year's Eve party in Sixth Year that Tara and I hooked up. I can't say I had anything to do with it – she seduced me, and I was unable to resist her charms. I'd say I was absolutely awful – I shudder to think about my performance. I don't know why she chose me that night – everyone at the party was mad for her. I was powerless as she took my hand, led me to the bathroom and confidently deflowered me. I don't think it was her first rodeo – she knew exactly what she was doing.

Looking back, I remember now that Tara's mam was sick at the time. Maybe she needed a distraction herself, maybe she felt my own vulnerability, maybe I just looked good to her that night. I think now that Tara recognized something in me, an innocence of sorts. I was more in awe of her than anything else. I soon found that she became somebody important to me over the years and we would occasionally meet up for no-strings-attached sex. I can't say how often it happened, but I'd bet more than two dozen times.

There were lonely nights in London before we both made it really huge, times of comfort in New York when an audition had gone badly for her or the pressure of being in a band was getting to me. We understood one another, but were pursuing different types of career. We could be close, but not too close.

After a few years, I started seeing less of Tara. She was already starring in romcoms then, being billed as the next Julia Roberts, or Lindsay Lohan (before Lindsay went off the rails). I didn't want to lose her; Tara always felt like a bit of home, no matter where I was. I did make sure to lean on her less, and to open myself up to other women more.

I was with her the night before she won her Oscar. She'd called me, freaking out, telling me she couldn't handle the pressure. I was in LA because it's the place to be when the big awards ceremonies are going on – loads of parties, mingling, glad-handing. I left the soirée I was at as soon as she called. I knew it might be my last chance with her – if she won, this thing between us was on borrowed time. She was becoming so much more famous than me.

Our arrangement only really stopped once and for all, though, when she met her husband the following year. As soon as she fell for Rory Vaughan, we were donezo.

I remember feeling put out when Tara told me she was in love with him and couldn't meet up any more. It wasn't like getting dumped exactly, but it did make me feel cheap – like I was a stopgap until she fell for her perfect action man. It activated that old feeling of never being good enough.

I remember my mate Ciaran telling me to cop on. He was the one person I told about my thing with Tara, and he said the only thing really hurt was my ego. I guess he was right, because I bounced back pretty spectacularly with Charlize Theron, the first of several high-profile relationships I would enjoy and endure.

I'll always remember Tara incredibly fondly. I'm so proud of her, and I guess I'll always have a lot of love for her. Even though I've been intimate with her numerous times, when I see her on the big screen it's like watching a stranger, someone larger than life. I can't believe how successful she is. I've won awards, sure, but they're for Higher Power, not just me. I wonder if she ever has imposter syndrome, like I do.

Tara gave me confidence and support, despite us not being in a conventional relationship. A part of me will always long for her. Part of me even feels like a big shot admitting that I've slept with the woman every guy wants to bed. Maybe if her marriage ever goes down the drain, we can revisit things. I'd never say never – and yes, lads, she is as sexy as she appears on the big screen. Sexier, even.

5. Tara

The thought of getting home to New York was the only thing that got me on to that tiny private plane the next morning. I was still shell-shocked and fragile from accidentally overdoing it on the pills, terrified of even looking at medication or a drink. I knew I'd have to endure the cruel torment of witnessing Alex's heartbreak stone-cold sober, in a confined space hurtling over the Atlantic.

We'd just boarded from the private terminal at Dublin Airport when Alex whipped out Sean's book and grimaced. 'I guess I have to finally read this,' she smirked. 'I wonder why Sean didn't ask me to ghostwrite it. It is my specialty, after all. Award-winning, don't you know.'

I attempted a smile. Poor, sweet Alex thinking that Sean Sweeney would know that about her, or remember anything about anyone from That's D'Amore who wasn't in his A-list orbit.

I cursed him internally once again, not only for his shocking indiscretion but for his really shitty timing. I didn't think I could feel any worse than I had the past few days, but somehow the thought of Alex hating my guts was even scarier than being deserted by my husband. The two combined, well, it was a wonder I was still breathing.

It crossed my mind that Rory wouldn't be best pleased with Sean's revelations either, but then I remembered that Rory didn't love me any more. He was hooking up with his very own pop star, perhaps even at that very moment. My stomach rolled and I wanted to throw up. How could all of this be happening? My husband was my rock, my world. We'd sworn to stay together for ever, no matter what.

I first met Rory at an incredible time in my life. I had just won the Oscar (and the BAFTA and the SAG) for Best Actress at the relatively tender age of twenty-four. Well, I was really twenty-six, but that's beside the point.

As far as the world was concerned, I was the hottest starlet in Hollywood, and the offers were coming in thick and fast. Over the years I'd been in three or four well-received romcoms, graduating from sassy friend to leading lady with ease. But I had really burst on to the serious acting scene and swept awards season thanks to *Rita*, the biopic of the beautiful Golden Age star Rita Hayworth. I was lauded for my ability to play her from a teenage ingénue through to the woman in her mid-thirties who divorced a Pakistani prince and returned to the movie business. Critics called me 'a chameleon who seems wiser than her years'. They were sort of correct – that little age reduction really was a great move by my mom.

Anyway, that's all to say that I was riding very high when I was introduced to the enigmatic Mr Vaughan at a mutual friend's dinner party in my honour. Lorraine Staffetta was a Big Deal in New York society, the wife of a publisher and a maven of the city's jet set. I'd just been revealed as *Mister* magazine's Sexiest Woman on Earth 2013, and the Staffettas threw me a lavish dinner party at their Upper East Side home to celebrate my cover of their most-esteemed title.

Lorraine is widely known now as one of the cast members of hit reality show *Ladies of New York*, but back then she was more low-key and cultured, preferring to fly under the radar. Her parties were known for being simultaneously hedonistic and elegant, and attracted the cream of the crop. People aren't quite so keen to attend Lorraine's shindigs these days, afraid their letting loose will be filmed for *LONY*.

I knew it was a set-up the second I sat down at the table next to Rory because he was exactly my type – sexy and macho but sweet with it, and seemed a little melancholy. He had light hair and fair eyebrows but the darkest black lashes I've ever seen on a man. It was a jarring combination, even more so up close.

'I owe Lorraine one,' I announced as I went to take my seat next to him. 'I lucked out with the seating arrangement.'

'Tara O'Toole, it's great to meet you.' He stood up and pulled out my chair, his height and manners instantly turning me on. 'Huge congratulations on a stellar awards season – you're the toast of Hollywood.'

I knew he was putting on the act we all do, but there was something that felt genuine about Rory. We kept brushing hands – accidentally-on-purpose on my part – during the starters, and every time we touched I felt a frisson of sexual energy I'd never experienced before. He regaled me with tales of growing up in Boston, and even asked me lots of questions about myself – unusual for an actor.

'I'm Irish too, you know,' he said during the main course.

'Let me guess,' I teased. 'You have third cousins twice removed in Wexford?'

'No, my mother is actually Irish,' he laughed. 'I'm not one of those Yanks who just claims the heritage. Bernie Vaughan is from Leitrim. She was born and grew up there, and moved here to be an au pair when she was eighteen. She had the misfortune of hooking up with my pop not long after.'

I admired his self-awareness. 'Okay, so you're just as Irish as I am! My mom was from New York.'

If he noticed the past tense, he didn't let on. 'Ahh, that explains your street smarts. So we're the same, then – only I don't have the adorable freckles or sexy Dublin accent.'

I practically purred at him in response.

I'd heard about his wife's death in childbirth a couple of years previously like everyone else, through the press. Lorraine confessed afterwards that she'd seated us together because she thought I could cheer him up. I'll never forget his sad green eyes, and how they gradually brightened as the night progressed and I worked my magic on him. Only, it wasn't an act – I really was taken with him.

Meeting men has never been an issue for me, but meeting nice ones in the business was difficult, to say the least. But as soon as Rory and I got past the pleasantries and the flirting and actually started to talk properly I could sense his sensitivity, his injured soul. By the time we got to dessert, he was opening up to me about the loss of Lana, who had been his high-school sweetheart. She had passed away from complications due to pre-eclampsia, along with their stillborn baby. I couldn't imagine that level of heartbreak, of having to endure it so publicly.

Rory spoke so lovingly of Lana, to the point where I felt oddly jealous. He seemed to come alive when he was showing me pictures of their gorgeous young children, and I felt bereft at the thought of them growing up without their mom. I could feel a kinship with Rory then, his own palpable sense of loss mirroring what I'd felt in the years since I lost my mother.

We both said later that we knew right away we were meant to be together. Rory said I brought him back to life, resuscitated the man in him he thought had died along with Lana. He said he'd been like a zombie until I came along.

There was a raw attraction there, but it was about more than just a sexual connection. It was the intellectual and emotional match I'd been longing for. Looking back, though, it was our vulnerabilities that truly bonded us. I might have been at the peak of my powers in work, but inside I was still the bereft teenager who thought becoming an even bigger star would save her from grief and loneliness.

It all moved pretty quickly. We slept together that same night; I invited him in for coffee because he insisted on seeing me home to my brand-new SoHo loft rental, and before I knew it we were naked and writhing in the entryway. I momentarily feared he'd think less of me for coming on strong, but he was as captivated as I was. He told me a couple of weeks later that he'd had to stop himself proposing mid-cunnilingus the next morning. 'I thought I'd be alone for the rest of my life, Tara. I was content to be, after Lana. But all of a sudden, you've changed all that. I didn't know I could be so lucky.'

It was love, the true love I'd been longing for. And now it was gone.

Alex laughed at something in the book. 'The way Sean writes about Darius is gas,' she said. 'He has him down to a tee.'

Ugh, she was edging dangerously close to my chapter. My head felt all jumbled up. How was I supposed to care about what was essentially ancient history between Sean and me at this moment in time? If things were normal, I would of course be horrified about Alex finding out about our encounters like this. But things weren't normal. I'd been deserted, abandoned, betrayed. My husband had razed our life together to the ground. Now my closest friend, my biggest supporter, was about to find out a huge secret I'd kept from her, all because of a stupid book. The extra layer of drama was threatening to push me over the edge.

I needed to warn her, to tell Alex what was coming before she read it in black and white, but I just couldn't get it out. My tongue simply wouldn't allow me to tell her the truth. My dalliance with Sean over the years was the only secret I'd ever kept from Alex, but I kept it for her own good. It would only have hurt her.

The plane took off and I noted Alex's fingers curling tightly around the armrest, her knuckles white. She hates being out of control.

Yet she didn't stop reading. In fact, Alex seemed to be digesting Sean's words at a frantic pace. I couldn't just sit there and watch her turn the pages of the book, inching ever closer to revealing my deep shame. Once we were at cruising altitude and the Wi-Fi kicked in, I practically sprinted to the bathroom and locked the door.

Seeing Jen's face when FaceTime connected made me feel

a bit better. Darius was our showbiz dad and mentor at That's D'Amore, but Jen was its heart and soul. I've always looked up to her as a super-cool big-sister figure; of course, the age difference is minimal now, but when we were kids it mattered. She's one of the few people in the world who knows Alex and I equally well.

'Oh Christ, you look in bits,' Jen gasped, recoiling at the sight of me. 'I'm sorry, I'm just so used to you looking perfect. You're grey!'

'Jen, I'm going out of my mind on this plane and we've only been on it forty minutes.'

'Have you owned up yet?'

I shook my head, and Jen sighed. I'd sent her pictures of the pages mentioning me in Sean's book the night before, and we had a long and fiery text conversation where she totally chewed me out for lying by omission for so many years. I'm glad I still had some of the benzos in my system, otherwise I may not have taken her admonishments so calmly.

'I know you're considering denying everything, but there's no point ever denying the truth, Tara. That just expands the web of deceit. You must tell Alex yourself. You can't sit there and let her read his words.'

'Maybe there's a chance she won't believe them. She knows how the game works – she could think that Sean is using my name to sell books. I could stick to that story. What's she gonna do, call him to verify it?'

'Alex Curtis is no fool, Tara. It all makes a lot of sense when you think about it. I know you're clutching at straws here, hon, but you are going to have to come clean. She will understand, when you explain it. It was just physical, meant nothing, famous-person stuff, yadda yadda.'

'You sound like Darius.'

'Well, sometimes Uncle Dar is right. Alex gets that you don't exactly lead a normal life. And Tara, I know you won't mind me saying this, but you've never exactly been a model best friend.'

'What's that supposed to mean?!'

'It means that people like you are treated differently to mere mortals. You're not great at texting back, your schedule comes first, you don't pay attention to details. But that's all understandable. You're a movie star! You make up for it in other ways.'

I frowned. Was that true? I had no time to dwell, because Jen was still going.

'. . . as a normie, I would not get away with riding the love of my best friend's life for years and not telling her, but you?'

'He's *hardly* the love of her li—'

Jen cut me off. 'Tara O'Toole, Oscar winner and superstar? You'll be forgiven. The rules are different for the rich, famous and beautiful.'

I snorted. 'As if you're not rich or beautiful!'

'Would you go and shite, Tara. I can just about afford my oat milk latte addiction and I'm barely above average-looking, but I'm happy to play by the normie rules. If Brian cheated on me, he'd be out on his ear. One thing I don't tolerate is infidelity!'

Jen realized what she'd said immediately, her hand flying to her mouth. 'I'm sorry, pet. How insensitive of me, with Rory . . . My god, this is truly awful timing.'

'Tell me about it,' I moaned, tears spilling over on to my cheeks.

'Look, Tara. Alex adores you just as much as I do, maybe even more. She knows you're going through something awful. But what happened between you and Sean happened, and it will all come out in the wash eventually. My advice is to get ahead of it. Tell her everything about the friends-with-benefits arrangement, stress that it was ages ago and apologize profusely. Sure, you forgave her all those years ago when she broke your pact about him.'

A light bulb went on in my head. 'Say that again?'

'Your pact? That neither of you would ever shag Sean Sweeney, and she was eaten up with guilt when she did?'

'Ohmigod, Jen. I had forgotten all about that!'

'You forgot? That she spent that one weekend with him, one she's both romanticized and felt guilty about ever since? *See*, you've just proved my point. You have the rare condition of celebrity brain. There is no known cure.'

I nodded, dumbfounded at my own stupidity.

'Christ, Tara. I know you're very busy and important, but that was a pretty huge moment in the girl's existence. She was odd for ages after it, remember? She disappeared to France for a semester, out of nowhere!'

I sighed, nodding. 'That was the weekend of pure magic no other guy can ever live up to. I remember.'

Jen went on chastising me, prattling on about how Sean Sweeney has been the blueprint for Alex's romantic life, but all I could think was how much better I felt about confessing. Alex had broken our pact first. Sure, I'd slept with him before I suggested we both steer clear, but she didn't know that!

Alex had been horrified about the effect her brief fling with Sean might have on our friendship and was distraught at the time, terrified it was going to be a huge deal. But if I remembered correctly, I'd forgiven her instantly. In fact, I'd been very magnanimous about it all. Maybe she'd reciprocate? Maybe this wouldn't be as awful as I'd feared?

'Jen, I have to go. I'm going to tell her right now.'

'Oh, thank god. Get it all out at thirty-five thousand feet. I'll fill Uncle Dar in for when you land; he can play go-between if needs be. And if she murders you, well, Brian knows some very good morticians in New York.'

I said goodbye and practically ran back into the main cabin. When I saw how much further she'd got in the book, I froze for a moment, but the warm smile Alex gave me told me she hadn't yet reached the chapter of doom.

'Hey . . .' I managed, hoarsely. 'Can I talk to you about something?'

'Anything,' she beamed, closing the book and leaning forward. 'Always.'

6. Alex

'There's something I have to tell you,' Tara said. She seemed giddy, nervous even. 'It would be great if you just let me get it all out because it's kind of a long story. Okay?'

Finally, Tara must be ready to open up and tell me what had really happened between her and Rory. I'd sensed that there was more to the dissolution of their marriage than she was letting on. Relieved, I smiled and nodded encouragingly.

'It's about Sean Sweeney. The book you're reading, well, there's a chapter about me in there.'

'No way!' I cried. 'That's gas, but I'm not surprised. His editor probably made him include all of his super-cool famous "friends". All in the name of publicity, right?'

'Al, just listen, remember?'

'Sorry. Of course.' I gestured for her to continue, intrigued.

'Sean's rendering of the whole debacle in the book is pretty accurate, so you can read it if you want some of the gory details. But the main point is that . . . well, in our final year at That's D'Amore I realized I was developing a thing for Sean. I was suddenly hugely attracted to him. Out of nowhere, we had this crazy chemistry that was difficult to ignore.'

This was news to me, but Tara was still talking.

'Gloria was sick at the time, you were locked away studying for the Leaving Cert and I just wanted to get out of the house as much as possible. I couldn't sit at home and witness my mother waste away. Jen was older, she was out in the clubs with her college friends, so I started hanging around with other girls in the school, remember? We got pissed, had fun. Well, there was one particular party on a night when I was really going through it. It was New Year's, actually. I couldn't get my mom's pale, sick face out of my head, no matter how much I drank. She was in so much pain and I couldn't help her.' Tara paused for a moment and gulped back tears. 'Sean was there that night. I saw him across the room through my vodka haze and, well, I thought he might make me feel better.'

Tara's voice was like a narration, so much so that I could picture the scene she was describing like an old home movie, the kind Eamonn used to transfer on to VHS. I could see the crowded house party in my mind's eye – someone always had a free gaff back then – and imagine Sean and Tara clocking one another from across the busy, smoky room.

'It was close to midnight, and everyone was lining up someone to kiss when the clock struck twelve. I thought, fuck this, went over to Sean and grabbed his hand. We didn't talk, I just led him to the bathroom and I put on the taps to block out the noise of the party. I took his face in my hands and kissed him, and it was like fireworks went off. Thinking about it now, there could have been actual fireworks going off outside, but at the time I was just focused on him. Before I knew it, we were rolling around the damp tiles on the floor.'

My hearing went a bit funny then. How had Tara never told me this before? I felt hot and cold at the same time.

'. . . and I was so shocked when he told me he was a virgin. I wasn't – you know I'd been with Darryl the year before . . .'

Oh, I remembered it well. I hadn't even been kissed at that point, but Tara was incredibly worldly in comparison, having already been 'in love'.

'What was it like?' I interrupted. 'With Sean?'

Tara swallowed. 'It was . . . ugh, I don't remember! I was eighteen – I'm sure it was very wham bam thank you ma'am. I just know that when we were finished, we went back to the party and I didn't see him for the rest of the night. Sometimes I wonder if I imagined it.' Tara looked thoughtful, but then she clocked my bewildered expression.

'Alex, I knew how you felt about him, even then. Maybe not

the intensity of it, but I knew you liked him. And I was selfish! I was immature, deranged with lust and some sort of premature grief. We all do stupid things when we're teenagers. The pre-frontal cortex doesn't even finish developing until you're twenty-five – why does nobody tell you that when you're young?'

She smiled hopefully at me, but I couldn't bring myself to smile back.

'Look, the only explanation is that my stupid adolescent brain figured that I deserved Sean because of all I was going through, and that you would never, ever make a move on him anyway. The girls were all saying he was gay because he never tried it on with any of them. I think part of me came on to him that night just to see if my attraction was reciprocated. But Alex, I realized very soon after that you were actually *in* love with Sean. Once I fully understood the depth of your feelings, I felt horribly guilty. I swore to myself that he would never come between us. He was just a boy.'

'That's what you said, all right. When you suggested we make a pact to stay away from him.'

'I did, I know. I should have told you I'd already gone there, but it felt pointless to hurt your feelings when it was just a one-off.'

I sighed. What was I meant to do with this information now? Suddenly, I felt very old, and the complexities of teenagers having sex light years away. 'Is that it, then? He tells the story of losing his virginity to you in the book?'

Tara sat back and swallowed, and my heart began a journey to my throat. There was clearly more to come and, by the look on my friend's face, it wasn't good news.

'Life took some turns, as you know,' she began. 'Sean joined The Chancers that summer, and they got signed. Then my mother died two weeks after I got my first agent, remember?'

I nodded. How could I forget? Gloria's death had been hard for all of us, but, of course, devastating for Tara. Her dad, Christy, had gone to pieces when Gloria was in treatment; by the time his wife passed, he was drinking heavily and basically MIA. His body was there, in their house in Terenure, but he was no use to Tara or anyone else.

'I just wanted to get away from home, away from Dad's grief and my own. You know I was never studious – college wasn't an option. So acting it was, and I was out auditioning, flitting from place to place when you were in college.

'Eventually, I bumped into Sean again. We were both in London when I wasn't quite twenty-one. I was filming what I thought was just a low-budget gangster movie – I never thought it would be my biggest break. Sean was working on the group's third album, he'd had a bit of a glow up, and we were so glad to see one another. A familiar face, you know? We ended up sleeping together, and it was different to the first time. But I didn't plan it, Alex, I swear. He came to my shitty hotel to watch a movie and hang out, but it just so happened that the movie was *Cruel Intentions*, which is *so* sexy, and well, it just happened . . .'

I felt sick to my stomach, but I let Tara talk. If this was in Sean's memoir, it was all going to come out anyway. I may as well hear it straight from the horse's mouth, even if it made me want to vomit. I was frantically doing the sums in my head, trying to figure out what year she was talking about, whether it was before or after my own time with Sean.

'It happened again twice, maybe three times over the course of that year, and it was nice and familiar. I swore that was it, that I had just been lonely and under a lot of pressure. I didn't want to tell you because you were studying abroad. It was when you were in France on Erasmus, remember?'

Of course I remembered. So, it wasn't long after my own dalliance with Sean. I remembered watching from Lyon as Tara's professional luck changed and feeling very far away from her. If I'd known she was sleeping with him then . . . I shuddered, unable to imagine it.

The plane started shaking and the Fasten Seatbelt sign came on, but Tara didn't seem to even notice. She was still talking.

'And then the universe just kept bringing Sean and me together. The celebrity world is small and crazy insular when you're in it. This was the noughties, so no dating apps. I was finding it difficult to meet any guy that wasn't a total sleazebag. At the time, all the cool celebrities were into hard drugs and it just wasn't my scene. When I ran into Sean at awards shows and glitzy parties, it was sort of inevitable we'd go home together.'

I was resisting the urge to scream.

'Alex, I never planned to sleep with Sean. It always just happened, but it only ever happened once in a while. That was how I comforted myself, and condoned not telling you. But trust me, afterwards, I'd be *consumed* with self-loathing, promising myself it was the last time and that I'd stay away from Sean Sweeney. I'm so sorry that I never told you, Al. I'm so sorry that it's coming out now, because the timing couldn't be worse. But I will answer any of your questions, tell you whatever else you need to know, because I need you to forgive me. Please, Alex.'

Her monologue was over, and I felt a strange mix of rage and numbness. I didn't cry, didn't even really react. Some inner strength, an inviolable instinct, told me not to, no matter how livid I was. I guess years spent hiding my emotions from the bullies stood to me, because I kept my shit together.

I'd known there was something up with Tara. I'd felt her watching me since I got back from London, and she'd been jumpy, like a little red squirrel scampering around the apartment as we prepared to leave. I figured that she was mortified about the drama with the pills, and that she was hopping around the place to prove she was okay.

But no. She knew that her dirty little secret was going to be revealed, not only to the world but to me. Of course, being long-term fuck buddies with Sean Sweeney was nothing to be ashamed of – news of their affair would delight the gossip industry, and the Irish press would have a field day with it.

Yet, to me, it was a savage blow – not just the act of sleeping with a man we'd both sworn off multiple times over many years, but actively deciding never to tell me about it. That cut very deep. I mean, everyone has secrets. But this one involved me, sort of. I felt so bloody stupid.

'Alex, you know I'd never do anything to purposely hurt you, right?' Tara bawled as I remained silent, her face tear-stained and her nose snotty. If only her adoring public could see her now, I sneered inwardly.

'Once it happened the second time with Sean, I figured what does it matter if it happens again . . . and again? It was only sex, I swear to you. And I didn't tell you because, well, I didn't even know if you'd care!'

My composure slipped a little. 'Wouldn't care?' I seethed through my teeth.

'Not that you wouldn't care, but, like . . . Sean was old news for you by then. Water under the bridge!' She must have clocked my thunderous expression, because Tara turned contrite again. 'Look, I only ever suggested we both avoid him to save us both any heartache. I had already gone there, and I was very, very sorry about it when I realized that your feelings ran so deep. And then, you had your wild weekend with him after we'd made the pact—'

I cut her off then. 'It's not about him, Tara. It's about us. I thought I could trust you with my life!'

'And you can!' Seatbelt sign be damned, Tara leapt out of her seat and sat on the floor by my knees, grasping for my clenched fist. 'Alex, I swear to you – it meant nothing. It was stress relief with an old friend, one that had some sort of idea what was going on in my crazy world at the time. It was loneliness and fear of the unknown and not having faith in anybody new I met. Please, forgive me, Alex. I promise you, it's the only thing I've never been up front with you about.'

I looked at her, sitting on the plush carpet of a private plane with her long legs folded underneath her. She was still wearing my old robe and didn't smell great, but she still looked beautiful even with her famous hair a mess and those dazzling amber eyes red-rimmed. She was always a pretty crier.

I could feel myself mellowing ever so slightly. Tara was going through so much, and I just didn't have the heart to make her feel even worse. I was furious, but also worried about her. It would be churlish to punish her in her hour of need for a mistake she had made (repeatedly, purposely) when we were much younger. Wouldn't it?

Tara didn't even know everything that had happened between Sean and me. Nobody did, really. I felt a prickle at the back of my throat. Was that . . . guilt? No. Some things are just best kept private.

I squeezed the hand that was clinging desperately to mine and tried to soften my face. 'Of course I forgive you, you gobshite,' I managed. Tara slumped with relief, and then threw herself at me. She felt limp in my arms, like she'd had all the life sucked out of her.

'Oh, Alex, I don't think I could have coped if you'd hated me too. I wouldn't have handled losing you and Rory in one fell swoop!'

I hugged her back, because what else could I do? But inside, I was devastated.

Eventually, Tara fell asleep in her seat, but I knew that I wouldn't be able to. I tried to do some work, even listen to some rival podcasts, but I couldn't focus on anything. By the time we landed at Teterboro Airport I was exhausted, but I pasted on a serene expression as Tara stirred. 'Welcome home,' I said, and was rewarded with a genuine smile.

I had come to New York to help my friend through a catastrophic life event, so I swallowed my sadness and anger and told myself to cop on. Tara was in no fit state to discuss something that had happened years prior. And neither was I, really. It was too dangerous, too much like tampering with Pandora's box. For my own safety, I rarely let myself revisit what happened when I was twenty years old. If I did, the pain might entirely engulf me.

People.com

19 February 2025

SPOTTED: CO-STARS GETTING COSIER!

Despite doing their best to go incognito, actor Rory Vaughan and his co-star and rumored lover Allegra were spotted on what looked like a cosy couple's getaway in Santa Barbara this weekend.

Enjoying a couple of days off from filming in Los Angeles, it seems Vaughan (48) returned from ending his marriage in London and whisked Allegra (26) to the stunning Rosewood Miramar Beach, where they were seen canoodling on their way back from dinner at the upscale Bouchon restaurant.

News broke at the weekend that Vaughan had flown to London to end his eleven-year marriage to actress Tara O'Toole, and it seems the rumors that he's fallen hard for the sexy singer playing opposite him in his latest flick are true. Allegra was uncharacteristically make-up free in the photos, her waist-length black hair loose and her world-famous figure on display in a crop top and leather leggings.

Reps for both stars declined to comment, but a source in Santa Barbara says the five-star hotel has been a favorite of Mr Vaughan and his wife over the years.

7. Tara

'*Aaaargh!*' I screamed as I threw my iPad across the room. There was a crash and then a smash as it hit something, likely an antique Tiffany lamp, but I didn't care. I was blind with temper.

Storm came running into my room, concern written all over her beautiful face. She's so young and gorgeous; every time I see her, I marvel at the collagen almost bursting from her plump pores.

'You saw the latest, then,' she said, her chin trembling. 'I didn't hide your tablet! I'm an idiot!'

My fury flagged in the face of my stepdaughter's obvious devastation. My loved ones were all trying to protect me from any news about her father and his trashy little side piece; it wasn't Storm's fault I decided to masochistically seek it out.

Alex had put some sort of child lock on my phone to stop me tormenting myself, but not on my other devices. So when I found my tablet on my bed as soon as I arrived at my New York apartment, I googled my faithless husband's name in a fit of self-flagellation. My emotions were yo-yoing wildly, vacillating between wanting to know every titbit of news about Rory and Allegra and wanting never to hear either of their names again. This story, however, had me teetering on the brink.

I didn't even realize I was sobbing until Storm took me in her skinny little arms and held me tight. This isn't right, I kept thinking. I'm the adult here; I should be comforting her. I must have muttered that out loud, because she pulled back and looked at me.

'Tara, I know you think I'm still a pre-pubescent child, but I'm not. I'm horrified about Daddy and that girl, but he's not my husband. It's you that's been betrayed, and I'm here for you. Now, lie down. You're totally exhausted.'

I did what I was told, because Storm was right. Once I'd got my Sean secret off my chest on the plane, I had relaxed a little and the fatigue had hit me like a ton of bricks. I'd been in a high state of anxiety for days, and then reading that fucking book had sent me over the edge.

As soon as it was clear that Alex didn't absolutely hate my guts after my confession, my body finally unwound and the pumping adrenaline receding slightly meant I felt utterly physically depleted. Not too depleted to torment myself on Google the second I was able, though.

Still, Alex wasn't exactly herself – there was a stiffness to her body language, a faraway look in her eyes. She said that she forgave me and she was doing all the right things – getting me from the airport in New Jersey to West 76th street discreetly, holding my hand in the car, even calling my close friends to tell them I was safely home. Yet something in her vibe was off, and it was niggling at me. Perhaps she was still in shock after my revelation. Maybe I just needed to give her a little longer to digest it all.

Just looking at Storm made me feel ever so slightly better, though. She was fussing about my room, a whirl of tanned, tattooed skin and short, mirror-sheen platinum hair. She's always been a ball of energy, which caused some problems in middle school – all of her friends were on Ritalin or Adderall, but Rory refused to medicate what he thought were pretty mild behavioural issues. 'She's a kid with tons of energy,' he'd said at the time, his strong jaw set resolutely. 'She lost her mom young, and her dad is famous. Storm just needs some hobbies.'

So hobbies she got. Storm was enrolled in drama lessons, tennis, Mandarin classes, violin, and even had her voice trained, but the only thing she ever wanted to do was doodle on any surface she was near. I gently suggested that perhaps art would suit her, and that's when it all clicked. Eventually she realized that the surfaces she most enjoyed painting were faces, and her career as a make-up artist was born.

Now she concentrates all her energies on just that. She does the glam stuff and has a big following online, but her heart lies in special-effects make-up for the movies. Her transformations are awe-inspiring, and she's just finished working on her first feature film. We're so proud of her.

Realizing in that moment that Rory and I probably weren't a 'we' any more was like a physical blow, one I attempted to conceal from my buzzing, blustering girl. Hold it together, I told myself sternly.

Storm announced she was drawing me a bath, because, apparently, I didn't smell wonderful. That wasn't surprising; I was still wearing Alex's old T-shirt and feathery robe, clutching it to me like a protective talisman. There was definitely sick somewhere in my hair, but I didn't care. I'd refused to bathe until I was back in my own home. Now I was here, I still didn't fancy it, but it seemed I didn't have much choice in the matter.

Once I was ensconced in hot, bubbly water I had to admit that it wasn't so bad. Storm pulled up a chair so she could keep an eye on me – the poor girl probably thought I might try and drown myself in the enormous spa tub. There are worse ways to go than in Sisley-scented bathwater, though.

'How are you feeling now?' Storm fretted.

'I'm okay, baby. I swear!' I protested to her sceptical face. 'How are you doing?'

Her big blue eyes filled up and brimmed over. 'Oh, Tara. I'm just so shocked. I didn't think Dad was like this! I mean, obviously, he's a cishet man with biological desires, but you guys have always been so happy, so perfect. I never ever in a million years thought he would cheat on you.'

'Neither did I, kiddo. But perfection is a myth – haven't I always told you that?'

'Yeah, but it's been pretty hard to take, coming from you.'

I shrugged. 'Looks can be deceiving. Look at me now!' I attempted a laugh, but it came out more like a yelp.

'But really, Tara! Allegra is younger than Xav! I know she's like, sexy and whatever, but how can you be attracted to someone the same age as your kids? It's totally gross! I just don't know what's got in to him. Do you think he's having a breakdown?'

'No, darling, I think he's having an affair. Lots of men do it, but the old eejit thinks he's in love.'

Storm's eyes widened, her mouth becoming a perfect O. 'He said that? Love?'

'Oh, I can't remember his exact words, but that was absolutely the gist of it. Powerful feelings, or some such . . .' I groaned, somehow feeling both numb and nauseous at the same time. 'Have you spoken to him?'

'Not really.' She sighed. 'He called me on his way back from London to tell me what had happened, but I was so stunned I couldn't take it in. I know I told him he was a cliché.' She grimaced. 'But like, he is! I just can't believe it. And to say to your face that he loves her? No wonder you socked him! I mean, violence is never the answer, Tara, but at the same time, I totally get it . . .'

She kept talking, but I'd heard enough. I zoned out, comforting myself with the memories of the early days of my relationship with Rory.

We'd managed to keep our love affair a secret for almost three months. It was exciting, meeting up clandestinely around the world. He introduced me to the kids as a friend at first, but I fell in love with Storm and Xavier instantly and they seemed just as drawn to me. Well, Storm did. Xavier seemed to resent me taking up his father's time, but he soon mellowed when he saw how fun-loving Rory became with me in his life. We were a great team. I was young in years, but not in life experiences, and I knew right away I could be there for those poor motherless kids whether they thought they needed me or not.

The paps busted us on our first romantic getaway, and the word was out – there was an extremely hot new A-list couple on the block. A long lens captured us running hand in hand from a cabana into the Pacific surf, and headlines blared delightedly. We were engaged six months later and married the following April in Palm Springs.

That first trip had been to the Rosewood Miramar in Santa Barbara, and now my husband of eleven years was there with his mistress. Rory is a creature of habit; I had never believed him capable of deliberate cruelty, so reading exactly where he was conducting his sordid new love affair convinced me more than his own words had. Rory wasn't just having an on-set fling. He really was in love with somebody else. My marriage was over.

I exhaled and sank beneath the bubbles, letting the warm, sweetly fragranced water envelop me. Storm was right to stay and watch me. Succumbing to the void was very tempting.

I was eventually dragged from the bath with the news that Lorraine had arrived and was demanding to see me in the flesh. Storm coddled me out of the water, dried me and wrapped me in a fresh, fluffy dressing gown before guiding me into the living room, where Alex and Lorraine were sitting on opposite couches.

There was tension in the air; my two friends have never exactly been close to one another, but they try not to let on. Alex thought Lorraine was too bossy at my wedding, trying to usurp her as maid of honour. Lorraine thought Alex was prim and proper, and could do with removing the stick from her ass. Neither of them would dare say any of this to me; it was relayed via Darius, who loves a good bitch.

Both women were on their phones. Alex's face looked pinched, but Lorraine leapt from her seat when she saw me.

'My *god*, you poor darling!' she shrieked. 'You look like hell, Tara. I knew you weren't being looked after properly across the pond!'

Alex coughed pointedly.

'I'm so happy you're home,' Lorraine said. 'Is it true you took pills?'

'Who told you that?'

'Oh, sweetie, you know Darius can't keep his trap shut. It was an accident, though, yes? You know better, mixing downers and martinis,' she tutted. 'Uppers and booze, fine! Encouraged even, on special occasions. But not the benzos, sweetheart.'

Lorraine is a bona fide New Yorker. She was born and raised in Queens but moved to Manhattan at eighteen and started working in upscale gentlemen's clubs as a cocktail waitress. Her goal was to find a rich man, and she succeeded with her first husband in that he was indeed rich, but he was also overly fond of call girls.

Upon divorcing him, she struck gold with Harold Staffetta, who was both very wealthy and very kind, and perfect for her. It was a love and life match, and they were known in the upper echelons of New York society for being fabulous hosts and genuinely lovely people.

As a reality-television fanatic, it was me who convinced Lorraine to accept the offer to appear on *LONY*. I knew she'd be captivating viewing. That was before poor Harold was diagnosed with Alzheimer's; he went downhill quickly and died a couple of years back. Lorraine's devastation played out on the show and won her legions of fans, but she would have been a favourite regardless. Her no-nonsense manner and acerbic tongue mean the audience adores her.

Today Lorraine was wearing one of her trademark all-beige looks – floaty layers of Max Mara and Celine in various shades of neutral, topped off with impressively shiny diamonds, her helmet of strawberry-blonde hair and famous coral lipstick. There's an air of throwback about her, but it comes off more classic than dated.

As she released me from her hug I saw true concern in

Lorraine's normally flinty eyes. 'Tara, you must have had such an awful shock. Were there any clues that Rory was unhappy?'

I sighed from deep in my soul. 'We had our ups and downs like all couples, and we'd been spending less time together because of work keeping us apart. But honestly, I thought we were going to be fine. I thought I didn't have to worry about Rory!' I exclaimed. 'I would never leave him, and I was under the impression he felt the same way. I have no idea why he'd upend his own life like this. The sex can't be that fucking good!'

I closed my eyes, attacked by mental images of Rory ravaging Allegra. It wasn't hard to imagine; there are love scenes in most of his movies. What was hard to imagine was him wanting to actually be with her, to live with her, to choose this . . . foetus over me.

'It must be about more than sex,' Alex offered. 'Maybe a midlife thing – she makes him feel young. Maybe she reminds him of something from his past. Maybe he just needs to feel useful again, needed?'

Lorraine snorted. 'I can think of a use for him right now and it involves kissing my ass!'

I choked out a laugh, despite myself. 'We can rack our brains all we want, but he currently won't answer the phone so I am without answers. All I know is that he took the little harlot to one of our most special places, and I hate him for that.'

'Was it a special place of his and Lana's too?' Alex's voice was neutral, but her question hit me like a gunshot.

'I don't know,' I replied carefully. 'I never asked.'

'I'm just thinking maybe it's somewhere special for Rory that pre-dated your relationship with him.'

Alex wasn't being unkind, but neither was she mincing her words. I had always tried very hard to be super cool about the fact that Rory had a great love before me, one he was still very much *in* love with when she died. I didn't see how bringing up that fact right now when I was feeling so wounded could be helpful.

I was about to say that when the doorbell rang, and my three miniature dachshunds all went ballistic, barking and running as fast as their tiny legs could carry them towards the elevator. Seamus, Patrick and Oscar are all named after great Irish writers that Rory has read and I haven't.

The elevator doors opened and out sashayed Darius, flamboyantly dressed as ever in what can only be described as a tropical-print kaftan. Even in the biting cold of a New York February, Darius could be counted on to bring brightness and colour to any room. It was only once he was fully in the apartment that I noticed his husband, Francisco, trailing in his wake, a dramatic flower arrangement nestled in his muscular arms.

'Darlings, it's so good to see you all!' Darius exclaimed, air-kissing Lorraine before scooping me up and smothering me with kisses. 'Your big gay father is here now, fear no more!' he boomed, twirling me around. 'You feel lighter, sweetheart. Have you been eating enough?'

'Leave the child alone, Darius.' Francisco took me by the shoulders and planted wet kisses on both my cheeks. He's a big hunk of a man, tall and buff with the most beautiful caramel skin. 'You look wonderful, Tara. Just make sure you're getting enough protein.'

Francisco is hugely into health and fitness, while Darius is more fond of demolishing tins of caviar and quaffing artisanal cocktails. The most exercise he gets is washing his shoulder-length mane. They are my favourite couple and proof that opposites attract, in business and pleasure – they operate one of Manhattan's slickest events and wedding planning companies together, The Scene.

I smiled, truly delighted to see them both. I've known and adored Darius since I started at That's D'Amore, but Alex has known him her entire life because he's Deirdre's best friend.

'Now, really, Tara. How are you doing?' Darius enquired, suddenly serious. He swept his kaftan up and lay dramatically across three seats of the enormous couch, while Francisco perched on one arm looking like an Adonis carved out of marble. 'It's not terminal, darling, is it?'

'She's not sick, Darius,' Alex tutted, petting Seamus on his wiry little head.

'Darling, she's heartsick! That's the worst kind!' Darius looked at me again, probing my face with his eyes. 'Thank god you wrapped the movie before this all kicked off.'

That was Darius, always thinking about showbiz. He's long been my most faithful professional acolyte; after I won my Tony for playing Blanche in the Broadway revival of *A Streetcar Named Desire* and settled into married life in New York, Darius had decided to make the move here himself. He said that being my coach would mean he could make his fortune on the Great White Way, so he sold the Dublin school, paid an immigration lawyer a fortune for a visa and came to live in Manhattan.

Sadly, he didn't make much of a splash here, despite my best efforts. Darius can be a bit of a diva, so when the great and good of the theatre world weren't clamouring for his expertise, he was more than a bit put out. However, he did meet a divine Brazilian dancer at an audition for an off-off-Broadway show he was casting, and he and Francisco have been joined at the hip ever since. Well, Darius would say that he hasn't seen his own hips since 1997, but that's not the point.

A wave of exhaustion washed over me, and I felt like I was going to pass out. It was all too much, being around people, even people I loved so dearly.

'Guys, I love you, and I'm delighted to see you, but I'm wiped. I don't have the energy to be normal right now. Would you mind if I retired to my boudoir?'

Everyone made kind noises that amounted to agreement. Darius and Francisco both leapt up to help me and, supported on each side, I made the journey back to my suite, where I knew I'd lie in bed staring into space for the foreseeable.

8. Alex

As soon as Tara was out of sight Lorraine whirled on me. 'What kind of question was that about the Miramar?' she hissed, the composure she'd demonstrated in front of our friend gone. 'Don't journalists have sensitivity training these days? Did you have to bring up the dead first wife in this instance, Alex?'

'Keep it down. You don't want Storm to hear you referring to her mother like that, do you?' I snapped back. 'It's all relevant. I thought it might help explain Rory's behaviour, because otherwise it just seems like a nasty move, and he's not a nasty guy.'

'He seems pretty nasty right now. He sure had me fooled!'

'I think it's a little less black and white than you believe, Lorraine,' I countered.

We hide it from Tara well, but Lorraine and I have never exactly seen eye to eye. It's because each of us assumes that we are Tara's best friend, which sounds juvenile when you say it out loud, but women are territorial about these things. I've known Tara for ever, but she and Lorraine have notoriety in common as well as proximity. Oh, and vast wealth. Lorraine is forty-six, but she acts like she's a decade older – probably because she was married to a guy a quarter-century her senior for twenty years.

'That's the blogger in you, Alex. Always looking for an angle,' she sniffed.

She's also very put out by my profession, convinced I'm going to betray Tara in some way, or leak a *LONY* storyline. The first is insulting, because I would never do that to Tara. The second, because, as if I could be bothered? I'm also not a blogger, but I knew that was her trying to get a dig in.

It's not as if I actively dislike Lorraine; I'd just never hang out with her of my own volition. She's brash, she's commanding, and I find her kind of scary in person – once she gets riled up, all bets are off. This impression is perhaps tainted by her persona on *Ladies of New York*; on the show she acts as a mediator to a point, but becomes a wailing banshee once she's activated.

'Well, how has she really been?' Lorraine asked, plopping down on the couch and fixing me with her steely gaze. 'She wasn't seriously trying to meet her maker with the pills, was she?'

'I really don't think so, but I've never seen her quite like this. It's uh, well, it's not just what's going on with Rory. Has she ever spoken to you about Sean Sweeney?'

'That boy from that band? The adorable one with the hair who wears nail polish?'

'That's him.'

'Not that I recall. Is this one of those things where everyone Irish actually does know one another?'

I grinned. 'Sort of. We were all in stage school together growing up. Ugh, it's a complicated story, but basically—'

I was interrupted by Darius returning, dachshunds in tow. Francisco followed but headed straight to the bar to make us all drinks.

'Alex was just about to tell me a story about that rock star, Sean Sweeney,' offered Lorraine. 'Do you guys know him too?'

'*Know him?*' Darius boomed. 'Darling, I created him! He's one of my many protégés, just like these two little Irish madams. I was a Svengali in Dublin, a master of my craft. I take credit for this entire generation of superstars from the Emerald Isle!'

I laughed, even though he's kind of right. Darius must have some sort of magic touch, because a heap of current Irish stars attended That's D'Amore at some point.

'Yes, well. Sean has written a book about his life and Tara is, um, mentioned in it,' I said. 'She read an advance copy in my apartment and kind of lost it a little. It's quite revealing, and, well, she thought I'd be angry with her about it.'

'And are you?' Darius's gaze was direct – he managed to accept a margarita from his husband without diverting his eyes from my face.

I sighed. 'I'm not exactly thrilled. But I realize there are more important things happening right now than how I feel about ancient history between Tara and Sean fucking Sweeney.' It sort of shocked me, how easily I lied.

'I'm lost,' Lorraine complained. 'What's going on?'

Gratefully taking a very dirty martini from Francisco, I filled Lorraine in as best I could. My rapt audience gasped, gaped and wheezed as I recounted an edited version of what Tara had told me on the plane about her long-term friends-with-benefits situation with Sean.

'And what, you and this Sean have history too?' Lorraine queried.

'Yeah, you could say that.'

'My god, you all need to get out more. Meet different people!'

I noticed Darius was unusually quiet. Normally he'd be role-playing any scenario along with the storyteller, but . . .

'You knew about this, didn't you?' I accused.

He nodded sagely. 'I suspected over the years, and Sean let it slip once when he was pissed and bragging about his famous conquests. As if I'd be impressed by the women he's had his way with! Then I heard from poor Tara yesterday, distraught. She thought you'd ditch her as well, once you read it. I told her it was a million years ago and to just cop on and tell you herself.'

I felt a bit hollow in that moment, as if I didn't matter. Both Tara and Darius thought that because Tara and Sean's affair happened ages ago, I wouldn't care? There's no statute of limitations on betrayal. Was I wrong to have feelings about the secrecy, about the lying, even now?

And Darius, well, he knew more than anybody else how my encounter with Sean had affected me. I was stunned at his cavalier attitude. It seemed like my emotions just didn't matter in the face of turmoil with the goddess Tara O'Toole.

Darius had already moved on. 'Now, Lorraine darling. Tell me all about that party on Saturday before we toddle off for dinner. Were you guys filming? Did Sybil Simpson get pissed or is she still on the dry?'

The three of them fell into a lengthy conversation about a scandalous incident in their social circle, but I'd stopped paying attention.

I was twenty when I had my lost weekend with Sean. I was interning at a local Dublin radio station for the summer before my third year in college and was accompanying a colleague to one of the biggest music festivals in the country, EXTRAvaganza. Laoise Lawlor was a former Miss Ireland and fellow That's D'Amore alumnus, and as well as being the host of the weekend magazine show on FM93, she was also a friend of mine – a mentor of sorts.

'Let's go to the media area and do some work,' she suggested once we finally got our tent pitched. 'We'll get all the soundbites we need and then we're free to PAAAAAR-TTTTY!' she yelled, prompting some hooting from the lads on the plot next door.

I swallowed nervously. Festivals weren't really my scene and I was worried about Laoise ditching me for her cooler, older radio friends. I was also terrified somebody would force me to do drugs, not realizing then that people are actually pretty stingy with their stashes in real life, and all Deirdre's warnings of young girls being forced to take Ecstasy weren't exactly realistic.

I clocked Sean right away when we entered the huge VIP tent. It was pretty glam for a festival, with a bar at one end, myriad sofas and fake palm trees. He was sitting at one of the picnic tables outside the covered area, and it looked like he was doing an interview. Boy-band Sean was different than I'd remembered – he had what looked suspiciously like a spray tan, new ink trailing down his bare arms and a directional haircut. But my stomach still nearly fell out of my arse when I saw him.

I wanted the ground to swallow me up when he made a beeline for the impossibly glamorous and bubbly Laoise. I always felt like a shrew next to my more fabulous friends, with my glasses and fine, flat hair. Laoise was blonde too, but in a sparkly way, had the most perfect figure and spoke Irish fluently. She's the kind of woman who can pull off a cowboy hat, while I was worried that my knees looked knobbly in my denim cut-offs. I was also totally scarlet to be wearing a raincoat in a way that's so quintessentially Irish I'm not sure how to describe it. Really cool people just . . . got wet. It was inherently embarrassing to want to protect yourself from a downpour.

After a few minutes of bantering back and forth on mic with Sean, Laoise excused herself to go flirt with one of Kings of Leon – this was when the band were all still drinking, and they had staggered in looking for a bar. Laoise was a bit of a rock chick and also a bit of a star fucker; her eyes were out on stalks when the bigger names arrived.

After she zipped off, Sean looked a little bit lost until he clocked me packing up the equipment. 'Hey, it's you!' he said, obviously racking his brains to remember my name, and then clicked his fingers as he got it. 'Alexandra! Alex Curtis, how the hell are you? It's been years!'

Hearing my full moniker coming out of his beautiful mouth made me dizzy. He knew who I was! I thought a couple of years galivanting with a boy band would have made him forget his past altogether, a sort of cool-guy amnesia.

'Ahh, only a couple,' I'd simpered. 'But it probably feels like longer for you!'

'Fuck! It does, actually. Are you working with Laoise?'

'I'm a lowly intern. I'm still in college!'

'Wow, what's that like?' He slung a leg across a nearby picnic bench and I hoped I wasn't blushing a vivid red at the sight of his thighs straddling wood. 'Sometimes I feel like I missed out on the whole college experience, even though I probably would have flunked out in the first term.' He laughed, beckoning for me to join him at the table.

'I think touring the world is a more exciting experience?' I managed, trying to perch myself on the bench in the most elegant way possible.

'Not really. It can get a bit lonely,' he said, and looked me dead in the eye. That was the first time I really felt the sexy nausea that would set upon me every time I thought about Sean, a throbbing, flushed feeling where I both wanted to vomit and have sex with him at the same time. I swallowed, praying my thoughts weren't written all over my face.

Sean suggested a beer; The Chancers had already played their slot on the line-up. 'They schedule all the shite acts like us for Friday afternoon,' he confided, smiling, but not with his eyes. I noticed he was downing the watery lager quickly and hungrily, so I tried to keep up.

We must have sat in that press area talking for hours. I didn't correct him when he kept addressing me as Alexandra, even though nobody ever called me that. I liked the way it rolled off his tongue. Sean was delighted to be with someone from his old life, someone who knew him 'before'. He regaled me with sordid music industry tales and the realities of being in a manufactured band, while I filled him in on what college was like. He was aghast to hear that I'd changed my course from Drama to Film Studies and French.

'But you were the best actress in the entire school!' he crowed. 'Everyone said you would make it huge. I never forgot your Nora Helmer, I was in awe.'

I blossomed at his praise, and the fact he'd even remembered a performance of mine. 'I'd rather write about Ibsen than star in his plays,' I demurred. 'I don't have the personality to make it as an actor, trust me. Even the college course was so competitive it took all the fun away.'

'Wow.' He shook his head. 'You have such integrity. Being famous always felt like the only way out for me. I was crap at school.'

He looked sad then, so I attempted to make him feel better by being more open than I ever was. 'To be honest, I'd been struggling with stage fright. I've always had this anxiety problem; it wasn't really an issue at That's D'Amore because my best friend was there with me. But in college by myself, surrounded by far more confident people . . . it just wasn't working. It was making me miserable.'

'Alexandra, I can relate to that, believe it or not.'

'But you're so talented!'

'I could say the same thing about you.' He smiled, and I felt myself swoon.

We were surrounded by journalists and associated hangers-on, but they weren't taking much notice of us. There were bigger fish knocking around, and drinking to be done. Plus, there's a sort of unwritten rule that you never gawk at a local celebrity – it doesn't matter if they've had a number one in England, you wouldn't want them to lose the run of themselves.

After what must have been hours and countless beers, I noticed it was getting dark. 'Oh my god, we've missed the entire day,' I cried. 'Do you want to go to the main stage for Kings of Leon?'

'I want to keep talking to you,' Sean said.

'But . . . why?'

'Because you're not only gorgeous, Alexandra Curtis, but you're a really lovely person too.' I nearly fell off the bench, weak with desire and happiness. 'I don't care about this scene,' Sean gestured around. 'Do you want to come back to my hotel, order some food and watch a movie? You surely don't want to sleep in a tent. I'll have you back here bright and early tomorrow morning to meet Laoise, and there'll be no funny business. Scout's honour.' One look at the mischief and possibilities in his eyes, and I was a goner.

I can honestly say I hadn't thought about Tara or our agreement to steer clear of Sean once that whole day. Everything had changed; she was living the nomadic life of a working actor, while I was still living at home. We talked as much as possible, but while I was in lectures, she was filming a soap opera or auditioning for a BBC drama. We kept up over email and MSN Messenger when we could; I was thrilled for her, but also felt totally out of her loop.

So I went back to Sean's swish countryside hotel without a care in the world. We made love for the first time in a four-poster bed, an empty room-service champagne bottle on the pillow beside us. It never felt like I was just a notch on a boy-bander's bedpost. He'd undressed me carefully and gently, marvelling at my body. 'Alexandra, you little sneak,' he'd whispered in my ear. 'You kept this little pocket rocket of a body to yourself all these years? I had no idea you were so hot.'

It was so tender, so romantic, that it felt like nothing I'd ever experienced. There had been lads before him, but it had never been special. Being with Sean felt like coming home, like it was meant to be.

We spent the whole weekend at the festival together, walking hand in hand through throngs of revellers in our wellies. Laoise told me to go and enjoy myself, that everyone deserved a lost weekend with a pop star. I'd laughed, telling her he wasn't just some pop star, that I'd known him half my life and that this was the real deal. She'd given me such a look then, one I'd thought was jealousy but would come to understand later was embarrassment.

Sean and I couldn't keep our hands off one another, sneaking off to have sex in the nice bathrooms at one of the branded bars, in his bandmate's RV while everyone was watching Fatboy Slim, and backstage behind an electrical rig. I was a wanton woman, crazed with lust. I even lost my knickers, which made him howl with laughter.

All too soon it was Monday morning, and I cried when Sean

had to leave for Dublin Airport. He and the rest of The Chancers were heading off on tour in Eastern Europe, hitting the festival circuit there as well as a few supporting gigs for McFly. I was absolutely sure this wasn't the end of us. How could it be, after the intense and wonderful seventy-two hours we'd spent together? As far as I was concerned, we were an item.

I floated home on cloud nine, excited to tell my mother all about my new – well, not exactly new – fella. When I didn't hear from him the next day, I told myself he was busy. He'd just had a rare weekend off; it was back to a full-throttle schedule for the band. But by the following weekend I was a wreck. My texts went unanswered, my phone calls rang out to an international tone.

When I finally realized that Sean had no intention of getting back to me I was distraught. It slowly dawned on me that a twenty-one-year-old pop star was the modern-day equivalent of a sailor with a girl in every port. What was a once-in-a-lifetime experience for me likely happened at least monthly for Sean.

Looking back, he hadn't made me any promises. In fact, he had said nothing at all about keeping in touch beyond programming an English phone number into my pink Motorola RAZR.

It was only when I desperately wanted to confide in Tara that I even remembered our pact, and that only served to confound my heartache. Not only had I been taken for a ride by the first boy I'd ever loved, I'd betrayed my best friend in the process.

I was so nervous that Tara would eat the head off me that I told her in a handwritten letter, one I agonized over. I imagined every possible scenario, from her scolding me to never speaking to me again. I was terrified of losing her. But Tara had been gracious, far more than I would have been. She rang long distance and told me not to be so silly, that Sean Sweeney was small potatoes and, if I stuck with her, I'd be shagging Brad Pitt before long. I was weak with gratitude, so thrilled to have such an amazing friend who would forgive me my mistakes and stand by me, no matter what. If only I'd known.

I tuned back into Darius boasting about Sean. Of course, the conversation had turned back to the talented Mr Sweeney.

'. . . and I said to her, "Excuse me, madam! I have not one but *two* Oscar winners under my belt. What have you got?"'

'The kid has an Oscar?' Lorraine sounded impressed.

'Well, the band has one for Best Original Song, for a Bond movie. Not quite the same as Tara, but still. I said to this old bag, "I've an EGOT already between the two of them, darling." And that wiped the smirk off her pruney face!'

'Maybe I should read this book.' Lorraine laughed. 'I feel out of the loop, with all of you in there.'

Then it hit me. Tara hadn't said, but maybe I was in Sean's book too! Our lost weekend had taken place after Sean and Tara had first slept together, so there was a chance I just hadn't reached my chapter yet.

All lit up, I excused myself breathlessly and practically ran to my room. Well, technically, it was Xavier's room, but as he was never there, it felt like my home away from home. I rooted in my Louis until I found the proof copy, already tattered and dog-eared from sweaty hands and frantic flicking.

I turned to the index and looked for my name. A for Alex, C for Curtis . . . nothing. Okay, so I wasn't famous enough to warrant my own entry. I'd just have to read about the early years of The Chancers – surely I would come up?

A cough behind me jolted me back to reality. Darius was filling the doorway, a look of puzzled concern on his rosy face as he took me in, sitting on the floor flicking frenetically through Sean's book.

'What are you doing, child?'

I couldn't lie to him. 'I'm just trying to find the bit in the book when Sean talks about me. I've known him for ever – I must be in there somewhere?' I could hear myself, but my voice didn't sound like my own. It had taken on a shrill quality.

'Honey, I've read it. Sean sent me a draft early on to make sure I was okay with all of his stories, and to fact-check them. You're not in there.'

'I'm not?'

'No, doll.'

'So you . . . you've known about him and Tara?'

'Yes.'

'Why didn't you say anything? To either of us?'

'Because I didn't know the finer details of who knew what, and it's not really any of my business. I didn't get to where I am today by telling tales, my love – on either of you. I figured it would all come out when the time was right. I didn't realize that Rory was going to abandon Tara in the meantime. And honestly, I wasn't sure how big a deal it was going to be. I see now that it's not a small one, so I do apologize.'

'It's fine. I'm fine!'

'Yeah, you sure look fine,' he smirked, flicking his long locks. 'Alex, this isn't like you. You're normally so together, so in control. I know what happened with you and Sean was very difficult. But I didn't think he'd still have this kind of effect on you, what, twenty years later.'

'Seventeen and a half,' I barked, and Darius jumped at my tone. I sighed. 'Look, things aren't exactly normal at the moment. I've just upended my life to be with my friend as she suffers on the public stage. I'm tired, and it's been a rough few days.'

'It was the right thing to do, and Tara's so lucky to have you. So why complicate things further by allowing yourself to be so upset over something that happened way back when? I know you were so sad after . . . everything. I'm not diminishing that. But honey, it really was all a very long time ago.'

He didn't get it. Of course he didn't. Darius had never even believed in love until he met Francisco; he'd actually thought himself sort of asexual, attracted to men but not interested enough in being intimate to deal with their flaws and foibles. And he was a man. He could never really understand.

Darius hunkered down next to me as best he could. 'You're not going to let all of this affect things between you and Tara, are you?'

'Of course not. It was a long time ago, like you said.'

'That's my girl! Now, get some rest and get over the jetlag. I'm going to take my husband out for something filthy to eat – I'm thinking cheese, cheese and more cheese. And you'll be pleased to hear Lorraine is gone.' He winked, poking me in the ribs and blowing me a kiss goodbye.

I watched his heft retreating but stayed frozen on the floor. If everyone else thought my feelings were irrelevant in the face of Tara's trauma, how could I argue? Never mind that she'd lied to me for years. It was apparently up to me to suck it up and get over it because the famous, beautiful one was hurting so badly.

This must be what truly resenting someone felt like, and I didn't like it. I wanted to shake Tara, and scream. Stopping myself meant there was a weight on my chest and a pound of bile and fury lodged in my throat. I had no choice but to try to swallow for the greater good.

Standing up, I looked in the mirror. I could hear a keening coming from Tara's room, a guttural sound of distress and pain. I knew I should go to her, comfort her. Why else was I here in New York?

I adjusted my glasses, fluffed up my hair and painted on a serene, bright-eyed expression. There were times when my acting ability came in handy, and this was going to be one of them.

20 February 2025
From: jen@jencallaghanceramics.ie
To: taravaughan2014@gmail.com
Subject: <3

I'm emailing because you're useless with texts and time differences. Get back to me when you can and tell me, how did it go with Alex? I'm asking you before I ask her, btw. I refuse to play piggy in the middle, I've never had to with you two and I won't be starting now.

I'm sorry I can't be in New York with you guys, but Uncle Dar assures me he has it handled, and I'm always on the phone, okay? Call me anytime – we can do some breathwork together if you're feeling overwhelmed, especially if you wake up in the middle of the night because it won't be stupid o'clock in Dublin.

Love you, chick.

Jen x

21 February 2025
From: Jen@Jencallaghanceramics.ie
To: alex@alexknows.com
Subject: Big Apple?

You and Tara are both strangely quiet. Did you murder one another?? I told you, Brian knows lots of undertakers in NYC from conventions. Let me know if you need one.

On a serious note, how are things? Bad, good, indifferent?

Kisses!

Jen x

9. Tara

We'd been in New York a few days when I woke up to the sight of Alex standing over me proffering my iPhone. She was in charge of it, after I'd attempted to go live on Instagram the night after I got home. We'd had some vino with Darius and Francisco, but I hadn't really been eating. The result was me screeching about telling my side of the story but thankfully being too pissed to figure out how to use the app. Francisco wrestled the device from my hands, and Alex took custody of my phone.

Now she was holding it out to me, her brow furrowed behind her thick-rimmed glasses. Her Botox has worn off, I thought absent-mindedly.

'It's Giulia,' she said. 'I think you'd better take it.'

'Hello?' I croaked.

'Tara, *bella*. How are you holding up?'

'I've been better,' I said to my publicist, knowing I didn't have to pretend with her. Giulia Rizzi is a total pro – she does PR for some big names, and she also happens to be my co-star Chris Adams's partner. They've been together around eighteen months, and he told me they were looking for a place together in LA.

'How's Chris doing? Please tell him I'm sorry I scarpered so quickly after I wrapped.'

'Oh, he is grand,' she replied. Giulia's thick Sicilian accent is peppered with the most delightful Irishisms thanks to the fact that her sister-in-law is the iconic Dessie Daniels, who also happens to be my all-time favourite reality star. *Ladies of Los Angeles* was my gateway drug to a full-blown V Network addiction, and Dessie soon introduced me to Giulia, just as I was looking for a new PR. It was love at first double air-kiss; there's no bullshit with Giulia, she's my kind of woman.

'I am glad to have him back, if I'm honest. I missed the man, can you believe?' She laughed huskily. 'I never thought I'd see the day! But do not fret, Tara. Chris loves you and he understands. I will try not to be jealous of watching you making out with my lover when the movie comes out. Now, I'm afraid I have some not so good news.'

I swung my legs over the side of the bed, my heart creeping up my throat. I caught sight of myself in the full-length mirror and recoiled at the sight – my hair was frizzy and sticking up at all angles, my face gaunt.

'If it's about me appearing in Sean Sweeney's memoir, I already know.' I sighed, patting my cheeks to try to bring a bit of life into my complexion.

'Ahh, shite! That was actually the good news to cheer you up, *bella*. It makes you seem hot and sexy and desirable during this bad time, which of course you are! The not so good news is about Rory.'

I sat up straighter. 'Go on, tell me. Can it get any worse?'

'There's a . . . video going around. Of Rory and that girl. It's quite intimate, *bella*. I know this Allegra is behind circulating it, because it makes her look very good, very in control of him and powerful. But it's not so good for Rory, you know? His image is more classy than this. And well, he is your husband still! As Dessie would say, the neck of this ragazza is like jockey's bollocks.'

I swallowed. 'Giulia, are you telling me that there's a sex tape of my husband and his twenty-six-year-old mistress? And it's being made public?'

'More of an extended clip. Like from a phone. But yes, Allegra is the one behind the camera for most of it. And then in front of the camera too . . . And . . .' Giulia trailed off.

'What?' I was sharp.

'It involves some light bondage, and a blindfold. As in, I do not think Rory was, um, aware he was being recorded.'

'When's it going to hit the internet?'

'It's already on Reddit. Soon, everywhere.'

'Should I watch it?'

'Not unless you want to have a stroke.'

I fell back on to the bed. 'Thanks,' I whispered, and hung up. I felt vomit rising in my throat and just made it to the toilet in time to empty the contents of my stomach, which was essentially just water and coffee. I couldn't remember the last time I'd eaten a full meal – probably back in London, before Rory showed up and turned my world upside down.

Alex found me sitting on the bathroom floor in a daze, god knows how long later. The way she looked at me, I knew she'd watched the video – she was red-faced and her eyes were full of naked pity. It must have been pretty hot.

I allowed myself to be hauled up and deposited on the couch with a blanket. I already smelled again, but I didn't care. I was sleeping only sporadically, waking up sweating from nightmares twice or three times a night. Alex placed a black coffee and a plate of almond croissants on the table in front of me, but I couldn't even look at the pastries. Things were really bad if I was refusing baked goods.

'Samuel will be here in half an hour,' Alex said, sitting next to me with her own breakfast. 'Will you talk to him today?'

'I don't know if I can,' I whispered.

'You're paying him either way, Tara. He was very disappointed you wouldn't see him yesterday. You might as well try.'

'Do you think I care about the money?' I snapped.

Alex shrugged, but I knew what she was thinking. It was well for some, throwing cash around like it had no meaning. Well, she wasn't going to guilt me into talking to my therapist if I didn't want to.

And I didn't. Samuel is fabulous, the man knows many of

my deepest, darkest thoughts and can be trusted with them. It wasn't him I had a problem with, it was talking at all. For the first time in my life, I had lost my ability to converse. My voice was hoarse, my larynx numb.

And what good would talking do? Every day felt like a fresh humiliation as more came out about Rory and his little girlfriend. The afternoon prior, it had been more on-set photos from the paps. Now a mini porno on the internet. What would tomorrow bring, a live sex show? And how would therapy help with that?

I was in unbearable pain. I felt both utterly humiliated and thoroughly ashamed. The latter emotion was difficult to comprehend, but I knew what Samuel would say – that I felt I mustn't have been enough for Rory, for him to go elsewhere. In truth, I don't think I've ever really felt good enough for him. Unpack that, Samuel! I thought.

I was also angrier than I could verbalize, but I understood that emotion. Storm had spoken to her dad the previous day and reported back that he didn't think it was a good time for us to talk, that he would be in touch when he knew what to say to me and the shock had receded.

I felt so sorry for my angel girl, acting as messenger for her father. I heard her tell Alex later, when she thought I wasn't listening, that she'd really let him have it. This both pleased and perplexed me – he deserved a good talking-to, but not from his darling Storm.

I simply still couldn't fathom that Rory, my good, strong, kind Rory, could put me through all of this. He was meant to be my person, my other half. How could he be okay with demeaning me like this? And how hadn't I realized that my husband was capable of inflicting this kind of pain? Had he been lobotomized out in Los Angeles? Or was his dick making every single one of his decisions?

'You know, I don't think Rory is in his right mind,' Alex said, as if reading my thoughts once again. 'The man I know wouldn't behave like this, Tara. I don't even think he carried on this way when he was single!'

'Of course he didn't. He was out of his mind with grief until he met me. He's never really been single in any meaningful way.'

'Well, maybe that's it? He never got to have his wild phase! He and Lana got married right out of high school, didn't they? She was pregnant with Xavier?'

Alex knew the story well, so I didn't know why she was using an inquisitive tone. Lana had discovered she was knocked up her senior spring, and Rory had proposed immediately. Providing for a new family curtailed his opportunity to attend the University of North Carolina on a baseball scholarship where he'd planned to major in Musical Theatre. He'd stayed in Boston, quit playing sports and got a job at a playhouse, and also joined the amateur dramatics society. He was famously spotted by an agent when he was playing Sweeney Todd at the tender age of twenty-four, and was encouraged to move to New York. Rory was a hit on Broadway, and that was the beginning of his amazing career.

'He's not entitled to have his wild phase now, Alex. In case you've forgotten, he is still married to me!' I felt my voice box seize up again, and had a fit of coughing.

Alex rubbed my back gently until it stopped. 'I'm just trying to figure it out, Tara. I'm not making excuses for him. It's just all so baffling.'

I heard the doorbell chime, and Alex scooted along the hardwood floors in her socks to buzz Samuel up. Moments later, he was sitting in the chair opposite me and she'd made herself scarce.

'How are you today, Tara?' he asked in his calm, clear voice. He's fifty-six, divorced, and has three beautiful grown daughters. I've made these spurious assumptions on the basis of a single photo he keeps on his desk from his fiftieth birthday, which appeared six years ago, and the fact that he doesn't wear a wedding ring. I'm very observant; it's a good quality for an actor.

Samuel won't talk to me about his personal life, though, says it's not relevant to our work. He has kind, dark brown eyes and big hands, and he wears comfortingly nerdy sweater vests and loafers. He's my longest-serving psychotherapist and he deals with everything regarding my psyche, but I also have a mind/body/spirit specialist called Elspeth who keeps everything energy-related in check, and a life coach for work stuff. Then there's the counsellor, Barbara, I see (saw?) with Rory, but I don't count her. She doesn't feel like mine.

'Vaguely hysterical, if I'm honest, Samuel.'

'Well, being able to speak feels like progress?'

'I only feel able to speak when I'm so angry I want to burst out of my skin. Did you see the video going around?'

He shook his head. Samuel doesn't really do the internet, which I find reassuring. 'Why don't you tell me about it?'

'Oh, I haven't seen it. I've been advised not to. But I believe it's my husband fucking a woman younger than his son, and it's on social media. Oh, and he's tied up and blindfolded, by the sound of things.'

Samuel's face remained impassive. 'And how does that make you feel?'

'Are you kidding?' I screeched. 'It makes me want to stab him, and his little whore! It makes me feel like a huge piece of shit! Like I'm a failure as a wife, like he's a pathetic excuse for a husband, like the whole world is laughing at me! And pitying me, and I don't know which is worse.'

'I know you and Rory were having some problems before he left for LA, but you haven't really gone into detail about them. Do you feel comfortable explaining exactly what was going on between the two of you?'

'This isn't my fault, Samuel.' I was getting riled.

'Nobody is saying it is, Tara. I'm just trying to get the facts.'

'Well, the fact is, I had no idea my husband was going to fall for his co-star, fly to London to dump me, and then proceed to parade his new relationship around for the whole world to see. He won't answer my calls, seems content with every man and their dog gossiping about us and is barely even speaking to his own children. Honestly, Samuel, if I had the courage and strength I would fly out there and confront him, get some answers. But I don't. I just feel . . . dazed. Lost. Terrified.'

He nodded solemnly. 'That's totally understandable. And you have your own career to consider.'

'Samuel, I don't give a flying fuck about my career right now!'

'Why not?'

I gaped at him. 'Because my heart is broken? Because this feels like a death in the family?'

'Tara, your work has always been of the utmost importance to you. It's the pinnacle of your self-worth. I've been trying to encourage you to find satisfaction in other things for years now, but your career is what makes you feel strong and balanced. I don't think it's true that you don't care about it; I think you're still in shock.'

I shrugged. 'So, what, do you think I should get back out there and book a new movie? Organize a tearful interview about being cuckolded with Katie Couric? What do I do, Samuel? Right now, I'll try anything to feel better, but I really don't think I can pretend to be easy, breezy romantic heroine Tara O'Toole anytime soon.'

'I'm not telling you to do anything, Tara. I'm telling you that when you feel ready, I think work might provide some solace for you. Rory can't avoid you for ever . . . I think when things calm down a little, he'll reach out and you'll get your answers.'

Samuel leaned forward, and there was kindness in his eyes. 'I know it feels like you're in the eye of the storm right now, and in many ways you are. But Tara, this is just the beginning of a new phase in your life, with or without your husband. Change has been forced on you. You've had a bad shock, you feel out of control, and that's totally understandable. But the reality is that it's up to you what way this chapter goes. You are not completely powerless.'

I nodded, trying to take in what he was saying.

'I'll leave you now for a couple of days. Call me if you need me, but otherwise I expect you in my practice next Thursday morning, okay? Let's try to get a sense of normality back.'

I sat there for a long time after Samuel left, thinking about all he'd said. He was right: my work has always been very important to me. Since I was eighteen years old, it was my reason for being – until I met Rory.

When I got my first agent and started going out for roles, I was the saddest I had ever been. My mother had just died, my dad didn't know what to say or do, and being at home alone together it felt like the walls were closing in on us. Dad was drinking a lot, and I was frightened seeing him passed out every night.

The only way I could move out would be if I made my own money, so success became my primary goal. I used my grief as motivation, pouring all my jumbled-up emotions into my acting, and somehow it worked. There was luck involved; of course there was. But the reason I made it as an actress was pure unadulterated tenacity and resolve.

And I really did make it. I wasn't just a working actor, I became a star. Before long my name could open a movie around the world, and people loved me – well, they loved the persona they saw onscreen.

I even exceeded my mother's expectations and won my Oscar years before I turned thirty, which was bittersweet, because my mom was always my biggest fan. Gloria Lopez O'Toole was Puerto Rican on both sides, but born and raised in Washington Heights. She would have loved nothing more than to be a superstar herself, but sadly, her parents didn't have the money to support that dream, and Gloria wasn't exactly Barbra Streisand in terms of raw talent.

She met Christy when he was in New York staying with family for the summer in 1984. They fell madly in love, Christy whisked Gloria back to his homestead in Terenure, and there she remained. I was born in 1987, an only child and the light of their lives. Gloria says I got all of their best bits, and none of the bad ones. I had talent, chutzpah and a stage mom willing to encourage my dreams.

Now I was at the peak of my powers. I could choose my own projects, command any fee I wanted, work with the best of the best. But I would have traded all the success and accolades in that moment for Rory and me to be okay. Without him, I felt empty.

I shook my head, trying to dislodge the image that was stuck in my mind's eye from the morning he left for Los Angeles six weeks previously. The last look Rory gave me before he walked out was haunting me.

It felt like a lifetime ago, but also mere moments. At the time I worried that what we were going through was more than a rough patch. Had I been naïve not to realize things were critical? Had I been taking our marriage for granted, or was I just secure in it? A fresh wave of terror washed over me, and I wanted to crawl out of my skin.

I tried to practise a therapeutic meditation exercise Elspeth had taught me for those tricky times when life got too much, but in seeking zen, all I could hear was Alex. She was on a call on the balcony, standing on the terrace overlooking Central Park, gesturing and laughing while on the phone.

Things were still a bit weird between us. Alex was looking after me, but she was also keeping a sort of distance. She was staying in her own room instead of hanging out with me at night, and our conversations were stilted in a way they never had been before. She was also working a lot, and I felt oddly jealous of her productivity. She'd even found a midtown studio where she could record her podcast. Wasn't the whole point of her being here to be with me 24/7?

Part of me thought Alex just didn't know how to handle what I was going through – scary emotion has never been her strong suit – but in the pit of my stomach I had the feeling she was more upset with me about the whole Sean Sweeney debacle than she was letting on. She knew I couldn't handle arguing about it, and she's confrontation averse, so we were just . . . saying nothing.

That got my back up a little. Me and Sean, it was forever ago. She had no right to be annoyed with me still; I'd told her everything and apologized. You can't say you forgive someone and then still make them feel like shit. I bristled with irritation.

I crawled over and picked up Sean's book from my side table, the very thing that had kickstarted the strange tension between Alex and me. I'd had my own copy couriered over from his publisher so I wasn't caught sneaking looks at Alex's proof. I had a strange sensation holding it, like it held some kind of mystical power – Rory would have called it a horcrux, and believe me, I only know what that means because he makes me watch those fecking Harry Potter films every Christmas. But it did feel like it contained a piece of Sean's soul, or maybe even a piece of my own.

I opened the back jacket and looked at Sean's author picture. He hadn't really changed in the dozen years since I'd last seen him properly. There were a couple of new laughter lines around his eyes and mouth, but otherwise he looked much the same. Better, even. There was a new air of maturity, of wisdom, about him in the photo. A sort of knowing expression under the floppy hair. My heart warmed a little at the sight of him, familiar and comforting.

I shivered. What if, all those years ago, I had ended up with Sean instead? He'd been upset when I told him I was getting married, but I'd given him no indication I wanted him to fight for me. In my mind, it was a done deal with me and Rory – but what if Sean had actually wanted more?

I'd been so crazy about Rory, right from the get-go. He wasn't just sex on legs, he was a proper adult man with a ready-made family for me to love. He respected my drive and ambition and he cherished me . . . until he didn't. Had I been too hasty when I accepted his proposal, too blinded by lust and hormones? Should I have taken time to consider all my options?

My mind was racing, wondering madly about the road not taken. It was like that movie *Sliding Doors*. You know, the one where Gwyneth Paltrow misses the train in one scenario, and gets on it in another? Her life diverges and I think she dies in the end, but that's not the point.

What if I was fated to miss the proverbial train? What if Sean Sweeney had been The One, and I'd picked the wrong guy? Was all this pain a sign that I'd made the wrong decision? Was the universe trying to bring me back to the man I was meant to be with?

Life was so much simpler back then. Sean knew me when I was just plain old Tara from Terenure. I racked my brains, wondering why I'd written him off as a potential suitor. Was it the naff boyband thing? No, he was moving on from that by then. The sheer unlikeliness of ending up with a guy you met when you were twelve? Perhaps. But no, it was something else . . .

I knew, deep in my gut, what the real reason was. I was looking out my French doors at her. It was Alex, and her continued feelings for Sean. By the time I met Rory and called it off with Sean, it had been years since her magical festival weekend and subsequent heartbreak, yet she still winced whenever his name was mentioned and turned off the TV or radio when his songs came on.

The truth was, my love for Alex was always there in the back of my mind whenever I thought about Sean, and it had always prevented me from fully falling for him. He was off limits, which definitely made him more exciting – forbidden fruit and all that. I knew that if I wanted to remain close with Alex Curtis, I could never seriously date Sean Sweeney. And so, it wasn't really a decision at all, because Alex was like a sister to me, closer than close. It didn't matter where I was in the world, what I was doing, we would always make it our business to talk. WhatsApps, phone calls, even just sending memes back and forth – if I didn't communicate with Alex at least once a day, I felt off kilter.

When I met Rory, I had a proper, solid reason to break things off for good with my long-term fuck buddy, my old fallback. I was going to be a wife and a stepmother, and that meant no more messing.

But what if I'd been wrong? Sean still had some sort of feelings for me; that much was obvious from what he'd written in his book. He'd made me feel better all those years before; could he do the same now? Or was there too much water under that particular bridge?

I shook my head again, trying to snap myself back to reality. I was deeply humiliated – of course I was questioning everything. Rory had stunned and devastated me; my head wasn't on right. Sean Sweeney was not the cure for all my problems. He was a human painkiller, a familiar reminder of the days when life was easy.

I looked out at Alex, who had finished her call and seemed to be admiring the view. It was well for her, really. I was always giving out to her for avoiding relationships, but perhaps she had the right idea, not bothering with men in any serious way. She seemed to be flying it on her own.

A strange sort of resentment had crept under my skin. Was Alex preventing me from my own destiny, when she wasn't even arsed taking risks with her own love life? Things were great for her – she had a high-flying media career, a nice low level of fame, enough money to have a comfortable existence, and two adoring parents. Who needed a husband if that was your life?

I dragged myself off the floor and confronted my reflection in the mirror fully. I was a wreck, there was no doubt about it. My eyes were haunted, my skin dull and patchy; even my neck looked drawn. I'd have to do something about it. Looking awful didn't help with feeling awful. It sounds shallow, but minding your appearance is often the first step towards feeling good – at least, it is in my line of work.

I texted Felicia to arrange for my beauty therapist to come over. A massage, peel and pedicure might help me feel less dogged, or at least look it.

A text pinged on my phone – my daily affirmation from Elspeth. 'If I work on my mind, body and soul, my energies and intentions will align,' I read out loud. In other words, what was meant to be would be, given enough sweat, time and introspection.

That's what I would do – work out, journal and figure things out. No more lying in bed moping and overthinking. It wasn't helping.

I glanced at Sean's book lying on the bed. Part of me couldn't help but think it was a sign, coming when it had. What if the answer to my quandary was staring me right in the face, and I was stubbornly ignoring it? I offered a desperate plea to the universe to show me the way to peace of mind – no matter what direction it took me in.

10. Alex

I'd been in New York a week, and I was feeling antsy. I was up to date with my regular work schedule, even perhaps a little ahead of myself, due to sheer panic about being far from home, so I was trying to relax a little, catch up on my reading and watch American TV. But it was no use; I couldn't really switch off.

Tara was showing tiny signs of improvement in that she was talking a little – short, succinct sentences – and caring about how she looked, which was positive. She's no vainer than I imagine any actress is, but when she was walking around looking like the Crypt Keeper, it was deeply unsettling.

She was still sleeping a lot and weeping at the drop of a hat, but overall I was a little less worried than I had been. And in the space worry had occupied, a sort of jittery hyperactivity was settling in.

I did what I normally do when I'm feeling a bit off, and rang my mother. Deirdre works a lot of night shifts in the Rotunda; she likes the slower pace of the darker hours and comforting the expectant and new mammies in that scary time during the dead of night when everything seems extra frightening. Unless she was mid-delivery, she'd be able to chat, even though it was 2 a.m. in Dublin.

'Ah, sweetheart, how are you?' The warmth in her voice was instantly soothing.

'I'm okay, Mam. How's your shift going?'

'Good, a blessedly quiet night so far anyway.' I could hear her thumping on what I presumed to be wood. 'How are things in the Big Apple? How's Tara?'

'Grand, grand. She had a facial last night, which was reassuring.'

'Anything from Rory?'

'Nothing. It's so weird, Mam. I asked her yesterday if anything had been wrong between them before all of this, and she just sort of glazed over. He's in contact with Storm a little, but that's it.'

'Mark my words, pet, there's more to this than meets the eye. Sure we never know what's going on in other people's minds or marriages, do we? No matter how well we think we know them.'

I murmured, feeling uneasy.

'And how are you, love? Is New York suiting you?'

'I'm feeling a bit bored, if I'm honest. It's too soon to come home, like I'd be abandoning Tara if I left, but I also feel like I'm twiddling my thumbs out here. I can't exactly relax, you know?'

'Oh, I know what you're like! Always on the go, never sitting easy. Would you put that energy to good use and try and do a bit of work out there?'

I paused. 'What do you mean?'

'Well, love, it's New York! There are celebrities on every corner, aren't there? Premieres, plays, paparazzi!'

I could hear her getting excited. My mother whiles away the long hours on the night shift reading celebrity magazines and is always very excited by my proximity to showbusiness.

'. . . those morning shows are full of stars shilling their new project or brand. The chat shows, the sketch shows . . . sure even Hugh Jackman is always being papped picking up his French bulldog's poo! I'm sure he'd be very nice if you just went up to him!'

'Mam . . .'

'The point, Alex love, is that you're in prime position to set up a few interviews, aren't you? There are loads of Irish working in telly and papers out there. Why not get in touch with them and offer your services to the New York media as a "talking head"?' I could hear the air quotes again, but maybe she had a point.

'Deirdre Curtis, I think you missed your calling. You could be a big-time publicist if you weren't always busy catching babies, you know.'

'Oh no, darling. I was fated to deal with vaginal tears and blocked milk ducts for a living. You're the one who can handle the real fannies of the world!' She was wetting herself laughing, delighted with her own joke. 'I must go, love, and check on my ladies. Think about what I said!' I could hear her laughing to herself and muttering 'fannies' as she ended the call.

I lay in my big, squishy bed in Tara's apartment and smiled. My mother was absolutely right. Why not use the proximity to celebs in the city as an excuse to expand my professional horizons? I would still be there to be a calming, supportive physical presence for Tara, of course, but it was also an opportunity for me to meet some people I'd never get access to back home. I couldn't let my own stuff slide, not on an island so ripe with opportunity.

Plus, if I was honest with myself, I wasn't enjoying actually being around Tara that much. She was oscillating between moping and rage, sloth and bursts of frantic activity, and I didn't know how to help.

After a few lick-arsey emails and phone calls to publicists the next morning, I quickly secured an interview with *the* rising star of the moment. I was pleased my journalistic credentials seemed to travel well, my listenership impressive enough even in the buzziest city on earth. I managed to nab a slot the very next day interviewing a gorgeous thirty-year-old actor called Lincoln Powers. He was already huge with Gen Z after his turn as a meth-addicted high-schooler on *Nirvana*, but now he was going mainstream, playing Sidney Poitier in a new biopic.

The following afternoon I was hanging around the film's junket HQ in the Beekman Hotel, where the studio had commandeered an entire floor. I spied Lincoln heading outside for photos on the pretty but blustery roof terrace, and as he walked by I instantly felt that rare X-factor vibe that some stars just have in spades. Tara has it. Rory has it. I do not have it.

Telling the PR assistant I was just getting some air, I followed Lincoln and his entourage and watched his little shoot with interest from the doorway. That's when I noticed a guy staring at me from behind the camera.

New Yorkers are a weird bunch. In Ireland or even in the UK, if you clocked somebody gawking at you, they'd instantly look away, mortified. In this city, they have zero shame. When I made eye contact with this man, he smiled and waved. Waved!

He looked my age, maybe a little older, and was slick and polished in a way that instantly told my professional brain that he was an agent. A decent one, judging by the cut of his fancy suit. Oh Jesus, he was coming over. I thought about darting back indoors to the safety of the junket, but he was calling my name. Did I know this guy?

'Alex? Alex Curtis? Jordan Jones!'

Ahh, I remembered his name from the multiple email chains I'd been cc'd on. He was indeed Lincoln's agent, and he was pretty damn good-looking in the flesh. Short, but sturdy with it, and with very nice thick black hair.

'Hi, Jordan. How did you know it was me? Were you googling me?' I surprised myself with my flirtatious tone.

'I am actually a big fan. I represent Sasha Wu here in the States, and she raved about your podcast when she was on it last year. I've been listening ever since, Alex.'

'Wow!' I was truly flattered. Imposter syndrome frequently had me believe that my podcast was but a blip on a very crowded landscape, so this thrilled me.

'I'd love to grab a drink and a chat. Do you have representation in the US?'

'Uhh, no . . .'

'Great!' He was proffering his card: nice, weighty stock and a chic minimalist design. 'Let's do it after you record with Lincoln. Do you like negronis?'

I must have managed a nod.

'Fantastic. I know just the place. Text me so I have your number, in case I lose you in the chaos.'

And just like that, Jordan Jones was whisked back into the fray surrounding his star client, and I was left standing there stunned, the card feeling like an unexploded bomb in my hand.

It's not that I'm afraid of success, per se. Quite the opposite, really – my work brings me a lot of personal satisfaction, and if it's not going well it has a big effect on my self-esteem. I've always liked flying slightly under the radar. I'm quite content being the one who asks the questions, the one who's in control. Jordan Jones had piqued my interest, though. I wondered what he could possibly want with me, and it was distracting.

Nevertheless, when I was finally called into the suite to meet Lincoln, I put my professional hat on and got down to business. God, he was gorgeous up close, and very charming – I made a mental note to tell Tara to watch out for a role opposite this guy.

'Lincoln, we've talked about playing an addict and playing an icon, but how does it feel to be a sex symbol in real life?'

'Well, Alex, do you know what? It feels pretty damn good.' He grinned, clearly flirting. 'Of course I want to be taken seriously, but I'd be lying if I said I didn't want people to think I'm hot, too.'

'They certainly think that, and you're as popular with the LGBTQ community as you are with the girls.'

'I love my gays!' Lincoln laughed. 'You know, they got behind me early on. You could say I have the thirsty gay brothers to thank for my career, and I live to serve them.'

'So we can expect more shirtless shoots in your future, then?'

'Alex, it's difficult to keep my shirt *on*.'

My listeners would love this, I thought. This guy was a star.

I didn't see Jordan again, but I texted him as he'd asked, and he pinged me back a location in the Village and a calendar invite for a thirty-minute meeting at 3 p.m. I was due back at Tara's before too long because Storm had to work and we still weren't leaving her alone. But what harm would another hour do? And sure, it was on the way back uptown. I soon found myself sitting opposite Jordan in Caffe Dante, a super-chic little Italian spot with a negroni happy-hour menu.

'Mind if I order for you?' Jordan offered. 'I'm sort of a regular.'

'Sure, because I have no idea what half these words mean!' I laughed.

'Two Americano 2.0s, please,' he twinkled at the server, who visibly swooned. 'It's the best drink ever,' he said, turning his perfect smile back on me. I noticed he was greying at the temples, but it sort of suited him. His eyes were very blue. 'So, Alex. It's great to finally meet you!'

I grinned back, unable to help myself. 'You too, even though I didn't know you existed until today.'

'What brings you to NYC?'

'Uh, I'm staying with a friend. She's . . . she lost someone.'

'Oh, that's tough. But you're working out here?'

'I'm dabbling where I can, I guess . . .' A tall, icy drink was set in front of me, and I took a long draw on the straw. My tastebuds exploded – Jordan was right, this was an incredible cocktail. He noted my approval, and we clinked glasses.

'Do you have a US visa?' Another thing about New Yorkers – they get straight to the point.

'No. Am I about to be deported?' I mugged, but he looked serious.

'Alex, I think you have a lot of potential. You have great instincts, excellent connections, and I really dig your look and whole vibe. It's the sort of sexy intellectual meets cutesy blonde thing, and you don't pull any punches in your questioning. You're commanding – people respect you. I think, with the right help, you could really do well here.'

'I'm flattered—'

'I appreciate this is all a bit out of the blue, but my job is to spot talent and nurture it. Who represents you overseas?'

'Trevor Greenwood, Greenwood & Associates.'

'I'm not familiar, but I'll be honest – you need a real power-player. I can see you on TV, hosting documentaries. I have a great idea, and I've been waiting to find the perfect person to collaborate with. It could be you. You have that air of cool authority, but then every so often your warmth comes through and you light up . . .'

'Uhhh, thanks?'

'It's a rare quality. Look, think about it. If you sign with me, I'll arrange your work permit with an immigration lawyer, set up meetings with the streamers and put you together with a development exec to hone some pitches. From your Instagram, I know pop culture and social media are your thing. You've got that potential, Alex. The journalistic chops, the distinctive image . . .'

I held up a hand to stop him. 'Jordan, this all sounds unbelievable, but give me a second to digest it all. I'm Irish – we don't take compliments well.'

'See, this is exactly what I mean! You're all flushed – it's adorable! Everyone here is so hard-nosed and corporate. I want someone fresh and unsullied by New York City.'

I gulped.

'Look, Alex, I know it's a lot to take in. But I really like your style. Go have a think about it, a really serious think. See if you want to take a chance on yourself. I'm interested in you, but I don't have all the time in the world. Things move pretty fast here.'

I drained my drink. 'I promise, I will likely think of nothing else. I really appreciate the enthusiasm, Jordan. It's just all a bit of a surprise.'

'I get it,' he said, signalling for the cheque. He pulled out an actual money clip – not only was he carrying cash, he was carrying large bills secured in what looked like a Tiffany holder. 'I have to run to meet Lincoln now, but I'm so glad we got the chance to have this talk. I expect to hear from you soon? Take care.'

And with that, he was gone. He'd left a hundred-dollar bill for two happy-hour drinks and a dish of olives, and disappeared on to the street. I felt like I'd been ambushed, but in a good way. Potentially a very good way.

The server came to clear the table and beamed at the cash. 'Mr Jones is the best tipper. Would you like another cocktail?' She grinned at me. 'On the house, of course. You look a bit overwhelmed. A lot of his companions look freaked out after he leaves.'

I nodded, trying to communicate gratitude with my expression because I felt too stunned to speak. And people said New Yorkers were unfriendly!

Moments later, another Americano 2.0 appeared in front of me. 'What's your name?' I asked the girl. She was so pretty, with long, red, curly hair and freckles.

'I'm Mona, thank you for asking! So many customers don't even look up when they're ordering.'

'Pleased to meet you, Mona. I'm Alex. Does Mr Jones come here often?'

'Not really, maybe once every couple of weeks? But he always leaves an impression. He's so cute, and friendly too. It's usually guys he meets, though.'

'I feel like I've just been speed-dating and at a business conference all at once.' I laughed.

'Girl, enjoy it. He's not a sleazy dude, trust me. I've been trying to think of a way to give him my number without getting fired!'

Pleasantly buzzed half an hour later, I said goodbye to my new pal Mona and decided to walk some of the way back to Tara's. For the end of February, it was very pleasant out.

I love New York. It's a place where I've always just felt at ease whenever I visited. I adore the efficient grid system of streets and avenues, the chic little boutiques along Bleecker, how some things there are forever changing and others are eternal. I even love the weather – the natives complain about freezing winters and stifling summers, but the city has actual seasons, unlike home.

Could I really spend some time here working? It had been a dream, a sort of hazy, unformed one in the back of my mind since I first came to visit Tara in 2009, but it always felt too scary to actually take seriously. Living in London had been a lot for me, and it was a place I now identified with stress, burn-out and the kind of daily commute that almost-thirty-eight-year-old me would loathe; I always hated the mass trudge to the Tube, everyone shuffling like automatons. New York was even more fast-paced, even busier, even more expensive than the English capital. And it was so far from my parents, my apartment, my car . . .

But really, what was tying me to Dublin besides Deirdre and Eamonn? I could rent out the apartment and make a killing, and let my dad have a loan of the Mercedes (he'd been hinting). I didn't have a boyfriend, nor a wide circle of friends. I didn't even have a pet, ostensibly because of the allergies, but really because I was becoming more and more aware of the cat-lady proclivities. Did I want to live alone in the city where I was born for the rest of my days, safe in my own bubble, but also hiding myself away from possibilities?

No, I was losing the run of myself. How could I even think of taking Jordan up on his offer? After all, I had no proven track record in front of the camera and a history of clamming up at big moments. But I couldn't deny there was a buzzing in my veins at the thought of it. Sometimes, it was hard to tell the difference between excitement and anxiety in my brain, as they both produced the same physical response.

School was letting out in the Village, and a group of teenage girls spilled on to the street in front of me. They couldn't have been more than thirteen, chattering away and brandishing their phones excitedly, but the sight of them made me uneasy. Even as an adult, packs of girls intimidate me, and their giddy ease with one another just reminded me of how lonely and isolated I'd always felt at school. How I was forever the odd one out.

I overtook the giggling gaggle on the sidewalk, and as I did I smelled a familiar, cloying perfume that felt like a time machine. *Happy* by Clinique is known for its zesty fragrance and had been a favourite of teenagers since my day. It was also my biggest bully's signature scent. A memory came to me then, from a remote part of my brain I hadn't accessed in forever.

I was twelve years old, and it was the week I was making my Confirmation. I'd been excited, not to receive a religious sacrament, but because my parents were throwing me a little party at the house to celebrate with family and some of the That's D'Amore crowd. The rite of passage had also marked an ending of sorts for me – come September I'd be attending a new secondary school in the city centre, one without any of the girls from my current class. I felt like First Year would be a fresh start, one I was truly ready for.

My classmates and I had been in the church rehearsing for that weekend's ceremony. The school decreed we'd all wear our school uniforms for the Mass itself, but the popular, pretty girls didn't let that deter them. As we practised, they were chattering about the fact that a mobile hairdresser was coming to one of their houses to make sure their manes looked perfect for the bishop. I doubted the bishop would give a damn about the butterfly hair clips they'd bought in Claire's Accessories, but I'd learned to keep my opinions to myself where the girls in my class were concerned.

As we finished up, I gathered my stuff and got ready to walk home in just my shirtsleeves. It was a balmy early May day and Tara was taking the bus over for dinner in my house so my spirits were high. I was skipping as I rounded the corner away from the church when suddenly the ground came flying towards me and my face made contact with the footpath.

'Oops!' a voice sneered, and I heard giggling. Seeing stars, I sat up, knowing instinctively who the laughing girls were. Sinead O'Neill and her cronies, Jessica and Amanda, were the meanest of my school's mean girls, and had been tormenting me for years.

'Now, Alex! You must learn to be more careful!' Sinead said in a faux-concerned voice. 'We know you think you're great now off in stage school, but really, you're obviously just as clumsy and embarrassing as ever.'

I remember seeing blood on my hands as my eyes tried to focus, and I started whimpering when I realized my face was cut and my glasses were broken. 'You tripped me!' I cried. 'I'm bleeding!'

'No, she didn't,' Jessica insisted. 'You fell over your big stupid feet because you can't see where you're going, Specky Four Eyes!'

'At least the cut on your face is a bit of colour, Alex,' sneered Amanda. 'The rest of you is so white!'

They all laughed at their stupid jokes, which were infantile even to my ears. But I was hurt, both physically and emotionally. I was worried my mam would go mad when she saw the state of me, and I hated to upset her. She told me every day I was her pride and joy, and not to mind the silly girls who must be jealous of me, but I knew she was just being nice; I'd heard her telling Darius that she blamed herself for me being bullied. 'Maybe I coddle her too much,' she'd said. 'Those little bitches can smell how gentle and innocent she is a mile off.'

I was still stuck to the ground, trying desperately not to cry, when a shadow fell across me and suddenly Tara was there, helping me up. 'Come on, Alex, thatta girl. Don't let them see you cry,' she whispered, folding my smashed frames and putting them in her pocket. She whirled on Sinead. 'How dare you lay a finger on her?' she seethed.

'It was more like a foot,' snickered Jessica, but Tara wasn't having it.

'Slagging her is one thing – you're all too thick to even hurt her feelings with words. But violence? What kind of pathetic idiots want to make someone else bleed?'

'What's it to you what we say about Alex?' Sinead countered. She was tough, not the sort to back down easily. 'And who the hell are you?'

'I'm someone that will kick the head off you if you don't leave her alone,' Tara said, her voice low and menacing. I had never seen my friend like that before; normally, she was sunshine personified. But in that moment, I wouldn't have messed with Tara O'Toole. She seemed older than her years, and streetwise. In fact, she reminded me of Gloria.

'Look, girls. Alex has some weirdo ginger sticking up for her! Where'd you find her to fight your battles, Alex? Is she another stage-school nerd?'

Tara's eyes went hard. 'See you, you little bitch,' she snarled at Sinead. 'You don't want to mess with me, or you'll find out just what kind of weirdo I am. If you ever touch another hair on this girl's head, you're mine. Do you hear me?'

Sinead wavered, but only ever so slightly. 'Come on, girls,' she said. 'We don't want to be seen associating with the local oddball and her pit bull.' Tossing her long blonde hair over her shoulder, Sinead huffed off, with the other pair following her. I saw Jessica sneak a wide-eyed look back at Tara, though.

Tara took my face in her hands. 'Ah shite, Alex. That's a nasty cut.'

'Don't tell my mam how I got it,' I pleaded. 'I'll just say I tripped.'

'No, Alex. We're telling the truth, and we're telling the school too. You'll have to wear a plaster on your face for your Confo now. You might even need a stitch!'

Tara's expression softened as she saw the horror on my face. 'Ah, look. It's not that bad. Maybe we can convince Darius to do the *Phantom of the Opera* for the next show. You can wear a mask, hide your hideous scar.' She stuck her tongue out at me, and I managed a laugh through my tears.

I shivered on the street corner in New York, touching my cheek, where a tiny mark was all that remained of that incident – on the outside, at least. Remembering my school days was never easy, and I bore a lot of emotional scars long after the cuts healed. One thing was constant, though – Tara O'Toole had always been there for me.

I knew in my soul that I was no longer the frightened little girl who never fitted in. But I also knew that Tara had been my saving grace, the person who bolstered me when I needed it the most. Could I really step out of her shadow and into the spotlight on my own steam? Did I have it in me to conjure what kids today call Main Character Energy?

The sun was disappearing, so I ducked into 14th Street subway station to catch the 1 train uptown. As soon as I descended the stairs, I was greeted by a poster advertising Higher Power's summer gig at Madison Square Garden. Sean Sweeney stared out at me from the life-size image, and it felt like a taunt. I could never escape him, could I?

I boarded the train feeling utterly flummoxed – excited, scared, sick, horny and angry all at once.

US WEEKLY

28 February 2025

DEATH OF A SUPER-COUPLE

A look back at RORA's relationship over the years

2011

Fresh-faced Irish actress Tara O'Toole has been making waves in Hollywood, and releases back-to-back movies thanks to a Best Supporting Actress Oscar nod for gritty British drama *Geezers* in '09. A new fashion idol, young fans and paparazzi mob the starlet shopping on LA's Robertson Boulevard and hitting the star-studded clubs of West Hollywood.

Rory is also riding high on the A-list with the release of action megahit *Helicopter*, but tragedy would strike his family with the death of his wife, Lana, and unborn baby before the year was out.

2013

After high-profile flings with Usher and Robert Pattinson, tabloid darling Tara is introduced to older man Rory through mutual friends. The dazzling new couple go public in late summer, prompting widespread glee from watchful fans. Tara was hot property after winning her Oscar for *Rita*, while Rory was back to work after taking time off to be with his kids, drawing rave reviews in the musical spectacular *VIVA!*

2014

The couple marry in an intimate ceremony in LA, and Tara cements her chick-flick-queen status leading the star-studded romantic comedy *Going to the Chapel*. Endorsements for Neutrogena, New Balance and Möet & Chandon for Tara, and Lexus and Omega (Rory) mean the newly-weds are rarely out of the spotlight and are making bank.

2015

The couple star together in the sexy thriller *All For You* to great box-office success. They buy their family home in Beverly Hills, which was formerly owned by the late Liz Taylor, and Tara is frequently photographed with her teenage step-daughter, Storm.

2016

Tara wins a Tony Award for playing Blanche DuBois in *A Streetcar Named Desire* on Broadway, and steals hearts in the smash-hit comedy *Two Can Play at that Game*. Rory takes on the iconic role of Lex Luthor in the dark and twisty reimagining of *Superman* helmed by Guillermo del Toro.

2019

RORA appear together in a series of sexy ads for Armani fragrances and celebrate their fifth wedding anniversary with a joint cover of *Vogue*. Tara's appearance on James Corden's 'Carpool Karaoke' is a revelation, showcasing a singing voice she's kept hidden all these years. She hints at a possible single release.

2022–4

As the movie world opens up again post-pandemic, both stars busy themselves on myriad postponed projects. Tara shoots the detective adaptation *Cuckoo*, romcom *Try Me* and Steven Spielberg's war epic *Protest*, while Rory works on *Superman: Extraterrestrial* and the presidential action flick *Oval Office*.

2025

The world is stunned as Rory separates from his wife and romances his co-star, Allegra, on the set of *Embroiled*. Meanwhile, singer Sean Sweeney lifts the lid on a previously unknown years-long tryst with fellow Irish star Tara before she met her husband.

As we write, Tara has yet to break cover, having fled the London set of her latest film. Another A-list couple crumbling – are any of our faves safe?

11. Tara

On Thursday morning, I left the apartment for the first time to go and see Samuel at his office. I didn't really feel up to it, but Storm insisted, and I'd rather die than let her down.

My stepdaughter was still sleeping at the Alphabet City walk-up she shares with two make-up artist friends but coming over to drag me out of bed and cook me whatever I could stomach each day. Sadly, I was only interested in toast or Irish chicken curry, so she was mostly preparing sachets of McDonnells sauce I'd ordered online.

I bathed and washed my hair, but I drew the line at glam. My cashmere sweatpants were hanging off me, and it felt strange stuffing my feet into outside shoes, but I managed to leave the building safe underneath a baseball cap and my biggest sunglasses. The blacked-out town car I preferred was waiting for me kerbside and whisked me away without anyone seeing me. Ramon is my favourite driver – he talks when I want to talk, stays mute when I don't feel like conversation. Today he remained quiet, and I thanked him silently.

'You look brighter,' Samuel said as I entered his cosy office. The mid-morning light was soft and pretty, and I sank into my favourite chair.

'I don't know how. I dream so much every night, I wake up feeling exhausted.' I took a deep breath, inhaling the familiar scent of leather and wood. It actually felt good to be in Samuel's office and out of the apartment. Storm had been right.

'Tell me about the dreams,' Samuel encouraged.

'Well, there are two different types. The first are about Rory and that woman. I'm walking in on them, catching them in the act, and Rory is sort of nonchalant about it. And I'm always trying to lash out at them, physically, but I can never touch them. It's so frustrating, and I wake up missing him so much it hurts, and also wanting to strangle him.'

Samuel nodded in the way I'd come to know means that I should continue.

'The other dreams are about a guy from my past. I hadn't really thought about him in a long time, but he's come back into my life . . . sort of. Anyway, in the dreams he's singing to me from the stage in a crowded arena, but I can't reach him. I can't get through the crowd.'

'What do you think all that means?'

'I don't know, Samuel. You're the professional here.'

'I've never held much belief in dream theory.'

'Then why ask me about it?'

'Because your subconscious mind is trying to tell you something, Tara, and you should try and work out what it is.'

'Jeez, Samuel. That's what I pay you for.'

He laughed, a rare occurrence. 'Okay, let's practise some CBT techniques, shall we?'

By the time Ramon deposited me at Lorraine's brownstone on East 62nd two hours later, I felt depleted and was regretting agreeing to lunch at my friend's house. She ushered me inside in her usual brisk fashion. 'Honey, you look a wreck,' she exclaimed as I unwound my scarf and removed my shades. 'Do you want me to send Dr Markarian over? You could do with a little filler under the eyes, maybe some of those salmon-sperm injections in your neck. You're getting sort of haggard, God forgive me for saying so!'

Darius appeared, his hands flapping. 'Leave her alone, Lorraine. She's been through the wringer. Well done for leaving the house, sweetie.' He enveloped me in his great girth, and I instantly felt a little better. Darius always smells amazing, like a bouquet of fresh flowers.

He led me through to Lorraine's palatial dining room, which

was set for afternoon tea. She thinks that all Europeans love finger sandwiches and tiny cakes, and I've never had the heart to tell her that I'd prefer a cup of Barrys in a chunky mug. Darius was in his element, though. That man loves fine bone china and a floral centrepiece.

'Alex not with you?' Lorraine enquired. 'I wasn't sure, so I set her a place just in case.'

'She's not. I actually haven't seen much of her the last couple of days; she's been in and out.'

'Is she not meant to be providing moral support?' Lorraine's tone strove for innocence but didn't quite get there.

'Sure, but that doesn't mean she has to be glued to me. I think she and Storm have determined I'm no longer a risk to myself,' I said grimly. 'Others, though? It's possible.'

'Well, I'd be a risk to the safety of Rory Vaughan if I got my hands on him!' Lorraine declared, pouring me some chamomile tea. 'Has he called you yet?'

'No.'

Lorraine saw my expression, and wisely left it at that.

We whiled away a pleasant couple of hours not discussing the elephant in the room. Darius regaled us with tales from the front lines of Manhattan wedding planning – New York bridezillas are in a league of their own when it comes to demands. Lorraine confessed that she'd signed up with a matchmaker; she finally felt ready to get back on the dating scene two years after poor Harold's passing. 'I'm too young and sexy to be alone for the rest of my life, you know? But I have to be careful – with all my money, I can't exactly go on an app. Mariah Friedman is the best of the best in New York at matching high-net-worth individuals. My friend Susan told me Mariah set her up with Aaron Sorkin back in the day! He could visit my West Wing any day.'

I smiled, letting Lorraine prattle on happily, trying my best not to fully dissociate. I could feel Darius watching me, though. For a flamboyant braggart (his words in his own Instagram bio, not mine), he can be pretty intuitive, and I knew I wasn't fooling him for a second.

When Lorraine excused herself to go to the powder room, Darius spoke. 'Sean Sweeney is doing *The Kelly Clarkson Show* today,' he announced airily. 'Francisco set the telly to record it.'

My interest was piqued, but I feigned nonchalance. 'Oh, he's in New York? Do you still keep tabs on all your graduates?' I asked.

'Only the megastars! How else would I know if they mentioned me or not?! And no, I believe he's dialling in from whatever rural bolthole he hides out in these days.'

I hoped Darius didn't notice me breathing a sigh of relief. I could not handle close proximity to Sean right now. Him being in the same city as me and Alex was too complicated to contemplate.

'I never miss Kelly anyway,' Darius was saying. 'Those pipes! She could sing the phonebook.'

'Well, let me know if he drops my name. I'm sure he will.'

Darius pursed his lips. 'Are you feeling sore about the book?'

'What book?' Lorraine had returned. 'Oh, that Irish kid's memoir again?'

'He's hardly a kid – he's older than Tara!'

'He's a kid to me. I'm used to older dogs. Is that who you're talking about?'

I nodded. 'I'm not sore, exactly. More irritated. What he wrote about me has caused this weird tension between me and Alex. She won't admit it, and I haven't the energy to get her to, but things feel . . . strained.'

Lorraine looked thrilled but, in fairness to her, she attempted to hide her glee.

'It's made me think about the past a lot, in a way I normally try to avoid,' I said. 'With my life turned upside down right now, it's just crazy timing that Sean would appear out of the blue and start reminiscing about our non-relationship.'

'But was it really a non-relationship?' Darius had an eyebrow cocked. 'The way I remember it, you were close for years.'

'You don't know enough about it to say that.'

'I suspected at the time, and now I know for sure. It made sense you'd lean on one another, and it'd be foolish to presume you weren't also at it like rabbits. Two hot young stars ascending to the peak of fame!' Darius was getting carried away, his voice starting to boom. 'In a time before smartphones and social media, you could provide comfort and companionship to one another, darling. It's not rocket science.'

I bit my lip. 'I've been wondering, you know . . .' I hesitated.

'Oh yes?' Darius leaned forward.

'What it would have been like if I'd been with Sean properly. Never married Rory, and given me and Sean a real chance.'

'Hah! You'd have hated it!' said Lorraine. 'Honey, the only way to love a rock star is from a distance. The reality of being a musician's girlfriend is dealing with constant infidelity, even more hectic schedules than actors and the whims and mood swings that come with being onstage for a living. I had a dalliance with one of Hootie's Blowfish after my divorce, before blessed Harold. They were as softcore as musicians come, and he was still an asshole!'

'I hate to agree with Lorraine' – Darius winked at our hostess – 'but she's right. If you think Rory is bad – and we do, right, Lorraine? Very bad – pop stars are way worse. If you'd fallen for Sean properly, you'd have never known a day's peace. The man has demons. Well, he used to. I think he might have exorcized most of them by now.'

I heard what they were both saying, but they didn't know Sean as intimately as I did. I looked at my watch. I'd consumed enough television over the past week to know that *The Kelly Clarkson Show* aired at 3 p.m., and it was now two twenty.

'Thank you for a beautiful lunch, Lor. You're both angels. But I, eh, have to go. I'm suddenly wrecked. I'll call you both!'

'Don't let yourself look any more cadaverous,' Lorraine called after me. 'Or I'll inject you with filler myself!'

I legged it out the front door, where Ramon was, thankfully, waiting.

Alex was in the apartment when I got home, and she seemed cheerful, humming as she vacuumed. I had told her to leave the housework. I didn't need anyone clearing up after me. Well, except the actual cleaner. With her anal retentiveness, though, Alex can't even look at a dust bunny. If running the Dyson over the place made her happy, who was I to interfere?

She'd been interviewing some actor – Lincoln something – the day before, and I'd forgotten to ask how it went. From her bubbly demeanour, I guessed well, but I wasn't in the mood to talk about it. I wanted to watch Sean on TV in peace.

'How are you feeling?' Alex chirped, dropping a kiss on my cheek. 'Any better today? Fair play for getting out of the house – I was started to worry you were turning agoraphobic.'

I wanted to thump her for being so patronizing. God forbid her husband ever publicly ditched her for a slinky woman-child! Oh wait, I thought nastily. That would involve her ever having a relationship. Stop it, Tara, I chided myself. None of this is Alex's fault.

But I couldn't shrug her off and I just wanted to be alone. When I went into my suite to change back into pyjamas, she followed me and sat on the bed.

'How are Lorraine and Darius?'

'Good. You were missed.'

She snorted. 'I'm sure. Hey, I met an agent yesterday. Jordan Jones. Ever heard of him?'

'Rings a vague bell. Who does he represent again?'

'Well, he wants to represent me.'

I walked out of my closet and looked at her. 'To do what? Act?'

'God, no. As a broadcaster, a host. He wants me to front some documentary projects about social media and celebrities. Isn't that gas?'

'Gas' was one word for it. 'Are you going to do it?'

'I'm going to take more meetings. You don't seem excited?'

I caught on. 'Oh, Al, I totally am. That sounds amazing! I just didn't know you wanted to do that kind of thing, in front of the camera. It's a surprise is all.'

'To be honest, neither did I until Jordan said it. But the prospect has lit something inside of me, Tara. I really want to see where it might take me.'

'Well, then, you will! I'm proud of you.' I squeezed her arm, and she blushed in that cute way she always does. She was showing no signs of leaving, though. I yawned theatrically.

'I'm exhausted after all that human interaction. I'm going to take a nap.'

'Oh, of course! You must be wrecked. Sleep well.' She hopped off the bed and skipped out of the room, and I let out a sigh of relief. Alex getting an agent in the States? I'd unpack that and why it was irritating me later. I just wanted to focus on Sean.

I put my TV on at a very low volume and sat on the floor in front of it. I didn't want Alex to hear what I was watching. Finally, after an excruciatingly long opening monologue, Kelly Clarkson introduced Sean in her typically bubbly style.

'You know his music, you've seen him model for the biggest fashion houses in the world and you probably had his poster on the wall of your college dorm. But now, he's adding "author" to his resumé with the release of his memoir, *Interview with a Rock Star*. Joining us remotely from his ranch in the mountains of the Wild West, please put your hands together for the sexy, talented Sean Sweeney!'

My heart was in my throat at the sight of him, gorgeous in a sleeveless T-shirt, even through a shitty Zoom connection. Sean was ageing well, and it didn't look like he was hitting the injectables, either. Maybe some laser work, definitely some chemical peels, but whatever it was, it was working. His hair was still thick and messy and he had more tattoos than he'd had way back when, but he still looked very much like the guy I remembered.

He waved at the audience through the screen and blew kisses, something that might have seemed contrived coming from a lesser star, but not from Sean. He's always had this friendly, genuine-looking face, not so traditionally handsome that it's bewildering, like Rory – Sean is more like a very attractive normal guy with a truckload of charm.

'Sean, it's great to see you!' Kelly bleated. 'We wish you were here with us in New York. Where are you right now?'

'I'm coming to you live from my own little slice of heaven, my ranch in the wilds of rural Montana. I'm here with the band, rehearsing for our upcoming world tour, a bit of calm before the storm.'

'Is that where you spend most of your time?'

'Ah, I'm something of a nomad.' He smiled, his eyes twinkling. 'I have a place in London and a little seaside hideaway back in Ireland, but I'm here a lot. I keep animals, ride horses.' This elicited a couple of screams from the audience.

'I thought that was an urban myth!' Kelly enthused. 'Are you telling us that you moonlight as an actual cowboy?'

He laughed. 'You could say that. I find it very peaceful here. I live in the middle of nowhere; it's where I write my best stuff.'

'You heard it here first, ladies and gentlemen! Now you can imagine Sean Sweeney wearing chaps astride a magnificent beast! Speaking of writing, tell us all about your new book. Why was it important for you to put pen to paper and tell your life story?'

'Well, Kelly, I've been doing a lot of work on myself over the past few years. I didn't exactly have it easy, growing up. My family didn't have a lot of money. My dad left when I was young, my mother had five boys to raise and I had undiagnosed dyslexia, something that made me believe I was stupid. For a long time I was carrying that burden with me, deep inside. I felt like I didn't deserve the success I had, you know? Like it could all be snatched away at any moment. I was always chasing my tail. I've never been married, I don't have any kids. The pandemic was a lonely time for me, so I wanted to take that time to look deep inside myself.'

'And what have you learned?' Kelly was spellbound, God bless her.

'Ahh, it's all in the book.' He grinned flirtatiously. 'I've learned that I want to be less of a lone ranger, though.'

'Are you telling us that you're looking for love, Sean Sweeney? Are you about to become the world's most eligible bachelor?'

'Not looking, exactly . . . I may have already found it, long ago, and let it go. I messed it all up.'

'Stop the presses – are you saying that there really is a One That Got Away?! Is that where the new Higher Power song title comes from?'

He made intense eye contact with Kelly – well, as much as one could via a webcam. 'You could say that, maybe. I met someone when I was much, much younger, back home in Ireland. She was amazing, but I thought happiness couldn't be that simple, that easy. I thought young love would never last – that the right woman wouldn't have been right there in front of my face, all that time. Then I realized that I'd never forgotten her or the magical time we spent together. I ruined it because I was immature, and I let her go. Maybe it's too late, but I often wonder if I should call her.'

The audience were in raptures. Kelly herself was misty-eyed. I felt like I was going to pass out. Was he . . . was he talking about me?

'Do you want this mystery lady to get in touch, if she sees this?' swooned Kelly.

'I'll seek her out, when the time is right. I think she's long overdue a grand, romantic gesture.'

'There you have it, ladies and gentlemen! You'll have to buy Sean Sweeney's new book, *Interview with a Rock Star*, to look for clues as to who the hell this lucky woman is! After the break,

I'm going to perform an exclusive acoustic rendition of his song "Feeling You". Don't go anywhere!'

I switched off the TV and sat there in a daze, wondering if I'd somehow conjured the entire interview. But no, I definitely wasn't imagining things. Sean Sweeney had basically told the world that he was still in love with an old flame, an old flame from Ireland who he let go. An old flame who could only, realistically, be me.

I felt a serenity descend on me, the type of calm I hadn't felt in ages. Since before Rory came to London, even since long before that. Suddenly, I felt like everything was going to be okay. I was right where I was meant to be.

The universe was telling me that I had been correct about choosing the wrong path way back when, but it was all right – I just had to hold tight. Sean Sweeney was coming to save me.

12. Alex

I knew instantly that Sean was talking about me, even as the clip on my phone auto-cycled to the next video. I went back and watched the interview again, and again, and again. My journalistic brain flicked through everything I knew about Sean's life in Ireland and eliminated all other possibilities as to the mystery woman's identity. Someone with whom he had a magical experience that he ruined? Someone who was right there in front of him at a time when he thought the world was his oyster, someone he regretted letting go? Who else could it be? There was no doubt in my mind whatsoever; I was the girl he'd let slip through his fingers. I stifled a squeal.

For a long time, I hadn't allowed myself to be taken in by Sean's image on TV, or even to listen to his songs on the radio. I had his name and profiles muted on social media because I just didn't need the constant reminders of his existence.

But this was different, even from a work point of view. This was a moment in pop culture that would go down in chat-show history, along with Tom Cruise's loved-up couch-jumping, or Matt Damon announcing his break-up with Minnie Driver to the world when she had no idea they were over. This was an A-list star purposely laying themselves bare, for all to see and discuss.

It was an instant talking point, taking the celebrity gossip world by storm – who was Sean Sweeney's long-lost love? Journalists were already penning think pieces online; was he a true romantic, or an arrogant bastard, to think this special lady would drop everything when he came calling? Why a grand gesture all on his terms? Did the flame still burn bright for her, too?

My initial feeling was relief. I wasn't crazy. I felt a sudden peace that told me I hadn't imagined everything all those years before, that I hadn't been mental to feel so broken-hearted for so long. I wasn't stupid or pathetic. I felt a blanket of calm descend like a sedative, so rare in my anxious mind it was actually disconcerting.

But what did this mean? Was he going to come and find me? Was I to be on high alert at all times in case Sean Sweeney appeared out the sunroof of a limo, like Richard Gere in *Pretty Woman*? Did he want to rescue me, so I could rescue him right back?

I was getting carried away. I needed a voice of reason, someone to confirm that if there was any Irishwoman alive that Sean Sweeney was holding a candle for, surely it had to be me.

When Jen answered my FaceTime, she was beaming. 'Seany boy has done it again!'

I must have looked confused. 'He's grabbed every headline in the world!' she said. 'It's like that time he posed for Gucci wearing only a pair of loafers. Or the time he was photographed with Hailey Bieber when she and Justin were on the rocks. The guy knows how to operate, I tell you. That book will sell like hotcakes.'

I smiled back. 'I can't believe it, Jen. After all these years! I just had to see your face to prove that this is really happening, that I'm not having a stroke or a manic episode.'

Her brow creased a little. 'What do you mean?'

'I mean, he's finally realized what he gave up. He's finally realized that I'm The One!'

Jen laughed nervously. 'Okay, I can never tell when you're acting . . .'

'I'm not acting!' I enthused. 'Jen, do you not realize that he must be talking about me? I mean, who else is there?'

'Give me one sec, I have to get away from my children.' Jen walked into what looked like her bathroom, shut the door and sat on the toilet with the lid down. She positioned the phone so it was in front of her and she had her hands free. 'Alex, I mean this with all the love in the world, and I'm not doubting your instincts, but do you actually think he was talking about you? Sure, you haven't seen him since you were twenty years old.'

I felt myself getting flustered. 'But . . . why not, Jen? I haven't forgotten about him after all these years. And everything he said, well, it just fits. It makes sense in a way that nothing made sense at the time when he ghosted me. I just . . . I just feel strongly, like from my gut, that he's talking about me. Is that mental?'

'I'm not saying he's not, it just wasn't my first thought, that's all.' Her eyes were kind, but I could see that I'd shocked her with my initial certainty. 'You know, you went a bit loopy after everything that went down with him. Everyone was concerned – you decided to go on Erasmus and basically just fucked off to France not long after having your heart broken. You've never exactly been rational when it comes to Sean.'

I laughed, but it was high-pitched and verging on manic. 'Stop, I didn't go loopy. I just grew up, is all.'

'Alex, have you considered the possibility that he might be talking about Tara?'

It was like a punch to the gut, and the realization must have shown on my face.

'I'm not saying he is' – Jen was trying to cushion her words – 'I'm just saying, the book comes out tomorrow. Everyone is going to read what he wrote about Tara and just assume he's talking about her. Part of me thinks he's a marketing genius; the other part thinks he just seriously lucked out with timing . . .'

I let Jen go on as my brain clicked through information. It pained me that Tara would even be part of the conversation, and while what Jen was saying made sense, it still didn't seem to me that he could possibly be talking about my best friend.

'It's not Tara,' I announced, cutting Jen off mid-sentence. 'They had a long-term casual arrangement. It wasn't love, it wasn't magical – it was convenient. And he didn't mess it up, she met somebody else.'

Jen didn't look entirely convinced. 'I guess you could be right, if you parse what he said exactly. It might not be Tara.'

'It's not, Jen. I just feel it in my soul that it's me. There's a reason I've never gotten over him, a reason nobody else ever lived up to him. It's because of this unfinished business.'

'Okay, let's say you're right and Sean Sweeney has realized you're the only woman for him. What are you going to do about it?'

'Nothing!' I exclaimed, coming to the realization at the exact moment I said it. 'I've waited this long. I'm not going to chase after him. I'm going to let him figure it out and find me when he has.' I sounded so serene, even to my own ears.

Jen nodded slowly, seemingly lost in thought. 'Alex, I just don't want you getting ahead of yourself and getting hurt all over again, you know? You have to entertain the notion that a) Sean is full of shit and b) he could be talking about another woman entirely.'

'You're absolutely right: both of those things could be true. It would be stupid not to consider that, and I'm not stupid. I can't explain it, Jen. I just know he means me. I feel it deep inside, this sort of strange knowingness and vindication. Do you think I'm insane?'

'Noooo. I think you're a hopeless romantic who's been stifling the impulse for years. I think that man got under your skin in a way nobody else ever could. I just want you to consider all the options.'

I nodded and smiled. 'I am, Jen. I know you worry about me, but I just feel good about it. And even if he chickens out or changes his mind and I never see him again, I feel like now I know that weekend meant something to him as well.'

My friend seemed appeased. 'I hear you. Maybe just don't go saying any of this to Tara? Just because you said things have been tricky since everything in his book came to light . . . and with everything going on with Rory, I mean, her name is going to get dragged into the guessing games either way.'

I decided to make dinner for me and Tara. We hadn't sat down and had a meal together, just the two of us, since we'd been in New York. She'd made such great strides in the past few hours, maybe she'd actually eat if I whipped up her favourite pasta dish.

The apartment was quiet because Storm had taken the dogs for the day, so Tara didn't have to worry about them as she faced the outdoors for the first time. It was peaceful without the sound of their claws on the hardwood floors. Watching their little legs slip and slide on the varnished surfaces was amusing, but further reinforcement that canines caused too much of a ruckus for me to own one.

I felt much better about the whole Tara-and-Sean debacle. It didn't seem important now, I thought as I chopped garlic and fresh chilli. I even felt a bit sorry for her. Spending all those years in his bed and none of them in his heart. Someone had to keep him occupied in the meantime, until he was man enough to have a proper relationship. Until he'd done the work required on himself to be able to commit fully. There was something noble about it all, about not subjecting his true love to the mistakes he'd inevitably make along the road to emotional maturity.

I knocked gently on Tara's door as the garlic sizzled in olive oil, and from the scrambling I heard behind it, I knew she was awake. 'I'm making your favourite, spaghetti aglio, olio e peperoncino,' I called. 'Aka carbs in oil.'

The antique walnut door swung open, and Tara's face appeared. She looked properly alert for the first time in ages, so much so that I wondered had Rory finally got in touch.

'Sounds great!' she chirped. 'And smells even better. Just give me two minutes.'

I busied myself setting the table, feeling a warm glow inside. Maybe New York City really was my kind of town and my luck was changing in Manhattan. After only a few days here I'd had an offer from a high-powered agent, and the only man I'd ever loved had given a pretty strong signal to the whole world that he loved me too. Now Tara was perking up under my care. I'd never really believed in the laws of attraction or the power of the universe, but perhaps I'd been too cynical. Maybe I'd just needed to change my circumstances to change my life.

Tara appeared, back in my feather-trimmed robe over her own silk pyjamas. The dressing gown had been dry-cleaned, but she seemed quite attached to it, so I said nothing. She'd brushed her long hair and seemed to have an energy about her for the first time in ages.

'You look well!' I said, stirring the spaghetti into the infused oil.

'Do I? Maybe today did me some good.'

'Did anything happen since you got home? Any calls?'

'What? No, no. I just feel a bit more human, I guess. It probably won't last long!' Her voice seemed shrill, but she was smiling as she accepted the bowl of pasta and tucked in with gusto. 'Thanks, Alex. This is delicious.'

'Welcome.' I smiled, feeling I could afford to be benevolent. Poor Tara, she really had been through the mill.

'I guess you've heard the news about Sean Sweeney,' she said, swallowing hungrily. 'Giulia called and told me he's riled everyone up with stories of long-lost love. What an eejit!'

I was momentarily thrown by Tara uttering his name but recovered quickly. So this was how we were going to play it. Okay, I could go along with this.

'Yeah, mad, isn't it?' I replied breezily. 'I swear, if another tortured artist credits the pandemic with changing their life . . .'

'I know! And everyone clamouring to know what poor, unfortunate woman he's on about,' Tara laughed. 'He's always been good at self-promotion. The book will make a fortune. Maybe I'll write one, tell my own story and get my side of the whole thing out!'

'I'll ghost-write it for you.' I grinned, matching her energy.

'I might take you up on that, you know. Lord knows I have enough tales about Hollywood to fill an encyclopaedia.'

Tara prattled on, talking more as she sucked up oily tendrils of spaghetti than she had in the entire time since she'd come to me from London. I wasn't going to question it – something had energized my friend, even temporarily.

And more importantly, we'd addressed Sean Sweeney and, by extension, the strange awkwardness between us. It felt as if the coolness had dissipated suddenly, like we were back on an even keel. I wasn't going to rock the boat.

I drained my glass of Montepulciano and reached for Tara's hand, giving it a squeeze, and was rewarded with what looked like a genuine smile. There was warmth in those amber eyes again. We were back on track.

13. Tara

It was like a spell had been broken, a grimy filter removed from my inner lens. Suddenly the world seemed like a better, brighter, more hopeful place. I felt an enthusiasm I hadn't noticed in forever, an eagerness to rejoin planet earth.

Alex seemed happy too, and I guessed it was all down to her exciting prospects. I was so glad the coldness between us had thawed. God knows what she'd make of Sean and me actually being together, but I'd cross that bridge when I came to it. For now, I was just relieved things were better between us, and found myself freshly soothed by Alex's presence in my home. It was so good of her to come to New York with me, I thought fondly. She was such a dote.

The Monday morning after Sean's revelation, I leapt out of bed at seven thirty and decided to do one of my favourite things – walk to Zabar's. When I first moved to New York full time and lived in a crappy serviced condo in the West 90s, walking was my only exercise in the city. Back then I was auditioning, self-taping and learning lines 24/7, so getting out for a stroll in the neighbourhood was like free therapy.

It's a little trickier now, being well-known, but not impossible. The reality is that unless you want to be noticed on the street, most people in New York won't even look at you. Rory and I together always caused a stir because he's so tall and striking, but if I have a hoodie or hat and sunglasses on and I'm not dripping in designer labels, I'm not that distinguishable from the next Upper West Side resident. Still, I dressed particularly low-key in black athleisure and hid my hair under a beanie. Patrick and Oscar were snoozing in their crate, but Seamus wanted to come with me so I popped on his little tartan coat and leash and headed out.

It felt good to be outside. The first signs of spring were showing, buds on the trees and daffodil shoots emerging from the softening ground. It was still relatively early; New York may be the city that never sleeps, but above 59th Street, mornings are quite peaceful. Kids were being dropped off at nursery or school, locals were out jogging and the smell of fresh doughnuts and coffee was in the air.

They know me in Zabar's. It's something of a New York institution, largely unchanged after ninety years, and I find the vintage vibe comforting. They sell everything there, from kitchenware to groceries and freshly ground coffee, but they're known for their smoked salmon and traditional bagels. Alex hates the place: it's too chaotic for her.

'Morning, Rocco!' I greeted the barista cheerfully, taking off my Gucci sunglasses.

'Miss O'Toole, it's good to see you!' he beamed. It was impossible to tell if this friendly guy had any idea what was going on in my life, so I chose to believe that he didn't. It's the only way I can handle fame, to pretend it doesn't exist. You can get very paranoid otherwise.

'I'll take two large drips, half a dozen wholewheat everythings, some scallion cream cheese, and give me a couple of knishes as well.'

'Certainly, Miss O'Toole. A feast for you and the family! How is Mr Vaughan? I haven't seen him lately.'

I tried not to let my stomach plummet, to keep a smile on my face. There was my answer: this lovely guy behind the counter had no idea my husband had left me.

'Good, good. Thanks, Rocco.' I busied myself on my phone until my order was ready, granted the barista my best movie-star grin as I grabbed the paper bag and made off towards home. I tried to find my earlier buzz again, to enjoy the outdoors. But one mention of Rory from a kindly acquaintance had totally tainted my good mood.

My phone rang then, and the display told me it was my stepson. 'Hi, Xav,' I said, balancing the phone between my ear and my shoulder. 'I'm sorry, we keep missing each other.'

'I'm just calling for our weekly check-in,' Xavier said. 'Wanted to make sure you were doing okay.'

'Aw, you're sweet. I'm all right. Have you been talking to your dad much?'

'A little. He seems, uh, preoccupied. Tara, I'm so sorry about all of this. I thought it might have been a momentary blip, something that would die down. It's embarrassing for me to have my dad running around with some girl my age; I can't imagine how it is for you.'

'You don't want to know, Xav. Just promise me one thing, will you?'

'Sure.'

'Don't get married unless you really, really, really want to, okay? Not unless you're a hundred per cent sure that you want to stay with one woman until you're old and blind and deaf and incontinent.'

He laughed softly, and it sounded so much like his father that it made my heart hurt. 'You take care of yourself, Tara.' And he was gone.

I passed my favourite street kiosk and glanced at the magazines on offer. It had been ages since I'd bought one, and disappearing into the new *Vanity Fair* could be a delightful way to spend the morning. But then I saw the new issue of *Us Weekly* next to it on the newsstand. *HOLLYWOOD LOVE TRIANGLE!* it screamed. *Tara v Allegra, at war for Rory's heart!*

I groaned. Why did they always pick horrible pictures of the injured party for these salacious covers? I swear they'd photoshopped a grimace on to my face, because I'm only ever smiling on the red carpet. And they'd chosen a stunning shot of my husband's mistress in which she was practically oozing sex appeal. Ugh. I pulled my hood up and kept moving.

I heard a clicking noise behind me as I reached my street. That noise signalled only one thing: the camera shutter of an early-rising paparazzo. I decided I'd roll with it, pasting on my toothiest grin so he'd get his shot and go away. Lucky you, I thought as he waved thanks and scuttled off. You've got the first photos of the abandoned A-lister; it was worth getting out of bed in the dark.

Alex was on Zoom on her laptop when I let myself and Seamus back into the apartment, but she finished up when she saw me and my bounty.

'I was worried when you weren't here!' she exclaimed, letting out a squeal of delight as she unwrapped the bagels. 'You should've left a note.'

I bristled. I wasn't a child who had to let my mommy know where I was going. But I didn't say anything. I half-heartedly spread a schmear on a bagel, but I'd lost my appetite.

'That was my agent in London on Zoom,' Alex was saying. 'I had him ask around about Jordan Jones, and he seems totally legit. My crowd don't have a US branch because they're a pretty small operation, so they think I should totally go for it.'

'Mmm? That's great, Al.'

'Yeah, I feel really good about it. Excited.'

'That reminds me, I have a call with my own agent later. I've been putting it off, but I told Giulia to arrange it last night.' I groaned. 'I hate the business side of being an actor. It's so boring.'

'Oh, poor Tara and her multimillion-dollar movies and endorsements,' Alex teased, but her eyes were kind.

'You're right, you're right. How bad could it be?'

An hour later, I learned just how bad. The producers of *Mind the Gap* were eager to get the movie out asap, which meant facing a promo tour sooner than I'd have liked. Nobody would admit it, but I knew they were trying to capitalize on my very public heartbreak.

Giulia was level-headed as I ranted and raved after the others left the call. '*Carina*, this is Hollywood. To them, you are a commodity – you know this. They want to piggyback off your publicity, and you have to agree, it is the smart move.'

'No, Giulia, it's not. This is my life we're talking about! A few weeks after my marriage ends and they want to plan a world tour to promote a romantic comedy? I'm not in any fit state!'

'It's months away, *bella*, just leave it all to me. I will arrange, and Chris and I will take care of you when it happens.'

'This isn't fair, Giulia! Using my personal tragedy to sell a movie – I'm disgusted! I'm an actor, not a chattel. My life is not for sale!'

If Giulia was perturbed by my dramatics, she didn't let on. She watched me imperiously through the iPad screen, waiting for me to calm down. That only made me madder.

'Just when I was feeling a little better, Giulia. This is complete shit.'

'I know, *carina*. Showbusiness is nasty, but it's made us very rich, no? They use us; we use them right back. Now, I have press requests coming out of my arse for you about this Sean Sweeney.'

I laughed, despite myself. 'Coming out of your ears. Yeah, I'm not surprised.'

'Everybody wants you. Between this blind item, Rory's antics . . . we could get big money. Oprah, Drew Barrymore, Anderson Cooper . . . take your pick.'

'Not yet, Giulia.'

'Are you going to be okay for your big Covet shoot next week? You know they will be expecting you to do press for when the new campaign is coming out . . .'

'I know, I know. Yes, I'll be fine to shoot. With media stuff, I guess I'll know when the time is right.'

'Don't wait too long. Ciao, *bella*.' And she was gone.

I lay there, my earlier sunny disposition utterly vanquished. Had I been foolish to feel optimistic? Everything was still totally crap – my husband had left me, it was affecting my work and my team was starting to get antsy. What's more, Sean hadn't called yet.

I was staying away from the internet, but I knew it was still alight with the details from his book and the aftermath of his appearance on *Kelly Clarkson*. As soon as Sean's memoir had hit the shelves the story of our entanglement was out there, and speculation about me and my love life was at an all-time high. If everyone else had already guessed that I was the long-lost mystery woman, why hadn't he reached out?

Maybe he thought it would be crass right now. After all, the Rory story was ongoing. Maybe Sean didn't want to be seen as a homewrecker, or a vulture swooping in on the rotting carcass of my marriage.

I was interrupted by a knock on the door. 'Shanice is here to see you,' Alex said. 'Can I let her up?'

Shanice! I'd forgotten I'd arranged for my stylist to come over, but her timing was perfect. A former model-turned-fashion-editor-turned-dresser-of-the-stars, she's French, fabulous and gives no fucks. She was exactly who I wanted to see.

Shanice swept into the apartment, six feet tall, with braids past her bum and a regal air. She barely glanced at Alex, who seemed irritated to be breezed past without acknowledgement.

'Darling, you don't look half as bad as Lorraine said,' was her greeting, accompanied by three kisses on my cheeks. 'Thinner, yes, but this is never a problem with fashion.'

Alex rolled her eyes behind Shanice's head, but I pretended not to see.

'Shanice, this is my best friend, Alex. She's visiting from Dublin, taking care of me.'

'*Enchantée.*' Shanice turned, her hand extended, and looked Alex up and down with her trained eye. '*Très chic* – love the frames.' She squinted at her feet. 'Those look like the Chloé loafers, but something is not quite right?'

'Eh, they're a dupe, actually. Vegan leather.'

Shanice barked. 'I just love that we call fakes "dupes" these days. So quaint.'

I saw the sneer on Alex's face and steered Shanice away from her and towards my closet. She came over once every month to go through it, removing anything that was already outdated to ensure I was only ever seen in the hottest styles. I wasn't often present when she edited my stuff, which was for the best. Shanice can be honest to the point of offence.

'She is cute. Is she gay?' Shanice nodded towards where Alex was banging around the kitchen. 'I can never tell with you Irish.'

'No, she's not one of yours,' I laughed. 'Not even a little bit bi, despite the loafers.'

'Shame. I like that petite-blondie vibe.' Shanice shrugged. 'And how are you, *bébé*? The talk of the town, as always.'

'Surviving. Have you heard anything on the grapevine that's not about me I should know about?' As a hotshot stylist, Shanice was privy to the kind of information disclosed in the intimacy of fittings and shoots, when people are vulnerable and their guard is down. As much as I enjoyed hearing her news, I was always wary of being the subject of it.

'Margot Robbie is playing Bardot in a biopic. That girl is going to play every famous blonde there ever was, but I don't think she can do the French accent justice.' She sniffed. 'And that other Irish girl whose name I can never pronounce?'

'Saoirse Ronan?'

'*Oui*, her. She is signing a beauty contract with Dior.'

'Do you only keep abreast of French-centric news?'

'If I can help it!' Shanice trilled. 'Now, gather all of your Triomphe bags, please. It is out; *le* Celine Victoire is now in.'

'But I love my Triomphes! They're, like, $4,000 each!'

'I will sell to the RealReal. They are *passé* now – the plebs are wearing them on TikTok.'

One thing about Shanice, she always makes me peal with laughter. One could assume she doesn't mean to be so rude and harsh, that her bluntness is down to the fact that English is her second language, but nope – anyone not famous or rich is a pleb or a peasant to her. She's like the devil on my shoulder, the person who can say anything they want and get away with it.

We chatted as she decimated my closet, bemoaning the fact that, in mere weeks, all my autumn/winter clothes would be packed up and either sold or archived. 'There is so much you did not get to wear, Tara. What a waste of couture, of tailoring!'

'Well, I haven't exactly been out and about, have I? But we have that Covet shoot next week – anything pink or purple will work for that,' I said, indicating a beautiful lilac satin Prada. 'And that black Tom Ford? Keep that for Alex.'

'*D'accord*. And this Alex, she is here to work for you?'

'No, no. She's my oldest friend, she's here for moral support. Saying that, though, she seems to be doing a lot of work of her own.'

Shanice caught the edge to my tone. 'This displeases you?'

I sighed. 'I don't know. I thought she was here to kind of be my right-hand woman, you know? But she's busy, while I'm not, really. She's been here a wet week and she's already got an offer from an agent.'

'She is an actress? Does she require the services of Shanice?' Her interest was piqued.

'No, you bitch. She's a podcaster, journalist sort of person.'

'They are very hot right now. The new influencers, they say.'

'Who says?'

'The people.' She waved her hand airily.

I felt my hackles rise. Alex, an influencer? Was she going to start doing brand deals on social media and attending fashion shows? There was a poisonous feeling in my stomach. It was bad enough that these online people were invited to the Met and crawling all over the red carpets during awards season. I couldn't have Alex joining their ranks.

'I miss the days when movie stars were the only real celebrities,' I moaned, fingering a Valentino dress Shanice had flung on the bed. 'Pop stars too, if they were huge. Now? Everyone is an A-lister. If I'd known it was going to be so easy to be famous in 2025, I wouldn't have bothered killing myself as an actor.'

'Movie stars are the peak of the A-list, Tara. That will never change.'

'Hmm, we'll see.'

'Well, movie stars and Taylor Swift. And Beyoncé. And Kylie Jenner. Actually, maybe the movie stars are sliding down the list . . .'

I growled and threw one of my discarded Triomphe bags at her as she cackled.

Shanice worked efficiently, taking clothes off hangers and unpacking a suitcase of new pieces into my closet. I picked up the iPad I had flung on the bed after my call with Giulia. There was a red notification icon on my personal email, the one only close friends and family use.

I tapped into it, and my heart nearly stopped beating when I saw there was an email from Rory. It was succinct and to the point, and I moaned so loudly, so gutturally, when I read it that Shanice came running from the closet to see what was wrong.

3 March 2025, 11.07 a.m.
From: rory@roryvaughanllc.com
To: taravaughan2016@gmail.com
Subject: <no subject>

Dear Tara

There is no easy way to say this, so I felt I should put it in writing. I wanted to notify you that I am filing for divorce citing irreconcilable differences. I feel like it makes sense, and draws a line in the sand. I'd rather not drag this through the courts, and I'm sure you don't want to either, so I hope we can resolve everything amicably.

I hope you're doing okay. I know Storm is in New York with you.

Take care,

Rory

3 March 2025, 11.08 a.m.
From: rory@roryvaughanllc.com
To: alex@alexknows.com
Subject: A heads up

Alex,

My daughter tells me that you're staying with Tara in New York, so I wanted to tell you that I informed Tara this morning that I'm initiating divorce proceedings. I know what she's like, and that she may conceal this information, to her detriment, so I wanted you to be aware.

My children have also been informed as of this morning. I'd like to keep this information among as tight a group as possible, to avoid any public leaks.

Thank you for being there for Tara.

Rory

14. Alex

On Wednesday, 5 March, I officially signed with Jordan Jones. I'd never signed a legally binding contract with a man before, and wondered briefly if that was what getting married felt like. Then I realized how alien that sounded, comparing a business partnership to a wedding; I guess that's how sceptical I am about relationships – or should that be *was*? Anyway, as a woman as far away from getting hitched as one could get, I took it as a good omen that I was taking control of something in my life and following a seemingly impossible dream of working in America.

Jordan and I met for lunch back at Dante, where, this time, he sprung for a bottle of Ruinart Blanc de Blancs.

'Congratulations, Alex. Here's to the beginning of a wonderful partnership,' he toasted.

'I have to admit, Jordan, I feel a bit hard done by not actually signing on a dotted line.' I pouted as I took a sip of champagne. 'I brought my favourite fountain pen.'

He laughed. 'You are so old-school! Everything is done digitally these days. But as soon as my assistant got your paperwork this morning, she engaged the services of a top immigration lawyer in Los Angeles. Very soon you will be the proud owner of a work permit and, in the meantime, we'll start pitching you around. You should prepare for many, many meetings.'

'Oh goodie, my favourite!' I snorted, and then could feel myself blush.

I felt oddly nervous under Jordan's cool gaze. 'You know, I had some second thoughts about signing you after our last meeting,' he said, absent-mindedly fiddling with his napkin.

'What? Why?'

'Because you're gorgeous, Alex. I just want to get that out of the way – if you weren't my new favourite client, I would absolutely be trying to hit on you. But you are, so nothing can ever come of this chemistry we seem to have. Pity.'

I was slack-jawed. 'You Yanks are so forward, it is bizarre. Why couldn't you just let us have a nice, simmering undercurrent of sexual tension, a sort of will they/won't they vibe? It would have made me much more productive.'

'You are so funny, Alex.'

'I am very suspicious of people who say something is funny but don't laugh.'

'Honestly, you're a ticket. But you're much too smart for me anyway, so it's definitely for the best that our relationship stays professional.'

'Oh, you like your women a bit dim, then?'

Jordan guffawed. 'No! Not dim. Just not smarter than me.'

Mona appeared then with some small plates we hadn't ordered. 'I could see you guys were celebrating, so I thought I'd take the liberty.' She beamed, placing down anchovies on toast and a dish of warm focaccia.

'Now there's someone you could ask out.' I nodded at her retreating back, her curls trailing down her back.

'Oh yeah?'

'Do you think Mona is giving us free food for the good of her health?'

'No, it's because I way overtip her always. It's good for business, always gets me a table and great service.'

'You're a cynical man, Jordan Jones.'

'And every ounce of that cynicism will be used to get you the greatest deals possible.'

We clinked glasses, and that moment felt like the first of the rest of my life. Everything was coming up Alex.

Back in the apartment, the mood was considerably more subdued. I was trying not to rub my happiness in Tara's face, but also keen to continue celebrating. Jordan had wanted to take me to dinner to keep the party going, but I felt like I had to go home and check on my friend, who wasn't doing well.

Tara had been in bed since Rory's email arrived, and refused to get up. When I poked my nose around her door she looked like she was asleep, so I left her. Feeling at a loose end, I looked at my watch. It was 11 p.m. in Dublin, I might just catch my parents before they went to bed.

Dad answered my FaceTime with a huge smile on his face. 'There's my American *star*!' he boomed, causing me to gesticulate wildly for him to be quiet.

'Tara's sleeping, Dad,' I laughed in a whisper, letting myself on to the terrace. The view of Central Park from out there never got old.

'I'm sorry, love, I'm just so happy for you. Hang on and I'll get your mother. She has something to tell you, actually.'

Dad kept the camera on his face as he walked through my childhood home, and I felt a pang at both the earnestness of his expression and the sight of the familiar wallpaper. Only an Irish person could feel homesick after a few weeks, I thought.

He eventually located Mam in the spare room, where she was playing Farmville on their ancient Windows desktop. 'Alex, love, we are so proud of you! Are you heading out on the town?'

'Oh, I don't think so, Tara is a little under the weather.'

'But it's your big day!' My mother looked distinctly put out.

'Yes, but I told you about Rory's email . . .'

My dad tutted loudly. 'Dreadful business, that.'

'But love, surely Tara wants to celebrate your good news? It's not every day a girl from round here signs up with a fancy US agent.' Deirdre was upset on my behalf.

'It's just the way it is, Mam. Don't worry, I had a lovely lunch with Jordan and I'm going to treat myself to some more wine and some internet shopping. Apparently, I'm going to be meeting a lot of important people over the next few weeks, so I have to look the part.'

'You always look the part! My girl has been a star for ever. For god's sake, buy yourself a dress, will you? Your legs haven't seen the light of day in eons.'

My dad nudged her softly. 'Tell her, Dee.'

'Tell me what?'

'Well, love, Aer Lingus has a great deal on. If it's not too much of an imposition, I think I'm going to come over to the Big Apple next week! I'll stay with Darius and Francisco – I won't be any bother to you at all, I promise. Just if you're going to be there for a while, I can bring over some more of your stuff . . .' She trailed off. 'Alexandra, what's wrong? Are you crying?'

'No,' I sobbed, well aware of the tears falling freely down my face. 'I don't cry.'

'Ahh, love. You'll have me going next!'

My dad took the phone as Deirdre started bawling as well. 'I don't know what to do with the pair of you. Love, I can't get away from work just yet. Your mam has lots of time owed to her, but I can't just up and leave, you know? I might follow her over if I can sort it out, if that's okay? I'd love to see New York again. I haven't been since the 90s, when you'd go over with a spare suitcase and fill it up with designer brands . . .'

I let my father reminisce without interruption. They really were the sweetest people alive. I was so damn lucky.

By the next morning I was officially worried about Tara yet again, and called in reinforcements in the shape of Darius and Storm. Tara was refusing to get up or eat, she looked like hell and her big Covet shoot was only a few days away. They were not going to be pleased if their multimillion-dollar spokesmodel showed up looking like a boiled shite.

Storm told me she had also received an email from her father, a lot less formal than the ones in my and Tara's inboxes. He told her that he needed to make the separation formal so he could begin to move forward. 'I just don't understand it, Alex. It's all so sudden. It seems too soon to be making things official!' Her big blue eyes were troubled.

'It definitely feels that way,' I murmured, giving her a hug. 'I'm just glad the press hasn't found out yet.'

'Knowing my dad, he probably filed in a tiny district that doesn't tip off the media. He's considerate like that.'

I thought that, if he was so considerate, he'd speak to his estranged wife. Storm must have seen the look on my face. 'Dad's not a bad guy, you know. This is all extremely out of character. He must feel very strongly to be doing this, but he won't tell me what went on between them.'

'I know, hon. Tara's convinced things were perfect until they weren't. I'm none the wiser either.'

Darius came out of Tara's room and shut the door behind them. 'Is she on something?' He looked pale with concern.

'No, she's afraid of pills since she accidentally overdid it in Dublin. Why do you ask?'

'She's not herself at all. I caught her googling facelifts. You're not to let her touch that face, Alex. It's priceless!'

'She's just having a rough time, Dar. When a woman of a certain age feels lacking in confidence, the plastic-surgery industry is poised to pounce.' I sighed.

'Well, she was also giggling manically at something on her phone, and when I tried to look, I swear I saw a dick pic.'

'Gross!' squealed Storm.

'Okay, it's my turn to go in.' I stood up grudgingly.

Tara was sitting up in bed, and she was indeed gurning at her phone.

'What are you doing?' I asked, picking the feathery robe up off the floor.

'Just having a bit of fun with Todd Kramer. Remember him?'

'Hmm, former co-star?'

'Yep, from a few years ago. He was always trying to get in my pants, and of course he was in touch as soon as he heard about my . . . business. So I've decided to engage in some light sexting with him. It's good for a girl's ego.'

'Isn't he, like, twenty-eight?'

'Twenty-seven, actually. And what's good for the gander . . .'

I got her drift. 'Do you feel like getting up today? We could grab some lunch, go to the beauty salon?'

'Oh, sure, why don't you just call TMZ right now and tell them what time to expect us?'

'I'm only trying to help, Tara.'

She sighed. 'I know, I know. I just can't face anybody just yet. I'm raging that photographer got pics of me the other morning – I swear I looked jowly in them. I'm just conserving my energy for when I'm contractually obliged to talk to people next week.'

'Fair enough,' I said, sitting on the bed. This was a relief: she was still thinking about the shoot. The jowls comment explained the facelift googling; I wouldn't have to alert Giulia just yet.

'I didn't want to disturb you when I came in yesterday, but I signed my contract with Jordan.'

'Who?'

'Jordan Jones, the agent?' I felt stung. I'd told her all about him.

'Oh, yes. That's great, Alex.'

I decided to change tack. 'Have you replied to Rory?' She knew he'd emailed me as well; I thought it best to tell her.

'No.'

'Are you going to?'

'What is there to say, Alex? I know you've never been married or even in a long-term relationship, but once your husband files something in a court of law, it's not exactly good news.'

'Hey, now. There's no need for that.'

Her face softened, then crumpled. 'Oh, Alex. I'm sorry. I don't know why I said that. I'm just . . . I'm not in my right mind.'

I scooted closer and put my arms around her. 'Have you ever been?' I whispered into her forehead, grinning.

'Oh, fuck off.' She gulped, but I heard the hint of a laugh in her voice.

'Things will get better, Tara. I promise.'

'I really believe they will, Al. Honestly, I can actually see a path forward for myself; I'm just impatient to get there. Feeling this pain, well, it's not good for my complexion. I have four new wrinkles!'

I started to laugh properly, and then Tara did too. It was contagious, to the point that we were soon jabbering like a pair of feral monkeys.

The door opened wide, and Darius and Storm stood there, gaping at us. Tara's face was purple, and I was struggling to breathe.

'See, this is exactly why I married a man,' Darius cried. 'You women are fucking crazy!'

15. Tara

By the time my big Covet shoot rolled around I was feeling slightly less unhinged, but still impatient to hear from Sean. The email from Rory had come as an enormous shock, but thanks to days of convalescence, face and body treatments and emergency sessions with both Samuel and Elspeth, I had pulled my shit together. I'd instructed my business manager to hire the most shark-like divorce lawyer imaginable and let them deal with it all. If I was going to end up as Mrs Sean Sweeney, of course Rory and I would have to formally end things eventually. I just didn't think he'd get the ball rolling quite so quickly.

As I got myself up and ready to face what would surely be a big, busy day, I practised mindfulness techniques that were meant to ground me in the moment, but I knew it was no use. As I washed my face, all I could think about was the fact that my marriage was over and, today, a reporter was coming to talk to me about it.

How had it all gone so badly wrong? The early years of my marriage to Rory were idyllic. I was a relatively young bride, both of our careers were red hot, and I had tons of energy to devote to Storm and Xavier while simultaneously doing a million other things. Xavier didn't actually take much raising – before long he was studying Visual Arts at Columbia and he didn't hang around in New York after he graduated, preferring the peace and quiet of the house on the Cape. He'd always wanted a low-key life and has been content there, tinkering with his boat and worrying about the environment.

Storm and I always had an incredible bond, though. When I met her she was at the precise awkward age where she needed a mommy figure to tell her about boys and periods and pubic hair, and I loved that I could be there for her. She filled some gap in my soul, something that cracked open when Gloria died, and I guess I did the same for her.

I'd always heard that marriage was work, but mine never felt like it. It was easy between Rory and me, but I wasn't going to rest on my laurels. I made sure to carve out time for the two of us, keeping our relationship romantic and spontaneous. We had the best sex life of any couple I knew, still as hot for one another as we'd been that first night.

Then I turned thirty-four towards the end of the pandemic, and my biological clock began to scream. It was physically deafening, like my ovaries were roaring at me for waiting too long – I swore blind to Rory that I could actually hear them, and dying eggs were all I could think of. All of a sudden, my body was telling me I needed to have children of my own immediately, that I had prioritized my career for too long and I needed to get cracking, like, yesterday.

So we started to try. Rory and I had always wanted more children in theory; he would have been happy to have ten kids. I had my IUD removed, started tracking my cycle and began pouncing on my gorgeous husband at any given moment. It was fun, at first. I'd meet him off the elevator in nothing but heels, surprise him at work for a quickie in his trailer.

But after several months, I still wasn't pregnant. I was warned it could take a while, but I was impatient. I'd spent my youth being told that it only took one microscopic sperm, one unprotected dalliance, to seal my fate. We were riding like rabbits with zero contraception, and nothing was happening.

I started worrying that it was my fault. Rory suggested all sorts of fertility treatments and screenings, but I had a visceral reaction to the idea that I couldn't produce children for my husband. After all, Rory's virility was evident from his offspring; it must be me that was defective, useless.

Telling Rory we hadn't conceived was awful every single time, watching his bright eyes dim with disappointment as I reached for the tampons in the bathroom cabinet. 'Next month, babe,' he'd say, putting on a brave face. I'd smile back, but inside I was terrified I was failing him.

Eventually the excitement of daily sex dulled; it went from fun and novel to automatic, timed, scheduled. After a while, it all did start to feel like work.

In the dead of night since the separation, this was what was tormenting me – that I had ruined what Rory and I had by asking for too much. We'd been so happy, but it wasn't good enough for me, I wanted more. I'd made our lovemaking boring and routine and, in turn, destroyed our beautiful marriage. No wonder he had left me for a nubile sylph who screamed sex, a younger woman who looked fit to burst with natural fertility hormones and primo eggs.

I looked at myself in the mirror. Really, you'd never be able to tell what was going on inside. I'm always good at getting my act together when it's important, of turning on the Tara show. And it was true that Sean's declaration on TV had helped me feel a little less frenzied and overwrought. Perhaps there had been no baby for Rory and me because it just wasn't meant to be. We weren't supposed to be together, so the universe was showing us that in a harsh and unavoidable way.

The fact that I now knew I was fated to be with Sean Sweeney made me feel calmer, less useless and redundant. And if Rory wanted to wash his hands of it all quick smart, that left the coast clear for my new (old) love.

However, Fate would want to get its fucking act together, because every day that went by without Sean and I together, time was ticking and eggs were dying off. I was turning thirty-eight soon. Maybe Sean and I would be a better fit, a more successful match.

Patience has never been my strong suit, though, and I was considering reaching out to him to get this show on the road. But every time I went to send a text or an email, I forced myself to rewatch the part of the interview in which Sean said I deserved a grand gesture. I wouldn't deny him that, or ruin any part of the fantasy he clearly had in his head. All in good time, I told myself. It had become my most dearly held mantra.

Still, I wasn't above moving things along a little if I could. The night before, I'd told Giulia that I would do the cover of *People* to promote the new Covet campaign, and also let the world know that I wasn't some cuckolded, pathetic spouse. If the studio wanted *Mind the Gap* to be a summer romcom, then I needed to get some practice in before the publicity tour. The message would be clear – I was moving on, looking great and ready for whatever came next. Surely that would be a red rag to the bull Sean Sweeney? A green light of sorts.

Giulia quickly arranged for the magazine's chief reporter to come and observe the shoot and interview me that evening right after we wrapped, probably in case I changed my mind.

When I arrived on set, Shanice was fussing over accessories and arguing with the make-up artist about my undertones. 'She cannot wear a warm eye, Sabrina!' she was shrieking. 'Her palette is cool! Cool winter!'

I find it oddly comforting when Shanice goes off on my behalf. It means I don't have to do it myself and get a reputation for being a bitch.

Alex had come with me, claiming to want to see the inner workings of a huge beauty campaign. I hoped she wasn't getting any ideas about fronting one herself; ever since she had signed with this new agent, I was feeling territorial about my work. But that was silly, right?

'Tara, darling,' Alan the photographer cooed once I was all dolled up. 'Pop into your little dress and we'll start shooting.' He was British, gorgeous and incredibly camp, which is just how I like my snappers.

I do three Covet shoots a year, and have done for ages. It was initially all about my hair, but the success of my endorsement meant we expanded, and now I'm known as the brand's de facto face. There are other models, of course – the cosmetics industry today is all about inclusivity, and rightly so – but when people think of Covet, they think of Tara O'Toole, a fact that means I'm paid handsomely for my likeness. This shoot was a big deal, the summer season fast approaching. I had to bring my A game.

Much to my relief, I clicked instantly into model mode as I replaced my stand-in in front of the backdrop. There had been a niggling noise at the back of my brain telling me I couldn't possibly perform as usual, not with everything going on. I needn't have worried. I threw back my hair, cooed and smized for the camera, and did my very best to show off Covet's latest launches in all their glory.

Before long, it was nearing the end of the day and time to capture the video close-ups required for television ads. Shanice, Sabrina and my hairstylist, Yan, were fussing around me, and I was starting to feel a little tired, the weight of make-up on my face becoming uncomfortable. This was no time for flagging, though – these were the money shots.

'Covet covers, Covet comforts,' I breathed, gazing down the camera. 'Covet colours, Covet cares.' I winked mischievously, blew kisses and laughed at nothing, all par for the course. Then it was time for the big catchphrase. 'Covet Cosmetics. Crave What's Yours.'

It was all nonsense, of course, but solid-gold nonsense nonetheless.

'Fabulous, Tara!' Alan beamed. I could tell from how he'd relaxed over the day that he too had been worried about my ability to give what was necessary. 'Let's just get that one or two more times from different angles. Everyone, reset the cameras!'

As even more sticky lip gloss and hairspray were being applied, I noticed some unusual activity behind the camera. Alex was reading something on her phone, one hand on her hip and looking serious. Shanice was gesticulating wildly, and Sabrina kept shooting me guilty looks as she painted lacquer on to my mouth. Felicia was on her laptop, iPad and phone simultaneously.

'Sabrina, what's going on?' I asked, as best I could without moving my mouth. I sounded like a ventriloquist, but I knew she had heard me. The make-up artist was pretending she hadn't, though. As soon as she finished her work, she flounced off away from me and my questions. Yan wasn't so lucky, still coiffing my hair when I regained full use of my voice. 'Tell me what's happening, Yan, or you'll never work with me or this brand again.' It was dramatic, but it was intended to be. The poor guy's eyes widened in horror.

'It's your, um, husband, I guess?'

My eyes narrowed. 'What now?'

'Alex!' Yan called, clearly terrified and dying to get away from me. 'Ms O'Toole has some questions!'

Alex approached me as you might a rabid dog, timidly and with great caution. 'Spit it out, Curtis,' I snapped.

'Rory and Allegra are walking the red carpet as we speak at the Brit Awards in London. Together.'

'And?'

'And, well . . . it's their first public appearance as a couple. She's nominated for a rake of awards, and she's giving interviews to the press about how madly in love she is with Rory. She's performing the new single she wrote about him.'

'Okay, thank you for being honest.'

'Are you okay?'

'I'm fine. Can we wrap this all up now?'

'The journalist from *People* is due to arrive any minute. Felicia is on the phone to Giulia now. Should we postpone?'

'Why on earth would we do that?'

'Um. It just might not be the best time.'

'No better time. If my estranged husband is out flaunting his new romance, there's no point in me hiding away any longer.'

Alex shrugged, nodded at Alan, and I flipped my internal switch once again. Showtime.

Two hours later, I was sitting in the Polo Bar on East 55th. I much prefer the Polo Lounge in Beverly Hills, but this Manhattan outpost was good for interviews – quiet, reassuringly antiquated and expensive enough that the clientele weren't the type to gawk at you.

People had sent Emily Rutherford, their top correspondent to the stars. I've known her for years, but it would be foolish to ever think a celebrity journalist is your friend. They all have an agenda, all are waiting for you to slip up. Still, Emily is a relatively good egg and I could feel ever so slightly comfortable with her.

At that moment, she was looking at me with naked pity in her eyes, and I was keen to disabuse her of the notion that I was the devastated party. I would not be 'Poor Jen' Aniston in this scenario, no siree. 'Emily, let's get the theatrics out of the way, shall we? I'm aware that Rory Vaughan is right now at a music industry event in the United Kingdom with his new . . . co-star, and that they are romantically involved. No, their relationship is not responsible for the dissolution of our marriage, and no, I will not be talking about what happened between us because, of course, the end of any relationship is complicated. It's still a bit too fresh to go into detail, but I am doing well.' I made sure my eyes were glistening with a hint of unshed tears, my expression brave yet humble.

'I've always admired your balls, Tara. You've got chutzpah. What is the message that you want to send to the world?'

'That I'm doing okay, I haven't gone to pieces. I am looking forward in life. How things between Rory and me officially ended and came to light was a shock, and of course it's never easy to see a former partner move on publicly. But really, our relationship had been over for a while.' I lied with such ease, I almost believed myself. 'Right now, I'm focusing on myself and making plans for the future. Rory and I had a wonderful marriage for a long time, and I remain utterly devoted to Storm and Xavier. That will never change.'

I could tell Emily was unprepared for my candour, but she seemed to be buying it and decided to chance her arm. 'And what of the murmurs that your old friend Sean Sweeney may have been talking about you in his now iconic interview with Kelly

Clarkson? After the details revealed in his new book, everyone seems to think you are the old flame that never extinguished.'

I laughed. 'Oh, Emily, you devil woman. Sean and I do go way back. But I don't comment on gossip and rumours. You know me better than that.'

'Fair enough.' She knew when she was beaten. 'So what's next for you, Tara? I've heard *Mind the Gap* is coming out earlier than expected?'

'Yes, the studio is so impressed with it, they want to share it with the world in July!'

'And do you have any projects in the pipeline?'

'Of course. I'm always developing something, Emily. I'm reading scripts, in talks with my agents. As you know, just today I shot the Covet Cosmetics campaign that's dropping this month.' It didn't sound like enough to my seasoned ears. I wanted to sound so booked and busy there wasn't time to mourn my soon-to-be ex-husband. I had a brainwave.

'I've also just decided to take the Academy up on their offer of presenting an award at the Oscars this year. I'll be heading to Los Angeles very soon and attending all the big events and parties. A girl deserves a good time, don't you think?'

'I don't know anyone more deserving, Tara.' Emily beamed at me, delighted with her scoop and totally taken in by my tall tales. I had just in that moment decided to go to LA, and I prayed the Academy would be receptive to me presenting. I made a mental note to get Giulia on that the second I left the interview.

As for being in California for the tail end of awards season, well, why the hell not? If Rory and his side piece were walking red carpets as love's young dream, why couldn't I as an independent, successful and highly in-demand star?

I smiled at Emily as she prattled on, making lists in my head of everything that would need to be done before I headed west. It was time to come out of hibernation, time to reclaim my life.

@TMZ

🤗 14,576 Likes

SPOTTED! Actress Tara O'Toole was photographed leaving the Polo Club in New York City, radiant in purple Prada and all smiles. Rumour has it she's back in action and has just shot her latest campaign for @covetcosmetics.

@RoryLover1987_: Tara looks amazing!

@trickster77 @RoryLover1987_: are you insane? She looks ancient

@trickster77: Team Allegrory!

@susansmith64526: I love Tara's movies. I feel sorry for her.

@RORA4eva: I am sooooo sad about RORA, I might k word myself

@brentwood_babe_99: Who is this

@heroinchic1994: She looks fat ew

@marymag2024: I'm worried about Tara, very thin

@godisgud2me: Godless heathens, all of them. Satan's minions.

@preciousbabyyyy: chill out dude

@seansweeneyscanadiangf: Slut

16. Alex

On Saturday morning, my mother arrived in New York. Darius insisted on picking her up from JFK, a task I wouldn't wish on anyone, but he owns a vintage Volkswagen Beetle that he loves to take for a spin every now and then, caring not a jot that he barely fits in the thing. It's pale lemon and very cute and often makes an appearance at his events and weddings.

I was waiting in the guys' apartment in Chelsea with Francisco when Deirdre and Darius bustled in, my mother raving about everything she laid eyes on. 'Alex, my love! You look fantastic!' she said, holding me to her like she hadn't seen me in months. 'New York agrees with you, pet.' She was so elated to finally be here; her big trip in 2020 for her sixtieth birthday had been cancelled due to Covid.

'Oh my god, the sights I've already seen!' Deirdre said, her eyes wide. 'Darius took the scenic route, so I got the full effect of the city skyline, and wowee. The last time I was here, your father made me get a manky train from the airport.'

'It's not every day my oldest friend comes to stay!' Darius shrieked. 'I went absolutely arse-ways, across the Queensboro bridge, to give my visiting queen the best view.' He blew a kiss at Mam, and she blushed.

Deirdre and Darius have been close since they met in secondary school when Mam was head girl and Darren, as he was known then, a sweet little first-year. He's always been the flamboyant person that he is now, and Deirdre was instantly protective of him. They formed a bond that carried them through their teens and twenties, Mam meeting Dad and getting married (Darius was Man of Honour before such a thing was commonplace), and Darius setting up That's D'Amore.

My mother was walking around the apartment oohing and aahing at everything. Tara had kindly upgraded her fare to business class as soon as she heard Deirdre was coming, so Mam was refreshed and raring to go.

'Right, what would you like to do first?'

'Whatever you think, love. Darius is getting us Broadway tickets for tomorrow night, isn't that exciting?'

'She wants to see *Mamma Mia!*' Darius rolled his eyes dramatically.

'That is my favourite!' squealed Francisco, jumping up and down. 'You cannot beat Abba.' He clocked Darius's thunderous expression. 'Uhh, but darling Deirdre, may I make a recommendation?'

My mother adores Francisco; she is putty in his hands. She nodded obediently.

'Let's go see something new and a bit different? I have a friend of a friend who will get us into *Gypsy*! Audra McDonald will blow your head off.'

Deirdre looked uncertain. 'I don't know those songs.'

'Francisco, I don't think my mammy is a seasoned enough musical theatre aficionado to know about Stephen Sondheim's canon.'

'A disgrace!' boomed Darius, but he was laughing. 'Call yourself my best friend, Deirdre Curtis? A lifetime of being your closest ally and you have next to *no* musical theatre education – I cannot.'

'I just like the normal stuff. Andrew Lloyd Webber and that.'

Darius pretended to keel over and landed awkwardly on the sofa. For a man of such great size, he's surprisingly graceful.

'Fine, fine,' he moaned. 'But please God, not *Mamma Mia! Chicago*, maybe? *Wicked*?'

'Ah yes, I've heard of those!' Deirdre beamed.

I was so excited to show my mam around, but I was more than a bit irritated that Tara wasn't going to be in the city to help me play tour guide; she was leaving for LA in a couple of days. Tara was hyper about the trip. She and Giulia were on calls constantly, deciding which events she should grace with her presence and how to strike the right tone.

Tara did seem more energized since she'd decided to go; that couldn't be denied. I wasn't thrilled about her leaving New York, mostly because I feared she was using it as an excuse to go and throttle Rory, but also because I couldn't just up and leave with her and get some Californian sunshine. Not only was my mother visiting, but Jordan had set up a big pitch with Netflix for the very day Tara left. Then it occurred to me that even if I was able to go with her, Tara hadn't actually asked me to.

I filled my mam and Francisco in on all my news while Darius busied himself making tea; he'd already heard about Netflix, helped me decide what to wear to the meeting and gone over some vocal exercises with me. 'This is an audition, Alex!' he'd boomed the previous evening. 'And auditions are my specialty.' He wasn't wrong, so I let him cajole, corral and coach me as he had since I was a tween, and in his own special way he had imbued some sort of confidence in me. I was terrified and anxious, of course, but I was also excited.

'So the project is all about social media,' I told my rapt audience of elders. 'The idea is a series in which every episode is based on a year in pop culture since MySpace launched, and how the world of entertainment has changed because of how connected we all are. It's basically exactly my wheelhouse,' I said. 'Recent history, music, film, TV, celebrities, all through the prism of social. Get it?'

'I think so, love. Like *Reeling in the Years*, but about the internet?'

'Yes, exactly, Mam!' I was thrilled Deirdre could sum it all up so succinctly. If she got it, surely the streaming executives would too? 'And it won't just be me – we'll have all sorts of expert talking heads, celebrities, and industry people too.'

'But you'll be the frontwoman?'

'That's the plan.'

Mam had hit on the part I was feeling iffy about. I had confidence in my own abilities to research and structure a show like this, especially with Jordan assembling a crack production team around me. What I was less sure of was my ability to host and sell such a big project. Why would anyone tune in to watch little old me? Why weren't they getting someone huge to front it? I feared that Netflix would say exactly that and I'd be relegated to the background.

That in itself was no bad thing, but I had allowed myself to dream of being a presenter and documentarian, like a blonde lady Louis Theroux. As soon as I gave myself permission to dream big, I was opening myself up to those dreams being squashed.

I was comforted that Mam, Darius and Francisco all thought it was the best idea they'd ever heard, though.

'You're a natural performer, Alex. I've said for years that you should be onscreen – the camera loves you,' Darius declared. 'And if you'd rather do it as yourself, well, all your acting skills are transferable! I'd personally rather you were doing Shakespeare at the National, but beggars can't be choosers.'

'He's right, Alex,' Francisco agreed. 'You're far too pretty and clever to not be on TV!'

My mam was beaming proudly. 'I feel it in my bones, this is your time, pet.'

'Stop, stop, or my head won't fit through the door,' I laughed, waving away their praise. But their confidence in me bolstered my self-esteem.

'And Alex, you have such great connections,' my mother said. 'You know everyone! Surely Tara will come on? And that fella Sean Sweeney? They both have huge international appeal.'

The mere mention of his name made me woozy. Little did Deirdre know, before long Sean would be doing much more than appearing on my show. I was also vaguely irritated by the mention of Tara. Like I needed her to boost the calibre of the project, that she'd be doing me a favour by being a talking head. If my mother thought it important that Tara O'Toole, superstar, would deign to help out her good friend Alex, maybe it was? I mentally shook it off. Now wasn't the time to give in to intrusive thoughts.

'Okay, enough about me,' I said. 'It is my mother's first visit to New York City in twenty-odd years, and the first ever with me. I have devised the perfect Deirdre-centric itinerary, if you're open to trusting me, a mere blow-in. Who wants to hear it?'

They all nodded enthusiastically.

'Okay, first we are going on the *Sex and the City* tour, but my own version. There will be cupcakes at Magnolia Bakery, of course, and we will visit Carrie's stoop, but I am not taking my mother to a sex shop to buy a Rampant Rabbit, so don't even ask.'

They nodded again.

'Then we will go and see the *Friends* apartment and have an early dinner at Emmett's on Grove. Mam, they do the most amazing deep-fried olives that you just have to try. Then we'll visit Christopher Street and the famous Stonewall Inn, and finally end up in Marie's Crisis Café, where the drinks are strong and the singing around a piano is loud. Sound good?'

My mother's coat was already on. 'What are you waiting for?' she roared. 'Let's go!'

The following afternoon, I cried off any more tourist activities in order to prep for my big pitch. That morning we'd been to the 9/11 Memorial, Brooklyn Bridge and the Empire State Building observatory, and Deirdre showed no signs of flagging – years spent in midwifery gave her stamina to beat the band, along with calves of steel. Unfortunately, I had to work, so I left Darius, Francisco and my mother to their NBC Studio Tour and visit to Broadway; tickets for *Wicked* had been procured, and everyone was happy.

However, the atmosphere back at Tara's place wasn't exactly

as peaceful as I'd hoped it would be; Shanice, Storm and Felicia were all present, helping her to pack for the big trip to California. All three were accompanying Tara, and even with my headphones on I could hear shrieking and stomping coming from her quarters.

I was irked because I had a lot of work to do, but then quickly shook myself. This was Tara's apartment; I was merely a guest. I considered heading to the coffee shop downstairs, but I'm also incredibly nosey and wanted to feel part of the excitement, even in a peripheral way.

Just as I was about to go and investigate the squeals, the elevator pinged and the doorman emerged, dragging something. 'Ms O'Toole is expecting Ms Staffetta,' he said to my inquisitive expression. Lorraine appeared behind him at the tail end of a jam-packed clothes rail and clattered into the apartment.

'Thanks so much for your help, Simon,' she said, tucking a folded-up bill into his jacket pocket and patting it. He smiled obediently and departed.

'What do you need all that for?' I asked, flabbergasted, gesturing to the rail. 'And how did you even get it here?' Tara had access to the biggest designers in the world, so why was Lorraine Staffetta dragging a rack of dresses across town?

'Not that it's anyone's business, but I've decided to go to LA with Tara,' she sniffed, clearly displeased at having to explain anything to me. 'I think she could still do with a lot of moral support, and she tells me you're staying here to work.' There was a definite accusation in both her tone and her flinty eyes.

Instinct told me to kill her with kindness. 'Oh, Lorraine, that makes me so happy! I'm delighted you have time in your busy schedule to travel with her. It's crap that I have to stay in New York, but this Netflix pitch is such an amazing opportunity for me, and of course Tara understands that.'

She softened a little at my effusiveness. 'Oh, well, it's my pleasure. And you never know, I might meet a nice man out there. Hence the clothes.'

'Seriously, Lorraine, how did you get that rail here?'

'A Manhattan woman moves in mysterious ways,' she called over her shoulder as she wheeled her dresses into Tara's suite, where she was greeted with cheers. Curiosity piqued, I followed her.

The scene before me was chaos. Tara was sitting on the floor in just a skimpy thong, there were clothes, shoes and bags everywhere, and Shanice was throwing items out of the wardrobe on to the bed. Three large suitcases and a Louis Vuitton trunk were open on the floor, all in various stages of fullness.

'Geez, how long are you going to LA for – a month?'

I was greeted with blank stares. Storm saw my confused expression and clearly felt sorry for me.

'Tara has to be prepared for any eventuality out there. Chat shows, red carpets, photo ops, dinners, lunches, drinks, workouts. It's been raining and chilly there lately, so that means bringing something for every possible scenario. It's endless, really!'

'We don't have time to shop or style out there, Al,' Tara continued. 'We'll be hitting the ground running. This is the reality of Oscar season.'

I nodded, chastened. I felt silly and naïve, and Tara could sense my embarrassment.

'Hey, how was the touring with Deirdre? Is she having fun?'

'Oh, she is having a ball. Thanks for hooking her up at NBC – Mam will be thrilled to meet Jimmy Fallon! She loves him.'

'He owed me a favour; it's no biggie. We should be done here by about eight—' She held up a hand to silence Shanice's protestations. 'Or at least, I'll have had enough by then. How about we have dinner, you and me? To make up for me ditching you for the City of Angels. You can tell me all about your pitch. I'll order in?'

I instantly felt better. That's the Tara effect; when she shines her light on you, it can seriously change your mood.

'Sounds perfect.' I smiled, trying not to grin smugly at Lorraine. 'I'll get back to work and leave you guys to it.'

'We'll try to keep it down!' Storm called after me, but within seconds the ruckus ensued once again. No matter, I thought. I had an evening with my oldest friend to look forward to.

Crazy Days and Nights

Blind Item # 2

Which A+-list beauty is playing hard to get? Her marriage may have recently gone down the tubes, but her former flame, an A-list singer, is trying to reach her to make her an offer she can't refuse. Our beauty isn't staying long enough in one place for him to reach her, though. Sources say she's open to reconnecting, but wants to make him work for it.

Blind Item # 1

There's trouble in paradise for this surprising new coupling. The hot popstrel loves her new older man, but doesn't love living among his ex-wife's things. She wants to redecorate, he's refusing and it's causing strife. Will this romance end because of his reluctance to renovate? Watch this space!

SPOTTED

Sean Sweeney and the guys from Higher Power in Las Vegas. Word on the street is that they were hired to perform for a billionaire high-roller's joint bachelor and bachelorette party in Sin City, and Sweeney seemed very cosy with a supermodel guest.

17. Tara

By 9 p.m., I was exhausted. Spending all day with your team packing for a glamorous and exciting work trip sounds fabulous, of course. It was definitely something I dreamt about when I was on the way up and begging friends to lend me clothes to wear for auditions. The reality of being a Fashion Girlie is less fun and more intense than you could ever think possible, though.

By the time the team left I felt like a human pin cushion and a Barbie doll at the same time, but I knew it would be worth it once I was in Los Angeles looking my very best. My outfits were chosen, suitcases were packed and ready to go for the early flight out of JFK, where I'd meet the others. We were flying commercial because, honestly, it's a bit more fun in a group. Private jets get boring after a while – no people-watching, no fellow travellers surreptitiously sneaking pictures of you.

Felicia had tactfully mentioned that she'd booked us all into bungalows at the Beverly Hills Hotel for the duration of the trip; of course, Rory was using our home there as his primary residence. I'd been aware of that, but it still really stung, especially when I thought of Allegra's enormous arse sitting on my favourite burnt-ochre sofa, but I swallowed the rage. Use it as motivation, I told myself. And anyway, I love the Beverly Hills. It's kitsch and luxe at the same time.

I flopped on the couch in my living room next to Alex, who was sitting cross-legged in her favourite chair and writing in a yellow legal pad.

'Ugh, I'm wrecked,' I yawned. 'Thank god that's all done.'

'Have you ordered dinner? It's getting late.'

I sensed a tone from Alex, and then remembered my earlier promise of a meal, just us two. Shit. I decided to style it out.

'Oh, I thought I'd cook!' I squawked. 'Treat you to a bout of food poisoning to remember me by.' I flashed Alex my most dazzling smile, which seemed to appease my friend, and stalked towards the kitchen, praying there was something edible in it.

I was in luck – Felicia had been keeping the freezer and pantry stocked, so I could whip up one of my few specialties. 'Shrimp risotto sound good?'

'Sounds complicated! Are you sure? We can just get sushi from the place around the corner?'

'No, I'm in the mood, and this is quick, I promise. I won't get to cook for ages now.' I actually meant it; when I'm in the right humour, I enjoy the ritual of making a meal. I'd lost so much weight over the past few weeks from feeling too nauseous to eat that I could do with a creamy, decadent dinner – Shanice had to pin a few of my LA looks so they weren't hanging off me.

After a while, Alex joined me in the kitchen and busied herself uncorking a bottle of Gavi and setting the table while I chopped, poured and stirred. I found a loaf of fresh sourdough and sliced it, while Alex grated some Parmesan. Before long, we were clinking glasses in front of steaming, unctuous bowls.

'Nothing like a home-cooked meal to celebrate a friend,' I said, and Alex beamed. 'I'm sorry I've been so all over the place, Al. I'm very excited for your new chapter and wish you all the success in the world here in the States. Tell me everything.'

That was all the encouragement Alex needed. Her excitement fizzed over as she told me about the big Netflix meeting the next day to pitch the docuseries, and her hopes, fears and dreams about the project. 'It was Jordan's idea, of course, so we'll be co-executive producers, but I've already brought so much to his initial proposal that I've started to believe him that the project needed me!' Alex looked so happy, and I had to admit the series sounded perfect for her. I murmured encouragingly, hoping that I sounded more enthusiastic than I felt.

For some reason, my friend's new opportunities were rankling a little. I wasn't lying when I wished Alex success, of course I did, but the timing was strange – like the universe had been waiting for my life to take a dip so she could soar. Alex had never even really expressed a desire to work in TV before – her stage fright meant she had never wanted to take acting seriously – and how was this different? I thought Alex was happy as she was, so hearing that she wanted to be more visible was surprising. It was stirring strange feelings in the pit of my stomach, ones I couldn't quite identify.

'Tara, I need to thank you too,' she was saying as I tuned back into the conversation, purposely pushing the negativity out of my head. 'If I hadn't been right here, right now, this may not have happened for me. So thank you for bringing me here, for digging me out of a rut I didn't know I was in.'

I took a large glug of wine. 'Well, I'm very glad my crisis came exactly when it did!' I bleated. I'd been going for airy, nonchalant, but it came out sounding kind of bitchy. 'I mean, look, it's a silver lining to a shitty situation, right? And you deserve some good karma, Alex.'

She smiled prettily. There was something different about her, I thought. Some air of youth, of vigour, that hadn't been present even a fortnight before. She seemed softer, gentler somehow. Her smile reached her eyes, her clothes were more relaxed – she was wearing leggings, for god's sake – and her hair was a little longer and shaggier than she ever normally lets it get. If I was being unkind, I might have said that the stick in her ass had been dislodged a little, but as a nice person I conceded that Alex had simply chilled out a bit away from home.

'New York agrees with you,' I said, and I meant it.

'My mother said the same!' Alex said, her smile twinkly. 'I don't know, I just feel really happy lately. Like everything is slotting into place.'

I stood up to get another bottle of wine, my appetite suddenly gone. How could she say to my face that she felt really happy when I'd been going through so much? Smug bitch! Had she no tact, no empathy? I didn't need Alex to be dishevelled and rocking back and forth on my behalf, but she could at least have the decency not to rub how thrilled she was with life in my face.

The nasty feeling was back. Was I . . . was I jealous of Alex? No, surely not. How could I be? It dawned on me then that, perhaps for the first time ever, I truly was on the back foot in comparison. Wow, was this what it felt like to be envious of my best friend? If it was, I really didn't like it.

I mean, I'd always been a bit jealous in some ways – does anyone have a friend they don't feel spiteful towards sometimes? At different times in our lives I envied her brains, her talent, her naturally blonde, straight hair. The fact that she had two adoring parents felt unfair; my mam had died, and I'd been basically estranged from my own alcoholic father ever since. Whenever I saw Alex with Deirdre I experienced a pang of longing for Gloria, but that was only natural. Right?

In so many other ways, I was the one always coming out on top. Alex may have been the 'better' actor, according to those who knew us as kids, but she got in her own way and then gave up. She may have gone to university, but she didn't even stick with her drama degree! I was the one who persevered, who was brave enough to see a career onscreen through to fruition. I was the one with the awards and accolades to prove that I'd done it. I was the one on the cover of the magazines she wrote for, and that dynamic had always worked for us.

Ugh, that must be it, I realized. Our dynamic was changing. Alex's stock was rising, while I was stagnating at best, heading towards washed up at worst.

I turned on the radio to drown out my thoughts and practised one of the techniques Samuel had taught me. I was not washed up, I affirmed. I was taking action and going to LA, where people would be very happy to see me. I was still a star.

Repeating those sentences in my head, I brought the fresh bottle of chilled white wine to the table. I'd steer the conversation back to more neutral territory. 'So tell me about this Jordan Jones, is he a looker?'

'He is, actually. Very handsome in that buttoned-up, slick way. But he's already made it clear nothing will be happening between us. It's all strictly professional.'

'What do you mean?'

'Well, he let it be known that he finds me very attractive, but I'm his client and I'm too smart for him. Or something like that!' Alex laughed, accepting a top-up of her glass. I noticed I was downing two pours for every one of hers.

I felt another surge of irrational jealousy. I wanted hot guys to tell me I was very attractive! As a married woman, nobody had even attempted to hit on me in ages. Sure, I knew I was a 'sex symbol' to some, but that wasn't me they fancied. It was Tara O'Toole, the star. I swallowed the bitter feeling again and pasted a smile on.

'Wow, look at Alex, making waves with the New York crowd!' I croaked. 'You know Shanice was interested as well, so you have options.'

'Lesbians always like me – it's the glasses!' She threw her head back and laughed again. I didn't think I'd ever seen Alex so relaxed, so open.

'What's going on with you?' I asked, unabashed. 'It's not just the work stuff – you have a glint in your eye.'

She flushed. 'Oh god, is it that obvious?' I could see her mind whirring, wondering whether or not to reveal what was clearly a secret she'd been keeping.

'What is it, Alex? Spill, you little wench!'

She bit her lip and began to talk. As I listened, I could feel my face getting hotter and hotter with each word that passed her lips.

'Oh Tara, it's been such a strange few weeks, but something happened recently that just changed everything. It's Sean, Sean Sweeney. I can't believe it was just a few weeks ago you were so upset about his book and what he wrote about you – and I'll admit, I was furious, far angrier than I let on about you two and your . . . arrangement. I couldn't believe you could be so blasé about him when you know how I felt, and I was so angry you kept it from me all these years . . .'

I swallowed nervously. So that was it. Alex must know that Sean was still in love with me. Maybe it had given her closure, allowed her to move on. She was going to accept us as a couple! But, hang on. No, she seemed much too happy for that to be the case.

'. . . anyway, it doesn't matter any more . . . I know you've been out of the loop, so you might not have heard, but Sean basically went on TV and told the entire world that he's still in love with me. That he messed up all those years before when he ghosted me, that he's never gotten over me and basically that he's planning a grand gesture to get me back. Tara, I'm his One That Got Away!'

Suddenly I was struggling to hear Alex over a loud buzzing in my ears, so I leaned in closer as she continued.

'. . . I don't know, Tara, it's just been so liberating. I realized that I've spent years and years feeling stupid about loving him, feeling pathetic for never getting past what happened between us. I've been wondering what the hell is wrong with me, why I couldn't just fall for somebody else. But now I know why! Because it was the real deal, Tara! I wasn't mental! I just had to trust the timing of the universe.' She hugged herself, completely oblivious to my horror.

I coughed, trying to dislodge what felt like a piece of cement sitting in my throat, but Alex didn't seem to notice my distress. She was still chirruping happily about an imagined future with Sean. My Sean. 'Are you saying what I think you're saying?' I managed.

'I'm saying that I feel like, on the cusp of thirty-eight, my life is finally starting to make sense, Tara. It's my birthday this week, my career is clicking into a higher gear, and I'm at long last getting the big romantic ending I deserve because Sean Sweeney still loves me. Maybe I really can have it all!'

She broke out of her reverie and looked at me properly for the first time since she'd begun her soliloquy. 'Jesus, Tara, are you okay? You're puce!'

'I think I must be living in an alternative universe, Alex,' I stuttered.

She frowned. 'What do you mean?'

I took a deep breath. 'I mean that when Sean Sweeney went on Kelly Clarkson's show and told her about the old flame he still holds a candle for, he was absolutely, one hundred per cent, without a shadow of a doubt, talking about me.'

18. Alex

'Wh—what do you mean?' I repeated, giggling awkwardly. Was this a joke?

'I mean, I'm the old flame. The One That Got Away,' Tara enthused. 'Me, not you.'

I stared at my friend across the table. Tara's famous eyes were alight, her lips drawn back so it was almost like she was baring her teeth. People have compared her to a leopard in the past, and I was seeing the likeness now for the first time – I'd always thought they meant slinky, feline and sexy, but in that moment she looked every inch the predator, coming for my throat.

I could only laugh, but it came out sounding like a goose's honk. 'Sorry, I don't know what to say. From what you told me, you two just had an arrangement. Me and Sean, it was . . .'

'It was what, Alex?' Tara snapped. She was so flushed she looked almost purple. 'Really, tell me honestly what you think it was. Because from where I've been standing all this time, it was a weekend-long fling like, seventeen years ago. One you've just refused to even attempt to get over.'

I must have looked horrified because her tone softened, her mouth looked normal again. The high colour in her face receded; it was like someone had taken a pressure cooker off the heat. 'Look, Al, we've all been aware of how that weekend with Sean affected you. I know more than most how magnetic he is, how special he makes you feel. And I know it's almost impossible to get over a guy who is essentially everywhere – you can't escape him. But this has been going on too long now. We want you to move past it, to get on with your life.'

'We?' I baulked. 'Who's "we"?'

'Jen and Brian, Darius and Francisco, your mother. We've all been worried about you.'

I couldn't take in what Tara was saying. My friends and family had been talking about me behind my back? They were worried about me? 'But why?' I rasped, my breath betraying me. 'I've been fine!'

'Fine? Alex, you've never been in a proper relationship. You have your life in such perfect order that it's verging on obsessive compulsive.'

I went to protest, but she shushed me. 'I get it, you were hurt badly once at a young age, and it made you retreat into what you perceived to be safety. But in reality, you've just been hiding yourself away. And now you think that Sean Sweeney is on television talking about you, a woman he hasn't seen since he was twenty-one? Alex, make it make sense!'

I don't know if it was the jab about OCD or the incredulous tone of her voice, but all of a sudden I was angrier than I'd ever been in my life – so livid that I couldn't speak. Tara took my silence as assent, and continued. She sat down next to me and took my hand in hers.

'Alex, I've just always wanted you to be happy. I know you had it rough growing up with the bullying – your skin is still paper thin and you're sensitive. You close yourself off from other people in order to protect yourself, and I get that. But everyone just wants you to open up a little to the possibilities of life, you know? To settle down with a nice guy, or even just to make more friends. You deserve a full life!'

I snatched my hand back. 'How dare you,' I seethed. 'What gives you the right to judge me? Do you think because you have an Oscar in your bathroom, you're an expert on what constitutes a full life?'

Tara reared back as if I'd slapped her, but I was on a roll.

'You've all been worried about me, when I've been busy working, fending for myself and being independent? I've been a good daughter, a great friend. You wish I'd meet a nice man, because you think that's the pinnacle of a woman's experience. You are such a hypocrite,' I spat. 'You met a man, got married young. Fat lot of good that did you! Look at you now, alone again!'

'I'm not doing this!' Tara yelled, standing up and attempting to stalk into her suite. 'This is a misunderstanding, a shock. We've had too much wine—'

'No, *you've* had too much wine,' I grabbed her arm and forced her to look at me. 'I've had a perfectly normal amount with dinner. But you don't eat much, and you're getting a bit fond of the sauce. Don't try and blame this faux concern about me on booze, because that's not it. The fact is, you think I'm pathetic. You didn't think for one second that Sean Sweeney could be in love with me, did you?'

Tara twisted away from me, freeing herself, and threw her hands in the air. 'Of COURSE I didn't think Sean could be in love with you!' she roared. 'Alex, I don't think he even remembers who you are!'

It was like she had slapped me right across the face. I felt physically stung, winded and hot and cold at the same time. In that moment, I was doubting every single thing I'd thought to be real. I couldn't believe that my oldest, closest friend and I had such different perceptions of . . . everything.

But Tara hadn't finished. 'He never once mentioned you to me over the years, not once! Sean and I had a relationship, a casual one, but a relationship nonetheless, over years and years . . .'

'Why would he mention someone he had feelings for to his fuck buddy?' I shouted. 'Especially when said fuck buddy was supposed to be my best friend! He's an asshole for sleeping with you, but I get it. Why wouldn't he, when it's right there on a plate, no strings attached?'

'The only reason I never allowed it to become more serious with Sean was because of you.' Tara looked triumphant, her voice returning to a steady level. 'Because I knew you had this . . . obsession with him, and you wouldn't cope well. Looks like I was right.'

'Take that back!' I said, seething. 'You have never done a damn thing in your life for anybody else, so don't make out for one second that I had anything to do with it. You were his friend with benefits, someone he used to get off with from time to time. That's hardly the stuff of great romance!'

Tara lunged at me then, and I stepped forward, knocking my glass of wine on to the rug. Both of us ignored it as we stood almost nose to nose. I could see the tiny hairs inside her nostrils as they flared, and the needle mark on her upper lip from the filler she swore she didn't have.

'You have always been jealous of me,' she snarled. 'Always wanted what you couldn't allow yourself to have.'

'And what would that be? A cheating husband? Meaningless awards? An ego the size of Manhattan?'

'Guts!' Tara screeched. 'Gumption, spunk, courage! You are a coward, Alex Curtis, and you've hidden behind me your entire life!'

'No, *you're* a coward! You've been the one hiding in bed because your husband left you, allowing him to destroy *your* entire life! You've always given your power away to men. You live your life for the masses, never for yourself. You are inauthentic and full of yourself, and that's why you have always been a shitty friend.'

'If I'm so shitty, why have you leeched off me for so many years? You've gotten a few opportunities off my back, haven't you, Alex?'

Thrown by the swerve in the subject matter, I didn't know how to respond and my silence made her gloat.

'Yeah, remember when your great friend Tara made those calls for you in the early days?' Tara crowed. 'Remember those favours I called in? Do you think you'd be successful without any of that? Maybe you'd have got there eventually, but don't ever forget the benefits my name has had for your precious career.'

She had hit a sore spot. We never discussed it, but I'd always felt a mix of grateful for and resentful of the fact that Tara's name had opened doors for me. She never asked for or even accepted my thanks, but clearly she felt some bitterness too.

'It was the least you could do, knowing full well you were keeping a huge secret from me,' I blustered. 'Did you ever feel guilty, Tara?'

'About having sex with Sean? Yes, I did, actually. You think I'm selfish, that I don't care about you, but you're wrong. I felt very guilty, but more than anything, I felt sorry for you. Sorry that you couldn't let bygones be bygones, sorry that I felt like I couldn't tell my best friend about a man who was important to me. And let's not forget, Alex. You were the one who broke the pact first.'

'The pact we made as kids after you'd already fucked him, you mean?'

Tara stuck her chin out, a tell of hers that she's feeling culpable but defiant. 'I didn't realize the depth of your feelings when we were eighteen, Alex. If you remember correctly, my mother was dying a long, slow, painful death at the time. And I certainly didn't think you'd still be carrying on about Sean Sweeney nearly twenty fucking years later.'

This row was officially out of control. I was feeling every negative emotion at once – shame, fear, guilt, embarrassment, rage – and I knew Tara and I were in uncharted territory. If we wanted to still be friends at all, we needed to walk this back, and fast.

I attempted a conciliatory tone. 'Look, Tara. We've both made mistakes. And if you've been as convinced as me that Sean was talking about you on the show, all of this must have come as a complete shock. I get that. But he simply couldn't have meant you. All the clues point to me.'

'Alex, I'm truly worried about your level of delusion here. Let's get Jen on the phone, she'll make you see sense—'

'Jen knows exactly how I feel already, because she's a real friend who I can tell anything to.'

'Oh, she's a fucking wimp if she's encouraging you. You probably put her in a ridiculous position. Jen is not going to tell you you're insane on FaceTime, with a kid swinging out of each of her arms!'

I felt like Tara was gaslighting me then. That whatever I said, and no matter how much sense it made, she would tell me I was crazy, irrational and wrong. And what's worse was, I was starting to think I *was* all of those things. It made me cruel.

'Tara, get real. The only reason you have any kind of friendship with Jen still is because of me. You're a fucking bitch to her – do you know her children's middle names? You might if you'd bothered to come to their naming ceremonies. When are their birthdays? Ever gone to one of their parties?' Tara's mouth was opening and closing, but no sound was coming out. She looked like a goldfish. Encouraged, I continued. 'Jen said herself only last week that you're utterly self-centred, that you've never had to behave like a normal human being because you're famous and pretty.'

'Is that all I am?' Tara's amber eyes narrowed at me. 'How reductive. Famous and pretty, adjectives that could be applied to just about anyone on Instagram these days. Wow, standards have really slipped in your writing if those are the best words you can come up with.'

The goldfish gaping was gone, and a sneer had replaced it. 'I'm powerful, Alex. That's the truth. My money and status have allowed you to live out your American dream from a room in my New York penthouse fucking apartment. I'm not some little ingénue you can disregard. I've been working in the business you were too chicken shit to even attempt to break into for nearly two decades and, what's more, I'm very fucking good at it.'

'You work in a business that's as fake as you are,' I shot back. 'I saw through it when I was barely an adult, and knew it was too phoney for me. You play make-believe for a living, Tara. You play pretend to the point where you're pretending you don't know what's going on with you and Rory.'

It was a low blow, and I knew it, but I couldn't have Tara staring me down all high and mighty. I had to force her to acknowledge her own flaws. But she didn't react as I'd expected. The mention of Rory's name seemed to calm her down, actually.

'You have no idea what it's like to have a husband, Alex. No idea whatsoever what it's like to share your life with somebody else, or to be selfless enough to think about another person. You're a lone wolf, and you think it makes you strong. But it doesn't. It makes you pitiful and weak. I do feel sorry for you. I'm sorry you don't put yourself out there in life, allow yourself to get hurt, to feel pain. Because those are the things that make you grow and evolve. You are still the same twelve-year-old girl wounded by people calling her Specky Four Eyes, fantasizing about your teenage crush and clinging on to your parents for moral support.'

It was the mention of my family that did it. I looked Tara right in the eye and uttered the sentence I knew would hurt her the most.

'You might be powerful and successful, Tara. But your mother would be ashamed of you.'

19. Tara

I'm not a violent person, but I've never wanted to maim somebody like I did right then and there. I had a visceral urge to claw at Alex's stupid face, to wound her physically and inflict pain so she might understand the way her words had just lacerated my heart.

My voice was dangerously quiet, a whisper. 'You've gone too far, Alex.'

From the look on her face, I could tell she was shocked by what had come out of her own mouth, but she doubled down. 'Gloria O'Toole was kind. She was a woman who valued friendship, and she was loyal. You didn't inherit any of those qualities.'

'You think you knew my mother because you came over for dinner a few times, Alex? You think because she was nice to you, she liked you? Gloria thought you were a hanger-on. She used to tell me not to waste my time protecting you, that you were too meek and prissy to be my friend and you were holding me back.'

'I don't believe—' she attempted to protest.

'No!' I barked, stunning Alex into silence. 'You weren't by her bedside when my mother was in agony, losing her fight for life in front of me. You didn't hear the things she said to me then, how she encouraged me to be great no matter what the cost, told me not to waste my looks and talent. And you couldn't possibly understand the loss when she was gone, how I wanted her back even if it meant she was suffering and bald and shrivelled. You don't know how I attempted to fill the hole she left in my life – with sex, with fame, with hard work – because it wasn't just my mother that was gone, my father might as well have been too. As usual, you haven't got a clue because you haven't experienced anything.'

'Oh, so, because I have two supportive parents who didn't tragically die, I haven't lived? Get real, Tara!'

I laughed then, a nasty sound I'd never heard emerge from my own throat before. 'You are the one who needs to get real. You think that because I'm an actress and famous, I don't understand real life? I understand it more than you'll ever know!' I roared.

'This isn't real life, you idiot!' she screeched, gesturing around the apartment. 'You are wealthy beyond most people's wildest dreams! You are privileged beyond belief, and utterly tone deaf if you think any of this is difficult!'

'You think having money cures everything? You try living your life under a microscope! Try financially supporting everyone in your life, everyone expecting too much from you. Sure, I can afford to take care of my drunk father, but maybe if I couldn't, he'd sort himself out.' I was crying now. 'You try always being perfect, never gaining an ounce or getting a wrinkle or a pimple. You talk about other people for a living; I have to cope with people like you reporting on my most private, intimate life for entertainment.'

I was in a fugue state then, a flow I'd never experienced before. 'I see the underbelly of the mediums other people use to escape, Alex. I know what it's really like. Those movie posters you have hanging on your walls? I know the stories of what really went on – the abuse, the assault, the greed. The movies are a mucky business. Art is filthy. You are so painfully, tragically naïve.'

Alex looked at me then, really looked at me, like she was seeing me for the first time in years. I could practically see the scales falling from her eyes, the realizations dawning. 'Have you been . . . have you been hurt?'

'I've been everything!' I shouted. 'Used, belittled, demeaned, discarded. But I've also been celebrated. Most actors don't get that.' I felt a burning sensation in my chest that I could now identify as shame as I remembered those early days, the frightening men and what they expected of me. The stars in my eyes rapidly extinguished by the smells and sounds and tastes that haunted me, the resilience and courage I'd had to build up. 'It could have been a lot worse, but it wasn't easy, even though it looked that way from the outside. I was an overnight success to so many, but I thought you of all people would know I was nothing of the sort. But no. You judge me from the sidelines, just like everybody else.'

'Tara, I'm—'

'If I'm a shitty friend who doesn't retain information the way you'd like me to, my apologies. I've kind of had a lot going on. Now, I'm going to my room. I'll be leaving early in the morning, and I'd like you to be gone from here by the time I get back from LA.'

I left Alex sitting on the sofa, and as I walked away from her I truly understood what it felt like for a heart to break.

I was up and out early, as planned, feeling numb. I'd succumbed to the lure of benzos the night before for the first time since Dublin, knowing I wouldn't have gotten a wink of sleep otherwise. Thankfully one pill knocked me out, and into a dark, dreamless world. I'd woken dry-mouthed but relatively calm just before my alarm went off.

There were no signs of life in the apartment. I didn't know whether or not Alex was still there. I thought I'd heard her leave moments after I'd gone to my suite last night, but I wasn't sure. My ears had still been filled with the unbearable buzzing, a rush of adrenaline that I knew wouldn't subside without chemical help.

I was relieved that I had my own car to the airport, that I wouldn't have to deal with the excitement of my LA-bound posse just yet. When Ramon passed an Americano into the back seat, I started to shake. One act of kindness, of friendship, and my body reacted with tremors so strong the hot coffee spilled all over my SKIMS pants.

Despite my burning thighs, I assured him I was okay the best I could, and tried to get myself together. My breath was coming rapidly, so I concentrated on my exercises to regulate it. My brain didn't want to address the catastrophic fight with Alex, but it seemed like my body was going to.

I really wanted to go to Darius. I needed his wisdom, the comfort of one of his hugs. But I also understood implicitly that Alex was probably already with him. Even if she wasn't, her mother was staying at his apartment. In this instance, he wasn't mine to run to. That realization made me feel more alone than I had since Gloria died.

I could call Samuel, or Elspeth, but I didn't want to rehash what had happened, what was still happening inside my mind. I was stunned at the viciousness of the row, at the venom that had spilled out. They say the line between love and hate is a fine one, and I understood that now.

'Are you okay, Miss O'Toole?' I saw Ramon's concerned dark brown eyes in the rear-view mirror.

I took a deep breath. 'I'll be fine, Ramon. Just some pre-flight jitters!'

He didn't believe me, of course. But that was fine. I didn't have to answer to Ramon, or to anybody else.

I had to call Jen, but I waited until I reached the private terminal at JFK and locked myself in the bathroom. Something Alex had said was sticking in my craw. When Jen answered my FaceTime, I looked at her bright, warm face and burst into tears.

'Tara! What the hell is wrong? Did something happen?'

I couldn't catch my breath to tell her, which she seemed to understand. As a yoga teacher and a mother of young kids, Jen knows how to deal with a sobbing fit even if she doesn't know what's caused it. She guided me through some breath-work, made reassuring, soothing noises and waited for my tears to slow to a trickle.

'Now, love. You're okay. Tell me what's going on.'

'You . . . you haven't heard from Alex, then?'

'No, why? Is she okay?'

'We had . . . we had a huge fiiiight,' I sobbed, the tears coming again.

'Oh, Tara, what happened? I'm sure it will be forgotten in no time. Alex loves you so much.'

'Jen, it was really, really bad. We were both so horrible to each other. It was like all of the worst things I've ever feared about myself coming out of the mouth of the person I trust most in the whole world. I was so mean to her too!' Another fresh round of bawling ensued, but Jen just let me cry.

'I know you won't take sides,' I managed, eventually. 'And I wouldn't want you to. But Alex said that you think I'm a shitty person and a shitty friend, and that really hurt me, Jen. I love you so much, and I know I'm not always available and my head is often full of other stuff, but you're like family to me . . .'

'Ah, shush now. We're not like family, we *are* family. I told Alex not to take things so personally with you, and explained that you're held to a much higher standard in life than us mere mortals. You don't always retain the finer details because you've never had to. I didn't mean it in a bad way; it just is what it is. I'm sure she was just trying to hurt you in the fight.'

'Well, she succeeded,' I sniffed. 'Jen, she thinks Sean Sweeney is still in love with her. I told her she was delusional and it did *not* go down well.'

Jen made a face. 'Eh, yeah. I knew that. I mean, it's not outside the realm of possibility . . .'

'Oh, come on!' I yelped. 'Jen, you know better than that.'

'I hoped she was right!' my friend protested. 'Alex seemed so happy, so at peace, believing it was true. But I did tell her that he's always been utterly full of shit.'

'Has he?' I was genuinely surprised. 'I don't remember.'

'He's a born charmer, Tara. He tells people what they want to hear.' Jen paused. 'Wait, don't tell me that's what you pair of absolute gobshites were fighting about? Whether or not Sean Sweeney loves Alex?'

I felt like such a fool, then. 'Well, that's how it started. We, er . . . we both think he was talking about us on Kelly Clarkson.'

'Oh, for the love of—'

'No, Jen, come on! It's highly likely he still has feelings for me, and far more likely I'm the mystery woman. And I've been wondering, you know, if I got it wrong all those years ago. If Sean is really The One and I fucked things up by choosing Rory. When I heard him talk about an old flame, well . . . it just made me see things differently.'

Jen looked at me with such naked pity I recoiled. 'Do you think I'm a complete eejit?' I asked.

'No, actually. That's the worrying part. You both have a point. Look, Tara, I don't want you to think I don't care about you, but I have to go and collect the littlest from playschool. I'm sorry – can you call Uncle Dar?'

'I can't. Deirdre is there, and Alex will be before long if she's not already.'

'Ah shite, okay. Where are you?'

'Hiding in an accessible toilet in the airport. I'm heading to LA. Storm and the glam squad are in the lounge.'

'Okay, good, you're not alone then.'

'I can't talk to any of them about this!'

'No, don't. Try and figure it out for yourself a bit first. Decompress before you put the dilemma to anyone else. Is Lorraine there?'

'She's flying out tomorrow.' I hiccupped sorrowfully.

'Right, that's something. Tara, I love you ferociously. I know that people presume that you don't need to hear words of affirmation and affection because you're famous and fabulous, but I know the real, beating heart that lies under that glossy exterior. And listen to me when I tell you this – whatever happened between you and Alex, I know in my soul that you'll sort it out.'

I nodded and attempted a watery smile for Jen's benefit. We

rang off, and I sat there for a few minutes trying to get myself back together.

Jen had made me feel slightly better, and her confidence that this was just a blip was soothing, but utterly incorrect. This fight wasn't just a passing thing. It had been the most raw, most devastating and cruellest argument I had ever had. Things had been said that could never be unsaid. This row was the kind you never come back from.

@TaraOToole [verified ✓]

Hello, sunshine! I've landed in LA for a couple of weeks of work and play, and it's just what the doctor ordered. Come see me at the Grove this weekend, where I'll be revealing @CovetCosmetics spring/summer line at a special meet-and-greet event. Details on how to enter at the link in my bio! #AD

960,859 Likes

@AllegrasHugeAss: hope you're not here trying to get your husband back, he's @allegra's now!

@RORA4EVA: omg omg omg I have to win the chance to meet you! @covetcosmetics my dog just died and this would really cheer me up

@LAgirl94x: you're a slut

@cinephile2k25: get back to work tara, movies will cure ur broken heart <3

@dariusdamore: bon voyage sweetie, have a ball

@glitterbbz_123: I don't know how you can show your face, you've just been dumped for a younger woman #awkward

@TarasBFF_NYC: you're a perfect goddess who don't need no husband!

20. Alex

I felt like I'd been bereaved. The overwhelming emotion in the days after Tara left for Los Angeles was grief, like somebody had died. And in a way, they had. The person I thought Tara was to me was gone. I was mourning a friendship I was sure would never – could never – be the same again. Not after everything we'd said to one another.

I also felt an intense guilt. I had never been so horrible to another human being in my life. Throwing her dead mother in her face? Mocking her crumbling marriage? I was so ashamed of myself, at times I could barely breathe.

But Tara had been just as cruel. It was shocking that she thought Sean loved her, of course, but the revelation that she thought I was truly pathetic had been eye-opening. She had accused me of never having lived. Every time I remembered that I saw red again.

I fled the apartment as soon as Tara locked herself in her room that night and went straight to my mother's side. Of course, it occurred to me that this was yet another action Tara would deem pitiful, but I didn't care. I needed Deirdre, and I was so grateful she was nearby. Otherwise I would have been on the next flight home.

It was only when I said this while weeping in my mam's arms that Deirdre brought me back down to earth with a bang. 'But you couldn't have come home, Alex. You have your pitch tomorrow.'

I froze. I had totally forgotten about the Netflix meeting. How on earth was I meant to pull myself together and be professional in a matter of hours? I was in bits, a shell of a person, and I also knew the enormity of what had gone down between Tara and me hadn't even fully hit me yet.

I looked at the clock on the wall of the guestroom my mother was occupying. It was close to one in the morning. I hadn't even scratched the surface of what had happened yet; all Deirdre knew was that there had been a huge fight and that I was devastated.

'Oh, Mam, I have to call Jordan. I can't go to a meeting in twelve hours like this.'

'You can and you will, madam. I don't know what's gone on between you and Tara, but I know that it is not going to stop you from making your dreams come true. You are going to that meeting even if I have to drag you there by the hair.'

In the end, I went willingly. By the time I woke up the next morning, what had happened the evening before felt like a bad dream, utterly removed from reality. I knew I had to focus, to keep my eyes on the prize, and that actually felt possible in the bright light of day.

Knowing Tara had left for the airport early, I went back to her apartment and got myself ready, collecting all my materials for the pitch. The three dogs were there, waiting for Francisco to collect them, and I took a minute to lie on the floor and allow their waggy bodies to crawl all over me. I'd become quite fond of Oscar, in particular; his funny little frame and wet snout were comfortingly cute.

When I saw the dirty dinner plates still on the table my stomach lurched, but I talked myself down. While I was upset, I presumed I was also in shock. Perhaps the ambitious part of my brain and an instinct of self-preservation were preventing a complete meltdown, or maybe it just hadn't fully hit me yet.

I pasted on a smile a couple of hours later as I met Jordan in the impressive midtown lobby that housed the biggest streaming network in the world. I should have been daunted by the giant, familiar Netflix logo on the wall, but all I felt was determination. I was going to succeed, and nail this pitch. I was going to show Tara what I could do.

Maybe I was operating on another plane, but I strutted into

the boardroom, guns blazing. My presentation was a mix of posterboards and digital slides, which suited the subject matter's journey from paper to screen. Once Jordan and I were organized, I clapped my hands together and a hush fell over the assembled executives.

'Thank you so much for meeting Jordan and me today. We want to talk to you about the biggest advancement of our collective lifetime, for better and for worse. Without it, well, none of you guys would have jobs.' A ripple of laughter echoed around the room, giving me confidence. 'Of course, I mean the internet and the digital revolution. Despite all its positives, being so connected has also presented myriad issues. As well as bringing us all together, social media and online culture has seen us become divided along political, social and cultural fault lines like we've never experienced before. With traditional media all but decimated, social media has become not only a powerful political tool, it has deconstructed the ways we consume entertainment. Being online is a non-negotiable. I plan to examine this phenomenon, assisted by some of the most interesting, well-known and influential people alive today. Allow us to present to you . . . *Caught in the Web.*'

I wasn't sure how it had gone afterwards. The execs seemed into it, and they weren't what I expected when you imagine a table full of important media types – there were as many women as men, from all different backgrounds, and nobody was wearing a suit. I was prepared for them to be polite and enthusiastic and still pass on the project.

Jordan thought it went great, but I had the feeling he'd say that either way – it's an agent's job to lie to you when necessary. I wasn't sure I'd smashed it, and part of me didn't even care. As the high of the pitch wore off, the horror of the fight came creeping back in. I was having flashbacks, my brain remembering slivers of the awfulness out of context and feeding them back to me like little electric shocks. With the pressure and stupor simultaneously receding, I was free to feel my feelings fully.

Jordan wanted to have lunch, but I told him I had a headache from the intensity of it all. In truth, I needed to lie down and cry. By the time I got back to Darius and Francisco's place, I was bawling.

My thirty-eighth birthday three days later was one of the saddest occasions of my life. Mam and Darius tried to cheer me up; Francisco even baked me a gorgeous coffee cake. I was too depressed to care, swiping through well wishes from friends on Instagram without even reading them. There were only two people I wanted to hear from, and neither Tara nor Sean got in touch.

Still, having my mother in New York was a godsend. Deirdre extended her trip and over the following days she minded me as only a mammy can, which made me feel even worse because Tara didn't have that in her life. I was feeling a mix of red-hot bile and enormous pity towards my (former?) friend, with added lashings of guilt, shame and anger.

Darius spent his time hovering in doorways, totally unsure of how to behave. Crying, desolate women are not his forte, but he supplied a steady stream of tea and snacks that went largely ignored.

After a few days, I felt brave enough to ask him if he'd spoken to Tara. I knew he had an idea of what had happened, but I didn't tell anyone the gorier details. He understood that it was a very big deal, though, and by the sheepish look on his face, I knew he had talked to her. It made me irrationally furious. Darius belonged to both of and to neither of us. He should be neutral in this war, like Switzerland.

'I didn't tell her anything, I swear,' he protested. 'And I didn't ask for any details. I was worried – she's so far away, and Lorraine is not exactly a kindly and benevolent support system!'

'No, it's fine.' I sniffed. 'You don't have to ignore her for me.'

'I would never ignore either of you, Alex.' Darius was stern, reminding me suddenly of his teaching days, except he was holding Patrick the dachshund like a baby and stroking his silky fur. 'You are both my girls. And you're probably both wrong in whatever this is that's going on between you.'

I went to protest, but he held up a hand. 'There are three sides to every story. Your side, her side and the truth. And actually, I don't want to hear any of them, to be quite honest with you. I'm too old and too unfit to carry the emotional baggage.'

I understood, but I wasn't happy about it.

'What I will do for you, though, is continue to entertain your mother so you can mope in peace,' Darius huffed. 'I will also house and feed you. But if I want to talk to Tara, I will. Do you hear me?'

I nodded sadly. Darius blew me a kiss and trundled down the hall, leaving me alone in my misery.

I hadn't felt this bad since . . . well, since I was twenty. Sean Sweeney's ghosting had been the opening act of the most turbulent, difficult and formative year of my life. We didn't even have succinct language to describe such a thing at the time; ghosting was a thing that only happened in horror movies.

Sean may have disappeared from my orbit, but I was faced with unimpeachable evidence that he was out happily living his life. I couldn't even fantasize that he'd been hit by a bus and was unfortunately in traction, his jaw wired shut and unable to text or call. I watched him on *E! News*, heard him on the radio and saw his photo in the paper. He was alive and kicking, and just . . . not interested in me.

Something like that happening completely fucks with your head, because where do the feelings go if there's no real closure, just constant reminders of what you lost?

In those few days after the fight between Tara and me, I did a lot of soul-searching. I came to realize that maybe there were some painful truths she'd brought up that were accurate. I couldn't deny that longing for my first love for the rest of my life was unusual, especially when our affair had been so short and sweet. But its brevity had only made it worse – this idealized, perfect, crystallized weekend that only got shinier and more magical as time went by. How could anything else live up to that? Plus, Tara didn't even know all the painful details, the things I'd kept almost entirely to myself for so long. So who was she to judge me?

It was true that I had been hypervigilant with my heart and mind ever since. It was also true that I put up walls and did everything I could to protect myself. But Tara's utter certainty that Sean wasn't thinking about me, that he wouldn't even remember who I was – well, that I couldn't believe or forgive.

Tara had such a big life she couldn't understand what it was like to be me. She went on to marry a movie star, but Sean Sweeney was it for me, the pinnacle. And as much as I loved and longed for him, I also fucking hated him. He came to represent all men to me – if he was the best of them, and he was a bastard, they must all be like that. Sean was both on a pedestal in my mind and a symbol of a species I must never trust again.

But I did *try*. It's not like I lived a celibate life, wasting away like Miss Havisham. Tara had implied I was some sort of nun, but I dated, I had sex, I even really, really liked a couple of guys over the years. Just not enough to overcome my gut feeling that if I couldn't have Sean Sweeney, I'd be better off alone.

Tara had made me sound like a deranged fan, some lunatic who longed for a person who didn't know I was alive. That was what had hurt the most, how she had dismissed one of the most important experiences of my life as barely worth remembering.

My mother wanted me to call Tara. 'Be the bigger person, Alex,' she enthused. 'She doesn't have the kind of support system you have – she doesn't even have her husband any more. She needs you. I know you both said horrible things to one another, but that means you're both guilty. You'll regret it if you don't reach out.'

Mam's pleas started to get to me, especially when I remembered what I'd said about Gloria, and I burned with shame. I was just about convinced I should send an email to Tara asking could we talk when I turned on *Access Hollywood* and saw her face beaming out of the television, taunting me. There I was, miserable and moping on the couch, while she was looking flawless on the red carpet at the Screen Actors Guild Awards without a care in the world.

Mario Lopez was saying in voiceover that she'd been a last-minute addition to the presenters roster, and we'd be seeing a lot more of the luminous and newly single Ms O'Toole right up to the Oscars the following weekend.

'Tara, welcome back to LA!' the red-carpet reporter was simpering. Tara was radiant, her skin glowing and her red hair long and lustrous. To look at her, you'd think she had no problems whatsoever.

'Thanks, Angélique. I love your dress!' she twinkled. 'I'm thrilled to be here. Having been a recipient of a SAG in the past couple of years, I know just how excited all the nominees are.'

'And are you here to promote a particular movie?' Angélique wasn't as green as she looked – she wanted to know exactly why Tara was showing her face.

'Not really. I'm just enjoying awards season without any pressure, which is actually so lovely.' Tara beamed, not letting on for a second that she was annoyed by the question. 'I've a couple of movies coming later this year so hopefully I'll be back soon with a nomination. In fact, I believe the trailer for my new romantic comedy, *Mind the Gap*, is premiering next week during the Oscars telecast.'

'And there you have it, folks,' Mario was saying back in the studio. 'We know Tara O'Toole is also appearing in Steven Spielberg's dramatic ensemble film *Protest* this fall, and it seems we'll be seeing a lot more of Tara on the promotional trail alongside the movie's huge, all-star cast. We can't wait for the outfits! Now, up next – we talk to Lavinia Rizzi about her brand-new Pilates app, PLANK.'

I turned off the TV. So, Tara was fine. Thriving, even. She

wasn't a good enough actress to put on a show like that, I thought nastily. When Rory left her, she had been unable to function. But a huge fight with her oldest, closest friend and she was absolutely grand? It beggared belief.

I knew logically that she must be hurting, even if she'd buried it very deep inside. Tara was human, which was easy to forget when you saw her in all her superstar red-carpet glory. But if Tara was coping this well on the surface, then I had to as well. I couldn't allow myself to go entirely to pieces. I had to adopt the 'fake it till you make it' attitude and hide my pain behind a mask. One thing was for sure, though. I would not be the one to reach out, to cross the battleground with an olive branch.

Just as I went to get in the shower, my phone rang. Jordan.

'Fantastic news, Alex. Netflix adored our idea. They want you back for another meeting this afternoon to figure out some things they're not sure about. Can you make it?'

Could I? 'Give me an hour, Jordan.'

I hopped under the stream of hot water and raked my mind for a mantra. My brain settled on one that made me laugh – the inimitable words of RuPaul. I could hear her in my head. 'This is your big chance, Alex. Now, don't fuck it up.'

VOGUE.com

24 March 2025

Tara O'Toole's Defiant Dressing

The Irish A-lister is putting her marriage woes behind her with what can only be described as a revenge wardrobe.

It doesn't matter where she's going or what she's doing, actress Tara O'Toole is pulling no punches in showing her ex, Rory Vaughan, what he's missing. Ms O'Toole has been photographed around Los Angeles this month as awards season builds to its climactic grand finale with the Oscars on Sunday, and whether she's exercising, grabbing drinks with friends or attending a star-studded party, Tara has been looking ripped, radiant and right on trend.

Paparazzi captured O'Toole (35) flashing rock-hard abs in an ALO two-piece on a hike, serving cleavage in a slashed Giambattista Valli minidress for dinner with her entourage at Craig's in West Hollywood, and showing off her long legs in leather leggings by Balmain when she swung by *Jimmy Kimmel Live*.

Overall, it's giving sexy coquette, a woman who is perhaps not yet single and ready to mingle but certainly not sitting at home licking her wounds. We're excited to see more of her on the red carpet as the movie industry's celebratory season comes to a close. Sources say O'Toole is wearing Loewe to the Oscars, custom-designed by fellow Irish star Jonathan Anderson.

21. Tara

They say you should be careful what you wish for, and I felt that old saying deeply as dawn broke on the morning of the 97th annual Academy Awards. Giulia had indeed got me the presenting gig I'd claimed to *People* I already had, and I was due to hand out the Oscar for Best Animated Feature alongside Dwayne Johnson later that day. My nerves were gone, though.

The Oscars is not for the faint of heart, and when I attended in the past it was always because either myself or Rory was nominated. It's a chaotic event; there are crowds on the red carpet itself, from publicists to security to stars and associated hangers-on. There's also a public section full of roaring fans, and hundreds of photographers from all over the world shouting for your attention.

Of course, you want to satisfy everyone. You want to look your best, pose professionally and be poised and elegant even as your heart feels like it's going to burst from your chest with nerves and adrenaline. It's the kind of event you never get used to attending, a complete sensory overload – and that's just the pre-show.

The year I won, I truly wasn't expecting it; the pundits said odds were split pretty evenly three ways between me, Anne Hathaway and Viola Davis – Annie and I had both won at the Golden Globes, but Viola had taken the Critics' Choice. I was so young back then, nothing fazed me, but the red carpet is still a blur in my memory. When I look back at videos of my win all I can think is that I was just a baby. I remember really, really wanting my mom that night.

This time I was going to the Oscars as just me, trying with all my heart and soul to appear happy, well-adjusted and doing great without the 230lbs of handsome movie-star husband that normally accompanied me on red carpets. I had Giulia check twenty times to make sure that Rory would not be making a surprise appearance, and I was assured that he was in fact not even in town. I wouldn't let myself go down the rabbit hole of wondering where he actually was.

I also made discreet enquiries as to whether Sean Sweeney would be in attendance at any of the parties, but nobody knew for sure. Rock stars have a habit of dropping in to events to which they haven't been invited to an uproarious welcome, so I'd just have to wait and see.

I had been in Los Angeles almost a fortnight at that point, and it had flown by. I felt worlds away from New York, rather than just three thousand miles. The weather had finally started behaving itself and the city was balmy and vibey. My Covet event at the Grove had gone well, with hordes of screaming fans mobbing the upscale, touristy mall to catch a glimpse of me. I always feel super-reassured when I get to meet the real people who go and see my movies and buy the products I endorse. It's weirdly grounding.

All in all, the feeling in town was buzzy in anticipation of Hollywood's biggest weekend, because nobody loves congratulating themselves more than people who work in the movie business.

A knock at the bungalow's door meant my glam squad was starting to arrive. I flung it open and screeched with delight at the sight of my beloved West Coast hairstylist, David, who screamed right back. He used to be my New York guy too, until he'd moved to LA the year before, and I was still mad at him for leaving.

'Salon O'Shea Soho isn't the same without you, you bitch,' I teased as we hugged and kissed.

'Well, of course it's not!' he laughed. 'But your hair looks amazing, so my girlies are doing something right in my absence. Ooh, I love my favourite natural ginge – I can't wait to make you look like a mermaid!' he trilled, giving me a tight squeeze.

That was the style we were going for, a sort of beached siren look – salty, messy hair, a Loewe gown that could have been fashioned from the sails of a yacht, and luminous, dewy skin that would make my freckles pop. It screamed youth, vitality and sex appeal – or at least we hoped it would when it all came together.

'How's Dessie?' I asked after my favourite reality star, who is married to David's father. 'Does she love being back home in Kerry?'

'My wicked stepmother is in her element.' David winked at me in the mirror. 'She has revitalized the women of Dingle – apparently everyone there is flat out on the filler now. She hosts a monthly book club and they all get pissed and make TikToks.'

'I haven't been back to Ireland in forever. Well, apart from the few days I spent locked up like Rapunzel in Alex's apartment, but that doesn't count.' I shuddered.

'Well, I don't know what the hell is going on, but us Paddies are totally taking Tinseltown. I've never seen so much pink-tinged skin on the red carpet out here – it actually totally clashes. There are so many going tonight it'll be like the VIP Style Awards. Let me see, there'll be you, Saoirse, Cillian, Paul, Barry . . .'

As he rattled off the names of our compatriots, I felt myself relax a little, the way I always do around other Irish. Hollywood feels far less daunting when it's populated by your people, and there really was an invasion from the Emerald Isle these days.

I filled David in on everything I'd been up to since I'd arrived to enthusiastic oohs and aahs. 'I had a meeting about potentially anchoring the forthcoming season of *The White Lotus* – oh, and I filmed a cute little cameo for *Abbott Elementary*. Then I met with a couple of producers and screenwriters, but nothing feels quite right, Dave. I'm not getting that zing of anticipation that means I just *have* to sign on to something.'

'Well, what do you normally do when you feel like this?'

I grimaced. 'Talk to Rory and Alex.'

'Ouch.' David gritted his teeth. 'Well, I feel like you'll know when you find your next gig. You won't need anyone else's opinion – it'll just kick you right up the arse and demand you do it.'

David was probably right, but it was really bugging me that I couldn't ask Alex for a vibe check on a project like I normally would. I went to text her almost hourly, before remembering the things she'd said to me and feeling devastated all over again.

There wasn't any time to mope, though. I'd been flat out – *Vanity Fair* spent a couple of days following me for their annual Hollywood issue's digital coverage, and the paps were on my tail constantly. Shanice was delighted I was getting seen in so many new looks, and the media coverage was hugely positive. 'Single, sexy and sashaying around town' had been TMZ 's take.

All in all, Giulia and I thought I'd been playing things very well. You'd never know my heart had been broken and then stamped upon until pulverized. Perhaps the double whammy of losing both my husband and my oldest, closest friend meant I just wasn't feeling anything any more. Maybe the pain was so intense I was in a sort of shock that protected me. I was able to carry on, to put on a show. I was a professional.

But when I was alone, my mind always went straight to Alex. My split with Rory was easy to dissociate from because it didn't even feel totally real yet. It had all been such a blur, happened so fast. When I thought of my best friend, though, it was like drinking a cocktail of fear, rage, shame and guilt all shaken up with a glug of horror.

'Did you text Alex on her birthday?' David asked as he brushed out my clip-in extensions.

'No. I was mulling it over, as you know – I didn't want her to be able to say I forgot, another example of me being the worst friend ever. Then I remembered what an absolute bitch she was about my mom. That was such a low blow. I don't want to give her the satisfaction of being the one to reach out first.'

'As someone also in the Dead Mams Club, I get that. But I also don't think Alex would have any idea how much that hurt you.'

'She's not a complete dope, Dave. She knew the second it left her lips.'

I was glad to be in Los Angeles, both because it put physical space between Alex and me, and because it had given my confidence a boost. When you're an actress the wrong side of thirty-five and have been laying low, it's very easy to think everyone has forgotten about you. This trip was a reminder that I was still hot property and that people were excited to see me.

I was having sleeping panic attacks, though. Three nights in a row after I arrived I woke up gasping for air, something that hadn't happened since the months immediately after my mom died. I was doing daily sessions on Zoom with Samuel, practising yoga and cutting back on caffeine to try and help, but I drew the line at meditation, which I had decided was an absolute swizz – it's basically sitting there doing absolutely nothing with better marketing, and so not my vibe. Thankfully the attacks lessened, but no matter how zen I felt when I went to sleep, I'd often be jolted awake in the wee hours, panting and frightened.

'Sooooo . . .' David was saying in the tone he uses when he's about to start gossiping, 'has the press out here been asking you all sorts of questions about the ex?'

'Not really, because Giulia has put the fear of God into them.'

'Do I hear my name being taken in vain?'

Both David and I whipped around to where the heavily accented voice was coming from, and my heart leapt at the sight of Giulia Rizzi leaning on the doorframe. She held out her arms and I ran into them, reassured by her warm hug and enveloped by her spicy signature scent. She planted a big red-lipsticked kiss on my cheek and held me at arm's length. 'Let me get a good look at you . . . hmm . . . *bellissima*! As always, *carina*.'

It was so great to see her. Giulia has a commanding essence; when she's around you just feel taken care of, and that's what makes her so good at her job. She's not just a publicist, she's an advocate and a protector – provided you stay on her good side.

'Now, what were you saying about Giulia?' she enquired, settling in on the armchair beside my makeshift glam station.

'That you frightened all the poor journalists so they wouldn't ask about Rory.'

'Frighten? Me? No, no. I just tell them that if they do, it will be the last question they ever ask you.' She winked, a devilish glint in her eyes.

'From you, Giulia, that could either mean they're blacklisted from interviewing Tara, or they're gonna sleep with the fishes.' David chortled.

'You do mafia jokes, I do the gay jokes. It's your choice.' She shrugged.

David and Giulia have the most charming dynamic. They're not blood-related but are both part of a sprawling brood with Dessie at its heart. It's the kind of huge, messy family I always wanted as an only child, and I'd still love to be in their gang. If things with Sean didn't work out, maybe I could marry in, I thought absent-mindedly. If I remembered correctly, David had a hot little brother . . .

Then I had a light-bulb moment.

'Dave, is Portia in town?' I asked.

'She sure is. It's my ugly stepsister's first awards season!'

'Dah-veed-ay, the Cinderella comparisons, they get tired.'

'Shut up, Giulia. You're just raging there's no role for you in the fairytale.'

'But of course there is, I am the fairy godmother!' Giulia laughed. 'I wave my wand and *allora*! Magic happens.'

David ignored her. 'Can you believe the girls won the Golden Globe for *Starting Over*? Best Musical or Comedy! Pity they didn't get the Oscar nod too, but that's the Academy for you. Snobs! Anyway, Portia and Katie are doing the party circuit after the ceremony. I'm glamming them after you. What do you want them for?'

'I loved *Starting Over* so much. Starring in their next project, now that would be a kick up the arse! I wonder if they'd let me be in their movie? That's if there's a role for me, of course.'

'If there is not a part already, I'm sure Portia will write you in,' Giulia said, and my heart leapt a little. Giulia doesn't say things she doesn't mean, ever.

'Really, you think so?'

'Do not act the eejit. You are romantic-comedy royalty – I am sure the women would be thrilled to work with you, if the timing is right. They have not cast yet, correct, Dah-veed-ay?'

David nodded. 'They're literally about to. I'll hook you guys up. So wait, back to Rory – do you think you'll get questions about him tonight?'

'I might,' I sighed. 'I have a couple of lines prepared, just in case some little shit springs a surprise question on me live on air. G can't control the red carpet, sadly.'

There was a commotion at the front door of the bungalow that signalled the arrival of both my stepdaughter and Lorraine. Storm was carrying a suitcase, no, two suitcases of make-up.

'Storm Vaughan, do *not* tell me you need that many cosmetics to do my face!' I yelped.

'Nah, only one of these is for you; the other is for Lorraine.' She winked, dodging a slap from my friend. 'I'm kidding! I have three other clients to see to after you two – I'm in demand!'

And so we settled in to the fun part of big awards ceremonies – the before, when everyone is excited and the look your team has envisioned finally comes to fruition. Shanice landed with the dress, shoes, accessories, undergarments and tape and worked her magic.

The designer, Jonathan, swung by to make sure everything was to his liking, Felicia documented the entire process for socials, and then it was time to go. Lorraine was playing the role of hype woman admirably, and I really tried to get into the swing of things.

As I walked to the limousine, I felt the lack of Alex so acutely it winded me. Strange, I'd expected to miss Rory, who was normally my companion at industry events; it wasn't like Alex would even usually be with me on a night like this.

But I knew that she would be eagerly anticipating the

ceremony and getting ready to report on all the goings-on for the world's press. Alex lived for the Oscars, for the best- and worst-dressed lists, the winners, the discourse and the glamour. If things were different, maybe she would have been here with me.

Shit, I thought. I should have brought her before! It would have been the highlight of any year for Alex. Maybe I really was a terrible friend. Selfish and self-obsessed, like she'd said.

As I settled into the car and my glam team fussed around me so I could exit at the Dolby Theater looking perfect, I felt a deep sense of unease descend. What was I even doing out here, attending the Oscars just for attention? What was I hoping to achieve – for Rory to see me and feel terrible, for Sean to see me and realize he needed to act fast?

I could claim it was all for my career, and of course it was in a way. But if I was truly happy in my life, I wouldn't feel the need to show off. Samuel and I talked a lot about my ego and how it affected my ambition, but it had never felt so obvious until now.

My presence at the awards ceremony would likely sour Alex's enjoyment of Hollywood's biggest night. But then I remembered the horrible things she'd said to me about the empty, shallow business that was the movies. If it was empty and shallow, why was she so invested in it?

As the limo pulled off into the LA traffic I made a conscious decision to put all thoughts of everyone else out of my head. I would live in the moment, play my part and reap whatever I sowed. This was my job. This was what I was good at.

Lorraine was fizzing with excitement as she popped a bottle of Dom Perignon, and I decided to make an effort to get on board with her good mood. What was it Darius always said? Oh, yes. Too much thinking is bad for the complexion.

22. Alex

'Are you sure you have to go home?' I whined, sounding eerily like my fifteen-year-old self. It was Oscar Sunday, and I was sitting on the bed in Darius and Francisco's spare room watching my mother pack her suitcase ahead of her evening flight back to Dublin. Normally the Academy Awards is my favourite night on the calendar, my All Ireland final, but I just couldn't get excited.

'Yes, love. I've left your dad to his own devices for far too long already. God knows what unholy state the house is in. Anyway, I have to get back to work.'

'You're retirement age!' I whined. 'You should be enjoying your golden years!' It occurred to me that I'd always claimed not to be a spoilt only child, but I was really sounding like one. I didn't care, though. I didn't want my mother to leave.

'Now, stop that, Alex. I love my job, and I'm as fit as a fiddle. I've been away for a fortnight! It's time for you to get your own act together – I've been here mollycoddling you for too long. I have to get back home to mollycoddle your father instead.'

I pouted, silent, and saw Deirdre relent a little. 'Love, I know it's a really strange time for you. But you've always coped with difficulties by working hard, right? I know you're waiting for the official green light from Netflix and you don't want to count your chickens, but there are other things to be done! Have you all your Oscars coverage planned out?'

I made an indiscernible noise, but she was on to me right away.

'Don't even *think* about not working tonight, Alexandra Curtis. You need to grow up and do your job. You're self-employed – you're letting yourself down if you don't! And think how sad your listeners will be if they wake up tomorrow and you're not there analysing the big event like always? It's the best night for "traffic"!' – the air quotes again – 'You always get writing commissions from the Oscars, don't you?'

She was right, of course. Awards season is very much a huge chunk of my bread and butter as a pop-culture commentator, but how could I happily watch a show I knew Tara was going to be on? It all seemed sullied somehow, like I had seen too much of the inner workings of the showbiz world and the illusion was shattered.

Deirdre seemed to read my thoughts. 'Doing what you love isn't always easy, pet. But it's already bad enough you didn't review Sean's book. "The streets are talking," as they say.'

My mother had been watching too much V Network if she was picking up sayings like that, but she wasn't wrong. My Instagram was ablaze with comments from subscribers wondering why I hadn't covered *Interview with a Rock Star*. I always made it a point to talk about Irish celebs; it was part of my USP. Well, except for Tara.

If I wanted to retain my crown as queen of pop-culture podcasting, I would indeed have to swallow my pride and cover the Oscars as usual. I insisted on watching the telecast alone, though, so after a tearful goodbye with Deirdre I called an Uber back to Tara's place just as the pre-show coverage was starting. It was a good time to pack up my stuff once and for all, while everyone else was out of town.

It had been a tricky few days, and I was feeling frustrated and a little frightened. Waiting for my work permit to come through was holding up the signing of the Netflix deal, and I was behind on podcast work and distracted in general. I was also afraid I'd outstayed my welcome with Darius and Francisco. Their place isn't exactly as palatial as Tara's in terms of space, and while they had been so kind letting me stay when Deirdre extended her trip, I knew I couldn't feasibly work from there.

Maybe I could look at getting a short-term let, or even move into a cheap hotel for a week or two while I figured stuff out. I wasn't made of money, but I could dip into my savings. If I was going to stay in the States for a while, I would have to rent out my apartment back in Dublin. It sitting empty was like setting fire to a pile of cash.

I rolled down the window of my Uber because I was suddenly feeling nauseous and needed a blast of fresh air. There was just so much to think about, so many unknown factors. I don't do well without a concrete plan. Tara had been right when she'd said I had a cushy place to stay in the city thanks to her, and now it wasn't an option any more I realized just how cushy it had been.

Nodding at the doorman, Simon, I was lost in my thoughts as I entered the elevator which climbed from Tara's lobby to the penthouse.

As the lift doors opened up right into Tara's entryway, I thought I heard someone in the apartment, probably the cleaner. I stepped out gingerly and went to call out, but before I could I collided with a man coming from the bedroom. I screamed at the top of my lungs before I realized it was Rory Vaughan.

'What the fuck, Rory?! You frightened the shite out of me!'

'I'm sorry, I'm sorry. I heard the elevator coming and didn't know what to do so I just ran out!'

'Jesus,' I panted, one hand on the wall steadying myself while I caught my breath. 'You're too tall to be surprising people like that.'

Once the shock had abated and I realized I wasn't in any danger, I stepped forward at the same time he did and we awkwardly hugged. He smelled of Creed, and his back felt alarmingly large and strong under my hands. 'Rory, what are you doing here?' I asked, still incredulous at the sight of him. 'I mean, I know it's half yours, but . . .' I trailed off.

'I didn't think there would be anyone here,' he replied. 'I wanted to come by and get some of my things, but it appears they've already been moved somewhere else.'

'Yeah, Storm did that so Tara didn't have to see . . .'

'. . . my belongings everywhere. Got it.'

He looked tired, but still gorgeous. Rory is the kind of man who is so dramatically good-looking he was always going to be famous in one way or another – similar to his estranged wife, I guess. He's got this towering, athletic build and winning-smile combination that makes him so attractive, but it's also something in the way he moves. A lack of self-consciousness, a lightness on his feet.

But in the apartment he looked strange, and I realized it was because I'd never seen him feel out of place before. He always fits in every scenario, but he was clearly deeply uncomfortable. 'Where are the dogs?' he asked. 'I miss them.'

'Francisco is looking after them. Darius has become very attached to little Seamus.'

Rory was eyeing me warily. 'Go on, say it,' he said, and I copped that I must have been frowning at him. 'Tell me I'm a bastard, an idiot, an old fool for leaving Tara. I can take it.'

'Rory, I have nothing to say to you about any of that. It's your business. And if you're Tara's least favourite person in the world right now, then I am a very close second. So I haven't got a leg to stand on.' I sighed and flopped down on the couch.

'What? What happened?' he asked, genuinely perplexed. 'You're the love of her goddamn life! And the last I heard from Storm, you were here looking after Tara. I presumed you were in LA with her, too.'

I felt tears threatening and tried to swallow them. 'It's a long, horrible story. But we had a huge fight the night before she left and our friendship is over. I came over here to get my stuff as well, because I have to figure out somewhere else to stay. I can't go back to Dublin because my passport is with a lawyer waiting for a US working visa; I've signed with an agent here but nothing can happen until my permit is approved and . . . basically, I'm in a horrible limbo with a broken heart and nowhere to live.'

'Geez, Alex.' Rory sat down next to me. 'I'm so sorry to hear that. And Tara . . . wow, she must be devastated too.'

He saw my scowl and wisely changed the subject. 'Hey, I'm also really happy for you about the agent! I'd heard, and I'm so glad you and Jordan worked out.'

My head snapped up. 'Excuse me?'

'Jordan Jones? He used to work as an assistant for my guy, but now he's out on his own in the big leagues. He mentioned he liked your podcast a while back, and I texted him when you were in town, told him to look you up.'

'You mean, you're the reason he signed me?'

'Noooo, no, Alex. That's not how it works. He wouldn't have even met with you if he didn't think you were great. Besides, when I texted him he told me you were already interviewing his star client the very next day.'

I was simultaneously irritated and grateful. I had wondered how it had all happened for me so seamlessly and seemingly out of nowhere, and it made sense to hear that I had a powerful ally in the industry. I didn't want to be in Rory Vaughan's debt, though. I was sick of my famous friends helping me out with opportunities they could then throw back in my face.

I was also puzzled. This was yet another example of Rory being the best, always caring and supportive. It just didn't fit with what I was being told about him, or with the fact that he was flaunting a new relationship with a much younger woman mere days after ending things with Tara.

'Why did you start seeing Allegra, Rory? I know I said it was none of my business, but it's so confusing and I haven't been able to get my head around it. You have always been such a great guy, so everything that's happened feels hugely out of character. Is it a mid-life crisis? Did it only take a few weeks around a younger woman for you to forget your great marriage?'

He barked a harsh laugh then, and it took me by surprise. 'Is that what Tara told you? We had a great marriage? Wow.' He laughed again, shaking his head and wringing his hands.

His jaw was twitching, but his eyes were sad. 'My wife has always been an unreliable narrator. I learned that when we started couples therapy. She doesn't like to admit it when she's at fault; she'll find any way around an issue besides saying sorry.'

I was confused. 'Couples therapy? But she said everything was fine with you guys . . .'

'Alex, come on. If everything was fine, why would I have left her?'

'Because, like all men, you were chasing your dick!'

The word hung in the air between us, and I felt my face flush. 'You had an affair, Rory. That's why you left her.'

He hung his head. 'I can't deny what happened with me and Allegra. It was wrong, and I take full responsibility. But Alex, there's so much more to the story – you know that.'

He was looking at me expectantly, but I had no idea what he meant.

'What's been going on for the last three years? It's been tough. Hard on Tara, hard on me.'

'What are you talking about, Rory?'

He looked baffled. 'Wow, you really don't know, do you? My god.' Rory rubbed at his jaw, and I was suddenly afraid he was going to burst into tears. 'I can't believe she didn't tell you. Maybe she was never serious about any of it.'

I was still none the wiser, but he seemed completely heartbroken. I was just about to press him gently for more information when Rory sprang up and made for the door.

'Look, I'm not going to get into it all. It's complicated, and painful too,' he said, shrugging on a leather jacket. 'If Tara has been keeping this kind of information from you, she's clearly not doing great and I'm even more worried now. What you're saying is suddenly making a lot of sense so, if you don't mind, I'm going to go and call my daughter. Something tells me she doesn't know the half of it either.'

I nodded, mute, as he stalked towards the elevator.

'Hey, Alex.' I looked up. 'Did you say you needed a place to stay?'

I nodded again, feeling like one of those dog ornaments on a dashboard.

'Why don't you go out to our place on the Cape? It's off season, so it'll be quiet. Xavier sleeps on his boat or in the pool house; he doesn't like being in the main place alone. It's a quick flight if you need to come back to the city in a hurry.'

I must have looked pathetically grateful. It sounded perfect – I knew the house on Cape Cod was in a ritzy area by the sea where I could go and work in peace, where nobody knew me and I could be alone with my thoughts.

'Wow. Thank you, Rory. That sounds amazing.'

'It's nothing. I've been wanting to thank you for being here for Tara. I'll have everything you need messengered here first thing tomorrow.' He gave me a curt nod and was gone, leaving me feeling unsettled.

Not long after Rory left, the elevator pinged again, but it was only Simon. 'Forgive the interruption, Ms Curtis, but some dry-cleaning came back addressed to you a few days ago.'

I was confused. I hadn't sent anything out. The doorman was holding something wrapped in plastic, so I took it and thanked him. My breath caught when I realized it was my feathered robe, the one Tara had become so attached to.

Why would she be giving it back to me this way? I'd thought it was obvious I'd relinquished it to her. Was she rejecting it now, along with me? Had she arranged to have it cleaned and delivered to send me a message, or was it just a horrible coincidence? My insides gnawed, and I felt bewildered but also strangely hurt. Sure, it was only dry-cleaning, but it felt like a sign. Tara didn't need me, or the comfort I provided, any more.

Maybe I was overreacting. It was just a robe; the cleaner could have found it on her floor and sent it out. But then why was it addressed to me? I shook my head to dislodge the negative thoughts. I had to focus – I would gird my loins, watch the

Academy Awards on the enormous apartment TV and do my job to the best of my ability.

Rory was true to his word, and a courier dropped off a bulky set of keys early the next morning. But by then, I wasn't exactly excited to head to Cape Cod, and I wasn't confused any more either. I was furious, livid, seething once again, and all because of Tara O'Toole.

Radar Online

30 March 2025

Tara O'Toole hints at new romance with old flame Sean Sweeney

Hollywood vixen Tara O'Toole walked the red carpet at last night's Oscars looking radiant in Loewe, but it was the tea she spilled at the Vanity Fair *after-party that has everyone buzzing. After a star turn at the awards ceremony presenting with Dwayne 'The Rock' Johnson and flirting up a storm onstage, Tara showed up to the magazine's infamous shindig in custom Valentino.*

Reporters were keen to ask the newly single actress if any of the rumours about her love life were true, and while she'd been coy on the official Oscars red carpet, she was clearly feeling a little more open later in the night.

'I think everyone expected me to be an absolute wreck,' the star laughed when interviewer Ashley Graham told her how great and happy she looked. 'But I feel fantastic! You know, a new year can bring a sense of renewal and revitalization, and I think that's what's happened to me in 2025 so far . . . I know it seems like my life is moving on very quickly, but trust me, the public only see the headline parts, you know?'

Ashley pried a little further, asking if the gossip about a new relationship with Irish rocker Sean Sweeney had any truth to it. Tara didn't say much with words, but she beamed at the camera, winked and blew a kiss down the lens of the camera, her body language leaving little doubt as to how she feels about her former flame . . . or is that current?

Sweeney wasn't spotted at any of the parties in Los Angeles last night, but Tara made it her business to spend the night on the dance floor. We're sensing a new showbiz power couple on the rise . . .

23. Tara

'Well, *carina*, the internet is abuzz with sexy rumours this morning after your antics last night,' Giulia trilled. 'You are a minx, Tara!'

'Ugh, go away,' I moaned as she opened the curtains in my bedroom at the bungalow. I was deeply, thoroughly hung over.

'No can do,' my publicist said, placing a large iced coffee on the bedside table. 'I came over to rouse you because there is work to be done. I want you papped today looking wholesome, please, otherwise the bloggers will say you are partying too much.'

I knew she was right; there's a fine line in Hollywood between enjoying yourself and requiring a trip to rehab. It would be good to be spotted looking fresh after my late night. I sat up in bed, groaning; my head felt fit to burst. 'I need Tylenol,' I croaked.

The Oscars was fun, but the after-parties are always far more craic. I'd gone to the Governors Ball and to *Vanity Fair*'s with Lorraine, and danced my way around both events, air-kissing all and sundry. After a while I'd noticed my companion was nowhere to be seen, and I had a sudden flashback of spotting her sitting on the lap of a very well-connected producer. I had a vague recollection of them leaving together not long after.

The floodgates of memories of the night before opened and I remembered selfies with the Irish crowd, slut-dropping with Jonathan Bailey and scoffing In N Out Burger with Florence Pugh. After that, it got a little patchy, but nothing sinister struck me in my waking moments, like it sometimes did after a Big Night Out. I was certain I hadn't done anything very bold.

Giulia was still talking as my brain quickly combed over the events of the night before. 'It is your last couple of days in LA, so let's make the most of it, *sì*? Covet called – your new billboard has just gone up on Sunset, so we must go visit. And let's do a little hike for Instagram.'

'Stopppp,' I cried. 'I am too hung over to talk about hikes and billboards.'

'This is why Giulia is the best, darrrrrrling. In five minutes, the ladies with the little bags arrive to perk you up.'

'Huh?!'

'The bags of fluids, *mamma mia*! What did you think I meant?!'

'You don't want to know. You got me an IV drip?'

'*Sì, certo*. Dah-veed-ay is insisting on coming for one too. He was at Elton's until the crack of dawn.'

All this news made me feel better. I sat up, slurping my iced coffee hungrily. Touching my face, I realized I'd had the foresight to scrub off the war paint before I went to sleep, although I had no memory of doing it.

'How's the press from last night?' I asked, wincing as the sun caught my face through the window.

'You were stunning, *bella*! On all the best-dressed lists. People are so happy to see you out and about. And that little stunt you pulled about Sean Sweeney was inspired. Saying a lot while saying nothing!'

Ugh, I'd been tipsy when I'd done that. On the spot, I'd felt confident sending a body-language signal to Sean, wherever he was, but now I had The Fear. 'Oh, god. Did I come off desperate?'

'No, no. Cute. Sexy! Most importantly, youthful.'

I dove back underneath the covers.

'Stop that, Tara. Trust me, I'm your mouth and ears in this town. I would tell you if you'd fucked up.'

'Alex is going to be so mad,' I moaned from beneath the duvet. 'I should have just said "no comment".'

'Alex already hates you,' said a male voice. I peeked my head out to see David making a running jump for the bed. 'So you might as well get the guy anyway!' He grinned as he landed and held up a paper bag. 'I brought greasy hash browns.'

'She doesn't hate me,' I pouted, accepting the delicious fried food. 'We just had a fight.'

'Um, well . . .'

'What?'

'New York is three hours ahead, so she's been up for a while. And, er, she posted something on Instagram just now that makes me think she definitely hates you.'

I went white as the Egyptian cotton sheets on the bed. Giulia was fussing with her phone, seething. 'I hate the social media – I just cannot keep up!'

Alex's voice filled the room from Giulia's device. 'Hi guys! I know I've been MIA on Insta lately, but I'm still Stateside, working on something very exciting. I'm off for a little seaside break today, but I'm bringing an old friend with me.' She held a book up to camera, and of course it was Sean's. In a very un-Alex-like move, she winked lasciviously next to the cover shot and I felt my toes curl with a strange mixture of second-hand embarrassment and rage.

'I'll need some tunes to keep me company as well, and I'm feeling very Allegra today! Let me know in the poll on the next slide which of her albums I should go in on. My favourite song of hers is a no-brainer – it's obviously "Love Bite".'

Alex's story changed to the poll, and the song filled the room. The excerpt Alex had chosen? 'Oh, that Rory, makes me so horny.'

I screamed so loudly that Giulia dropped her phone.

An hour later, I was hooked up to an intravenous drip that was pumping me with fluids, vitamins and minerals, but I felt like death. It wasn't just the hangover; I simply couldn't believe that Alex could be such a fucking bitch. Of course, only a handful of people would know what her story was getting at and how much it would hurt me, but that's what it was designed to do.

I was surprised, because it was an immature and nasty move on Alex's part and she wasn't normally either of those things. Only, things were far from normal.

I knew Alex would be pissed with me for encouraging rumours about me and Sean when she still vehemently believed that she was his long-lost love. I guessed her story was the equivalent of Alex throwing down the gauntlet – if I could use the world's media to flirt with him, well, so could she.

I had to admit, I was disappointed and frustrated that Sean *still* hadn't been in touch. I knew he was busy, but he could have sent a text by now, opened the lines of communication. I still had the same number, so he knew how to reach me. Why hadn't he called?

My blood ran cold then, and I sat up straight. Had he called Alex? Was that what she meant by taking an old friend to the seaside? And what seaside was she on about?

Jesus, was she *actually* the one he wanted? Why else would she feel cocky enough to basically mock me online? She must know she's already won. Oh god. Oh god, oh god, oh god.

No, it couldn't be. I tried to breathe deeply, to dislodge the horrible anxiety in my chest.

My heavy panting woke David from his little nap. 'Stop moaning, Tara. I'm not able for negativity right now.' In the time since he'd arrived, his condition had deteriorated rapidly.

'Oh, you were well able for negativity when you came in full of beans with your little Instagram news!' I seethed. 'Now you want peace and quiet?'

'I'm sorry,' he whispered. 'I must have still been drunk. Elton is an awful man for the shots.'

'Well, I have no sympathy for you. I'm now dying a death *and* freaking out. And Giulia wants me to go for a fucking *hike*!'

'Ssshh, ssshh. Just go for a little sleep, let the nice drip do its work. You'll feel better after a snooze.'

I didn't. I felt angrier, more hurt and more upset as the

morning rolled on and my head cleared. I was worried that Alex was with Sean, that she hated me more than I'd even realized and that I'd really lost everything – my past, present and future.

I needed to get some more information. Darius answered my call on the second ring.

'Hiiiii, darling,' he warbled, but I could tell right away he was putting on an act.

'I take it you've seen Alex's Instagram story?' I went straight in, no messing.

He sighed deeply. 'I have, and I don't know what to say, Tara. This seems very unlike her. But I know she saw Rory yesterday and then watched all the Oscars coverage . . .'

I froze. 'She saw who?'

'Oh, you didn't know. Okay, well, she went back to your place to get her stuff and, um, Rory was there.'

I couldn't take this information in. 'Rory was in my apartment? In New York?'

'Yeee-eeesss. And well, he told Alex she could use the house on the Cape for a while. So that's where she's going.'

I must have looked like I was going to pass out, because David sat up and put a steadying hand on my shoulder.

'Darius, what did he say to her?'

'I truly don't know, Tara. All I know is that she was flying out to Hyannis today. She's probably even there by now.'

'Did Rory contact you? Did he say why he was in the apartment?'

'I really don't know any details, my love. I would tell you if I did. I just know that they spoke, and that she's gone. Is Lorraine there with you?'

'No, she hooked a big fish last night.' My mind was racing. 'David and Giulia are here. I'm not alone.'

'Give them kisses from me. And mind yourself.'

I thanked Darius, rang off and leaned over my knees, sitting in the brace position you adopt when a plane is going through severe turbulence. That's what being inside my brain and body felt like – as if I was on an airplane hurtling through rough skies that were threatening to send me spiralling towards earth at breakneck speed.

Not seeing Rory at all in the past few weeks meant that I'd been able to compartmentalize him. How could he bother me if he didn't really exist? I've always had the ability to simply switch off from negative experiences, and I really honed it after my mom died and my dad hit the bottle. Samuel says it's meant to be a temporary protective measure, but I keep it going until I'm forced to confront reality. He says it's never good to put off your feelings, but when things are bad I really can't help it.

Well, reality hit hard upon hearing that Rory had been in my apartment, in our home, without me knowing. I was thrown for a loop, and felt drained of all energy despite the vitamins coursing through my veins.

What on earth was he doing, acting all pally-pally with Alex? Did he think he had an ally now? Were they going to gang up against me? Maybe he didn't know we were fighting – maybe she hadn't told him, I surmised.

I was breathing deeply, trying to calm my mind, but it wasn't working. No, it was far more likely that Alex had told Rory about our row and played the victim to get him to take pity on her. Big bad wolf Tara being mean to little fluffy sheep Alex – it was believable, at least to Rory.

And letting her use *my* beach house? Crazy! Well, in fairness, it had been his house for ever and I never wanted much to do with it. Still, it belonged to me too! She simply must have spun him a sob story about me kicking her out. Thinking of the two of them in cahoots made me momentarily wish I was dead. What else had he told her? No, surely he wouldn't go into detail about . . .

The door to the bungalow flew open at that moment and a very angry-looking Storm stalked in. She gave me such a frightening glare that I physically recoiled from her. I knew then that she had also been speaking to her father, likely in depth.

Glowering, she sat down opposite me with her arms crossed, her usually perky expression eviscerated by a scowl. 'You'd better start talking, Tara,' she commanded.

So I did.

Reddit.com/TaraOTooleSuperfans

Redzer1969: Did anyone see Alex Curtis's Insta story? She's meant to be BFF with Tara, but she posted about loving Allegra, and was being weird about Sean Sweeney. I smell trouble!

TOTWorshipper_2024: Ugh, what a bitch. With a friend like that, who needs enemies?!

Sunshinegirly886858: I started listening to Alex Knows *because I heard she's Tara's BFF and I really like it, but if they're fighting I'm unsubscribing!*

BeachcomberMA72: I came here to see if anyone else knew what was going on. I follow Alex because I like her podcast, and I saw her today in the town I live in – she's staying in Tara and Rory's house in Chatham.

LoveBiteList_xx: Finally everyone is seeing through the FAKE Tara!

TOTWorshipper_2024: you're on the wrong thread for sure
TOTWorshipper_2024: There's something fishy going on . . .

BeachcomberMA72: I'll keep you guys posted!

24. Alex

I briefly felt guilty about my Instagram story when I was mid-air en route to Cape Cod. It was childish and silly, but I was furious when I posted it. Anyway, Tara probably wouldn't even see it. She was too busy being fabulous and important in LA.

The Allegra dig had been a low blow, but so was Tara giggling and simpering on the red carpet about the very man who had ignited our blow-up. She knew I'd see it, and I felt like she was definitely sending me a message – so I'd sent one right back.

I tagged Sean in the story, thinking he'd recognize my name and see it – or that his social media manager would, at least, and maybe tell him. I was verified on Instagram; it wasn't impossible. But a few hours later, the message hadn't even been seen and I just felt pathetic – like one of millions of fans in his Message Requests. The mortification made me mean.

Tara would be mad as hell when she found out I was on the Cape at Rory's behest, and that gave me a nasty little thrill of vindication. According to him, his estranged wife had been keeping secrets about their marriage from me, big ones, judging by how hurt Rory was. Of course, she wasn't obligated to tell me anything, but as her alleged best friend it just felt like another incidence of Tara not being real.

Was it foolish to presume that our sort of friendship could persevere between adult women on different continents, with different careers and different types of families? Was it juvenile of me to presume that Tara and I could still be as close as we were as young women?

A cruel voice in my head chided me. 'Were you ever even actual best friends?' it said, mockingly. 'Or were you just always there, doing the heavy lifting and getting crumbs in return?' But then another one piped up. 'Be honest,' it was saying. 'Have you always told Tara everything that was going on?'

I shushed both sides of my subconscious. Why was I even surprised by Tara letting me down? It was just another example in a long line of incidents where she'd demonstrated little or no interest in how her behaviour affected me. Like that time she threw me a birthday party and didn't even show up for it because she got a callback for Broadway, or when she ditched my book launch for a front-row seat at Chanel during Paris Fashion Week. I was used to her disappointing me.

As my Uber from the airport pulled up to the Vaughan house, I looked out the window and my jaw dropped. I'd never been to the place in Chatham before, because Tara wasn't crazy about it.

I was completely blown away when I finally saw the property Tara referred to as boring. Or was that the town? The house was enormous, a Victorian-style mansion with an A-frame roof, tons of windows with painted shutters, a huge wrap-around porch – and was that a turret? It reminded me a bit of the house in *Practical Magic*, or maybe the one from *Big Fish*? Either way, it was magnificent. As I let myself in, my mouth was a round O of delight.

The house was beautifully renovated, with hardwood floors and huge wooden beams. The style wasn't what I'd call contemporary, but it had some modern flourishes – I spied a huge kitchen island with a waterfall-edge marble countertop, and a gleaming eight-ring range with brass hardware. There were sparkling chandeliers, expensive-looking art on the walls and the loveliest Persian rug in an alcove off the kitchen.

The house just kept going, and I walked through an enormous family room with multiple couches and a huge fireplace that I recognized from Christmas photos. I gravitated towards a pair of old-fashioned French doors hung with gauzy curtains. Flinging them open, I laughed out loud at the view before me – sparkling sea water, a small private jetty where a flashy boat was docked, and a gorgeous pool, seating area and fire pit. There was an outdoor kitchen, and wait – was that a granny flat in the back of the yard?

It was still a bit chilly on the last day of March, but I felt a rush of glee and freedom that was intoxicating. There was a smidgen of heat in the sun and the smell of salt in the air. If the weather was like this in Dublin, there would be lads walking around with their tops off, guaranteed. I whirled around the back deck with my arms in the air until I heard a pointed cough behind me.

I turned quickly, which made me dizzy, and my glasses slip down my nose. 'Rory?' I asked, confused. It certainly looked like him, but he wasn't meant to be there.

'No, Alex. It's me, Xavier.'

I blinked as my sight cleared, but all I could see was Rory still. Then I realized this man was younger, but surely not young enough to be Rory's son. This guy was thirty if he was a day.

He must have noticed my confusion. 'I swear it's me, I promise,' he laughed. 'I get mistaken for Dad about twice an hour around here in high season, which is why I spend a lot of time on my boat during the summer.'

'Xavier, I can't believe it. You're a man! You were a gangly seventeen-year-old the last time I saw you. What has it been, ten, twelve years?'

'Yep, I'm twenty-nine.' He smiled. 'Remember, I was conceived out of wedlock? I'm the one who ruined the sports scholarship and almost destroyed his dreams of stardom.' Xavier's voice was light, but I detected an edge.

He led me to a couple of Adirondack chairs on a little man-made beach next to the jetty. I couldn't get over how picturesque the scenery was, like something on a postcard.

Xavier grinned at my open-mouthed awe. 'Yeah, sometimes I forget that this place can have that effect on people. You take things for granted when you live somewhere beautiful full time, but don't be fooled. Winters can be rough.'

As my eyesight returned to normal, I took in this man-child of Rory Vaughan's. I'd never spent much time with Xavier, not like I did with Storm, anyway. He'd been largely absent; Rory's eldest was always away doing his own thing. Xavier was a graphic novelist of some sort, but I knew he didn't write under his own name.

It didn't look like he spent much time slaving over a desk, though. Xavier had an outdoorsy vibe, overgrown fair hair and calloused hands. I guess he fit the image of what I thought his dad would look like if he wasn't a manicured celebrity.

'The old man mentioned you were coming, told me to keep an eye out for you. I didn't think I'd find you doing a rain dance on the deck.' He was teasing, but his eyes were kind.

'Oh my god, I am so embarrassing. It was more of a freedom dance,' I admitted.

'Freedom from what?' He was direct, and it was disarming.

'Uhhh . . . years of being too nice, I guess. Keeping my mouth shut, letting Tara walk all over me. You've never been her biggest fan, right? So you'll get it.'

He frowned. 'Who said I'm not her biggest fan?'

'Well . . . nobody exactly, I guess, but you two have never been close? Not the way she and Storm are.'

'That doesn't mean I don't like her. She and Storm have always had girl stuff to bond over. But she's great. I guess I know her more as my dad's wife than as an actual woman, though.'

'What you see is what you get with her,' I said. 'So I'd say you know her pretty well.'

'Do you want to talk about it?'

'What?'

'Whatever is going on with you two.' He was very astute.

'I think a weight might have lifted off my shoulders. Hence the dance.'

Xavier raised an eyebrow at me, clearly wanting to know what I meant.

'I've learned a good bit about her this week. Not much of it very good. And I think I just got my own back on her a little.'

'On Tara?' He let out a low whistle, and I bristled.

'What, I shouldn't stand up for myself?'

He shrugged.

'It wasn't bad,' I protested. 'I'm just done taking all of her shit.'

He shrugged again. 'Look, not my circus, not my monkeys.' He grinned, cocking an eyebrow at me in a way that made my knees feel funny. 'But whatever you did, it will have consequences you need to be prepared for.'

I nodded, swallowing deeply. 'Are you also a psychiatrist out here, then?' I joked, poking him. Was I . . . flirting with Xavier Vaughan?

'No, just a former child raised by wolves in La La Land,' he smirked back. 'It's three o'clock. Around here we call that quittin' time in the off season. Want a beer?'

'Sure.' I smiled at him as he stood up and padded towards the main house. 'Although I haven't gone to the supermarket yet, so who knows what's in there!'

He laughed over his shoulder. 'There's always beer. I make sure of that.'

I lay back and breathed in the sea air deeply, taking in the island vista. There are worse places to face consequences, I thought.

25. Tara

'So, you've talked to your father, then,' I said.

'I have,' Storm glowered. 'He told me everything. It's fair to say you haven't exactly been honest about what happened between you guys, Tara.'

David and Giulia glanced at one another, and both stood up. 'I think we should get going,' David said, yanking at the IV still attached to his vein. 'If I can just get this thing . . . fucking ouch!'

'Sit down,' I said, and they both instantly obeyed me. 'You guys might as well hear this. No doubt Alex will blab to our friends if she's been talking to Rory too, but I'd rather you all heard my side of the story, and I'd prefer to only have to tell it once.'

All three nodded, surprised. I beckoned for Storm to come and sit next to me and took her hand. 'I never set out to intentionally lie to anybody. However, I've been going through a lot over the past couple of years, and quite honestly didn't feel like it was anybody's business outside of Rory and me. But I guess in not saying anything at all I've allowed people to believe that I'm . . . blameless in this dissolution of our marriage, and that's not strictly true.'

I sighed, trying to figure out where to begin.

'Just start from the very beginning,' Storm whispered. I nodded.

'Christmas 2021, I told your dad that I was finally ready to have a baby. He was delighted – he'd wanted another kid for ages – and we were both super-excited for this new chapter. I'd never felt the urgency to have a child of my own before, even though we'd been married about eight years at that point.

I had you guys.' I attempted to smile at Storm. 'But during the pandemic I spent a lot of time alone and not working, and I realized I did want to have my own baby – to be pregnant, give birth, the whole shebang. I became quite obsessed with the idea. If my biological clock had been dormant, all of a sudden it was wide awake.

'So we started trying. A lot.' I grinned, ruefully. 'We figured it wouldn't take long, but by that summer, I still wasn't pregnant. By Thanksgiving, there hadn't even been a brief moment of hope. The tests were always glaringly negative, even though I'd been charting my ovulation, taking the prenatal vitamins, doing it in the right positions for conception, even lying with my fecking legs in the air after sex . . .' I sighed, remembering my excitement turning to worry.

'I was turning thirty-six then – actually thirty-six – and when I went to see my gynaecologist she started talking about advanced maternal age and the complications that could ensue, *if* I were to conceive naturally. It was apparently a big *if* because we'd been properly trying for like, a year and a half by then, so I freaked out a bit.

'Then all of a sudden, the clock stopped screaming. It went so oddly silent I became convinced it was already too late. Every month when my period arrived, I'd be desolate. It just felt like further proof that I was dried up and done for. Rory tried to remain hopeful and optimistic; he said we just needed to practise more. Sorry, gross,' I said, glancing at Storm, who waved away my apology. 'But by then I was getting really stressed about it, even though I knew that stress was counterintuitive.

'I just had this feeling that my uterus was closed for business. I started my period when I was ten years old, so I thought if my fertility started young, maybe it would end young too. Plus, my mom died of ovarian cancer, so that brought up a whole load of feelings and worries. Was there something wrong with me? Was I going to die too? I was petrified, scared to even have myself checked out.'

I took a steadying breath.

'Around that time, I started getting all of these amazing opportunities at work that I took without thinking. I presumed it meant I must really, really want to work on those movies, but looking back, I think I just wanted to get really far away from Rory and the pressure of trying and failing to have a baby. It was tearing me apart, disappointing both of us every single month.' I shuddered at the memory.

'Oh, Tara,' David breathed. 'I'm so sorry.' I realized then that tears were falling down my face freely.

'I stopped wanting to even have sex, and that's when Rory said we had to start seeing a couples therapist. Sex has always been our thing. It sustains us even when we're apart. We've always been so good at intimacy, but I could feel myself pulling away from him. He felt rejected, so then he didn't want to have sex with me because he felt like he was forcing me. Sorry again, Storm.'

'I didn't know you guys were in counselling,' Storm said quietly.

'Nobody did, except the two of us. Oh, and Darius, because he recommended a friend who was very discreet. But it didn't help. If anything, it made things worse. It all got so bad between us that I was actually afraid of getting pregnant then, if it was even possible.

'By the time we had been actively trying for, like, two and a half years, Rory and I were just not on the same page and we were fighting about everything. The therapist was telling us to reignite the spark, have romantic nights, surprise one another, play games. In fairness, we really did try. Rory especially. But it all felt so fake. I felt nothing. And that's when . . . that's when . . .'

'You can say it, Tara.'

I started sobbing properly then. 'That's when I went on the pill, without telling Rory.'

David gasped dramatically.

'I know – I know it was an awful thing to do, but I couldn't take it any more!' I cried. 'The weight of expectation was suffocating me, and by then our relationship was coming apart at the seams. At that point, I truly felt like having a baby would make things worse. I still didn't even think I was capable of conceiving, and we were barely having sex, but I wanted to take the slightest chance of it off the table so that my period wasn't this horrible surprise every month. It was basically guaranteed I wasn't pregnant, so there was no point hoping even a tiny little bit.'

'When was that, *carina*?' Giulia asked gently.

'Last fall,' I whispered. 'And Rory found out during the holidays. He caught me taking my pill, had found the packet hidden in my drawer when he was looking for some pimple cream. He waited to confront me until he caught me in the act. I tried to deny it, swore it was an old packet, that he'd seen me swallowing a supplement, but he knew I was lying. I swear, I saw his heart harden towards me before my very eyes.' This admission prompted a fresh tsunami of tears.

'He spent a couple of weeks trying to talk to me about it, trying to work things out,' I sobbed. 'But I was so far gone by then, so confused and frightened and ashamed of myself for not being able to give him what he so badly wanted, and then for lying to him about it. I was just completely closed off. Then he went to California to work on the movie with that . . . woman. I went to London. The space actually did me some good. I realized how much I loved Rory, and how poorly I'd acted, sneaking around and lying.'

I wrung my hands in my lap, accepting the box of tissues Giulia handed me wordlessly. 'When he came to visit me the day after Valentine's, I thought he was making a huge effort to get back on track. I really believed he was coming to tell me he loved me, that we could work through anything. But no. Rory was coming to officially end things so he could frolic with Allegra in public and not feel guilty. I knew for sure it was really over when he took her to our special place in Santa Barbara. He was bad, I know he was bad, but it feels like . . . It feels like it was entirely my fault.'

There was a silence after I finished speaking. I looked at Storm, who was wiping her own eyes. 'Is that how he told it?' I said.

'Pretty much,' she admitted. 'He said at first, when he found out you were on the pill, he thought you were having an affair.'

I snorted. 'He did, and I was dumbfounded. As if, like. He couldn't see any other reason why I'd take contraception when we were supposedly trying to have a baby. Then when I got him to believe me that there had been nobody else, he didn't understand why I wouldn't just talk to him about how I was feeling. How could I tell him I needed to take a break from the pressure of trying, when I was already thirty-seven years old? In my mind, it wasn't going to be a break – it was going to be the end, because I truly didn't believe having a baby naturally was possible any more.'

'But Tara, thirty-seven is so young,' Giulia implored. 'Modern medicine is amazing, there is so much that can be done. Then there is surrogacy, and adoption—'

'None of you get it!' I said. 'Rory had a wife before me who could get pregnant at the drop of a hat! I have spent our entire marriage worrying about not living up to Lana, to your amazing mother, Storm. The poor woman died from complications of pregnancy. I wasn't going to put him through hospitals and tests and egg retrievals and gestational carriers. I was scared of hospitals, scared of finding out that what happened to Gloria was hereditary. It just all felt so wrong by then.'

Storm was freely weeping now. 'Dad loved you so much, Tara. I think you were actually the big love of his life, not my mom. He said you never believed that, you always compared yourself to her, and then you just totally shattered his heart by lying to him.'

I said nothing, horrified by my stepdaughter knowing so

much about our marriage. I was so embarrassed that it had come to this.

'He was a lot kinder about you than you are about yourself. And a lot tougher on himself about the whole Allegra thing. But he's angry, Tara. He's hurt you didn't even tell Alex that you were trying for a baby. He's wondering if you were ever serious about it all, and if you were taking the pill the whole time. I know now from listening to you that you *were* serious, but I can't believe you let us all think that his thing with Allegra came completely out of the blue. You had me convinced my dad was a heartless bastard!'

That wounded me. 'I'm so sorry, but he is a heartless bastard! How could he parade her around so soon? Yes, I'd broken his trust and things felt irreparable between us, but did he really have to rub this new romance in my face, in front of the entire world? It nearly destroyed me! Bad enough I wasn't woman enough to give him the kids he wanted, he also had to humiliate me with some young fertile girl? I was livid! I still am!'

Giulia scooted over and put a soothing hand on my thigh.

'Tara, you should have communicated with Rory about all of this. And Alex, too. She is your closest friend.'

'I couldn't,' I sighed. 'How do you tell someone you're a total failure? Alex wouldn't get it; she doesn't do relationships. She wouldn't have understood what I was going through, and I was already feeling totally misunderstood. I just threw myself into my work and hoped the situation would resolve itself.'

'Did you tell anyone?' David asked.

'Darius knew,' I said, wiping my tears. 'He's the closest thing I have to a parent, a conscious one, anyway. He's the best listener because he just doesn't really offer an opinion. Plus, he's like a vault. He heard me, he tried to help me where he could, and he doled out hugs when they were needed. But he couldn't really understand either. Who I really needed was my mother. She would have told me what to do. I deserve to have my mom, and I'm so angry that I don't.'

I don't think I'd ever admitted that before. Not to Samuel, not to Elspeth. Not to Rory or our irritating couples therapist, Barbara, or even really to myself. Saying it out loud felt like a weight off my chest, an admission I needed to make.

Giulia looked around the room. 'I've just realized something,' she said, smiling sadly. 'Every single one of us here has lost our mother.'

My head swivelled. David, Storm, me; Giulia was right. Recognition dawned on all our faces. A horrible thing for the four of us to have in common, but a meaningful one too.

'I was older when my mamma died, of course,' she continued. 'But it's never an easy thing to cope with. All three of you were far too young to be without yours. So we find mother figures in other people. Some people find it in themselves with their own children, that connection. Others in friends, in family members, in older gay gentlemen.' We all laughed softly. 'The point is that once we admit that we need others, they appear. They will not replace your mother ever – nobody will. But a piece of someone here, a piece of someone else there . . . they can all help fill the gaps she left behind. You, Tara, *bella*, have never allowed yourself to rely on anyone else since you lost your Gloria.'

In those few sentences, Giulia had summed up what I'd been trying to put into words during years of therapy. When Gloria died, I became an adult overnight. With my mom gone, my little family had fallen apart; my dad wasn't strong enough to take care of me, so I just told myself I was beyond being parented. Christy was only too happy to not have to deal with a bereft teenager when he was so destroyed himself. And now? The distance between us felt insurmountable.

Giulia was right; ever since I lost my mother I'd refused to let those closest to me get too close, just in case I lost them too. That had proved a futile exercise, because look at me now – no Rory, no Alex. A distant, silent father living in Dublin with his routine of going to the pub all day and drinking by himself all night. His sisters kept an eye on him, made sure he ate and slept, and sent me updates. But I might as well have been an orphan.

I was a huge success story on the big screen, but I realized I was an utter failure when it came to knowing myself and what I needed.

The enormity of it all was overwhelming, and we were all sitting there lost in our own thoughts when Giulia's phone pinged. She looked at it and grimaced.

'How do you say? It never rains, it pours.'

Los Angeles Times

Monday, 31 March 2025

Rory Vaughan Files for Divorce in Santa Barbara County

Actor Rory Vaughan has made things somewhat official in his split from fellow star Tara O'Toole, filing for divorce quietly earlier this month.

Vaughan is said to have been attempting to keep proceedings under the radar, but the Times *has obtained the legal documents after receiving a tip from a source.*

O'Toole and Vaughan have been married for eleven years, and were often cited as one of the stronger pairings in Hollywood. O'Toole is Vaughan's second wife – his first spouse, Lana, died in 2011.

Since news of the split emerged, Vaughan has been making headlines due to a high-profile romance with his Heist *co-star, Allegra. There has been speculation that O'Toole has been romancing Sean Sweeney of the band Higher Power, but the pair haven't been spotted together or confirmed a relationship.*

Representatives for Vaughan and O'Toole did not immediately respond to the Times' *request for a comment.*

26. Alex

I cut myself off after two beers with Xavier that afternoon because I wanted to go and explore the town. Chatham, Massachusetts, looks straight out of a story book even in the wintry twilight. There's a huge white lighthouse that's so quintessentially New England it seems sort of fake, like something an AI generator would spit out.

I breathed in the chilly sea air as I walked and admired the beachy view. The houses in Chatham were big, but not huge, and somehow understated, without the gloss and sheen of similar rich-people homes in the Hamptons. The Cape was more rustic than glam – the kind of place where people go barefoot in summer, porch swings are creaky from salty air and windows are adorned with nautical decor.

Rory had been smart to buy here in the late 90s; the house on Oyster Pond Lane backs right on to the water, and he could easily sell it now for over $15 million and make a killing. I remember Tara saying he paid something like ten per cent of that for the lot.

He won't sell, though – Rory always says this is his own little slice of heaven. He grew up on the mean streets of South Boston and it's far from Cape Cod he was raised, but buying this place was a dream come true. Tara prefers to spend her spare time in Lorraine's home in ritzy Bridgehampton, which I know pisses Rory off.

Xavier's a lucky guy to live here full-time, I thought; even in the off season with a distinct nip in the air when the sun hid behind a cloud, the place was breathtaking.

I strolled the few minutes to Chatham Village Market, but quickly noticed it's not really a place anyone walks and felt conspicuous in my Gazelles and Barbour jacket, stomping down the road. This outing was a treat for me because I absolutely adore a foreign supermarket, particularly an American one.

The grocery store was more low-key than a Manhattan one, but the sheer variety of brands and produce on offer was incredible, and thcy had so much stuff that we just don't get in the local Tesco or Aldi back home. I was going to while away at least an hour in these aisles, an indulgence I was allowing myself for being brave.

This being New England, I decided to stock up on local delicacies – Rory's favourite bluefish pâté that he flies in from Nantucket, fresh clam chowder, and more Sam Adams beer for Xavier. I piled my basket with eggs, dyed white as they are in the States, and grabbed fresh linguine, pesto and olives from the deli, and some scallion cream cheese. I treated myself to Cloudy Bay Sauvignon Blanc because it felt like the kind of wine a woman in control of her life would choose.

I finished my haul off with a visit to the bakery, where I tossed crusty bread, everything bagel, and sugared doughnuts into my basket, which was now full to bursting and weighing me down. I spied a case of the extremely bouji sparkling water La Croix at the tills, and added that to my pile, too. I felt like I was in a Nancy Meyers movie, and loved it.

After gagging at the total – Chatham prices make Donnybrook Fair look like Lidl – I was figuring out if I could walk home with my haul or whether I'd need to get an Uber. Before I made it even ten steps, though, my phone rang.

'Alexandra! You didn't, did you?'

'Mam? What are you talking about?'

'Don't take that tone with me – I raised you better than this!'

'Whaaa—' I sat down on a large, smooth stone at the entrance to the supermarket, heavy bags at my feet.

'One little fight and you throw out all your morals. What was the point of it? To make people think badly of your oldest friend? To embarrass her? To make a name for yourself by telling her secrets?'

My stomach plummeted. 'Mam!' I shouted, exasperated. 'I don't know what you're talking about!'

'You leaking the news about Rory filing for divorce! I'm really disgusted with you, Alex, and that has never happened before. I don't like the feeling. You've gone low when I've always taught you to go high, and quite frankly, I'm worried about you now. You must have lost your mind.'

Finally, she paused to take a breath. 'Are you finished?' I asked, but that was stupid because she saw my question as 'cheek' and launched into another tirade.

'No, I am *not* finished, how *dare* you say that to me! The brass *neck* of you to say that! You should be saying, *I'm sorry, Mam, it was a moment of madness, Mam, I feel terrible, Mam!*'

I stayed quiet, trying to digest everything that I was hearing. Was my own mother really accusing me of leaking gossip about Tara?

'Alex? Are you there?'

'I'm here,' I stuttered. 'And I don't know what kind of person you think you raised, Mam, but I didn't do any of the things you're saying I did. Quite frankly, I'm astonished you think I would.'

I heard Deirdre suck in her breath. 'It really wasn't you?'

'What on earth makes you think it would be?'

'Oh, love. Everyone thinks so. Between that story you posted earlier and then running off to Rory's house. We thought you were so angry, you were lashing out. Actually, I have to admit – Jen said you would never do it in a million years, to be fair to her.'

'Well, maybe Jen is the only person in the world who truly knows me!' I said.

'Alex, I'm sorry, love, but I'm worried about you. You're all on your own over there in some mad town for millionaires, and you're acting so out of character, taking Rory's side! I know you're hurting about fighting with Tara, but sweetheart, you just don't seem yourself. Nobody thinks you'd rationally lash out, but me and Darius were afraid you'd lost the plot a little bit. Giulia called him saying Tara was hysterical, ranting and raving about discretion and loyalty and, well, she definitely thinks you were behind it all. She said you were the only person who knew about the filing who would want to hurt her.'

My heart sank. So Tara presumed that I was the kind of person who would tell the press sensitive information to get revenge. That hurt, badly.

'Did it not occur to anyone that perhaps Allegra would be behind a leak like this?' I implored. 'Did everyone's thoughts just go straight to me being a huge bitch instead?'

'Oh, Janey Mac.' I could practically hear the truth clicking into place in my mother's brain. 'You're right, of course. It was probably that little rip Allegra. Oh, honey, I really do apologize. I just got caught up in the madness. I know in my soul you'd never hurt Tara like that, but I was afraid you'd gone a bit loo-laa.'

I let her prattle on about Madame Tussauds on Times Square separating Tara's and Rory's waxworks, but I felt sick to my stomach. If my own mother thought I was taking Rory's side and battling my ex-best friend through the press, what sort of vibes was I putting out into the world? Christ on a bike, I did one little Instagram story not licking Tara's arse and I was suddenly the devil. I hung my head, which now hurt. Here were those consequences Xavier had predicted, arriving right on time.

I waited for the screeching phone call from Tara that night, but it never came. Maybe word had got back to her of my staunch denial, but I felt oddly disappointed that she hadn't rung calling me every name in the book. In a way, her silence was more frightening. Didn't she care to confront me? And why did I care that she didn't care? Oh, Jesus. There was a lot to unpack there.

Jordan Jones was delighted, though. 'The conspiracy theories on Reddit about you fighting with Tara and leaking info about her means more US listeners for *Alex Knows*!' he roared down the phone over the noise of midtown traffic.

'Jesus! You say that like it's a good thing!'

'Alex, it *is* a good thing. The more people that know who you are, and what you do, the better. The context is largely irrelevant, as long as you didn't murder anyone.'

'No, just a twenty-eight-year friendship,' I muttered.

'Gotta go. Keep the chin up and stay off the internet tonight. Enjoy the Cape!'

I went to sit on the dock in the moonlight, my mind a jumble of conflicting thoughts. It was freezing now it was night-time, but still utterly beautiful, with a huge icy-blue moon suspended in a sky littered with glittering stars. I was well wrapped up, in my fuzzy Ugg clogs and a puffy parka I'd found in the mudroom, but the cold was creeping into my ears and up my nose.

It was eerily quiet; even the seabirds had gone to their nests for the night. Xavier was sleeping on his boat, a fact that initially worried me because I think 'boat' and I see a dinghy in my mind's eye. But no, it's a thirty-five-foot sports cruiser with a very comfy cabin and climate control, so comfy that Xavier spends more time there than in the pool house. Rory bought it as a gift for his son's twenty-fifth birthday, yet another reminder of how different the life of a celebrity's offspring is.

Xavier said he was going to take me out on the boat the next day after a whistlestop tour of the Cape. I had protested that he didn't need to babysit me, that I was more than happy to make my own way around, but he insisted. I surprised myself by how much I was looking forward to it.

The truth was, I could do with the company. I was used to being on my own and have always been fiercely independent as an adult – it's just been easier that way. But all of a sudden, I was feeling quite alone in the world. It wasn't surprising after all the upheaval and change that had transpired over the past few weeks, but I guess I took for granted just how much of a support system Tara was for me, even from afar. Without her in my corner, everything felt a little scarier.

I was surprised to feel tears threatening when I thought about her. I knew if I was to allow myself, sobs would escape from my choked throat. But I forced myself to swallow the feeling, willed my eyes to dry up. I wasn't going to cry about any of this any more.

I had made my own bed. I'd allowed Tara's personal drama to bustle into my life, and hustle me across the Atlantic. If I had a life of my own like Jen did, I wouldn't have been available to be at my best friend's beck and call. My mother was right; I had been so busy devoting myself to being Tara's rock I had forgotten about myself in the process. Meanwhile, Tara hadn't even deemed me important enough to tell me what was going on in her marriage. I was still none the wiser, even though Rory presumed I'd be fully up to date.

Realizing that truth was sobering, and frightening. I felt like such a fool, like I'd wasted so much of my own time. Shivering in the cold night air, I made a decision. I would focus purely on myself and giving my own life direction. I wasn't going to be anybody else's sidekick any more.

27. Tara

The day the news of Rory's filing was leaked passed in something of a blur. I was initially convinced that Alex was behind the story, but felt oddly delighted that she hadn't gone the whole hog and revealed the sorry tale of my barren womb to all and sundry while she was at it. Storm didn't believe it was Alex, but after my former friend's catty Instagram story I knew she was out to hurt me. I wouldn't put anything past her.

Not long after the story dropped, the ladies arrived to remove our IVs. Untethered, I was suddenly filled with the kind of nervous, harassed energy that only exercise can cure, so I told Giulia I would do the proposed hike if she and David came with me. They grudgingly agreed.

Lorraine called, but I hadn't felt able to listen to her screeching about Alex and gloating about how she'd always known my best friend was a bad egg, so Giulia spoke to her. Apparently Lorraine was going to spend a few days with the older man she'd scored the night before. 'She says she may have found a new West Coast lover.' Giulia shrugged. 'I hope the poor man has enough Viagra.'

I got dressed in my brightest athleisure and Storm gave me a fresh-faced look, taking the edge off any visible signs of a hangover.

After snapping some shots for social media with my enormous Covet billboard on Sunset Boulevard, Giulia graciously bowed out, claiming work duties, and I ended up practically dragging David up Runyon Canyon. When he eventually caught his breath, I had him take some more shots of me looking relaxed, happy and completely unbothered at the top. Seriously, I deserved my Oscar. We posted them all in a carousel on Instagram, and it felt good to pretend I didn't have a care in the world.

Inside, however, I was crumbling. It had been an exhausting day, opening up about all that Rory and I had endured, and I didn't really have it in me to deal with Alex being a weapon. The story had felt like a threat, like the beginning of something nasty. The thoughts of her and Rory being in cahoots made me want to peel my own skin off; it was perhaps a good thing that I didn't really have the capacity to take it in.

'Please, Tara. Please God, let me go home now,' David whined. 'I need some greasy fried rice from a strip mall and my bed.'

I laughed. 'That sounds so good, but I have to go and meet your stepsister. Are you sure you don't want to come?'

'I would on any other day, but I'm actually dying. And anyway, you and Portia will just be talking business so I'll be bored out of my tree. Now, be a doll and drop me at Panda Express on Santa Monica Boulevard on your way to the Chateau?'

I did as I was asked, and by the time I handed the valet my rental car keys at Chateau Marmont my hangover was all but gone. This was a good thing, because those who hang out at the iconic hotel overlooking the Sunset Strip on the day after the Oscars are looking to see and be seen.

I'd suggested it as a location for our meeting to Portia Daniels the night before in the full knowledge of that fact. If I wanted to stay hot and current, I should be spotted with the new maestro of my favoured genre.

Portia and I air-kissed and settled into seats in the bar for a cocktail. I like the Chateau because it's old-fashioned, and I like Portia because she's not. 'How's the head?' she asked in the way only an Irish-adjacent person could, her brown eyes twinkling. 'I believe David is in bits.'

'I dragged him up the Canyon, but it still didn't fix him!' I laughed. 'Forgive my leggings, but I know you don't expect me to be all gussied up for a quick drink. Fun night, right?'

'Oh, so fun,' she agreed, taking a long sip of the Aperol Spritz that had just arrived. 'You look every inch the superstar, even in athleisure. I need this drink to cure me – I'm getting too old for that much gallivanting. I love that word – "gallivanting",' she said, rolling it around in her mouth even though it sounded strange in her soft Angeleno accent. 'So,' she said, swirling her straw and suddenly a little more serious. 'How are you holding up?'

'About what, exactly? My husband leaving me, or my former best friend leaking sensitive information to the world's press?' I grimaced.

'All of the above.'

'Well, not great, if I'm honest. Portia, have you ever felt like you just don't have the headspace to deal with something painful, so you don't even entertain it?'

Portia coughed, choking on her drink. 'Uhh, yes. Yes, I have. I'm sorry you're going through it, Tara. You're getting it from all sides.'

'Maybe I deserve it!' I said shrilly, and she looked surprised. I recovered quickly and pasted on my famous smile. 'Now, please distract me by telling me all about your fabulous new project I may have the honour of being involved in.'

'The honour is all mine! So, it's a romantic comedy, but it's really about friendship. I feel like female platonic relationships are so often overlooked, but they're some of the most important love stories of our lives, right?'

I raised my eyebrows. 'Go on . . .'

'Well, the love between girlfriends is so interesting. It's such an intense relationship, the one you have with the women closest to you. I've always been drawn to writing about it . . . and I guess you could say the movie that's come out on to the page is sort of like a modern, fresh version of the female melodramatic comedy.'

I couldn't believe what I was hearing. A movie about female friendship, at a time when I was in the middle of my own shitstorm in that very arena? I must have been gaping at her, because Portia shook her head. 'I guess I'm not explaining it very well. Think *Bridesmaids*, *Beaches*, *The First Wives Club*, *Thelma and Louise* . . .'

'Okay, so public pooping, premature death, revenge and . . . more premature death with a smattering of crime?'

Portia threw her head back and laughed. 'See, this is why I love you, Tara. You're witty and you wear your emotions on your sleeve. If only you could see how perplexed you look. There will be no shit, and no premature death. But there will be lots of the heady emotions that come when you entangle yourself with other women in relationships that are meant to last for ever. The question is, can you handle digging into that right now?'

'Honestly? I don't know. But let's talk more. Can you send my agent the script?'

'Of course. I think you're perfect for it, Tara – honestly, I would have brought the project to you sooner if I'd thought for a second I could afford you. You have that quality, that likeability meets vulnerability meets sex appeal.'

'Well, put that on my headstone.' I smiled, batting away her compliments. I never like it when other people describe me to my face, mostly because it feels like they have me dead wrong. Giulia tells me it's not *me* they're talking about, it's the star Tara O'Toole. I knew that – well, I knew that when I wasn't feeling so raw, like I'd shed a layer or ten of my thickened skin overnight.

'Look, think about it. I know things feel tender right now. Katie and I are pretty much ready to go on this, but I've spoken to her and we are willing to wait for you. So much so that we'd cast the rest of the movie around you.'

'Portia, thank you so much. As soon as my head is on straight, I'll be in touch.'

I kissed her on the cheek and stood up to make a public exit, waving at industry contacts and fellow stars on the way out:

Quentin Tarantino and Uma Thurman were in the far corner; Glen Powell was having coffee in the lounge. From the outside looking in, I knew I appeared calm, cool and collected. Inside, I was burnt out – and I knew exhaustion was the only thing stopping me from breaking down altogether.

The next night was my last in Los Angeles, but I was done schmoozing. Shanice had gone back to New York, Storm was staying on a few days with friends and I was scheduled to depart LAX the next afternoon on a commercial flight. Lorraine still hadn't returned; her new lover must be quite the goer, I thought.

I was feeling jittery, though, and out of sorts. Word had reached me via Jen that Alex was denying leaking the Rory story, and I was confused. I'd been so sure it was her lashing out at me, but Alex wasn't a liar. If she was saying it wasn't her, then it wasn't.

Darius believed that Allegra was a more likely candidate, and with hindsight I was inclined to agree. That little wench wanted me out of the conversation asap. Still, I was incredibly mad at Alex for going to our Cape house. I knew she was angry with me, but running off to Rory's seaside bolthole felt like a huge middle finger right in my face.

Portia was as good as her word and sent over the script. As expected, it was brilliant and perfect for me, but reading it had given me a crisis of confidence. I'd thought I was ready to go back to work, but signing on to a film about friendship at this moment in time just felt crazy. What did I know about any of it?

But then, if I couldn't do a fun, relatable comedy, who was I? Those were the easy gigs, the ones I could do in my sleep. Maybe I should steer clear of anything to do with regular human emotions and any sort of kinship. Perhaps I'd get my agent to look for something in the fantasy or sci-fi genre, or maybe even an action movie. I could reinvent myself as a sexy, high-octane adrenaline junkie! It would be so easy to just fall into a new genre, to switch off my brain and let the costume and special effects do all the heavy lifting.

Ugh, enough thinking about work, I told myself. But without worrying about my professional life, all there was left to torture myself with was my personal life. Whatever way I looked at things, I was screwed.

Hmm, screwed. Maybe I just needed to have sex! It had been quite a while, after all. I hadn't even thought to bring any toys out to LA with me, that's how dormant my libido was.

Sure, I'd been sexting Todd Kramer on and off; he and I had worked together on a pretty steamy romcom in 2019 where he played my younger conquest. He had been distraught to find out I was faithful to my husband. While he was the recipient of my recent artfully saucy snaps, I was self-aware enough even as I was sending nudes (with my head cut off, obviously) that it was for validation, not titillation. I thought about summoning him for a second, but the truth was, I didn't actually fancy poor Todd.

Plus, I couldn't just make a booty call, not in this town – not unless I wanted the news everywhere by morning. Unfortunately, shagging Tara O'Toole at this moment in time would be currency for the opportunistic. I'd been out of the game a long time, so I didn't have anyone I could trust on speed dial like the good old days.

A familiar sensation scratched at the back of my mind. Ahh, yes. My most trusted former collaborator in the sexual arts was of course Sean Sweeney. Why hadn't that fucker contacted me yet? For the first time ever, I really needed him, both physically and emotionally. Who was he to drop bombs, blow up my life and then go silent?

Throwing caution to the wind, I decided to just call him. I wasn't going to sit around any more and wait for some bullshit grand gesture. I was impatient, tired of being strung along and suddenly convinced that a great sweaty sex session could cure me of my malaise, even if it was over the phone.

Luckily, I had packed some raunchy animal-print lingerie because Shanice wanted me to wear it with jeans and heels. I hadn't quite had the balls to pair my straight legs with the cheetah-patterned cut-out bustier in public, but at that moment I was glad I had it with me. I struggled into the corset, flipped my hair and added some blush to my cheeks and gloss to my lips. Assessing myself in the mirror, I was pleased with what I saw. I'd caught some sun at Runyon, and I looked far more vital and vigorous than I felt.

I scrolled to Sean's name in my phone and pressed the FaceTime icon before I chickened out. I hoped he still had this number. When was the last time I'd called him? Jesus, it couldn't have really been almost twelve years ago, could it? Time flies when you're married.

The call connected, but instead of messy hair and tattoos filling the screen, I saw a woman in her twenties, blonde and perky. I immediately grabbed the sheet to cover up my ample cleavage.

'Ohmigod! You're Tara O'Toole!' she squeaked, seemingly unperturbed by my semi-nudity. 'Hi, I love you so much!'

'Uh, yes, thank you. Sorry, do I have a wrong number? I'm looking for Sean Sweeney.' I hoped she couldn't see my face flaming, mortified.

'Nope, this is his cell. Well, one of them!' the girl tinkled. 'I'm Raphaela, his second personal assistant. Unfortunately Mr Sweeney is super off the grid right now. May I take a message?'

I bristled. 'What do you mean, super off the grid?'

'Mr Sweeney is currently not in possession of his own devices. He is hunkered down writing, and he doesn't like the distractions of the internet or people calling. His first assistant, Annabeth, and I screen all of his correspondence and send him a digest. May I take a message?' Raphaela sounded like an automaton. I wondered how many times a day she reeled off that speech.

'No, thank you. Well, maybe just tell him I called. Do you know when he's likely to be back on the grid?'

'I do not, I'm afraid,' Raphaela chirped. 'But I will inform him! I really am a big fan, great to meet you. Thank youuuuuu.' With that, she was gone.

I was furious. Sure, I hadn't seen Sean in a dozen years, so I wasn't at the top of his call log. But it rankled to only get through to what was essentially his human answering service, only perkier.

Where the hell was he? It made me nervous. What if he was with Alex? No, surely Alex Curtis wouldn't have the nerve to bring Sean Sweeney to *my* house.

I felt myself getting even more riled up until I forced myself to think rationally. If Sean was in suburban Massachusetts, he'd be spotted immediately. Chatham is a small place, and international pop stars high on the current news agenda wouldn't go unnoticed. Plus, surely Xavier would have told Storm if that was the case.

It gave me some comfort to know Sean and Alex weren't likely cooped up together. But I didn't really know why, seeing as Sean Sweeney wasn't with me either. For the first time, I seriously contemplated that he hadn't been talking about either me or Alex. Maybe there was a third Irish woman who had truly stolen his heart way back when. The bastard.

I took off the bustier and crawled into bed with my make-up still on. I wasn't even horny any more, just confused and feeling isolated. One more sleep, I told myself. And then you get to go back to New York and figure out the rest of your life.

@DEUXMOI

Sunday Spotted:
I saw Allegra flying out of Las Vegas this weekend. She was trying to go unnoticed, but you kind of can't miss that ass. She was flying with a hot girl I didn't recognize, and they looked very cosy – they were holding hands. Isn't she supposed to be dating Rory Vaughan? Are they in a throuple now?!

Sunday Spotted:
Rory Vaughan was having lunch alone in SoHo at Café Gitane. He was just staring into space, not even eating his roast chicken baguette. He is so hot for an old dude!

28. Alex

Is there a word for realizing that you fancy your former best friend's grown-up stepson? Unlikely, because I don't believe any other human being has ever experienced such a strange crush.

It hit me like a bolt from the blue, this intense, sudden attraction to Xavier Vaughan. I'd noticed faint flutterings of lust over beers the previous day but had wholly dismissed the notion of being into him. I wrote it off as momentary madness brought on by my heightened emotional state, and the fact that I hadn't had sex in an awfully long time.

I soon discovered that it wasn't a temporary condition. I woke up the next morning after a delicious sex dream about Xavier ravishing me on the kitchen island, and from that moment on I had it bad.

Part of me was sick to death of subconsciously pinning all my romantic hopes and dreams on Sean Sweeney. While nothing had changed in relation to my feelings for him, I was suddenly fed up with being so drawn to my old flame and in a perpetual state of waiting. Tara had told me to live my life; well, my hormones were telling me I wanted to have sex, and soon.

Thus, from the second Xavier walked into the kitchen that morning, my nerve endings were on red alert. This brand-new crush felt so inappropriate I didn't know if I could allow myself to spend the day alone with the new-found object of my desires.

For once I found myself listening to my heart (and hormones) and not my head, and quite literally leaning into Xavier Vaughan on the deck of his boat later that afternoon. His right arm was on the back of my seat, he smelled sweet and salty, and I felt an intense rush of longing.

It had been a gorgeous, mind-bending day that felt straight out of a romcom, one I couldn't quite believe had happened. Xavier had brought me fresh coffee and cinnamon rolls before 9 a.m., which made the house smell like a bakery. It was a sunny morning, so we ate together at the kitchen island, bathed in warm rays as they streamed into the house – the very same kitchen island I'd imagined him bending me over in my erotic dream. He looked incredibly hot in a white long-sleeved polo T-shirt, pale chinos and a waterproof jacket open to the waist.

'This is good coffee,' I enthused, for something to say, and Xavier laughed as he leaned over and wiped something from my nose. 'You've got a bit of icing on your beak.' He grinned, and I nearly keeled over with a strange mix of desire and mortification.

I half-heartedly tried to catch myself on. This was Tara's stepson, for god's sake. Sure, he was a grown man of twenty-nine and I wasn't even a full decade older than him, but I couldn't escape the guilt. It's baked into Irish people.

Xavier would have been very difficult *not* to fancy, even if I hadn't been sex starved and in turmoil. There was no denying the guy had pedigree – being good-looking is literally in his genes.

There was something else about him, and I soon copped that it was because he was *normal.* Rory is worldly, he's wealthy and well groomed, but that all makes him seem untouchable. The only physical clue as to Xavier's privileged upbringing was that his teeth were straight and white, the product of expensive American orthodontia. His hair is too long, and his skin is charmingly freckled. A good Hollywood aesthetician would laser such sun damage off, given half the chance, and that's why father and son don't look very far apart in age. If Rory Vaughan was movie-star unapproachably gorgeous, Xavier Vaughan was regular-guy super-hot – and right in front of me.

I told myself that these feelings didn't matter anyway; this man wouldn't fancy me back, and I'd just have to make do with him being the subject of my fantasies for the foreseeable.

All too quickly, though, it became clear that Xavier was in fact casting admiring glances my way. Maybe it had been a quiet, long winter on the Cape. Or maybe I was being a little hard on myself and underestimating my appeal. Okay, so I'd switched out my glasses for prescription sunnies and taken extra time doing my hair and make-up. I was wearing a T-shirt bra that made my boobs look perky under a stripy shirt, and this particular pair of jeans were more form-fitting than my day-to-day ones.

Still, my arse looking good didn't mean he automatically wanted to have his wicked way with me. And I wasn't trying to seduce him, not really. For all I knew, he already had a girlfriend. I put the mere prospect of finding out if he had a sixpack under his shirt out of my mind and decided to just try and enjoy the day touring the place I'd long dreamt of visiting with a hunky, flirtatious man.

'Where are you taking me?' I said as his jeep backed out of the driveway, and instantly blushed. Everything sounded dirty to my revved-up ears.

'We're going north to Provincetown. Another day, I'll take you out west to Hyannis and Falmouth. They're beautiful too. But your first real introduction to the Cape has to be P-town and all the beautiful beaches along the way.'

I was instantly enchanted by the scenery. The weather was bright and crisp, which Xavier said was pretty unusual for this time of year, with blue skies and pretty puffs of clouds above. Xavier's beat-up Defender was very him – strong and masculine and a little rough around the edges – and I felt safe next to him.

We made a pitstop at an adorable little market called Macs in the town of Eastham, and it was exactly the kind of cute seaside grocery store I'd envisioned in my fantasies. Xavier had brought a cooler, so we filled it up with delicious sandwiches, cheese, meat, bread and wine. He even insisted on buying me a Cape Cod hoodie. 'A touristy souvenir, and it'll come in handy if you get chilly on the water.' I gulped. So, he'd meant it: he was going to take me out on his boat. The boat where he slept. In his bed.

After a blustery walk on Campground beach, we returned to the Defender to feast on the sandwiches we'd bought – a lobster roll for me, turkey for Xavier. All the while, we talked about our lives but kept it perfectly surface. We chatted about our childhoods, but nothing traumatic, and our work, but nothing intense.

When we reached Provincetown, I was thrilled at the sights and sounds – rainbow flags everywhere, bustling businesses on Commercial Street even in the off season, and buzzy little restaurants. I knew Darius and Francisco loved it there, a fun LGBTQ+ haven 'for the gays too old for Fire Island'.

An older couple took a picture of us with the colourful shops in the background, and I almost keeled over when Xavier slung an arm around my waist. But that was the extent of our physical interaction; we really were mostly just talking. I told him all about Dublin; he told me what it was like growing up between the East Coast and LA with his famous family.

'High school in Beverly Hills was a trip,' he told me, grimacing. 'Dad moved us there full time after our mom died. In some ways it was great, because I wasn't unusual. Everyone's parents worked in the business. But everyone was so wealthy, so privileged, so stuck up. I never felt like I fitted in there, and as soon as I could, I headed back out east.'

The conversation was perfect; I sensed Xavier was a man who always liked to keep things light. I learned that he adored his career as a graphic novelist, that drawing had always been his true passion in life. 'Storm and I are both artistic in a way we definitely inherited from Mom,' he told me as he navigated winding roads. 'Storm uses her talent for make-up; I use mine for drawing. Thankfully, we're nepo babies who never had to get a real job.' He laughed, but again I sensed an edge to his humour.

'Why do you keep making jokes about nepotism?' I asked, all attempts at remaining relatively aloof out the window. I was so curious about this guy.

He flicked a sidelong glance at me that made my insides go mushy. 'Honestly? I can't speak for Storm, but me, I feel bad about it,' Xav said simply. 'There are heaps of talented people out there who don't have the opportunities I have. Not only the introductions or the interest in who my dad is, but the space and freedom to create that having money allows. I've never had to worry about making rent or putting food on the table. I'm afraid it makes me soft.'

I was struck by how open and honest he was, completely without guile. I totally understood what he was saying. He was in a different league to me in terms of family wealth, but I knew that having close, supportive parents had definitely given me a leg up in life. And having Tara, of course.

'I know what you mean,' I said quietly. He looked over at me again, but chose to let the moment go.

We arrived back at the house just before four o'clock, which Xav said was perfect timing. 'I want to show you Martha's Vineyard and Nantucket from the water,' he said. 'Another perk to having an A-list father.'

We walked down the private jetty where his boat was moored. 'I try to give back to the town as much as I can so people don't think I'm a complete spoilt brat – I pitch in at the local events, lend the boat for charity trips and stuff like that.'

I was touched by his determination to help out, and not just rest on his famous father's laurels. It would be very easy for Xavier to be a layabout, but Rory and Lana had obviously instilled a good work ethic in both their kids.

'My parents didn't come from much,' he said. 'They were new to having money, and they raised us just like their parents raised them. Well, at least until we moved to Hollywood.'

The boat was impressive, a long, shiny specimen with all modern conveniences. I tried not to watch as Xavier untied the ropes with practised hands; by that point of the afternoon, sexual tension was at an all-time high.

An hour later, we were floating in the Nantucket Sound with Martha's Vineyard to the right and the eponymous island in the distance. It was a calm evening for early spring, so we dropped anchor, popped open a bottle of sparkling rosé and spread out the goodies we'd bought at the market just as the hazy sun started to dip behind the clouds. It was so romantic, a chilly sunset on lightly lapping waves.

'So how are you really feeling today, Alex?' Xavier said, catching me unawares as I stuffed a slice of mortadella into my mouth. To avoid choking I chewed slowly and swallowed, realizing what he was getting at.

'Oh, you mean those consequences you warned me about?'

'The very ones. I googled you last night, you know. I couldn't help myself.'

I felt my face flame, and Xavier laughed. 'The internet seems to think that you've been leaking stories to the press about my family.'

'I have not! I swear, Xav, that's not who I am. Your family has been nothing but good to me. Tara and I . . . it's very complicated, but I would never—'

'Alex, I know. I was kidding. I know Tara trusts you with her life – you two go way back.'

'Way, way back. There's all this history between us, but it recently occurred to me that it's never really been an even playing field. I mean, sure, I've been successful in my own field, but I don't know how well I'd have done without her help – something that's been in the back of my mind and that she recently pointed out to me. If you're a nepo baby, then I've been a nepo best friend.'

'I'm sure that's not true. Dad and Tara always spoke so highly of you. She said you were an amazing actor.'

I nodded. 'I was good; everyone said so. But I had this stage-fright problem, this anxiety. It was always there in my life, this fear of everything going wrong, but it got worse as I got older and more self-conscious. I could never quite get over myself enough to enjoy performing. Tara, though – she took it all in her stride. She was made to be a star. Whereas I think I was made to study the constellations, you know?'

He nodded. 'It must be hard, when your best friend is *the* Tara O'Toole.'

I looked into his eyes to see if he was taking the piss out of me, but I was met with a clear blue gaze and not a hint of sarcasm.

'It is,' I admitted. 'Harder than I ever let myself believe.'

'So was the fight really over some guy?' He blushed when I raised my eyebrow at him. 'I was talking to Storm. She doesn't believe you're a rat either, by the way.'

I nodded, and Xavier continued. 'I can't imagine Tara giving a shit about anyone except my dad . . . those two have always been like love's young dream. I can't picture my dad with Allegra either. That's too awkward to even comprehend. I used to really dig her.' He shuddered.

'Well, Tara has as much history with Sean Sweeney as she has with me. Actually, she's more intimately acquainted with Sean than she is with me.' I snorted, rolling my eyes.

'And you're jealous?' Again, his gaze was direct and untroubled, and I felt I could be just as straight back.

'Yeah, I guess I am. More than jealous – I feel betrayed. I never knew about them, you know. Sean and Tara were carrying on for years behind my back. And we had a pact.' I laughed, because it sounded ridiculous when I said it out loud. 'If it seems juvenile, well, I guess it is. It's ancient history, really. Or it was until Sean brought it all back up again.'

I filled him in on the whole fiasco, wincing at the really embarrassing bits where Tara and I argued like schoolgirls over a man. Then I found myself crying real tears when I told Xavier how Tara had accused me of being afraid to live my life, and I'd told her she was a fraud. He let me cry, handing me a tissue and staying quiet until I finished.

'I think you needed that,' he remarked as my sobs became sniffles. 'Feel better now?'

'Oddly, I do.'

'Good! Because both you and Tara are way too good to be fighting over some douchebag who led you both on.'

'We are?'

'Of course you are! His behaviour screams loser, if I'm honest. And yeah, you and Tara have reverted to adolescence over him, but I'm not surprised. Tara is heartbroken, and you're feeling stuck.'

I gawped at his easy analysis.

'I can't imagine what it must be like not to follow your own dreams because you're too anxious to, and then to watch your closest friend achieve them all, and then some. Then she looks at you and craves your normality, your togetherness. Of course you're going to feel at odds sometimes, but you've never really got the chance to rub each other up the wrong way until you were in close quarters at a very weird time for both of you. It's a really strange situation, but it was just a fight, Alex. If you want to, you can get over it.'

I stuck out my chin, defiant. 'What if I don't want to?'

'You will. You're hurt right now. But eventually, you'll want her back. And trust me, neither of you really wants this Sean guy. He's just a metaphor.'

'For what?' I laughed out loud.

'For your rivalry. They exist in every friendship, Alex. You guys really aren't that unusual.'

'Wow,' I said, taking a long sip of rosé. 'Are you sure you don't have a sneaky degree in psychology?'

'Not sneaky; it was my minor at college. But I was never going to practise. I'm interested in human behaviour, but I don't want to listen to other people's problems all day, every day.'

The sun had set, the boat was softly lit, and even though I couldn't see him clearly I was very aware of Xavier's closeness – even more so when he got up to get a beer from the cooler and sat back down right next to me, so close that our thighs were touching. He slung an arm around the back of my chair, and that's when I caught his scent in my nostrils; he smelled masculine, sweaty from sailing, sweet from his shampoo, sexy from his very essence.

All of a sudden, I was very aware of the throbbing between my legs. It felt conspicuous, like Xavier could feel it too, or see it even. I turned my head to look at him and saw he had his face angled towards me, so close that our noses brushed. Oh, so he wanted this to happen too.

I felt a thrill shoot from my toes all the way through my body, but still I hesitated. I wasn't going to throw myself at him. When he leaned in to kiss me, I pulled back ever so slightly, even though every cell in my body was screaming for him.

'We shouldn't do this,' I whispered, my lips centimetres from his. 'It's . . . weird.'

'Weird I can handle,' he muttered, his voice thick. 'As long as it doesn't feel wrong?'

I felt another throb at my very centre and couldn't resist any more. 'Wrong?' I gulped. 'No, it actually feels very right.' I closed my eyes as his mouth met mine.

I'm not normally a woman who has sex on a boat in the middle of the sea, but maybe I should be, because it was probably the best sex of my life. Xavier was commanding, guiding me throughout in a way that told me this wasn't his first time seducing someone on the yacht. He scooped me up with one arm so I was straddling him, my hands in his hair and his palms on my ass as we kissed with a ferocity I don't think I'd ever felt. This wasn't romance, it was animal instinct. I could feel him hard beneath me and I couldn't help but rock up and down as my tongue explored his mouth. It was so erotic; I knew it was cold out, especially with darkness encroaching, but I felt so very hot.

When I reached down to unbutton his trousers Xavier grabbed my wrist. He stood up and led me inside, into the small cabin, where the bed was unmade and his scent seemed to fill every inch of space. He peeled off my coat and his own, and I flung off my shirt and jeans with urgency. As I stood there in my (thankfully matching) underwear, he sat down on the bed in front of me and took me in with his eyes, and then his hands. His rough palms caressed every inch of my body, removing my bra and lace-trimmed knickers as they went until I was standing there completely naked in a haze of euphoria, my nerve endings on fire.

Xavier parted my legs ever so slightly with his hands and began to stroke me with his thumb right where I was burning for him. As I came, hard and fast, I felt him suck and bite one nipple, then the other.

As the waves of pleasure ebbed, I pushed him backwards on the bed. I wanted him inside me immediately, and when I slid down on to him, he cried out. I took command then, with long, teasing strokes up and down his body with my own.

'Alex, I'm going to come,' he moaned, so I stopped moving and held him inside me.

'Not yet,' I purred, and he responded by flipping me on to my back. I could see and feel him resisting the urge to go all in, thrusting until he was done. Instead he started a slow, building pace until I was the one begging for him to go faster.

It was like a dance, one in which neither let the other fully take the lead. But when I reached the peak again, crying out as my body shuddered with waves of pleasure, I decided to be the one to initiate the climax.

I rolled Xavier over, and to his surprise started working my way down his body with my mouth. As he realized what was happening, a grin worked its way across his beautiful face. I reached his groin, covered in rough, fair hair, and stroked his thighs with my hands as I took the length of him in my mouth. He tried to pull me back up, to end it together intertwined, but I wanted to be in control. I expertly used my tongue until Xavier came with such intensity he shouted my name.

As we lay there panting afterwards, entangled in each other's slick bodies and in the sheets, I realized just how much I'd missed being intimate with someone. Afraid of overstepping, I tried to roll away and give him space, but Xavier grabbed me and held me tight. I surprised myself by falling asleep like that, curled up in his arms.

29. Tara

I was packing up my personal bits to check out of the Beverly Hills Hotel bungalow when I noticed another missed call from Jen. Shit, I thought. She'd been trying to get in touch with me all week. The West Coast time zone and my crazy schedule had meant that every time I tried to call her back, it was the middle of the night in Dublin.

I checked the time on my phone as I zipped up my toiletries bag and did some mental arithmetic – if it was noon in LA, surely it was past the kids' bedtime in Ireland and she'd be free to chat. I decided to chance my arm and call her.

'Well, if it isn't the woman who doesn't answer her WhatsApps,' was Jen's dry retort as she answered the phone.

'Ah, come on, Jen. I'm old – I prefer phone calls. My messages are always full of people looking for quotes or donations or threatening to murder me. I don't even read them any more.'

'Oh, what a life you live,' my friend laughed. 'Listen, have you been talking to Alex at all?'

I knew Jen well enough to know she was aiming for breezy, but she was coming across slightly manic.

'You know I haven't.'

'Ah . . . well. No reason, really. Are you in her Instagram Close Friends?'

'I didn't know she had one.'

'Mmm, I think it's new . . .'

'Jen, what's going on?'

She sighed. 'Look, something is going on with Alex. She's being weird, posting all sorts of strange pics.'

'What kind of strange pics?'

'Well . . . Tara, she's been on a date with Xavier for over twenty-four hours.'

I laughed heartily. 'Oh my god, Jen. Talk about getting sucked in by social media! You're absolutely gas. He's probably just been showing her around.'

Jen sounded annoyed then. 'I am not gas, I'm serious. She's still on his boat, since last night. She's very . . . happy-looking. Have you watched yet?'

'No, sure I'm on the phone to you! I'm busy, I've a flight to catch.'

'Put me on speaker and watch, please. There's been a big shift in their energy. It's obvious, no?'

'Jen Callaghan, are you telling me you can sense energy shifts through a phone screen now?'

'Well, I must be able to, because I rang her to see what was going on and Alex admitted to riding him!' Jen cried.

I must have blacked out for a few seconds, because the next thing I knew, I could hear Jen roaring, 'Tara, are you there?'

'What did Alex tell you, Jen?'

'That she and Xavier slept together last night, on his boat. I wanted you to watch the stories and see for yourself, though, instead of springing it on you!'

'You're telling me that she told you directly that she had sex with my stepson?'

'Um, I am, yes.'

'And you're telling me this information why exactly?'

'Because I think it's a sign that she's gone full mad, basically. Tara, this is not how Alex Curtis behaves. Our friend doesn't run off to upscale seaside towns and shag people's relatives.'

'He's only a child!' I yelled, the full gravity of what Jen had told me hitting me like a ton of bricks.

'Well, no, Tara, he's not. He's nearly thirty.'

'He's a child to me! And he should be to Alex! Jesus, if a man my age made a move on Storm, I'd cut his bollocks off!'

'Xavier is a good bit older than Storm,' Jen said, clearly

backtracking now. 'Look, while it is undoubtedly strange behaviour, it's nothing bad, really. It's just more that it's out of character for Alex. And wasn't she just saying that she only had eyes for Sean Sweeney? That's why you fell out!'

I sat on the bed with my head in my hands. On the one hand, I realized that this meant Alex definitely wasn't with Sean – good news. On the other, well, she was banging my stepson. Bad. Very bad.

'I thought Sean was the reason, Jen, but lately I'm not so sure. Jesus!' I said. 'What am I supposed to do about this? Is she trying to ruin what's left of my family? What is she thinking?'

'I don't think Alex is thinking at all, Tara. For once in her life, I think she's just acting on impulse.'

'Well, I'm going to act on impulse myself and go out to the Cape and confront her.'

'Oh Jesus, I regret telling you now.'

'Then why did you?'

'Because I was afraid you'd hear it from someone else. And because I'm worried she's lost the plot in a way that only you can fix. I'm close to Alex, Tara, but nobody is closer than you.'

I was already texting Felicia to book me on a flight to Boston. 'Oh, I'm going to get close to her all right. With my fist!'

'Tara!' Jen was laughing nervously now. 'You're joking, right? Tell me you're joking.'

'Oh, by the time I get to the East Coast I might have lost the desire to pummel her, but who knows?'

'Are you really going to go to Cape Cod?'

'I really am, Jen. What, am I supposed to pretend none of this is happening? I turned a blind eye to her bitchy little Instagram, but infiltrating my family with her vagina? I'm not letting her get away with it!'

'Infil—Tara, come on.'

'No, Jen! Alex always wants everything I have. I'm not letting my stepson get caught up in it all, even if he is allegedly a full-grown man. Warn her that I'm coming if you want, but Felicia has just confirmed my flight. I'll call you later.'

By the time I was mid-air, I'd calmed down a little – but only a little. I'd debated calling Rory, and then Storm, but they didn't need to know about Alex and Xavier's tryst any more than I did. I didn't want them imagining it, like I had been, very much against my will, since Jen called.

Getting to Chatham was always such a pain in the arse. Sure it was quaint and pretty, but it's bloody awkward and means either getting a car from Logan Airport and driving for two hours, or flying by helicopter, which I don't like doing. They're loud, scary and cramped.

I was having regrets then, thinking that maybe I should just get home to Manhattan and figure things out from there. Then I remembered that Rory had been in my apartment while I'd been gone, and it just didn't feel safe any more. Damn him, and damn Alex Curtis!

The flight east was largely uneventful, and I only noticed one woman attempting to take sneaky photos of me. They're always so obvious, I just let them at it. Felicia arranged for a driver to meet me at the airport so I didn't have to get behind the wheel and drive while fuming.

It was late by the time my car pulled up at the house on Oyster Pond Lane, almost 11 p.m. I thanked the driver and as he left I noticed the lights were on in the hallway. I typed in my code at the gate, and it hit me then that I didn't have any keys. I'd come all this way, and I'd have to ring the doorbell to get into my own house. A fresh wave of humiliation washed over me, and hardened to anger as it reached the pit of my stomach.

I pressed the bell hard, and heard footsteps and laughter inside. Alex threw open my front door, a smile on her face and a glass of red wine in her hand. She was wearing only a robe. My robe.

I could hear music filtering out from the kitchen as her smile dropped and she just stood there, staring at me. I don't know how long we stayed like that, me on the front step and her inside the door, but it must have been a while because Xavier appeared behind her. 'Hey, what's going . . .' He stopped short when he saw me. 'Tara!' he exclaimed. At least he was clothed, in a T-shirt and sweats.

'Well, isn't this cosy?' I snarled.

'What are you doing here?' Alex managed, eventually.

'You're honestly standing in the doorway to my house, asking me that?'

Xavier jumped in then. 'Come in, come in,' he said, moving a robotic-looking Alex out of my way.

The house felt different, more lived in somehow since the last time I'd been there. Of course, Xavier was here year round, but I was under the impression he used our home the odd time, not as somewhere to hang out entertaining guests. Or was he the guest in this case? After all, Rory had apparently told Alex to use the house as her own. Was I the interloper here? I shivered, feeling distinctly put out.

'Tara, I mean this with all due respect, but, um, what brings you to the Cape?' Xavier was polite but direct.

'Oh, I don't know, a little birdie told me that Alex was shacked up here and fucking my stepson.'

It was gratifying to see her flinch; Alex doesn't do confrontation – our argument in New York had been a complete anomaly. I was pleased to have caught her on the back foot, playing house with Xavier in such an obviously romantic setting. There were fecking candles lit!

He was instantly defensive. 'Tara, there's no need for that.'

'For what? Being blunt? I'd rather you didn't tell me how to behave or speak in my own home, Xavier,' I growled, and he held his hands up.

'I'll leave you ladies to talk,' he said, turning and padding towards the kitchen.

'It's not what you think, Tara,' Alex said meekly then.

'Oh? Are you denying having sex with Xavier?'

She turned purple, and I simultaneously felt victorious and queasy. She must have seen the flash of uncertainty on my face, because Alex sprang into action then.

'There's nothing wrong with it, you know. He's only a few years younger than me.'

'Of course he is. It's just, I used to catch him jerking off to internet porn when he was sixteen, so forgive me for feeling a little grossed out. Alex, he's our son!'

'Yeah, and the age gap between you and Rory is bigger than between me and Xavier. Don't be a hypocrite, Tara.'

She had me there. I realized then that Alex had basically zero relationship with Xavier when he was a teenager. Just because I'd heard him crying at night because he missed his mother, busted him underage drinking and cheered at his high-school and college graduations, Alex hadn't. To her, he was just a handsome guy with peripheral ties to her. A guy who was clearly hot for her too.

I couldn't shake the sting of feeling, like Alex always wanted my stuff. It was childish and puerile, but it came from my gut. I wanted to hurt her, like she'd hurt me. 'Have you always been attracted to my husband, then? Or is the fact that you're sleeping with his lookalike child just a coincidence?'

'Cop on to yourself, Tara.'

'No, you cop on, Alex. I know I told you to get a life, but can't you get one of your own? Why are you always obsessed with mine?'

My phone rang then. I was too far into this stand-off with Alex to even think about answering it, though. That is, I was until her own device started vibrating on the hall console table.

We broke eye contact to look at our mobiles for a split second. Francisco was calling me.

I glanced at Alex; the phone in her hand said Deirdre, even though it was the middle of the night in Ireland.

In that instant, we both knew something was badly wrong.

I met her eye again, and we both pressed the answer button at the same time.

'Tara?' Francisco was sobbing so loudly I could barely make out what he was saying.

'Francisco, calm down. What is it? What's wrong?' I cried, at the same time Alex was making a similar request of Deirdre.

'It's . . . it's Darius. He collapsed. Tara, he could not breathe. His lips were blue.'

I looked at Alex and saw my horror reflected in her own expression. 'Francisco, is he alive?'

'I think so – I think he was. I tried to do CPR, the 911 operator told me how to do it, but I don't know if it was right because he wasn't breathing. The paramedics are loading him into the ambulance now. Oh, Tara, where are you? Can you come?'

'Fuck, I'm on the Cape! Francisco, try to stay calm. I'm with Alex, and we're coming right now.'

30. Alex

Tara and Xav took action while I remained rooted to the spot after speaking to my mother on the phone. As a medical professional, Deirdre is always the calm head in a crisis, but I could tell that she was scared witless just from Francisco's description of what had happened to Darius. Mam said that it sounded like a heart attack, a big one.

I felt frozen, my mind racing at a million miles an hour but my body unable to move.

'Alex, come on, get dressed,' Tara was saying. 'We've got to go.'

'Are you sure you want to go by car?' Xavier was saying from what seemed like very far away.

'Absolutely. At this time of night, it's the quickest option. I'm not sitting around waiting to charter a plane or a chopper. Let's just go.'

'Okay, I'll drive.'

In a daze, I put on the jeans and top Xavier handed me. It was the Cape Cod hoodie he had bought me the day before. Was that really only yesterday?

I allowed Tara to take me by the arm and lead me to Xavier's jeep. I wasn't even wearing shoes, which I only noticed when Tara handed my Uggs to me in the back seat. She sat beside me and took my hand, and I didn't stop her. It felt comforting, familiar. Tara always has warm, dry palms; mine are always freezing. 'Cold hands, warm heart,' she used to smile at me.

Somewhere along the Massachusetts border I snapped back to reality when I saw a sign for Providence, Rhode Island. 'Rhode Island? Where are we? How long is this going to take?'

I bleated, my face burning and my hands tingling. I could feel my heart beating rapidly, panic setting in. 'What's going on?'

'It's okay, Alex. This is the fastest way. We're about three hours out from the hospital,' Xavier said, turning around and giving me a reassuring look. 'I'm going as fast as I can.'

And he was. Xavier was whizzing through the dark night over the speed limit as Tara and I sat side by side, white-faced and silent. When I noticed her furiously refreshing her phone, I rooted in my bag for my own.

'Jen's booked everyone on the next flight out of Dublin,' Tara said, to nobody in particular. I didn't ask who exactly; I knew my mother would be one of them. 'Your dad is coming too, Alex. And Brian. Jen is leaving the kids with Brian's mam.'

My heart lurched. Jen crossing the Atlantic without her brood in tow was something she'd only do in a matter of life and death.

We knew Darius was alive, but that was it. He'd been admitted to Mount Sinai's emergency cardiac department, and Francisco was waiting there for news with Lorraine. As we sped through the inky-black night I felt more afraid than I ever had in my life.

We arrived at the hospital just before 5 a.m. and were greeted by a feral Francisco, wild-eyed and hyperventilating.

'Oh, girls, it is not good,' he cried. 'He stopped breathing when we got here. They brought him back, but he could go again any minute!'

'Slow down, Francisco. What do you mean, brought him back?'

'He was dead, gone. Flatlined.' Francisco made a choking noise and dissolved into sobs once again.

Lorraine came around the corner, and I was surprised at how glad I was to see her. She took Tara in her arms and began speaking quietly and urgently to us both.

'I've been interrogating the doctors. It looks like Darius had a massive coronary in the apartment, and another one about an hour ago,' she said, her voice breaking a little. 'They had to resuscitate him. It took a while to get his heart beating again and they're not sure of the damage. They had to intubate him, I'm afraid. He's sedated.'

I moaned, but Tara was all business. 'Lorraine, is he going to be okay? Tell us he can come back from this.'

'Honey, it's touch and go right now. He's critical. We're not even allowed in to see him yet. Come, sit down.'

As Xavier took Francisco to get some water, Lorraine explained the information she'd managed to glean from him when he'd been calmer. Francisco told her that Darius had been complaining of a pain in his neck for a few days, blaming his new pillows, and said he felt a little nauseous after dinner. That was nothing new or worrying: he was known for his rich cooking and love of butter; food often repeated on him.

'Francisco left him watching the V Network around ten thirty and went to fold his laundry, but only a few minutes later he heard a huge thud and found Darius writhing in agony on the floor.'

I grimaced at her descriptive adjectives, but Tara pressed for more information.

'Francisco acted quickly, making sure Darius had an airway and calling 911, but by the time the paramedics arrived to their apartment, Darius was white as a sheet and barely awake. He lost consciousness fully in the ambulance, and his heart had stopped in the ER. The docs got it going again after fifteen minutes of meds and shocks, but he coded again not long before you guys arrived.'

I cursed myself for not having a serious talk with Darius about his health sooner, but I'd thought of him as young and vital still – I presumed the worst he had to worry about was gout. Chastising him about his cholesterol wouldn't have worked either. Darius often said that he wouldn't want to live without what he deemed to be the finer things in life – rare steaks, unctuous buttery sauces and sinful desserts. I felt winded as I realized how ominous and prescient that sentiment could be.

The men returned, and I could see Francisco was making a concerted effort to hold his shit together. 'I'm sorry, ladies, I was overcome. The main thing is, Darius is still with us,' he said, his teeth chattering. 'But he is asleep.'

'He's in a coma,' Lorraine said grimly, her mouth a hard line and her skin grey. 'The doc says it's not necessarily a bad thing – the heart muscle has to rest. They're debating surgery to repair the artery, but with his weight . . .'

'. . . the anaesthesia could be a huge problem,' I finished.

'It might do more harm than good,' Lorraine agreed.

'What can we do?' Tara asked, a sense of urgency in her voice. 'There must be something. Can I fly in a cardiologist? It's no problem – I'll pay anything.' Glancing at her, I saw her eyes were wild and desperate. She was terrified, and trying to throw money at the situation.

Luckily, Lorraine knew how to handle Tara, so I didn't have to. 'This is New York City, hon. They have the best doctors in the world here. There's nothing we can do, except wait.'

At that, Tara dissolved into anguished tears and I felt my own composure give way. I felt a strong hand on my shoulder and turned in to Xavier's chest, where I cried my heart out.

Tara's fame has its perks, even in critical situations. Knowing she couldn't spend long in the waiting-room chairs without being recorded or photographed, the chief of surgery arranged a private area for us to try and get some rest. It was right next door to Darius's room, and we were allowed to go in and see him briefly even though he was still unconscious.

A huge man, Darius looked somehow small in the hospital bed – shrunken, sort of, without any of his joie de vivre. His skin was frighteningly pale, and it was bizarre and horrible to see a machine breathing for him and tubes coming out of his mouth and nose. I wanted to brush his long hair because it looked a fright and Darius would hate that, but there were too many cables in the way.

Darius was stable for the moment, but his condition was very serious. The loud beeps and whirs from the hospital paraphernalia made me jump every couple of seconds, and I couldn't stop hearing them, feeling them in my own chest like a heartbeat even when I was out of earshot.

Francisco, Lorraine, Tara and I remained in a sort of daze. It felt like a waking nightmare as daylight broke and the hospital became filled with the light of a new morning. I thought I was dreaming when I saw my mother appear at the door. It wasn't even 9 a.m., still far too early for her to be here. But Deirdre was indeed right in front of me, and Jen too. I ran to them at the same time as Tara, and we all collided in the corridor.

'How?' was all I could manage, but Mam shushed me.

'A friend helped us,' she whispered, holding me tight and rocking back and forth.

I looked at Tara, wordlessly questioning, but she shook her head. 'It wasn't me,' she mouthed, seeming as shocked as I felt.

'It was Rory,' my dad said, appearing from behind the women and putting his arms around me and Mam. 'He arranged a plane. And young Xavier here came and got us from the airport.' I hadn't even noticed Xavier leaving, that's how dreamlike the entire morning had been.

Tara made a choking noise, disentangled herself from Jen and ran to her stepson. 'Thank you,' she whispered into his chest as he held her awkwardly. 'Thank you for telling your dad.'

'Of course,' he said softly. 'We're always going to be family, Tara.'

I looked away then, embarrassed and awkward at the display of familial love. I'd thought that Xavier was here to support me but, of course, he was here for Tara, too. I felt that familiar bubble of poisonous jealousy rise up inside me. Why couldn't I ever have something just for me? Why did she have to be involved?

Then it burst as quickly as it had inflated as I turned back and forced myself to watch the two of them embrace. All of a sudden it was much too clear to me that Xavier really did regard Tara as a mother figure. He was her family, whether I'd thought of them that way or not. Why had I assumed there was a coolness between Tara and Xavier? Had I imagined it?

Whatever I'd thought, I'd clearly been wrong. Xavier held his stepmother as if she was a child, his great height making her seem tiny in his arms. At a glance, you'd be forgiven for thinking it was Rory and Tara reunited. Right then, I felt like a complete outsider. Was Tara right? Did I always secretly want what belonged to her?

Maybe subconsciously I'd known exactly what I was doing when I slept with him. It's not like we'd met when everything was hunky dory and grown close; this had happened when Tara and I were at odds. Had even a tiny part of me been trying to get back at her?

I shook my head. No, I was crazy attracted to Xavier. It didn't matter that he was in Tara's orbit. Did it? Another wave of nausea hit, this one tinged with shame, as I understood why she'd been angry enough to come to the Cape.

I swallowed the sick feeling. The events of the past forty-eight hours were completely overwhelming, but in reality nothing mattered except Darius. I couldn't devote any energy to worrying about anything else, least of all Tara. I allowed my parents to walk me out to the waiting room, each clutching one of my arms, so I could catch them up on the latest.

PageSix.com

4 April 2025

ANOTHER CRISIS FOR TARA

Actress Tara O'Toole keeping vigil at friend's bedside at Mount Sinai

Hollywood star and Upper West Side resident Tara O'Toole has reportedly been keeping vigil at the hospital bed of her close friend and mentor, Manhattan party planner Darius D'Amore. Darius collapsed at home from a suspected cardiac arrest.

It was initially believed that Tara's estranged husband, actor Rory Vaughan, was also present at the Upper East Side hospital, but sources say that the tall doppelganger spotted among the group is in fact his son Xavier (29), a graphic artist who lives out of state. Friends and family from O'Toole's native Ireland were also there supporting the red-headed superstar, as well as D'Amore's husband, Francisco Campos, and LONY*'s Lorraine Staffetta.*

Staffetta has been seen pacing outside the hospital smoking cigarettes and talking on the phone, while taking deliveries of food for the assembled group and the healthcare workers of the intensive care unit.

More as we get it . . .

31. Tara

The hours after the Irish contingent arrived both dragged slowly and flew by far too fast. One minute I was waiting anxiously for the surgeon's afternoon bedside rounds thinking she would never appear, the next it was dark out and there was still no change in Darius's condition. I had lost all sense of time, and my body clock was shot.

When she did show up, Dr Sarah Wilson was Scottish and no-nonsense. She told us in no uncertain terms that she didn't want to have to operate on Darius, and only would if it was absolutely necessary. 'If Darius was younger or healthier, I'd have gone in right away,' she said gently, but firmly. 'His arteries are clogged, and his heart is struggling to circulate blood around his body and so depriving his brain of oxygen. The muscle has been under a tremendous amount of pressure, and I won't sugar-coat it – he could arrest again at any moment. If that happens, I will have to take him to surgery to put in an emergency stent. I think the best-case scenario is that Darius remains in a coma, we keep giving him a cocktail of drugs to clear the arteries and lower the pressure, and hope that another MI doesn't occur.'

'An MI is a myocardial infarction,' Deirdre offered. 'A heart attack.'

I knew what it meant. I did a six-episode guest-star arc on *Grey's Anatomy* a few years back playing a tough but sexy visiting cardio-thoracic surgeon. Now that I was witnessing a real-life emergency first hand, I was mortified that I ever thought I could do a person like Dr Wilson justice.

'If he comes out of this, Darius will have to make some serious changes. But we're not quite there yet. Let's just keep the faith, shall we?' Dr Wilson swept off, a trail of underlings following in her wake.

I felt so disoriented, and so absolutely alone. When her parents arrived, Alex snapped out of the trance she'd been in since we got the news, but also pulled right away from me. It was torture sitting across the room from her with this coldness between us, watching her in the bosom of her family. We were only feet apart, but the distance felt impassable.

I kept checking myself, remembering that we were here for Darius, for Francisco. This wasn't about Alex and me. But watching our dear, dear friend hovering between life and death made me wonder what on earth she and I were fighting about. Why were we wasting time? Then Xavier would appear with a coffee and go to her instead of me and a white-hot poison of jealousy and loneliness would spread through my chest.

The evening dragged on with no change in Darius's condition. Deirdre and Eamonn, and Jen and Brian, all left to go and check into the hotel up the block, to shower and rest. They hadn't slept in over a day apart from a couple of bumpy hours crossing the ocean in the middle of the night.

I kept meaning to call Rory to thank him for acting so quickly in getting our loved ones here, but I couldn't bring myself to press the call button. What if Allegra answered? A text would feel too cold, too impersonal. It was best to say nothing and let Xavier relay my thanks. I couldn't think about Rory or his mistress at a time like this.

Eventually, Francisco went next door to get some sleep and Xavier went back to the apartment, but not before giving Alex a lingering kiss goodbye, a sight that made my stomach turn.

I must have fallen asleep in the chair next to Darius's bed, because the next thing I knew it was light out and Jen was shaking my leg.

'Honey, time to wake up. It's Thursday morning. The doctor will be around soon.'

I was so tired and disoriented I felt nauseous. 'Where is everyone?'

'They're all round here somewhere,' Jen said, taking a seat next to me. She looked how I felt: completely exhausted and drained of all her usual healthy glow. I don't think I'd ever seen such fear and worry in my friend's eyes.

'It's not looking good, is it, Jen?'

'No, love, it's not. I'm praying to a god I don't even believe in for Uncle Dar, but I really don't know if he's going to pull through. If he does, he's going to have to live a completely different type of life, one he'll absolutely hate.'

'My god. I can't imagine the world without him, Jen.'

'So much for positive thinking,' a voice snapped from the door. Alex stood there looking ragged and angry. They were the first words she'd spoken directly to me since we'd got the call from Francisco, goodness knows how many nights previously. 'I thought we were here to provide support?' she said. 'Not to write the man off entirely. Don't put that kind of negativity into the atmosphere. You know better than that, Jen,' she scolded.

Chastened, Jen and I closed our mouths. Alex was furious, that much was clear. If she had to direct it towards us to get it out, we'd let her. She stalked off, back to her mother. Deirdre was white as a sheet, and Eamonn wasn't much better. Brian and Francisco were sitting with them, both quiet and silent as statues.

Another day dragged on at a snail's pace. Lorraine was in and out bringing food and coffee and trying to encourage me to go home for a few hours. There was no way I was leaving Darius's bedside. I just couldn't. Felicia was an angel, ferrying whatever any of us needed over from the apartment – clean clothes, fresh underwear, phone chargers.

Somehow it became night-time again, and I found myself still in the room with only Alex and Lorraine. Everyone else had taken the doctor's advice and gone to get some rest. From

Lorraine's frantic leg-jiggling I knew she was anxious to leave for work; she'd told me earlier on she couldn't get out of filming *LONY* that evening, and I understood. But her leaving would mean just Alex and me at Darius's bedside. I wasn't going to go anywhere, and I knew she wouldn't either, so it was a sort of stalemate. An Irish stand-off. I made eyes at Lorraine to let her know that it was okay; she could go.

'All right, sweeties, I have to get going for the night,' she cooed, kissing me on the forehead. 'We're filming at a Broadway after-party, and I know Darius would simply not allow me to miss it. In fact, he'd be absolutely fucking furious if I did.'

'You're going . . . to work?' Alex was incredulous, and sharp with it.

'Yes, Alex, I have commitments.'

'To reality television? Wow.'

I tried to communicate telepathically with Lorraine to drop it. Alex was furious with the world, and she wouldn't understand that everyone's life doesn't stop completely when something terrible happens, especially in a horrible limbo like this. Lorraine had contractual obligations to *Ladies of New York*; she couldn't just not show up to a planned filming.

She was right, too. Darius would absolutely want her to go and tell everyone he was sick so they could be sympathetic on camera. He'd popped up enough times on the show that the fans knew and loved him.

Thankfully, Lorraine didn't rise to the occasion as she might when confronted on screen. She chose to ignore Alex, squeezed my hand and slipped out.

By midnight, the only sound in the ICU was intermittent beeping. The hospital was quiet as the night shift rolled on, a skeleton staff of nurses keeping a watchful eye over their charges. Alex and I hadn't uttered a word to one another, both engrossed in our phones either side of the hospital bed.

Then, out of nowhere, Alex started to laugh. I looked up,

surprised at the sounds of mirth coming from her, but there was an edge to them; I realized she was crying at the same time. When she saw me looking at her, clearly perplexed, she only laughed harder.

'I'm . . . remembering,' she gasped, unable to stop guffawing, '. . . when Darius got arrested.'

Oh my god. I had forgotten about that incident. Alex and I had been about fifteen at the time and visiting London with Darius and two other girls from That's D'Amore to see a play in the West End. Some old busybody had thought Darius was a pervert bothering teenage girls and had called over a bobby on the beat to investigate.

'He was so furious,' Alex said, her face turning purple. 'He kept saying, "But I'm gay," as if that made a blind bit of difference.'

I felt laughter bubbling up in me as well; the memories and Alex's unhinged giggles were infectious. 'The PC was so rude to him,' I recalled. '"I don't care who you sleep with, sir,"' I acted, mimicking the copper's cockney accent. '"There are public concerns that you are sex-trafficking these young ladies."'

It turned out that a man matching Darius's description had been lurking around the theatre district and was suspected of myriad kidnappings of foreign teenage girls. It was serious, and Darius had been taken in for questioning, leaving us all without a chaperone.

Alex had taken charge, getting us to the theatre (because we weren't going to miss *Les Misérables*) and then calling her mother to tell her what had happened. Because we didn't know anyone else in London, Darius spent the night in the clink until it was confirmed he was actually our guardian and not the leader of an international sex-trafficking ring.

'God, I'll never forget what a lick-arse you were,' I said. 'Deirdre said to go back to the hotel straight after the play and not to move, so that's what you made us do. You were always a Goodie Two Shoes, when all the rest of us wanted to do was get pissed. Do you remember we emptied the minibar? And Niamh Whelan vomited all over the beds and we had to sleep on the floor?'

Alex had turned bright red from all the howling, but her laughter soon turned to sobs. 'Oh, poor Darius. It's only now I see how horrific it must have been overnight in the station. He's such a gentle giant. But it was the ponytail-and-goatee combo for sure,' she sobbed. 'He thought it was giving a heftier Skeet Ulrich, but it was giving sex offender.'

As we both came down from the high of the memory, I caught Alex's eye and instantly felt sombre. Our wheezes fully receded, I took my shot at something of a détente. 'Hey, how are you doing?' I asked softly.

She shrugged, tears still falling freely. 'Not great,' she managed.

'Me either.'

We were silent for a few moments, but then both spoke at once.

'Alex, I don't know—'

'Tara, I didn't—'

Then we both stopped as suddenly as we'd started. I chanced giving my oldest friend a wary smile. 'May I?'

She nodded reluctantly. Ever so slightly encouraged, I began to talk.

'In this moment, Alex, I can't really remember just why we're quite so upset with each other. Well, I know why, but it all feels sort of ridiculous. If Sean Sweeney walked into this hospital room right this second, I don't think either of us would really care. Am I correct?' I arched an eyebrow at her, but she remained stony-faced.

'It wasn't all about Sean,' she bit back.

'You're right, it wasn't.' I decided to be even more conciliatory. I wasn't too proud to apologize any more – I'd learned the importance of communicating the hard way, thanks to Rory. 'Al, I'm sorry about everything that happened between us. I've had the strangest few months – hell, the strangest few years – of my life, and I haven't exactly been honest about any of it. If you'd let me, I'd like to tell you my side of the story.'

'Well, I don't have anywhere else to be,' she acquiesced haughtily, but I could see a flicker of curiosity in her face that hadn't been there before. She may not have been warming up to me, but neither was she ice cold.

And so I told her absolutely everything. How Rory and I had been trying to have a child without any success, and how he'd caught me in a massive lie that was the catalyst for his desertion.

As I spoke, I saw every emotion pass over Alex's face – shock, surprise, horror, sadness, judgement and pity – but she said nothing, just letting me get it all out. It was clear then that Rory hadn't actually told her his side and she had been completely in the dark about the finer details.

There were tears streaming down my own face by the time I'd reached the part where Allegra entered the picture and Alex got involved. 'When Rory came to London to tell me he was leaving me, I just felt so ashamed. That's why I couldn't tell you, because I knew that even though he was behaving like an enormous shit, it was really all my own fault. I didn't want you to blame me as well, because I was blaming myself already so thoroughly. It felt good to have people on my side, for people to feel sorry for me and think I'd been treated so horribly out of the blue.'

'Tara, you *were* treated horribly. You taking the pill and lying about it, awful as that was, doesn't excuse Rory going off with the next young thing that shook her famous arse in his face.'

'I know that, but I had been icing him out for so long by then he must have been totally devastated. He thought we were still trying in earnest to have a baby, while I was making sure that we couldn't. I know he was probably just looking for comfort, and didn't expect it to get so . . . serious.'

Alex looked deep in thought. 'Why didn't you tell me you wanted to have a baby?'

'Truly, I don't know,' I sighed. 'I guess, at first, I was worried it wouldn't happen for us and telling you would have felt like counting my chickens. Then as time wore on and it hadn't happened I just felt like such a huge failure. I've never exactly wanted to admit my shortcomings to you, Alex.'

She gaped at me. 'Why the hell not? Are you afraid to not be Ms Perfect, even with me?'

I threw my head back and laughed. 'Perfect? There is nothing perfect about me, Alex. You are the one who has her shit thoroughly together. Everything in your life is perfectly organized, designed for maximum efficiency. If you decided you wanted to have a baby, you'd probably be pregnant in one cycle.'

'Aahh, but to have a baby I'd have to be capable of a proper adult relationship,' she said frostily, her mouth set. I swallowed, knowing I'd hit a nerve and hoping that wasn't the end of the conversation.

'I didn't think you wanted kids, you know,' she said eventually. 'I thought you were happy with Rory's, that you wouldn't sacrifice your career or your figure. Maybe I just don't think of you as a regular person with regular desires.'

'Well, I didn't really want them in any sort of tangible way for a long time. I was scared, you know? I lost my own mom so young, my dad is on another planet and I don't have any brothers or sisters. And yeah, I was busy being a star.' I gave a hollow laugh. 'But when the desire hit me, god, it was like being hit by a truck.'

'That hasn't happened to me,' Alex said thoughtfully. 'Maybe it never will. Maybe you're right and I'm just not cut out for all of that.'

'Alex, I'm sorry I said those things about you. I didn't mean all of them, at least not the way they came out. I have been worried that you cut yourself off from other people, I won't lie about that.'

'I don't know how to be any other way.' She sighed. 'My whole life, I've been so anxious. Such a worrier, so scared for no reason. Then some reasons came along. Watching you lose your mother frightened me too, you know. I couldn't help but soak up your emotions; I've always been such a sponge.'

'But Alex, it didn't happen to you!' I was exasperated. 'You had your mother, you have her still. People deal with rejection all the time – from family, friends, colleagues, lovers. You go through it, you move on, and it makes you stronger.'

'I've never felt strong enough,' she whispered. 'I don't know how people do it. Fall in love, break up, fail and then get back up and keep trying.'

I understood then. I'd always known that Alex was wired differently to me, but I didn't fully get just how risk averse she truly was until that moment – how her wonky fight-or-flight signals had impacted her entire life. My heart ached for her, for the little girl constantly watching from the sidelines as other people lived their lives, too anxious to join them in the realities of the world. Instead, she contented herself with observing from afar.

'I've always been jealous of you,' she blurted out then, seeming to surprise even herself. 'And not in the way you might think, not because you're beautiful or rich or famous. You are just so . . . able. Willing and capable, and ready for everything life throws at you. I've never felt like that, and I envy your ability to live full throttle so much. It makes me crazy.'

I smiled sadly. 'I've envied you. Your family, your normal life, your ability to not chase fame and fortune to fulfil yourself. I thought you were so content, so steady and stable. I guess the grass really is always greener, right?'

'You should have told me about you and Sean Sweeney,' Alex bit, clearly unwilling to let her anger go completely.

'You should have moved on from him a long time ago,' I countered.

'Maybe, but that's not the point.'

'But it is, Alex. It's exactly the point. In the grand scheme of things, he is so unimportant.'

'Then why have you been waiting for him to call you so desperately?'

'I guess I needed to believe that someone was going to come and rescue me! I wanted to truly believe that everything going wrong between Rory and me happened for a reason. That I was meant to be with Sean, and that's why my life is currently such a mess. That I had taken a wrong turn and chosen the wrong life, not that I had fucked it all up so royally.'

Alex nodded slowly, the truth dawning on her. 'And I've been using him as an excuse for never letting anyone else get close. Never wanting to get over him, because it would mean I had to move on. Look, Tara. There's something I haven't told you about me and Sean. I never told anybody except Darius, not even my mother. But . . . well, it's just that . . .'

She looked so forlorn, I was just about to reach across the bed for Alex's hand when all the machines started beeping.

'Code blue!' somebody called, and nurses immediately started rushing in with trolleys. I backed up against the window, feeling like time was standing still until a kid who barely looked old enough to be out of school appeared in front of me. 'Ms O'Toole, I'm sorry but you can't be here. I need you to wait outside.'

I nodded and obeyed, because he was wearing a white coat. Alex and I backed out of the room as our friend was swarmed with professionals trying to save his life.

32. Alex

Darius was taken into surgery. Dr Wilson's ominous warning that his heart could burst in his chest had come to pass, so the doctors rushed him to the OR. Tara and I ran next door and roused Francisco immediately. My parents, Jen and Brian rushed back to the hospital in the early hours when they were woken up by our frantic calls. We were sitting nervously in the communal waiting area, desperate for an update. Dr Wilson had been paged and scrubbed in somewhere around 2 a.m.; by the time the sun was coming up, we were all in various states of huddling and pacing.

At 7 a.m. Tara's stomach rumbled so loudly I heard it from across the room. I walked over to her then, ignoring the surprised looks from Jen and Mam. 'Come on,' I said. 'Let's go and get something to eat. I can't stand sitting here waiting. Someone will call us if there's any news. Right?' I directed the last part to my mother, who nodded emphatically.

'Go,' she ordered. 'It won't do any of us any good if one of you collapses from lack of sleep or food.'

Tara grudgingly stood up and let me lead the way to the cafeteria on the mezzanine level, which was just opening. I ordered us breakfast bagels and extra-large coffees and then joined her at a table by the railings overlooking a huge window where you could see the day dawning outside. It all felt unreal, like we were in a long, unrelenting nightmare.

'Darius is going to be okay, Tara,' I said, beckoning for her to start eating.

'He might not be okay, Alex. You have to face up to that.'

'I don't want to.'

'Well, tough. Shit happens. You have to learn to deal with it.'

'It's not that easy.' We lapsed into silence, both nibbling at our bagels. Mine tasted like cardboard.

'Darius is like a dad to me, you know,' Tara said suddenly. 'When my father checked out, he became my parent even though I thought I didn't need one. He was the one who came over and got me up in the mornings. I was so young and so scared, I don't know what I would have done without him.'

'You had me too, and my family. We were there for you.'

'It's not the same. You guys were a unit; everything you did was for each other. Darius and me, we didn't have proper families of our own, so we clung to one another.'

Was she trying to make out that she was closer to our friend than I was? 'Darius had Jen's family, her dad was his brother . . .'

'Darius had a brother who insisted on calling him Darren and never tried to understand him. Sometimes blood isn't thicker than water.'

'I love him just as much as you do, you know,' I said.

'It's not a competition, Alex,' Tara said gently. 'We both adore him.'

'But I've always felt in competition with you,' I blurted out. This was the second time I'd had verbal diarrhoea with Tara in the past few hours; my defences were clearly kaput. 'I always knew the competition was one-sided because you're Tara O'Toole, you were going to win. So I think eventually I just decided not to even compete. What would be the point?'

Tara slammed down her bagel. 'There you go again, giving up before you've even tried!'

'There was never any room for me when your light was shining, Tara! It's never been easy being your friend, you know.'

'Bullshit. You just wrote yourself off early because you never had any self-confidence.'

That stung, probably because it was true. 'You really think all my issues come down to low self-esteem?'

'Yes!' Tara cried, so loudly that everyone in the cafeteria

looked at us. I could see a few faces peering over, wondering if it was really her.

'You have never believed in yourself, Alex, and you've never been able to see yourself clearly. I was always in awe of your talent. Everybody was.'

'Then why didn't it feel like it?!' I cried. 'Nobody ever made a fuss of me! Nobody ever gave me any opportunities! I was always in your shadow.'

'Oh my god.' Tara's mouth was gaping open. 'You thought you were going to be handed a career!' She shook her head resolutely. 'Nobody is given anything in this business. You have to fight tooth and nail for absolutely every chance and nothing is ever guaranteed. But you try, if you love it. You keep trying.'

'I wasn't strong enough to try.'

'No, you just didn't bother.'

Her words hung between us, and I knew then that she was right. I didn't bother trying to become an actress, because it felt too hard. I told myself I didn't want to be a celebrity and I didn't envy Tara's lifestyle, but I could have gone a different route – Oliviers and Obies instead of Oscars and Tonys. The life of a working actor instead of a star.

'You're right,' I admitted. 'I wasn't brave enough.'

'It's not too late, you know,' Tara said simply. 'It's not over till it's over.'

'And what about you? Is it too late for you and Rory?'

She recoiled at the mention of his name but recovered quickly. 'Rory has made his choice. He's moved on. I guess I have to learn to be on my own.' She drooped then. 'I don't know how, though. It's so fucking scary.'

I took her hand. 'You're not alone. You have me.'

'Do I?' She looked right into my eyes.

Then I remembered I had one last thing to apologize for. 'I'm sorry about Xavier. I think it was all this pent-up emotion just exploding in the face of someone being kind to me. I never meant to sleep with your stepson. It's so fucked up.'

Tara sighed. 'He's a great guy, and he's clearly mad about you. You like him, don't you?'

I shrugged. 'He's lovely. He's hot. To paraphrase the great Shania Twain, man, I felt like a woman with him.' I smiled, but knew it didn't reach my eyes. 'But I'm so confused, Tara. I've never felt like this in my life. I don't know what I want.'

'It's a mess,' Tara agreed. 'But one we can clean up, if we want to. Do you think we can get past it all?'

'I don't know,' I said bluntly. 'But you've just ripped me a new one for never trying. So I guess we can try?'

She gave me a watery smile, and my heart lifted ever so slightly.

Both of our phones rang then, at almost the exact same time. We stared at them, unwilling to answer and hear something potentially life-altering.

'They'd text if it was good news,' Tara whispered.

'We don't know that.'

Both phones fell silent, like defused timebombs. 'They would text us now, telling us to come back. If they call again, it's bad news,' she said.

I couldn't bear the tension, the next few moments feeling like hours and milliseconds all at once. Then the phones started ringing again.

33. Tara

Darius died at 7.59 a.m. on Saturday, 5 April. Dr Wilson and her team did everything they could, but his poor heart was too badly damaged to save and the doctors had to let him go.

Due to my eerie premonition, Alex and I had mutually decided not to answer our phones, instead walking hand in hand back to the waiting room together to hear the unbearable news in person. When we got there Francisco was doubled over in grief, wailing, with Jen holding him. Deirdre looked at us both with raw devastation written all over her face, and we knew then that Darius was really gone.

Thank god for Lorraine, who had arrived while we were in the cafeteria and was business-like in her grief. She had after all buried her husband recently enough; she knew what needed to be done. Brian was really helpful too – Jen hadn't been joking when she said her undertaker husband knew the best morticians in New York City. He and Lorraine sprang into action, helping Francisco sort out paperwork, calling lawyers and basically taking the awful bureaucracy of death off all of our hands.

I'd barely let go of Alex since we got the news, and I was clutching her arm as we went in to see Darius one last time. He'd been tidied up, the wires and cables removed and the machines silenced. A kind nurse had combed his hair and he looked peaceful in a way he hadn't the night before when his damaged heart was still beating.

And yet I couldn't accept that Darius was actually gone; the finality was too overwhelming. The body didn't seem real, more like a realistic movie prop than my dear friend. It all felt like a cruel joke.

Alex was white as a ghost herself, her skin and lips leeched of all colour. She clung to Darius, weeping, while I felt utterly numb. There are unreal times in life when an actress wishes she had a script to tell her what to do, and this was definitely one of them.

Eventually it was time to leave the hospital. Stepping out into the brightness and bustle of Madison Avenue was disconcerting: life was going on around us while I felt caught in between worlds.

'Can we walk back to your place?' Alex asked. 'I need some air.'

'Yeah, let's go through the park. I mean, you're obviously coming back to stay, right?'

Alex nodded. 'If you'll have me.'

We were both beyond tired, like zombies in sweatpants as we plodded the paths of Central Park towards West 76th. I pulled my baseball cap low on my head just in case – I couldn't deal with a fan asking for a selfie.

It's actually a really nice walk from Mount Sinai to my apartment, taking in some of the highlights of my favourite green space in the city. It was a bright, clear morning and spring was in bloom; there were daffodils burgeoning at the base of old oak trees and the branches were budding. It felt so strange to see a new season thriving while Darius lay dead and cold in a hospital morgue. I shivered, and Alex noticed.

'It's crazy, isn't it? Life just going on without him.'

'It's utterly surreal.'

We walked in silence for a while. The route across the park took us past tennis courts where fit people wearing white were batting balls back and forth, and the waters of the reservoir shimmered in the sunshine. As we approached a playground full of boisterous children, I idled for a second, suddenly feeling winded. I felt Alex sliding sideways looks at me.

'It was so good of Rory to organize the plane,' she said.

'It was good of Xav to ask him to.'

'They're top-notch guys, those Vaughans.'

'Are you going to keep seeing Xav?' I was blunt, too tired not to be.

'I don't know. Are you going to talk to Rory?'

When I didn't reply, she continued. 'I don't think the door is closed there, Tara. He still cares about you too much.'

I'd been thinking the same thing, but my brain felt too full to give it any proper thought. So much had gone on, and everything was different now. 'He's a good, kind man, Alex. I'm not surprised he wanted to help. He loves . . . loved Darius too. I can't keep thinking that every nice thing he does means he wants me back, and I don't even know if I could forgive him. It doesn't change anything between us, you know?'

'What went on between you two seems to have been a terrible case of miscommunication. From my inexperienced vantage point, anyway.'

'It's not just that. I can't give him what he wants, which is another child.'

'You guys were fine before having a baby came into it. You said yourself, you wanted it more than Rory. Anyway, if he really, truly wanted to raise a baby with you, I don't think it would matter how the child came to be. Somewhere along the way, you guys stopped talking and started guessing what the other wanted.'

I watched the kids whizz down the slide one by one. 'Do you know the official name of this space?'

Alex looked at me quizzically.

'The Diana Ross playground. As in, *the* Diana Ross. Only in New York, I swear,' I said. 'No wonder Darius loved it here so much – this city is as camp and eccentric as him.'

'If you could have a kid tomorrow, would you do it?' Alex was direct, and not letting me get away with changing the subject.

I hesitated. 'I don't really let myself think like that.'

'Well, think about it now. If you could click your fingers and have a child to raise even all by yourself, would you?'

'Yes,' I answered instantly, surprising myself. 'I would.'

'Then why don't you? Tara, lots of women adopt. Look at Sandra Bullock! Charlize Theron, too. Madonna! You wouldn't be the first A-lister to give an abandoned child a dream life.'

'What if I was bad at it?' I whispered.

'Bad at what? Do you honestly think a child would be worse off with you than in the system? You're an amazing stepmom – I know you'd be brilliant. Darius would tell you that you could do it, Tara.'

'Darius would have helped.' A tear slid down my face.

'Eventually.' Alex looked thoughtful. 'He wasn't keen on babies and toddlers. Too sticky.'

A laugh escaped me, because she was right. Darius had no time for small kids pulling his hair or smearing his clothes. 'But as soon as they were coordinated, my god. He would have stage-mothered them to within an inch of their life.'

We smiled at each other sadly. 'Darius is the reason we know each other, you know,' Alex said.

'Do you think he knows we made up?'

'I think he was waiting for it.'

The next few days passed in a blur. In Dublin, funerals happen quickly and are the kind of occasions where everyone is welcome. My dad used to tell a story when I was young about his late cousin's mistress showing up to his burial and releasing a flock of homing pigeons at the graveside to make her presence felt. They had met at a club for racing birds and carried on for more than a decade behind his wife's back. I'd always admired her refusal to hide away, and the story had grown legs over the years. The last time I'd heard it, she'd trained a pigeon to attack the grieving widow. Good old Irish whispers.

In New York, though, it's a different story. Funerals are a lot more formal, invite-only and there are myriad options when the departed is an atheist, as Darius was. He'd left instructions on file with his attorney and his requests had been both outlandish and unsurprising. He wanted his wake to take place at the renowned Frank E. Campbell funeral chapel on the Upper East Side and for his remains to arrive in a horse-drawn carriage. Darius wished to be cremated, with half of the ashes to be scattered along the Royal Canal in Dublin by Deirdre and half to be kept by his husband in New York.

This all meant waiting for a day that his preferred suite at the funeral parlour was free. We also had to allow time for friends and relatives to fly in from the UK and Ireland, and Francisco's loved ones from Brazil, and the days were spent making arrangements, greeting those who arrived and trying to keep ourselves from burning out before the big send-off.

In his letter of wishes upon his death, Darius had requested that both Alex and I do readings, something that touched me, until I learned what had been planned. Alex had been asked to compose an original poem, 'like the sad one in *Four Weddings and a Funeral* that makes everyone sob'. For me, Darius had chosen the famous 'All the World's a Stage' monologue from *As You Like It.*

I was fuming – he knew well that I struggled with ye olde English and iambic pentameter and that Alex was the more natural choice for Shakespeare. Having her write a poem was hard work, and I knew she was panicking about doing him justice. Then I realized that's exactly why Darius had asked for this. To push us both out of our comfort zones, as he always had when he was alive.

I held a small reception for immediate family and close friends in my apartment on the morning of the service. We were all wearing purple, as decreed by the departed. Darius had once attended a memorial in Thailand and had been taken by the beauty of the traditional colour donned by mourners there. I remembered him telling us about it at the time, laughing as he declared the shade 'so much more chic than Grim Reaper black, darling'.

Shanice had leapt into action, armed with my credit card, dressing all of us in various shades of mulberry, plum, amethyst and violet, and everyone looked fantastic. I was wearing a particularly extravagant hat by Philip Treacy, and Alex was actually managing to walk in high heels. I hoped Darius could see us, and that he approved.

The inner circle assembled was a motley crew: me, Francisco, Storm and Xav, Alex and her parents, Jen and her mother, Angela, Brian, Lorraine, two senior staffers from The Scene and Ethel, his elderly Irish aunt. Francisco hadn't wanted his own family present. He was delighted that they'd made the journey for the service out of love for him but felt that this gathering was for those who truly knew and adored Darius. 'My parents, they tolerated our relationship but never considered us properly married, not in the eyes of God. They can meet us at the funeral home. That's enough.'

The widower had done a stunning job on the flowers – Francisco's own way of sending off his husband in style. There were ostentatious blooms in pink and purple everywhere, waiting to be loaded into the carriage with the coffin. Francisco was fussing with the florals now, and we were letting him – it was something to keep his mind occupied when he was unwilling and unable to give in to the enormity of the occasion.

Deirdre was pouring champagne for everyone, as Bollinger had been another request. After a little while, Brian clinked his glass to silence everyone. Darius had specifically not wanted to be eulogized in front of everyone, but for his nearest and dearest to share memories of him together before the ceremony.

Lorraine began. 'I met Darius when he first moved to New York, and I adored him on sight. He was a huge presence everywhere he went, not just because of his physical size but because he had a personality that was larger than life. Knowing him has changed me for the better, and I will never forget him. I'll also never forget that he told me he chose the Frank E. Campbell funeral home for the service because it's a great place to meet well-heeled men. Even planning for his own departure, he wanted to make sure the single girls, gays and theys in his life had opportunities.'

We all laughed softly and clinked glasses. Stories followed from everyone present. Alex told the tale of when she went mute with fear onstage when we were fourteen, and how her first thought had been about disappointing Darius.

'It was *Pygmalion*, and every word of Eliza Doolittle's dialogue just left my head. All I could remember were the songs from *My Fair Lady*! I was standing there like a deer in the headlights.' She dipped her head, a tear slipping down her cheek. 'I couldn't see Darius, but I could feel him willing me to get it together from the wings. Eventually, Tara as Mrs Higgins stepped in and finished the scene by herself. When I ran offstage I was so worried he'd be angry with me, but Darius just pulled me into one of his famous hugs and reassured me next time would be better.'

Deirdre recalled her best friend throughout the stages of his life, which had all of us in bits. 'He used to always tell me the men I fancied weren't good enough for me, that I could do much better. He didn't say that when I met Eamonn,' she recalled, squeezing her husband's hand in a tender gesture that made my stomach contract with loneliness. 'In fact, before long he was saying Eamonn was *too* good for me.'

My favourite part was eighty-nine-year-old Aunt Ethel from Dublin recalling a time Darius had requested to borrow her high heels aged seven. 'He was fabulous then, and he'll be fabulous for ever,' she wept. 'He never wanted to be called Darren – he liked the name Darius because it means "to maintain possessions well". Even as a little boy, he had a deep love of and respect for beautiful things. I didn't think I'd outlive him, and I'm sad that I have. To Darius.' We raised our glasses again, and I thought how lucky Darius had been to have a glam, liberal dame like Ethel in his corner as a child.

I didn't know what to say. For once, I was unprepared, but the story that came to me just felt natural. 'When my mother first got sick, Darius wouldn't let me sit around and pout about it. He told me that crying would give me acne, and anyway, there was nothing to cry about yet. I learned later that he was well aware of Gloria's prognosis – the cancer had been advanced when it was discovered, but he didn't want me to waste time grieving my mother while she was still alive. He spent hours on end with us, watching old Barbra Streisand musicals on DVD and listening to CDs he'd burned full of her favourite show-tunes. He never let on that she wasn't going to be okay. Darius was there for me in a way I couldn't, and still can't, comprehend at the worst time in my life. And then he just never stopped being there. He was like a father to me, and I'll miss him more than I can say.'

Jen was last to speak. Her own father had passed on during the pandemic, and Darius had been distraught not to be able to travel home for his older brother's funeral. She was just about holding it together. 'Darius never felt like a grown-up to me, always like a mischievous older brother. Much older, obviously. It feels unreal and unfair that he's been taken from us so soon, but I'm happy we could all be here together to celebrate my inimitable Uncle Dar so perfectly, just as he wished. The world is less glitzy without him in it, but he left such a mark on so many people. He'd have absolutely loved this send-off, and he'd want us all to get absolutely rat-arsed as well. So, let's go say goodbye and then get on with fulfilling his wishes.'

We formed a procession, all fourteen of us squeezing into the lift together holding flower arrangements above our heads. When we got downstairs, we collectively gasped at the sight of a magnificent black steed decked out with a purple feathered headpiece, and then felt the gut punch of seeing the mahogany coffin it was pulling for the first time.

We stood there in silence, paying our respects, before getting into the waiting limousines. Just as Brian had finished loading the flowers and was about to corral us, the horse let out a loud whinny and promptly took an enormous dump on the street.

I froze, mortified, and looked around the group open-mouthed. Then Francisco started to laugh loudly, and Deirdre joined in. Before long, we were all doubled over at this strange, shared merriment on such an awful day. It was so Irish, and so needed.

If there had been any lightness infused into an unbearable morning, it was quickly diffused as soon as we landed at the funeral home. As Alex and I entered the suite, already half full, we both looked up and sucked in our breath at the same time. There, decked out all in black, because he didn't bother himself with the details, was Sean Sweeney.

34. Alex

I sensed Sean before I saw him and nearly stumbled, but Tara had a firm grip on my clammy hand and didn't let me fall. She must have clocked him too but was paying him absolutely no heed, so I decided to follow suit.

Still, my body reacted as it always has to him – nauseous, aroused, nervous. I broke out in a cold sweat all over. For one split second my grief-addled brain was convinced he was there for me, and my heart soared. Quickly, I realized the truth – Francisco would have invited him, along with the other That's D'Amore alumni. Sean wasn't even glancing in my direction. Nor Tara's, interestingly.

Of course, it made absolute sense that Sean *should* be there – he and Darius had remained close – but it hadn't occurred to me that he would bother to show up, and I was wholly unprepared to be in the same room as him.

I hadn't thought about Sean much in the preceding days. The week since Darius died felt like we were all playing pretend as we waited to lay him to rest, and then I'd been thrown for a loop with my assignment from beyond the grave and fretting about writing this ode to my friend. I was sleeping at Tara's, in her bed; she and I were spending time together reminiscing, bawling and watching old videos of our That's D'Amore performances. When teenage Sean popped up onscreen, we said nothing. Seeing the real Sean Sweeney in person for the first time in eighteen years was a different experience altogether, and I wasn't prepared for how it made me feel. All of a sudden, I was twenty again and assailed by every emotion I'd experienced that year. An urgency came over me, and I squeezed Tara's hand so tightly she got a fright.

'Ow, Jesus! Alex, what's wrong?'

'Bathroom,' I muttered, making a break for the ladies as fast as my stupid purple high heels could carry me.

'Alex, what is it?' Tara was flustered as she joined me by the sinks. 'They're about to bring the coffin in. Oh my god, you're hyperventilating. Calm down, it's only a bloody poem!'

'I need to tell you something,' I wheezed, 'because Darius was the only other person in the world who knows about it, and he's gone. If I don't tell you now, it will be like it never happened, or even worse, like I imagined it. Sean's here, and nothing feels real, and I just have to get this out, okay?'

Tara nodded, her eyes wide.

'It wasn't just a lost weekend with me and Sean, Tara. He got me pregnant.'

I didn't notice that my period was late. It was always patchy, known to disappear in times of high stress throughout my adolescence, so I was never in thrall to my cycle. I had been stressed – Sean's ghosting and then having to tell Tara I broke our pact about him had each taken their toll. I was glad to have summer in the rear-view, to be back in college facing my third year. Academia soothed me, as did the autumn.

It was in a French tutorial in early October that I suddenly felt an urgent need to vomit. I never wanted to make a fuss, but I couldn't stop what was happening and practically ran from the room, just making it in time to the closest bathroom stall. Weird, I thought. I must have eaten something dodgy at lunch. I felt a lot better once I'd been sick, so I went back to class and forgot about it.

Then this propulsive desire to throw up happened again the next day. And then again the day after that. It was then that something horrifying clicked. No, I couldn't be . . . could I? Sean and I had been careful . . . ish. I scrabbled at my wall calendar, searching desperately for the familiar red marker dot I used to track my wayward periods. The last one had been at the beginning of August.

I felt sick then for an entirely different reason, but tried to convince myself everything was fine. I couldn't be pregnant; we'd used condoms. I mean, maybe we were a bit slap-dash with them when fornicating in a field, but no . . . it would be so horribly unlucky if they hadn't worked. This sort of thing didn't happen to girls like me.

I bought a pregnancy test in Boots in town where nobody would know me and tested in the loos in Brown Thomas for the same reason. I peed on the stick and sat there, listening to posh ladies making small talk while they waited their turn. When it was positive, I felt oddly calm. I was the least likely person I knew to get pregnant by an errant rock star. There must be a mistake.

Three more conclusive tests later, my student bank account was empty and my situation clear. I was definitely with child; I had been knocked up and abandoned, and I was absolutely terrified.

More than that, I was furious with myself. Why hadn't I been more careful? I should have tried to get the morning-after pill, difficult and mortifying as it was. And booked an STI test! Sean was probably riddled, I thought bitterly. Normally I was the type of person who took no chances in any situation, but everything about my behaviour with Sean had been uncharacteristic. And now this.

I couldn't tell my mother. I was mute with shock and horror at the mere thought, knowing it would break her heart. She was so proud of me studying at Trinity, and my parents had such high hopes for their only child. How could I possibly finish my degree with a baby? How could I get a job while looking after an infant? It was too much to even think about, letting them down because of a moment – okay, several moments – of blind, chaotic lust.

And I couldn't even blame naïvety. As a midwife, Deirdre had been lecturing me about safe sex and avoiding a crisis pregnancy before I even began menstruating. 'I see so many young girls in trouble, Alex,' she told me, shaking her head. 'Children raising children, and their lives are never the same again. Or else taking a horrible flight across the Irish Sea, and then coming in to us because they're scared and bleeding. The second you even think about having sex, you come to me and I'll get you on the pill. Do you hear me? Here are some condoms, just in case.'

'Mam, I'm fourteen!'

'Better safe than sorry!'

I hadn't heeded her. I was a late bloomer, and then I didn't want to do anything that would interfere with my body – I remembered friends having wild mood swings when they started taking hormonal contraception.

Well, weren't you very clever, Alex? I thought nastily to myself. An unwanted pregnancy will certainly interfere with your precious body, you fool.

Distraught, I did the only thing I could think of and went to Darius.

'Alex, are you sure?' His face was grey.

'The tests are all positive. I've taken four of them.'

'Do you know how far along you are?'

'The festival was the last weekend in August, whatever that means.'

'Oh, sweetheart. Well, we better get you checked out. Find out what your options are.'

'I don't have any options!' I cried. 'This is Ireland, remember? I have to have this baby.'

'There are always options, Alex.'

Darius made me an appointment at the Coombe – Deirdre had friends in Holles Street, and the Rotunda was out of the question – and came with me a week later. The throwing-up had stopped by then, but I felt nauseous constantly and had a dull ache in my back. Darius rubbed it soothingly as we waited;

we had concocted a story about unusual bleeding in case we ran into an acquaintance in the hospital halls.

'Have you got in touch with Sean yet?' Darius asked.

'No!' I whirled on him. 'And you are not to tell him a single thing! If he didn't answer my phone calls and texts before, he definitely won't want to now.'

'Alex, it's his responsibility as much as yours.'

'He doesn't give a fuck about responsibility, Darius. This is my problem, and I'll kill you if you as much as google him to see where in the world the fucker is.'

Darius held up his hands, my wishes clear.

Completely drained, I dragged myself into the consultation room to be examined, answering the doctor's questions mechanically. Yes, my period was irregular. No, the father was not in the picture.

'Let's see how many weeks you are,' the doctor said, pity in her eyes as she squeezed cold jelly on to my bare stomach. It was still flat, not yet betraying what was going on inside my body to the outside world.

She frowned as she ran the probe across my abdomen, pressing down here and there uncomfortably to get a better look. 'Alex, I'm going to have to do a different type of scan. I'm not able to see very well with the external ultrasound so I need to conduct a trans-vaginal examination. Try to relax for me, love.'

I closed my eyes and tried my best to think of a happy place, to escape from the present moment. Finally the doctor withdrew the device and placed her hand on my shoulder. I opened my eyes and saw concern in hers. 'Alex, I'm not getting a heartbeat.'

For a moment, I thought she meant from me, and it made sense – I felt completely dead inside. Then I realized she was talking about the baby. 'What does that mean?'

'I can't say for sure, but a heartbeat should be present, considering the dates of conception, and I'm not seeing one – see here, on the screen? It should be flickering. This can mean a few different things, so I want to take some blood to run a few more tests, okay? And I'm going to have to have another doctor come and examine you as well. Don't worry, she's lovely.'

I went through the same process as well with another, younger doctor, but the blood draw was the worst part because I'm terrified of needles. I insisted Darius be there to hold my hand, but the second the nurse pierced my vein I must have passed out. I came to in his arms on the bed. I lay there and he held me tight, making soothing noises for I don't know how long.

Eventually the original doctor returned. 'I'm really very sorry to tell you, Alex, but you've had what we call a silent miscarriage. We concur that, with what we can see on ultrasound and your blood results, this pregnancy hasn't survived.'

'So, what . . .' I blinked. 'It's just . . . not alive any more?'

She looked at me gravely. 'I'm afraid not.'

'When did this happen?'

'It's difficult to say. It could have been quite recent, days ago even.'

I didn't know what to feel. Part of me was relieved, because I wouldn't have to tell my mother. Part of me was devastated, because Sean and I had created something together and it had died. Mostly, I felt guilty for not wanting to be pregnant – had I wished the baby away? Did it know I was distraught at the idea of it? Was this all my fault? I felt pain then, all over. Even my brain felt sore.

Darius sprang into action. 'What are the next steps?'

'Because of the early stage of pregnancy, my colleague and I agree we can deal with this medically. I'm going to give Alex a tablet to take that will pass the foetus, so she doesn't have to have a D&C, but she will have to be monitored at home for complications and brought back in if there's anything unusual.'

'What do you mean, pass the foetus?'

'Well, Mr D'Amore, the uterus will have to expel the

pregnancy and this medicine will help it along. It'll be like a very heavy, painful period . . .'

I tuned her out, then. All I could think was that nobody else could ever know this had happened.

I allowed Darius to guide me out of the hospital, clutching some pills. He drove me to his house, where I took them robotically, and then heard him on the phone to my mother telling her we were having a good old-fashioned sleepover. 'No, she's absolutely fine!' he trilled, putting in a wonderful performance. 'I just bumped into her in town, and we both fancied a night of ice cream and musicals. Of course I'll mind her, Dee, don't fret. She's twenty years old, not five. I might even get her pissed!'

The pains were getting worse, and my stomach was in agony. I felt a steady, hot trickle between my legs, so I went to the bathroom, where I attached one of the massive pads the doctor had given me to my knickers. I don't know how long I sat there on the toilet, hunched over – I was terrified of standing up, of seeing something I didn't want to see. I just wanted all this to be over.

After a long while, Darius knocked at the door. 'Are you in a lot of pain, sweetheart? The doc prescribed nice strong tablets for you. I'd take them myself for a buzz, if I wasn't a responsible adult.'

I pulled up my pants and stood, feeling both dizzy and winded by the intense cramps. I opened the door and accepted another pill and a glass of water, and trudged into the sitting room, where I lay curled up on the cheetah-print sofa that was Darius's pride and joy.

He was watching me cautiously, but pretending everything was fine and wittering on largely to himself. 'Will we watch a movie, Alex? Barbra Streisand works in any situation! Or maybe you're not in the mood for singing . . . and maybe not a love story . . . I've got it! We'll watch *ET*. Safe as houses.'

As he busied himself with the DVD, I felt the edges of my consciousness start to dull. By the time Elliott discovered the alien in his shed, I had rolled over and fallen into a dreamless sleep.

'Why didn't you tell me?'

Tara was gaping at me, her huge purple hat dominating the small bathroom.

'I didn't know how to. You were so busy. You were far away. Obviously, I would have eventually, had there been anything to tell. But it was just . . . gone. Problem solved.'

'Would you have kept it? If you could?'

'Oh, Tara, I don't know! I didn't have to decide, did I? It was decided for me.'

'And nobody else knew? Not your mam, not Sean?'

I scoffed. 'As if he'd have cared! And no, I never told my mother. Only Darius. I don't exactly like thinking or talking about it, even now.'

Tara looked shell-shocked, just like I felt. I hadn't known I was going to tell her about the miscarriage. A sudden urge to confess all to her had come over me when we were alone in the hospital together, but fate had chosen that moment to take Darius from us. Rattled, I hadn't dared bring it up again.

It was seeing Sean that compelled me to tell Tara now, with an urgency to unburden myself immediately.

'In a way, it all makes sense,' she said. 'A horrible, awful sort of sense. Oh, Alex.'

Just then, the ladies' room door slammed open. Jen stood there in her mauve rigout looking angry. 'What the fuck are you two up to? The funeral is about to start – the coffin is idling in the hallway, for god's sake!' Then she clocked my face. 'What's going on? Alex, are you all right? It's only a poem, for god's sake!'

I managed a nod. 'It's . . . I . . .'

'We'll tell you after the service,' Tara said, springing into action and hustling poor Jen out of the room. 'Alex, do you think you're going to be okay? We have to do this now, for Darius.'

I exhaled, forcing myself to return fully to the present, and gave myself a little shake. 'Yes. I feel . . . not better, but better for telling you. Does that make sense?'

'Absolutely.' She took me by the hand and we walked out together.

It was a gorgeous service, just as Darius had planned. The funeral party followed down the aisle behind the coffin, which was another break from New York tradition. Darius wanted the drama of an Irish entrance, pallbearers carrying him to the front as chief mourners followed. A former student, a soprano named Gillian, was giving a powerful rendition of 'Over the Rainbow' – the Judy Garland version, of course. People were already bawling as we took our seats up the front, which was the desired effect.

Gazing upon Sean for a second time didn't hit me quite so hard in the solar plexus; in fact, I felt able to sneak looks at him from across the room, to take him in from thirty feet away. He was shorter than I remembered.

I saw then that it wasn't just Sean who had made the journey – his mother and two of the other lads from Higher Power were there, too. I recognized one of them, Ciaran, from That's D'Amore, and then saw clusters of other past pupils standing around the room, both older and younger than us. I was touched so many students had come so far, but that was the Darius effect.

I noticed Tara's publicist, Giulia, was there, and her mate David from LA. Shanice and Samuel, too, and Jordan Jones. Our friends old and new had come to support us, and it made me feel ever so slightly less frightened.

The room was jam-packed with purple-clad mourners, despite being the biggest the funeral home had to offer. Darius had insisted that the coffin would remain firmly closed, but there was a lovely photo of him placed on top of the casket from his wedding day, and it was exactly how I'd try to remember him.

Francisco stood up, supported by his very glamorous mother, and thanked everyone for coming. 'My husband was the great love of my life. I didn't know I could be so happy with another person until I met Darius, and I will miss him every day until I die.' He hung his head. 'He didn't believe in an afterlife, but I believe that I will see my Darius again someday. If I get my way, heaven will be a Broadway theatre with a standing ovation for my beautiful husband every night.'

Francisco sat back down, and Mam, who was acting as master of ceremonies, introduced Tara.

I knew my friend was nervous about reciting Shakespeare, but Tara looked every inch the movie star she was, her waist cinched to the gods and her enormous hat giving the drama Darius would have wanted.

Tara had memorized her monologue and, like any good actor, she gave it socks. Near the end, as she got to the part about a world too wide for his shrunk shank, she seemed to startle at the sight of something at the back.

I didn't have long to wonder why, because it was my turn to read. Unlike Tara, I wasn't looking up from the script because I was too afraid of catching Francisco's eye and bawling like a baby.

'For Darius,' I managed, taking a deep breath.

He's gone too soon, but it would have always been too soon.
The world's too quiet – I keep listening for that distinctive boom.
He filled up every space, in every room, unsubtle as an ostentatious bloom.

Never sure what to call him, but he was the best.
More than friend, more like family, more than the rest.
He held my deepest secrets close to his chest, lived and loved with zest.

How do I go on without his light? Even these words
feel trite.
He was passion, talent, gusto burning bright.
He was human, flawed, adored, nearly always right.

I chanced looking up and saw instantly what had thrown Tara. Standing in the back with Xavier and Storm was Rory Vaughan, handsome and solemn in a dark suit and tie. I gulped and continued, realizing as I read how Tara must be feeling. There's no funeral when a marriage is over, no public mourning. You just have to get on with it.

All we can do now is carry on as if he's still here.
Carry with us what we've learned, love as if he's always near.
Miss him every day that dawns anew, force ourselves to
persevere.
He's gone, and without him we are lost.
But knowing – loving – him was worth the cost.

When I finished, there wasn't a dry eye in the house except my own. I felt proud then, that I'd done Darius justice. My mother came up and gave me a squeeze, before announcing that refreshments and drinks would be served in the reception room and thanking the congregation again. I walked straight to Tara in the front row and fell into her arms, allowing myself only then to briefly fall apart and sob.

'I can't believe it,' Jen said, shaking her head. The three of us were still in our seats in the suite, deep in a hushed conversation as mourners mingled next door. I'd whispered the sorry tale of loss in its entirety for only the second time in my life, and the three of us wept quietly together as guests ate miniature bagels and drank champagne mere feet away. 'Alex, you poor, poor thing.'

I nodded. 'It took a really long time for me to acknowledge how traumatic the miscarriage was, even to call it that.'

'Is that why you went to France after Christmas that year?' Jen asked.

'I guess so. I just wanted to be far away. A semester on Erasmus in Lyon sounded perfect, but god, I was so lonely once I got there. I was also in complete denial that anything had actually happened. In my mind I was pregnant for about a week, and then before I had to decide anything, I wasn't again.'

'I can't imagine it,' Jen said. 'For all my messing in life, I've only ever been pregnant when I wanted to be.'

I felt Tara stiffen, so I moved things along. 'I think it's why I ended up moving to London after college too, you know. I didn't want to live somewhere with memories of it all. I threw myself into work and for years I was able to forget. Then I started having very bad panic attacks around the time you met Rory, remember?' I said to Tara, who nodded.

'Well, I started going to therapy when they became debilitating – I had one on the Tube once and was convinced I was going to die. I couldn't breathe, and my NHS doc referred me once he figured out it wasn't a physical issue. After a lot of work on myself, everything I'd been through began to come out in fits and starts. The counsellor diagnosed a generalized anxiety disorder but also PTSD, which I thought was crazy. I was under the impression then that only soldiers had that, from combat situations. The more I read up on it, I realized she was right. The whole experience of abandonment and then loss was very traumatic, and in trying to run from it all, I made things even worse.'

'Alex, you must have been so scared. No wonder . . .' Tara trailed off, and I let out a little guffaw at her suddenly guilty expression.

'No wonder I've been living in arrested development ever since? Does it all make sense now?'

'Well, I wouldn't say that exactly,' she said, but stopped once she saw my wry smile.

'No, Tara, you were right when you said that, even if you were being a bitch. I have been scared of living my life. A part of me is still twenty, abandoned, pregnant, terrified and madly in love with the boy who knocked me up and then fucked off. The girl whose baby died before she even had a chance to decide if she wanted it or not.' I sounded bitter, even to my own ears, but it felt so good to tell my closest friends the truth I'd been holding so tight to my chest. 'I'm still angry too. I think on some level I always hoped Sean would eventually come back to me, and I could tell him what happened. Once he got all the rock-star stuff out of his system, you know? We could be together, and all the trauma wouldn't have been worth it exactly, but it would have all made some sense.'

The girls nodded silently, unused to me being so open.

'That's why I wouldn't let Darius call him at the time – I wanted Sean to come back to me on his own. Then I thought he was finally going to, nearly eighteen years later.' My voice broke. 'I thought it was clear to him now, that he'd loved me all along without realizing. Even though there's no child, we could start over and just be happy. Jesus, our baby would be seventeen now. Can you imagine? My life would have been so completely different.'

Sometimes I allowed myself to imagine the child that might have been. Would it have been a boy or a girl? Would it have been blonde like me, or dark-haired like its father? Would it have been musical, talented in the arts? Then I remembered there was no point in wondering, because it hadn't happened. It was a world of possibilities stolen away.

Tara shook her head. 'Alex, I'm so sorry. I had absolutely no idea. I'm distraught I wasn't there for you, and had I known anything, I never would have carried on with him . . .'

I swatted away her apology. 'No, of course you wouldn't, but you didn't know because I didn't tell you. So I can't exactly be on my high horse about keeping secrets, can I?'

Jen's phone pinged then; a message from Brian. 'He's asking me to kindly get my ass outside and talk to the guests at the reception. He's stuck with Francisco's auntie.' She put her arm around my shoulders and gave me a firm kiss on the forehead. 'We have lots more talking to do on this subject, yes?'

I nodded. 'I'm only sorry it's taken me this long.'

Tara and I watched Jen stroll out into the crowd, always so at ease in herself. I envied her that comfort, that confidence. I felt hot and sweaty and cold and clammy all at once, and my hands were still shaking. But then Tara enclosed them in her own.

'Do you think you'll be able to face going out there if I'm there with you? It will mean facing Sean, more than likely.'

I nodded again, summoning a courage I didn't fully feel. 'Do you know what, Tara? I think it's about time I did.'

35. Tara

It didn't take long for Sean to pop up in front of us, like an apparition. It was so strange seeing him up close and in motion, this man I hadn't laid eyes on in twelve years but was now seeing in a whole new light after Alex's revelation. It was bizarre to realize that he had actually aged, like the mere mortal he was, pushing forty now, with thready wrinkles on his forehead and laughter lines around his eyes. He had no idea what might have been, and I felt sort of sorry for him and furious with him at the same time.

Sean was wearing a tight cashmere polo T-shirt and high-waisted trousers, and was still hot, of course. In real life, though, his painted nails and cartoonish tattoos looked a little bit ridiculous in such a sombre setting. The thought crossed my mind that he could've laid off the rock-star shtick for one afternoon, but I guess that's not really how it works.

When he leaned in to kiss Alex and then me, I felt her wobble beside me as I offered him my cheek and tightened my grip around her waist. Sean smelled of Gucci Pour Homme, an upgrade from his Cool Water days, but also cigarette smoke and . . . hash? Was this eejit stoned at a funeral?

'I'm so sorry, girls,' he said, looking between us. 'I loved Dar – the man was a legend. I just want to say, if it's not very inappropriate, that you both look absolutely stunning.'

There was that old charm, oozing out of every pore, but I wasn't letting him get away with it.

'You've a nerve, licking up to us after all your troublemaking,' I hissed under my breath, but kept my expression outwardly serene.

Sean looked perturbed. 'What? Me?'

'Yes, you. Do you not recall putting me on blast in your little book? The media circus that ensued?'

'Ah, Tara, I don't remember half of what I said in that book. I was jarred for most of the interviews.'

He looked so innocent I believed him. I had enough experience of famous people to know that he likely considered himself too busy and important to read the memoir bearing his name and life story.

'What about going on *Kelly Clarkson* and saying you were still in love with a girl back home from your past? Did you or your publicist not think that might lead back to me as well? I should sue, you little bastard.' I was inordinately angry with him, and I knew it wasn't about me, but on Alex's behalf.

He gulped. 'Uhh, yeah, well, that might have been accidentally on purpose. Look, I had books to sell. There were loads of girls from way back when – you were only two possible candidates. I knew you wouldn't have to actually confirm or deny anything.'

He was still beaming at both of us, attempting to worm his way out of any acrimony with his winning celebrity smile. Part of me wanted to smack the smugness out of him, and part of me wanted to smile back. I couldn't help it. That's the effect Sean has on people.

I looked at Alex and saw a pained smile painted on her face. I couldn't imagine what she was feeling. Then something seemed to click with her, and her complexion flushed.

'So you *were* full of shit, then?' she exclaimed, and Sean gaped at her. 'You did some real damage with your big mouth, do you know that?'

'I wouldn't say I was full of shit exactly. A man never forgets his early conquests, but, er, I'm kinda seeing someone pretty high profile and I wanted to throw the press off the scent. You girls didn't really mind, did you?' His eyes were a bit bloodshot and he had a dopey grin on his face. Yep, definitely stoned.

I caught Alex's eye, and the two of us started giggling. Within seconds we were hysterical, all the emotion of her confession and our grief mingling and combusting in laughter.

'What?' Sean asked, his eyes widening at our frenzy. 'Don't laugh. Look, it's actually a member of the royal family. The British royal family, and quite high up. Hey, it's not funny!'

Alex and I were howling, his protestations falling on deaf ears. It was suddenly hilarious, that we'd been squabbling like children over this absolute fool, while he'd been riding a blue-blood Brit on the DL. Poor Alex had never got over Sean, not because she was emotionally immature but because of so much I'd never known. It was awful and chaotic and unbearable, and we were frenzied. I clung to her and laughed until I wept, until Sean got sick of our carry-on and stalked off.

Then I looked up and stopped laughing. Alex was still going like a hyena as Rory took Sean's place in front of us.

'Oh, Jesus! Excuse me,' Alex breathed, her giggles abruptly subsiding as she realized I was face to face with my estranged husband. She released my hand and stumbled off as best she could in her ridiculous shoes, and I was left alone with Rory for the first time in weeks.

Had it really only been weeks? It had been what . . . a couple of months since the incident in London, yet it felt like much longer. When was the last time I had seen Rory clearly before that? Maybe it had even been years since we'd stood eye to eye and really looked at one another.

I couldn't really take him in up close; he looked so familiar, yet also like a complete stranger. He was wearing his funeral suit, a tailored Tom Ford number he's had for ever, and I wondered when he'd taken it from the apartment.

'Storm fetched the suit for me,' he said, and I realized I must have been frowning noticeably at his lapels.

'Th—thank you for coming,' I managed, all semblance of togetherness leaving me at the sight of him. 'And for everything you did for the family this past couple of weeks.'

He nodded. Rory was so tall and startlingly handsome, but he looked tired. He had bristly stubble on his chin, the kind I knew he hated. I wondered if it was a new addition to please his younger girlfriend. My heart ached then, because I longed to reach out and stroke it, but it was no longer my place.

'Can we talk, do you think?' Rory's voice was gruff, but his eyes were soft. I was already exhausted from Alex's revelation, but I heard Darius in my head saying I might as well be hung for a sheep as for a lamb. Our friend would also want to know about every word exchanged, so I hoped he was nearby somehow and had the ability to listen in from the great beyond.

'Do you want to get out of here?' I offered.

'No, there are photographers outside. I'm sure we can find an empty room.'

With that he strode off through the crowd and there was nothing else to do but follow him.

Down the corridor he tried a couple of doors, and when one eventually opened he ushered me inside. It was dimly lit, and as my eyes adjusted I realized we weren't alone.

'Rory!' I hissed. 'There's a body in here!'

'Shit! Well, it is a fucking funeral parlour.' He started laughing then, and my body betrayed me by joining in. I was still on the brink of hysteria.

'Look, at least the casket is closed and it's quiet. I don't mind if you don't?' His eyes were pleading, so I gave in.

I walked up to the coffin and read the order of ceremonies aloud. This woman's service had taken place earlier that morning; she had been ninety-two and was survived by her husband of sixty-six years.

'Sixty-six years.' Rory whistled under his breath. 'That's some going.'

I wasn't in the mood for laughing or joking with him then. That could have been us, together until we were old and grey, if we hadn't stopped talking to one another. I walked away and sat down in the first row of fold-up chairs, trying to keep my emotions in check long enough to have what appeared to be a necessary conversation with my soon-to-be ex-husband.

I wanted to be civil, convivial even. Yet when I looked up at him I felt overcome with poison and spite.

'Didn't bring Allegra with you, then? Funerals probably aren't her scene – the dress code must be too restrictive for someone who likes to wear so little.'

'It's over with her.'

That stunned me. 'Oh . . .'

'It's been over for a while. It wasn't about Allegra. It was never about Allegra, Tara.'

'Maybe not, but you sure seemed to enjoy your little sojourn with her.'

He sighed, raking a hand over his face. 'She was a reaction, a consequence. I felt betrayed by you, like less of a man or something. Not just for not being able to give you a baby, but for being such a shitty husband that you felt like you had to lie to me, like I wouldn't understand how you were feeling. Allegra was there, she was kind to me. And yeah, she barely wears anything and she threw herself at me. I'm not a fucking priest, Tara. It was good to actually feel wanted.'

'I don't need to know the gory details—'

'No, but you do!' he cut me off. 'Do you know what? It felt good to be the baddie for once. All my life, all my career, I've been your stereotypical nice guy. Caring, respectful, charming. Well, I was so mad at you I didn't give a flying fuck any more. I thought to myself, screw this! Bang the hot co-star! Give the paparazzi a show, the gossips something to talk about. I was so sick of being Good with a capital G.'

I was silent, letting him vent because I didn't know what to say.

'But then, as soon as it didn't feel good any more, it felt fucking awful.' He sat down heavily next to me. 'My kids were mad at me, the fans were shocked and disappointed. You slugged me in the jaw. And Allegra? Jesus, she's an absolute nightmare!'

He threw his hands in the air, gesticulating wildly. 'The woman is a bona fide, grade-A nutjob. She's a narcissistic harpy who isn't even beautiful up close, you know . . . and her personality, well, it actually makes her quite ugly. She's so mean, Tara, but I thought that maybe I deserved her. I said to myself, stick with her, Rory. You've blown up your world for this woman, you can't dump her in a hot second.'

He sighed deeply. 'Thankfully she got tired of me quickly. As soon as we finished filming the movie – which is a stinking turd, by the way – she discarded me like a dirty rag, and I never thought I'd be so happy to be dumped. She even dared to suggest we pick it back up for the movie press tour, that the relationship had been good for her career. I told her I was too old for her antics, and that was that. She'll probably write a break-up album about me now, but I don't even care.'

Rory leaned in towards me and I felt a surge in my chest at his physical closeness. It was a strange mix of desire and rage, so I tried to tamp it down because this was not the time to lunge at him – I didn't know if I'd strangle him or straddle him.

'Then there you were at the Oscars, swooning over Sean fucking Sweeney – who is a moron, by the way, and totally baked right now, if you hadn't noticed. I can smell it off him from across the room. I read the headlines about your past together and convinced myself you'd been carrying on with him the entire time. I was so fucking mad at you, Tara. I still am. Then I saw Alex, and talked to Storm and, well, I realized the truth of it all. How alone you must have felt in everything, how scared you must have been. I forgot just how thoroughly you clam up when you're frightened. I knew I needed to talk to you and I had just worked up the courage to get in touch when I heard about Darius.' He dropped his gaze then, and hung his head.

'So what is it you want to actually say to me, now I've listened to all your excuses?' I bit.

He swallowed hard. 'I deserve that. What I want to say is that

I miss you. I love you. I've never stopped loving you even for one second, even when I was so angry I hated you.'

I didn't dare believe my ears. I looked at him agog.

'Tara, my life isn't worth living without you in it. I want to come home, to go back to how we used to be.'

I snapped back to reality. 'Rory, it's not that simple. We can't just go back. You humiliated me, you've spent the last two months shagging your co-star. Do you think I'm going to forget that and welcome you back with open arms? You come here on the day I say goodbye to the only other man I've ever really, truly adored – did you expect me to just fall back into your arms because you say you love me?'

He hung his head. 'I'm so sorry. It was all so messed up and I wasn't thinking clearly. I'm obviously still not thinking clearly.'

'Well, I wasn't thinking either, when I went on the pill. Sure, it was a decision I made, and keeping it from you was another, but they were made purely out of fear, Rory. You don't know what it was like, feeling I was failing you every single month. Worrying that I was sick, like my mom.' I started crying then, and he reached for me. I let him hold me, giving in to the sensation of being cradled by the guy I loved.

'I don't need another child, Tara. I have two on earth and one in heaven. I know you always wanted to give me what Lana had, but the circumstances couldn't be more different. I loved my first wife, I'll always love her, but I knew her since I was fourteen years old. I didn't decide to make a family with her as much as it just happened.'

He took my face in his hands, wiping away tears with his thumbs.

'You are the woman of my dreams, the love of my life. I wanted a baby with you mostly because I wanted you to have that experience. I didn't mean for it to be so much pressure on you that it broke us.'

I didn't know what to say. There was so much water under

the bridge, so many hurt feelings and tangled emotions. I felt overcome.

'Tara, do you still love me?' Rory was hunkered down in front of me, beseeching me with his eyes. 'Because if you do, we can figure all this out. If you love me, we can forgive one another and move forward.'

I suddenly felt so tired, the weight of the exhaustion I'd been carrying around hitting me full force. I'd never known upheaval like the kind I'd experienced in the months prior, and everything just felt like too much. I'd only just endured the trauma of fighting with Alex, uncovered the anger I felt about my mother's death, and then lost my friend and father figure in quick succession. I couldn't have this conversation with Rory, not at Darius's funeral. I needed time and space. For the first time in my life, I had to figure out what was important to me. I had to put myself first.

Rory seemed to sense then how depleted I felt. 'I'm sorry, Tara. I didn't mean to overwhelm you. You're right, I can't expect you to fall back into my arms here and now, in a room with the corpse of a ninety-two-year-old woman. I'm just asking you to consider it.'

I smiled weakly at him. 'I can consider it. I have to consider everything, and I need room to do it. I need time and kindness and understanding, and I need to do it all on my own. Can you give me that?'

Rory sighed. 'I can.'

We sat there for what felt like ages, silent in the candlelight. 'I know what I'd like to do right now, though,' I said suddenly.

He raised his eyebrows at me.

'I want to get absolutely locked, Irish funeral style.'

Rory grinned, and I saw a glimmer of the man I adored somewhere in his eyes. 'Well, we better get to it, then.'

36. Alex

We all ended up in a traditional Irish pub on the Upper East Side called Ryan's Daughter, one that was actually pretty authentic, devoid of hokey paddywhackery and had decent draught Guinness, or so my dad said. It was the exact opposite vibe of the glamorous funeral parlour, but it was exactly what this particular congregation needed. Irish and Brazilian people have a fair amount in common, not least being historically Catholic nations with a fondness for a drink and a hooley.

The men had all taken off their jackets and loosened their ties, and Felicia had shown up with slippers for the women, much to my delight. By the time darkness fell, Xavier and I were chatting at one end of the bar while everyone else milled around drinking.

'I give it half an hour before the singing starts.' I smiled.

'Oh, can I do "The Irish Rover"? That's my party piece.' Xavier grinned back. It was good to see him; he'd been back on the Cape for a week, and while we'd been in touch we hadn't been discussing anything beyond the day-to-day.

'I have a feeling this particular wake will be more showtunes than sean-nós, but go off, sis'.' I winked.

'I can "defy gravity" from time to time, you know. I did inherit some of my dad's musical theatre talent.'

The mention of his dad deflated me a little. It was a lot easier to pretend that Xavier Vaughan was just some cool, sexy younger guy I'd met when we weren't in the bosom of his family.

'It's still weird, right?' he acknowledged, noticing my chagrin.

'It felt different in Chatham,' I admitted. 'It's definitely feeling weirder now that we're in the same room as your father. Kind of verging on wrong.'

'I really like you, Alex. It wasn't wrong, and it wasn't just a fling for me.'

'But . . .'

'But, you're too involved with my family for this to be a real thing, right?'

I bowed my head. 'I don't think I could ever feel comfortable being in a long-term relationship with Rory Vaughan's son. Christmas would be so weird.' I laughed, despite myself. I was emotionally exhausted but felt I needed to be honest with him.

'It totally would, now you mention it. I also don't think you'd be happy relocating to a peninsula in Massachusetts, and I wouldn't be thrilled living in a bustling metropolis. I've tried it – it's not for me.'

'We want different things.' I sighed. 'Bummer.'

'Is this the most civilized break-up of all time? Or were we even together enough to call it that?'

'It's very civilized, and let's just say we're calling it off – whatever "it" was. Maybe funerals just put things into perspective.' I cast my eyes down, so he couldn't see me tearing up. 'Can we still be friends?' I asked. 'Like, actual friends who talk and spend time together but don't complicate things with sex?'

'I really think we can. Let's be pen pals! I love writing a good old-fashioned letter.'

'Deal, until you meet some young, fabulous woman who doesn't understand your handwritten correspondence with a grizzly old lady like me.'

'Don't write yourself off, Alex Curtis. Right now, two fifths of the uber-cool rock band Higher Power are most definitely checking you out.'

I flushed. 'What?'

'Yep. I know they're just as old and grizzly as you are' – Xavier laughed as he dodged a swat of my hand – 'but they have been looking over here and whispering among one another for a good ten minutes. So I'm going to be the bigger guy, recognize that I shouldn't monopolize you and let them make their move, even if that's very inappropriate at an event such as this. Plus, I owe my dad a beer.'

He dropped a kiss on my forehead and turned to leave, but I grabbed his arm, serious all of a sudden. 'I want you to know that you brought me back to life, Xav.' He looked surprised. 'I'm sorry, that sounds very dramatic. I was really stuck for a very long time, and I had no idea. Being with you, no matter how briefly, woke me up to the possibilities. Thank you.'

He brought me in for a bear hug and gave me a tight squeeze. 'If I thought for one second that this could work out, I wouldn't let you out of my sight. You're one in a million, Curtis,' he said gruffly, and sauntered over towards Rory without looking back.

I stood alone at the beer-soaked bar and took in the scene around me. I'd never felt so tired, but also oddly peaceful, having unburdened myself. Talking about the miscarriage and seeing Sean hadn't brought back all the old feelings of pain and abandonment, as I'd feared; if anything, telling Tara and Jen had lightened the load ever so slightly. I knew I'd carry the loss with me for ever, but also that I had the strength to. It was all part of my story.

Tara and Storm were playing on the basketball arcade game in the corner, and I noticed Brian was beating everyone at pool. He's something of a shark; he gets away with it because he looks so nice and cuddly, people don't think he could be so nimble and dextrous with the cue until he takes all their money.

Francisco was huddled with my parents at a table, and Rory and Xavier were ordering a round of Baby Guinness shots for the entire bar. Jen caught my eye and mouthed, 'You okay?' and I nodded. She was busy entertaining Francisco's brothers; I didn't need to take her away from a brief opportunity for extra-marital flirtation. I was okay, and I would be okay. I knew that now.

I didn't dare look in the direction of Sean and his band-mates, though, especially after what Xavier had just said. I had surprised myself by not being completely physiologically over-whelmed by Sean Sweeney's presence in the room; I thought I'd be dragged to him like a magnet, but since our brief exchange in the funeral home he was having barely any effect on me at all.

Someone had brought the photo of Darius from atop the casket, and it was in pride of place behind the bar. I found myself looking around for him for a befuddled second, as I thought how much he'd enjoy a night like this, full of all his favourite people and where he was the centre of attention.

Darius was always there for me, not only in the immediate aftermath of my miscarriage but every second since. We never talked about what happened once it was over, but he hadn't left my side as I bled and wept, terrified and devastated. I knew he was always waiting for me to bring it up, but I never did. I also knew he'd kept my confidence and taken my secret to his grave. As I gazed upon his round, happy face, a wave of grief and loss threated to overwhelm me. Then I felt a steadying hand on my shoulder.

Lorraine was the last person I expected to console me, but she must have sensed my devastation somehow. She opened her Escada-clad arms and let me cry on her shoulder, and I was grateful for her compassion. 'Let it out, sweetie,' she murmured. 'I've got you.'

I bawled for several minutes while she patted me on the back and made encouraging noises. It had been a big day for me, and her kindness meant a lot.

'If there's one thing I've learned from burying two parents and a husband, it's that you never get over it,' she said matter-of-factly. I looked up at her, frowning, unsure how this was meant to make me feel better. Lorraine laughed.

'I mean, everyone we love takes a little bit of our soul with them when they leave. But what rushes in to fill that empty part is wisdom. The lack never goes away, but you learn to live with it and learn from it. Does that make sense?'

I nodded, wiping my eyes. I had to admit that I could see what Tara loved about Lorraine now that I wasn't so busy treating her as a rival for my best friend's affections. She was strong, empathetic and astute. I vowed there and then to start treating her with the respect she deserved.

'You Irish really know how to send someone off,' she observed as I pulled myself together. 'I thought sitting shiva was extravagant, but now I hope I come back in my next life as one of you guys.'

I snorted. 'Thank you for everything, Lorraine. I truly don't know what we would have done without you throughout all this.'

'Stop.' She batted away my thanks. 'Do you know how much Darius would have loved the *LONY* cameras here today? I kept them away out of respect for you, you know.'

'Oh, he's unforgettable anyway, without his funeral being immortalized on reality TV.'

'That he is, my friend.'

Giulia stumbled over, shots in hand. 'These are the *piccolo* Guinnesses – so cute,' she slurred. 'Rory bought one for everyone, for another *cin cin* to Darius!'

Lorraine and I took a syrupy glass each and the three of us chorused a *sláinte*, clinking shots before downing them. After we all wiped our sticky fingers on Lorraine's Hermès scarf, the two older women made a beeline towards Deirdre, as I had been correct – a sing-song was beginning at my mother's table. I looked over and instantly caught someone's eye, realizing it was Ciaran Doyle of Higher Power fame. I smiled, and he ambled over.

He gave me a big hug, one I reciprocated warmly. I'd always liked Ciaran. He was the least showy stage-school kid I'd ever known, attending That's D'Amore purely because of a love of music. He was the drummer in Sean's band now, firmly in the background, where I suspected he liked it. I hadn't seen him in person for twenty years, but that time melted away as soon as I looked at him up close.

'Some show for Dar.' He smiled.

'He was some man. How are you, Ciaran?'

'I'm great. About to embark on a world tour with Sean and

the lads. It's full on, but it's the stuff of dreams. I believe you were talking to the man himself earlier?'

'Oh, I expect Sean told you that Tara and I ate the head off him.'

Ciaran laughed. 'He deserved it, I'm sure. I don't know the details, nor do I want to. I'm glad you seem over it all now.'

I looked at him. 'What do you mean?'

'Ahh, you were always mad about Sean! All the girls were. I never blamed you – he's got it, whatever it is. It just meant the poor oul' lanky musicians like me never got a look-in.'

I took him in then. Ciaran was tall, towering more than half a foot above Sean but not bulky and muscular with it like Rory and Xav. I felt petite next to him, but not dominated. He had a couple of line-drawing tattoos on his forearm, visible beneath his rolled-up shirtsleeves, bushy reddish hair and kind hazel eyes. He was right in that I'd never paid him a blind bit of romantic attention growing up; I vaguely remembered him being a bit pimply and shy, and that's not exactly what teenage girls go for.

He was neither of those things now. The man standing in front of me seemed confident and seasoned, the kind of guy who's been around the block enough to know what he wants out of life, and smart enough to enjoy the trappings of fame without being a slave to it.

Jordan Jones came over then, sweaty and a bit sick-looking.

'Are you okay?' I asked, concerned.

'Too many shots. I can't keep up with you guys.' He shuddered dramatically. 'Alex, I gotta go, but I have great news just in from the West Coast office! Your work permits are all officially through. I'll make the requisite calls tomorrow and get the ball rolling again on our project. This is big, Alex. We are about to take off, you and me. Purely professionally, of course.' He grinned.

'That's amazing,' I enthused, kissing him on the cheek. 'Thank you for everything, Jordan, not least enduring an Irish wake on my behalf.'

'Hey, what are friends, agents and new business partners for?' Jordan gave me a squeeze and practically ran into the night, desperate to escape.

'Does that mean you're sticking around New York for a while, then?' Ciaran asked. He'd been standing to the side, clearly earwigging.

'I guess it does. Wow,' I said, as the reality of working in the Big Apple hit me. 'I'd better find somewhere to live.'

'I know a great realtor,' he offered. 'I spend the vast majority of my time here, so you'll have another friend in the city. One that would love to take you out for dinner sometime, if that's not totally inappropriate in the circumstances.'

His candour was unexpected, but perhaps that kind of self-assurance comes with being a global rock star. He handed me a card and laughed at my confused expression.

'Musicians do carry business cards, you know,' Ciaran said. 'I do some session work for other bands. I don't have Sean's endorsement deals.' He winked. 'But I do have a far more normal schedule than him, and the ability to show a beautiful woman I've always secretly fancied around my favourite place in the world. If she's up for it, that is.'

As I smiled up at him, I realized I felt something I hadn't encountered in a long time, if ever. Was that . . . confidence?

'Well, Ciaran, as an elder millennial with zero game, I realize you could be talking about absolutely anyone – I've learned not to presume about these things.' He looked confused, and I didn't blame him. 'But if the woman you're talking about is actually me, then I'd be delighted to let you show me the town sometime.'

I took the card he was still proffering, a smirk on his face. 'Let me get my head together, but I'll give you a call sometime soon. I promise.'

Variety.com

15 May 2025

Netflix commissions Ten-Part Documentary on Internet Nostalgia

Yes, you read that correctly – the internet is now officially old enough for you to feel nostalgic about it, at least according to Netflix. The streaming giant has just signed a deal with cultural commentator Alex Curtis and Curtis Jones Productions to make a ten-part series all about how pop culture has changed since we began logging on.

Caught in the Web *will premiere later this year, and mark twenty years since the phenomenon of social media really took off with MySpace and bebo. Each episode will focus on how music, film, television and how we live our lives altered alongside the growth of these social networks, which were soon joined by Facebook, Tumblr, Snapchat, Twitter, Instagram and TikTok, and all but decimated traditional media in record time.*

'This project is a dream come true, but one I never really knew I had,' says Curtis in her official statement. 'The past twenty years have seen digital and societal advancements at breakneck speed, and it's an honour to examine just how the internet affects what we consume and how we consume it.'

Co-producer Jordan Jones, an agent to the stars, said he has been mulling over a series like this for a while, but it took a chance meeting with Curtis to make it a reality. 'Alex has it all – she's intelligent, distinctive, warm and charming, and has a wealth of experience in digital journalism and podcasting. She is the perfect person to helm this docuseries and take it global with the help of our streaming partners.'

Caught in the Web *will feature contributions from titans of social media industry like Mark Zuckerberg and Jack Dorsey, as well as stars of stage and screen. Tara O'Toole, Sean Sweeney, Sabrina Carpenter and Jennifer Lopez have all signed on as talking heads, and social media influencers including Tinx, Lavinia Rizzi, Trisha Paytas and Amelia Dimoldenberg. Production will begin imminently in New York and San Francisco.*

37. Tara

I stepped outside into the morning sunlight, caressed by balmy air and soothed at the sight of swaying palm trees. It was late August and Los Angeles was baking hot, but at least California had swimming pools and wide open spaces – summer in LA is far more pleasant than in Manhattan.

It felt good to be back in my Beverly Hills house. I'd really missed it. I had it deep-cleaned before I came out west, to remove every trace of Allegra and her ass from the property. Even though Rory and I renovated before we moved in in the mid-noughties – mostly ripping out the shag carpeting dear departed Liz Taylor adored – the house still exuded that classic 50s mid-century charm, with huge windows, soft curves and high ceilings with exposed beams. It was a happy place of mine, and I was delighted to be back in it for a few weeks.

I was in Los Angeles shooting my latest film, *Reunited*, with the writing/directing/producing duo of Portia Daniels and Katie Carlton. Alex and I had considered the project in those hazy days after Darius's funeral and agreed it was perfect for me. David's stepsister was as good as her word, and Portia and her partner had indeed cast the story around me and fast-tracked production.

I was so glad to be back making a movie, and it was such a stark contrast to the last set I'd been on. Thinking back to London the previous winter made me shudder; had that really been only a few months ago? I'd been trying so hard to convince myself I was happy back then, acting far more in my personal life than I had been at work. Still, I'd pulled it off. *Mind the Gap* had come out a couple of weeks prior to rave reviews, and Chris Adams was everyone's new favourite romcom silver fox.

Shooting in LA meant I could stay at my own home and not in a hotel, which was a luxury I didn't take for granted now. I took my oat iced latte over to the cabana by the pool, allowing myself just a little sun. The make-up department would kill me if I got any sort of tan or even obvious new freckles, but I couldn't resist the feeling of warmth on my skin.

After I finished my coffee I slipped off my satin robe and eased myself into the cool water, where I began to swim lengths; it was how I liked to start my days before work out here, mostly because I didn't have to worry about washing and styling my own hair – that was David's job on the movie, a perk in itself. Storm was on the glam squad too, and it all felt like a family affair.

I found a refreshing skinny dip set me up nicely, and was surprisingly good exercise for something so relaxing. I liked to do my thinking in the pool, and that morning there was quite a lot to mull over.

It had been a few weeks since I'd last seen Rory. We'd spent a bit of time together in New York during the early days of summer, but it was purely platonic, on purpose. Rory was giving me the space I desired, but we'd talked a lot and had quiet dinners, just the two of us in the apartment and away from prying eyes. Still, we hadn't so much as shared a kiss. I was wary and hurt, and I knew he was afraid of frightening me off.

I don't know why we were suddenly able to communicate. It was like a dam had broken after so much holding back and everything was pouring out. There had been many difficult conversations between Rory and me that were painful but necessary. I wanted to know all about his liaison with Allegra; he thought the details were unimportant. He wanted to know why I'd ever thought Sean Sweeney was The One and couldn't get his head around my *Sliding Doors* logic. It was hard, but I found it far easier than talking in front of a third party. Both

Rory and I agreed that couples therapy had been more of a hindrance than a help; both being actors, we'd been performing for Barbara in an effort to get her to take sides.

This movie shoot in LA had come at the perfect time and provided much-needed relief, a chance to get away alone and clear my head. But, for once, I wasn't running away or avoiding facing up to anything. I was just grateful to focus on something other than the detritus of my marriage for a while.

Work was going well for Rory too; he was in rehearsals for a new musical onstage. He was going back to Broadway for his next project, his first professional love, and I was thrilled for him.

It all felt very adult. I didn't know if we were going to end up back together, or even if we really wanted to. For the first time in my life, I was trying to trust the universe and just see what happened, instead of controlling every situation I found myself in. I was vaguely worried that all this sexless friendliness meant our chemistry had disappeared, that there wasn't really any hope for us after all. If Rory and I were meant to be, we would be. Either way, I would be okay. We both would.

My shoot was going well, and it was a blessedly short one. Principal photography was only five weeks total, and working with Portia was as dreamy as predicted. The movie was a fun, chaotic and beautifully girly romp centred on my character and her two oldest friends meeting up again at their twenty-year high-school reunion.

My former besties were being played by Amanda Seyfried and Issa Rae, and we were having an absolute ball. The romantic lead was the delightfully eccentric and charismatic Andrew Garfield, and I was pleased that there was only the requisite amount of heat between us and nothing more. Part of me had been afraid that I would latch on to the next man I was in close physical proximity to out of sheer neediness, but it hadn't happened. This must be what growth feels like, I thought.

I was especially excited for that day on set because Dessie

Daniels was filming her cameo. She was in Los Angeles visiting her family, and she'd convinced Portia to cast her as a sexy former teacher of ours. Portia isn't able to say no to her mother, nor did she want to. 'Dessie is perfect for the part, but don't tell her that.' Portia had winked at me. 'She's a diva as it is.'

I showered and gathered my things, and as I hopped in my Bentley convertible I continued my new daily ritual by calling Alex on the way to the studio. She was filming her docuseries in New York and my drive usually coincided with her break.

'Tara! *I did it!*' my friend squealed as I answered the phone.

'Did what?' I teased, knowing full well what she was getting at, because Jen had already texted me. 'Did you finally shave your head?'

'Very funny. No, I spent the entire night at Ciaran's.'

'Hallelujah! Did the sky fall down because you had to sleep on someone else's pillows?'

'Quite the opposite, actually. I think his bed might be nicer than mine!'

I laughed, delighted to hear such joy in Alex's voice. She sounded giddy and youthful as she filled me in on the previous evening's events. For months, she'd been dancing around her blossoming relationship with Ciaran Doyle and trying to break her commitment-phobic habits of a lifetime. He was patient with her; he told me he'd always had a massive thing for Alex and was willing to tread lightly so she didn't flee. It was music to my ears.

I let my friend prattle on happily, her chat segueing, as it always did, from Ciaran to work.

'Today is very exciting,' she was saying. 'Zuckerberg is recording his segments.'

'Incredible, Alex! The father of social media on your show, in his own words.'

'I know, pinch me. Right, gotta go. Netflix waits for no woman. When are you coming home? You'll be our last star guest on the project.'

'Not long now, a week or so. Talk later.'

I was smiling as I drove on to the Apple lot in Culver City. It was a breezy half-hour drive from my house, which is nothing in Los Angeles. There was buzzy energy on set, and I went straight to the hair trailer so David could get started on taming my mane.

He seemed a bit jittery, something I attributed to too much caffeine. Then I noticed David's eyes shining every time he looked at me. Was that . . . a tear?

'Dave, what's with the waterworks?'

'Allergies,' he croaked. 'I'll be fine.'

'I can do my own hair if you're not feeling well—'

'Nonsense! I am going to make you look the best you've ever looked.'

'No better than yesterday, please. There's this little thing called continuity.'

Before long, it was go-time. There was an excited murmur as I reached the sound stage, probably due to the arrival of reality-TV queen Dessie. As I entered, there were no other actors present on the set and the stage lights were off.

'Where's Katie?' I asked a runner, looking for the director. The girl shrugged and hurried off, and I looked at my phone to make sure I had the call time right. I'd been summoned to set as usual; what was going on?

All of a sudden, the floodlights over my head came on and, as my eyes adjusted, I saw that the entire set had been practically carpeted in pink flowers. Roses, I noted. Magenta ones, my favourite.

I whirled around, taking it all in, and then my breath caught in my throat as I noticed a man standing at the other end of the stage. As he walked towards me with a familiar lope, I recognized my husband.

The last time Rory had surprised me on a movie set, my initial joy at seeing him had quickly turned to dread and despair. This time, though, he was wearing a completely different expression on his handsome face. He was smiling as he strode to my side.

'Hey,' he said when he got there, and I giggled nervously.

'How are you here?' I asked, awed at the sight of him. He was casual, in jeans and a striped shirt, and I felt a stirring I hadn't experienced in ages. 'Aren't you meant to be in New York working on your jazz hands?'

'Oh, I just flew three thousand miles to win you back.' He grinned, and my heart leapt into my throat. 'Women like big gestures, right?'

I stood there opening and closing my mouth until Rory put two strong hands around my waist and pulled me to him. I felt a zing at his touch. Yep, there was definitely something going on south of my belly button.

'Tara, you are the love of my life. It's only ever really been you. I'm so sorry for all the pain I've caused you, and for what went wrong between us. I've given you your space over the past few months, and I'm sorry to tell you that it's just not working for me any more.'

My breath caught in my throat. I was confused, and it must have been written all over my face because Rory laughed before continuing.

'I'm saying that I need to be your husband again. I don't want to be just friends any more, if that's okay with you. I want to wake up next to you every morning when your hair looks crazy and your breath stinks. I want to be the last thing you see at night. I want to be married to you for the rest of my days. We can even renew our vows in a ridiculously over-the-top celebration if it makes you happy. I'll do anything for you, every day, for ever. Can we please, for the love of God, get back together?'

I didn't need to hear anything else. Every single cell in my body yearned for him, and I wasn't going to fight it any more. We'd both fucked up. We'd both hurt each other. What mattered was that we'd found our way back.

I stood on my tiptoes, threw my arms around Rory's broad shoulders and kissed my husband deeply in front of the entire cast and crew, who had clearly been in on the plan and were now clapping and cheering. As he lifted me up and pulled my legs around his waist, I could hear David loudly crying to my left; his earlier tears now made sense.

Rory and I pulled apart, beaming at one another, and I heard a familiar voice behind me. 'Well, isn't love grand?' said Dessie Daniels, wiping away a tear. 'If you are doing the ridiculously over-the-top vow renewal, you have to let me handle it, pet. I'm very good at that kind of thing. Now, shall we get this show on the road before my make-up cracks?'

Epilogue

Alex

Six Months Later

On her birthday in February, my mother retired from a long, rewarding career as a midwife. Deirdre being Deirdre, she didn't want a fuss, but we were never going to let her go quietly into funemployment. In fact, Tara, Jen and I desired maximum fuss, because this was a woman who had spent her entire life helping other women and she deserved her flowers. Finally, Mam was going to get some real time to focus on herself, and we wanted to celebrate her working life and send her out with a bang.

She didn't let on, but everyone knew Darius's death had a lot to do with her decision to retire. As much as Mam loved her job, she had realized that life is short and for living with your loved ones. You could say we all realized the same thing.

Tara said money was no object for the party, but Deirdre Curtis isn't someone who goes in for all-out maximalism. I batted away Tara's outlandish suggestions of renting cruise ships or the Empire State Building and decided to commandeer a swanky Dublin city-centre restaurant and invite everyone we knew. I also insisted on paying half.

Of course, there would be one major gap at the table; Darius's absence was still sorely felt. But at his funeral, Deirdre had found a partner-in-crime in Giulia Rizzi. The two sixty-somethings had become firm friends who Zoomed and emailed and even watched *Bridgerton* together, but apart, marvelling at the wonders of modern technology.

Giulia had flown all the way to Dublin to celebrate her new best pal, and brought Tara's friend Portia, her mother, Dessie, and Giulia's boyfriend, Chris, along for the ride. Thus the party was super star-studded, and every Tom, Dick and Harry that Mam knew from the supermarket to Zumba wanted an invite.

'Let them all come,' Tara had said magnanimously. 'How much trouble are a few extra pensioners going to be?'

Jen said it was clear then that Tara O'Toole had been living away from Ireland and the real world too long and had forgotten that the oldies are always the boldest at any shindig. Still, Tara didn't care. She was feeling benevolent, and was far less careful about her image and privacy these days – my best friend was the happiest I'd ever seen her, and she didn't care who knew it.

Lorraine was very impressed with Dublin. 'Why didn't you tell me this place was so fabulous? I've been having the time of my life! The men are so fun and beardy! Francisco and I have our eyes firmly peeled.'

'Do not listen to her. I will never love again,' Francisco protested.

'Nah, but you'll definitely want to get laid at some point.' Lorraine laughed.

Storm and Xavier had also made the journey, which thrilled Deirdre because she saw them now as her honorary grandchildren. My mother didn't know about Xavier and me, and now never would; her maternal feelings towards him made me incredibly glad that he and I hadn't continued our dalliance. We had kept our promise to one another and remained in touch. I loved reading his long letters in scratchy handwriting, and especially loved it when he sent me drawings from his new graphic novel. I'm not sure I ever had a straight male friend before Xavier entered my life, and realized I had been missing out.

One thing I wasn't missing out on was regular excellent sex, though. It couldn't be denied that satisfaction was adding a certain sparkle to my own appearance. While my glow wasn't entirely down to the fact that I had fallen in love – I'm not that much of a sap – it was true that Ciaran Doyle had a lot to do with how great I'd been feeling.

We were taking it slow, but I surprised myself at just how much I enjoyed being a rock star's girlfriend – just not the rock star I initially thought. I rented out my place in Dublin and found a super-cute one-bedroom in Greenwich Village with his help. I was living my New York dream on my own terms, but I was open to the possibilities.

There was something in the air. Jen and Brian were on a rare night out without the kids and acting like teenagers, smooching at the table. Jen had confided in me in the ladies that she had a renewed sex drive thanks to a new supplement for perimenopause. 'I'm horny as a young wan! Brian doesn't know what's hit him.' I told her not to dare tell my mother about these vitamins, but that Lorraine might like them.

My dad stood up and clinked his glass. 'I would like to thank you all for coming here tonight to celebrate my amazing wife, Deirdre. For forty-five years, she has devoted herself to helping bring new life into the world. Countless mothers have her to thank for their little ones' safe deliveries. Now, rather selfishly, I am thrilled that she will be devoting herself to spending time with me and our own little one, who is not so little any more. Stand up, Alex. Our daughter has a hit show on Netflix, you know,' Dad bleated, unable to conceal his pride. 'She's a star!'

He was exaggerating, but Eamonn wasn't wrong. *Caught in the Web* had premiered in all territories the previous month and was a top-ten hit for Netflix in the UK and the US, as well as number one in Ireland, Greece and Japan. I had been bitten by the telly bug and Jordan and I were currently developing two more projects. *Alex Knows* was being revamped to reflect my new-found niche fame, and I was thrilled at how my career was turning out. Every time I felt nervous or overwhelmed I heard Darius's voice in my mind telling me to act as if my life depended on it. I was thoroughly proud of myself, perhaps for the first time ever. I may have been a late bloomer, but I was blooming, finally.

Tara and I were also back to being as thick as thieves; closer, even, given what we'd been through. We had no secrets and a promise to always be truthful, which was both good and bad – it meant Tara could tell me I needed cheek filler in the name of honesty and I couldn't give her a smack.

If Sean Sweeney's name came up in our presence, we'd catch each other's eye and smile. It was our code that everything was okay. His affair with a married princess had been exposed in the tabloids, but as usual Sean came out of it all looking like a feckless but loveable Lothario. He is the guy who falls into shit and comes out smelling of roses, and I could see now that he always had been. Thankfully, Tara and I had come to the point where we thought it kind of funny that we'd very nearly ended our lifelong friendship over such a gobshite, and we were allowed to joke about it.

Ciaran doesn't love the jokes, but he gets it. He's chill like that. I ended up telling him everything, even about the miscarriage, and the way he'd reacted – with compassion, kindness and love – told me everything I needed to know about him. I knew he wouldn't let on to Sean, or anyone else. My secrets were safe with him. I reached over and gave his hand a squeeze and was rewarded with a beaming smile. I was really lucky to have met Ciaran again, and I wasn't going to mess this up.

Tara and Rory weren't quite at the point where they could joke about Allegra, but everyone was enjoying the fact that the singer's revenge album had flopped quite spectacularly, as had their movie together. Taylor Swift she is not, and once #RORA was back together, nobody really had any interest in watching the sexy film that had been the catalyst for their marriage implosion. It was crap, anyway.

Rory's run on Broadway was receiving stellar reviews, and Tara's movie *Reunited* was due to premiere at Cannes. They were blissfully happy to be back together and were looking particularly sparkly in one another's company that night. They both clapped as my dad finished his toast.

As the dinner plates were cleared away I stood up and clinked my own wine glass. 'We're all here tonight to celebrate the wonderful Deirdre Curtis,' I began, and a hush fell over the assembled diners once again. 'My mam is an amazing person. Not only has she spent her life helping other women become mothers, she has also been the most wonderful mother not only to me but to my friends as well. Deirdre, I am so proud to be your biological daughter and I love you to the moon and back. But your honorary daughter Tara has a surprise for you tonight that I hope will make you very happy.'

Tara stood up then, Rory clutching her hand protectively as she steadied herself on sky-high heels. She looked around the room, beaming and clearly on the edge of tears. 'Thank you, Alex, and thank you for always sharing your mom with me. I lost my own mother when I was far too young, only eighteen years of age. Ever since then, Deirdre Curtis has been an important figure in my life, alongside other incredible women of all ages. Nobody can ever take the place of your mom in your life, but it really does take a village to raise a child. I hope you'll all become part of the village that helps raise the little one that Rory and I are expecting.'

A delighted ripple went through the room as the guests realized what Tara was saying. I already knew, of course. I was there when Tara got the call from her gynaecologist telling her the intra-uterine implantation had worked, that she was finally pregnant. All she and Rory had needed was a little scientific helping hand in getting his swimmers over the hurdle that was her tilted cervix; they hadn't even had to go through the IVF they had steeled themselves for.

'I'm currently growing a little life inside of me, and Deirdre, I know you're retiring, but I really hope you'll be by my side as I give birth, breastfeed and try not to drop your honorary grandbaby on its head!' Everyone laughed at that, but I knew it was a real fear of Tara's.

My mother was openly bawling, blowing kisses at Tara as she spoke. But my friend wasn't finished.

'This time last year, I didn't know if I would ever be happy again. While I'm deliriously thrilled now with my husband, our family and a new baby on the way, I'm also very sad because we have all been living with a huge loss since our dear Darius passed away. It hurts my heart that our baby will never know him in person, but I also know every one of us will have his head wrecked telling him stories about his namesake.'

Another pause for dramatic effect, and I saw my mam gasp as she realized what Tara had said. 'Yes, you heard me correctly. Our son will be named Darius D'Amore Vaughan, but it's okay, everyone – he won't be bullied, his parents are celebrities. It could have been much, much worse.'

Everyone clapped and cheered and cried happy-sad tears. Tara sat back down, and I signalled to the waiters to bring out the huge cake I'd organized to bring the party atmosphere back.

'Do you think Deirdre's happy?' Tara asked, wiping her eyes carefully with the corner of her napkin.

'Thrilled. The only thing that could make her happier was if I was having a kid of my own.'

'Ah, little Darius will keep her busy, so no pressure.'

'Maybe I could do with a bit of pressure.'

Tara's mouth fell open. 'Are you saying what I think you're saying? Do you want to have Ciaran Doyle's babies?'

'I don't think so, but never say never. I definitely want to keep him around. I might even give Deirdre and Eamonn a day out, an occasion to buy a hat.'

'Alex Curtis, as I live and breathe, I never thought I'd see the day.' We clinked glasses, hers of sparkling water, mine of champagne. 'Here's some news for you too – I've decided to go and see my dad tomorrow.'

I couldn't believe what I was hearing. Tara had never expressed any interest in rekindling a relationship with Christy before. 'I know,' she said, reading my mind. 'But apparently he's off the sauce. My spies on the ground said he'd be thrilled to see me when I suggested calling by. I've come to realize that there's blame to share between us – I ran off on him, too. Losing Darius Senior and growing Darius Junior, well . . . it's turning me into an old softie.' I squeezed her hand in solidarity. I was proud of my friend.

We sat there quietly, watching the party unfold around us. Jen and Brian were vigorously making out now, to the point of it being a bit inappropriate, and Lorraine was holding court with the older crowd.

'If I do ever go through with the whole wedding fandango, I can count on you, right?' I said.

'For what?'

'Moral support, hiring male strippers . . . standing beside me at the altar, trying your best not to upstage me.'

'I could never upstage you, Al. But please Jesus, at least do me the favour and wait until after I've given birth. Don't try and get me back for being a fabulous superstar by making me be a bridesmaid with swollen ankles!'

'Oh my god, that could be the perfect revenge!'

'What are you two wetting yourselves about?' Ciaran enquired, leaning over me to kiss Tara congratulations.

'Ah, just girl stuff,' she said, winking at me.

I turned to him and beamed. 'You've made me really happy, you know,' I said. 'I don't ever have to pretend with you. In fact, you're sort of perfect.'

'If only you'd realized that around the turn of the millennium, huh? Could have saved yourself a lot of bother.' Ciaran grinned.

'Something I've learned is that you have to endure the bother to get to the good part. You can't avoid it, unfortunately.'

'And I'm the good part?'

'You're a really big part of the good part. Is that good enough?'

He smiled at me then, a big, toothy beam that felt like coming home. 'You bet your arse it is.'

Acknowledgements

Ah, the 'difficult' second novel. Thankfully, it wasn't very difficult at all because of two things – first, the wonderful experience of my debut happening as I wrote it (I was buoyed by all the energy and kindness coming my way when *Reality Check* was released) and second, the amazing support I've received from the best teams and kindest people.

Thank you to all the authors, journalists, readers and booksellers that have so thoroughly welcomed me into the bookish world, and to the Bookstagrammers who have helped spread the word about my work – special shout-out to Sinéad and the Tired Mammy Book Club for being the very best hype girls. Being an author is an honour and a privilege and has been the happiest experience of my professional life.

Writing *Long Story* was cathartic for me. I've always had complex thoughts and feelings about the nature of female friendship, the highs and lows and intensities you experience when bonded to another woman platonically. It was only natural that Alex and Tara were both as obsessed with the film *Beaches* as I've always been; I think my cousin Trev and I wore out our nanna's VHS copy by watching it every single Saturday when we were kids.

Thank you to the editorial team: to Patricia Deevy, Deputy Publisher in Penguin Sandycove, and to editor Claire Pelly – your careful eyes, kind suggestions and endless encouragement made this finished book so much better than its first draft, and allowed me the space to give the story the true heart and depth it deserved. We make a great team, gals! And thanks also to Ellie Smith, editorial manager in London, and to copy-editor, Sarah Day.

Thank you to Louise Farrell for her expertise in publicity,

and to the entire PRH team in Dublin, especially Joyce Dignam (editorial), Finn Roche and Lorna Browne (comms), Carrie Anderson (sales) and Michael McLoughlin (MD).

I could not love the cover artwork more, so thank you to illustrator Bron Payne and Penguin designer Charlotte Daniels for making it so beautiful.

Huge thanks to my agent Faith O'Grady and all at Lisa Richards for always looking after me. My motto is to always have faith in Faith.

Thank you to my early readers – Denise Notaro, Shelley Carlyle Morgan, Sonia Harris Pope, Aidan Corcoran, Katie Gilligan and Patrick Kavanagh. Your texts and voice notes when you reached some of the climactic parts made me laugh and cry! I'm particularly grateful to Shelley, an incredible medical professional who in part inspired the character of Deirdre and who was a brilliant help with all the health-related terminology.

Thank you to my amazing family for all that they do – Denise, Eugene, Rita, Shelley, Jack, Billy, Síle and Yves – and also to my extended family and closest friends, who, as an only child, I would be utterly lost without. You know who you are, and I love yiz.

My elderly canine gentleman, Jacko, is still with us age fourteen, and I want to thank him for being the cutest furry co-worker a gal could ask for. It may seem strange to thank a dog, but he helps me in his very own special way, and gets me out of the house when I need a break.

The biggest thanks, as always, go to Joe. My better half, my support system and the reason I'm able to do what I do. I love you for ever.